PRAISE FOR ANNA

APART FROM THE CROWD

"Amusing and touching with a nice twist at the end."
—*Irish Independent*

"Truly absorbing from start to finish. It impressed me so
much that I will be reading it again."
—*Irish Mail on Sunday*

"A delightful roller-coaster ride of emotion."
—*Sunday Independent*

PACK UP THE MOON

"Refreshingly honest, laugh-out-loud funny
and heartfelt."
—Cathy Kelly

"Fascinating and hugely readable."
—*The Kingdom*

"Crisply written, insightful and moving."
—*Irish Independent*

Apart from the Crowd

Anna McPartlin

DOWNTOWN PRESS

New York   London   Toronto   Sydney

Downtown Press
A Division of Simon & Schuster, Inc.
1230 Avenue of the Americas
New York, NY 10020

Copyright © 2006 by Anna McPartlin
First published by Poolbeg Press Ltd. (Dublin, Ireland)
Published by arrangement with Poolbeg Press Ltd.

First Downtown Press trade paperback edition August 2008

DOWNTOWN PRESS and colophon are registered trademarks of Simon & Schuster, Inc.

For information about special discounts for bulk purchases, please contact Simon & Schuster Special Sales at 1-800-456-6798 or business@simonandschuster.com

Manufactured in the United States of America

10   9   8   7   6   5   4   3   2   1

Library of Congress Cataloging-in-Publication Data

McPartlin, Anna, 1972-
    Apart from the crowd / Anna McPartlin.—Rev. ed.
      p. cm.
    ISBN-13: 978-1-4165-6972-5
    ISBN-10:   1-4165-6972-3
    1. Man-woman relationships—Fiction. 2. Kenmare (Ireland)—Fiction.
3. Psychological fiction. I. Title.
    PR6113.C585A85 2008
    823'.92—dc22

                                                    2007050052

To Mom
I remember the days when the power in your legs
and arms had gone,
All hope for a bright future was lost and you in a home
with your radio playing on.
I remember your face and the smile in your eyes.
I remember your faith and the lesson that
hope never dies.

To my godchildren, Conor O'Shea and Laura Kerins
For you I wish the best this world has to offer,
but when the shit hits the fan, and it will,
Bannie will be there.

Acknowledgments

Thanks to my family: Mary and Tony O'Shea for being my aunt my uncle my mom my dad and all things during times good and bad. Denis, Siobhan, Brenda, Caroline and Aisling for taking me into your home and making me feel like I was a part of it; their significant others, Lisa, Paul, Mark, Ger and Dave, for all that you are to the people I love. Mary and Kevin Flood for being my home away from home and to Mary for being the eternal reminder that my mom once lived here; their sons, Eoin, Dara, Cónal and Ruaraí, for the eighties and being the people that never failed to make me laugh. Paudie McSwiney for your friendship which I hold dear. The McSwineys Kenmare for being the first family in Ireland to buy a copy of *Pack Up the Moon*. My grandparents Bertie and Nora McSwiney, no longer living but still in all our hearts—we loved you then and we love you now. Claire McSwiney, my half sister and some would say better half, thank you for your kindness.

Claire's mother, Mary—you were and always will be a lady. Don and Terry McPartlin for your enduring support, help and friendship.

To my husband, who fell in love with me even though I had a god-awful perm and a penchant for wearing polka dots—like Dolly P. once said, "I will always love you," and the day you bother to read one of my books is the day you'll get a dedication.

To my friends: Valerie K.—to me you will always be my Hallie and no one makes me laugh the way you do. Fergus E., I love you like a fat kid loves cake. Enda B., did you ever know that you're my hero? Sing it with me now—you're everything I wish I could be. Tracy K., I'd jig naked just to hear you laugh. Edel and Noel S. and Lucy and Darren W., you are sensible, forthright, intelligent, irreverent, funny and I'm glad I met you. Joanne C., you are me in a parallel universe except you get to be blond and have a better dress sense but I love our weird ways. John G., how can I not love a guy who married the blonde, better looking and better dressed me? Martin C., the first time I met you I was wearing baggy pants and bunny slippers and you didn't hold it against me—you are and will always be one of my best friends. To Trish C. for making me fill out forms on an Easter Monday—I know I moaned but without you we'd still be renting. Graham D., for those nights when the band was courting record companies in Reynard's or Lillie's and I was bored stupid—you always knew what to say; to your wife, Bernice D., for becoming a great friend. Angela D., the ultimate punk rocker with flowers in her hair. To Lisa and Warren: Lisa sings, Warren supports, and you can't beat that.

ACKNOWLEDGMENTS

To my friends from Kenmare: Leonie K., we laughed we cried people died we survived and through it all I love you. Dermot K., I love you, your wife and your kids. Cliff M., you are the only person in the whole world that I would watch a gardening show with. Gareth T., you get me on a whole different level. Mark L., thank you for being the first person to tell me a joke after Mom died—I'll love you forever for that. Nina B. for being one of the kindest and best people I've ever known. Bernice and Rosita, the C. twins, for our friendship through all those years.

To the buyers and sellers in Easons, Hughes and Hughes, Dubray and Tesco: your support has been overwhelming and much appreciated, thank you, thank you, thank you.

To Paula Campbell, Poolbeg's publisher—you have the hardest job of all. You find talent where others don't. Without you many of the writers in this country wouldn't have been heard of. Thank you.

To all at Poolbeg: Kieran, Lynda, Niamh, Claire, Conor, David. Thank you.

To Gaye Shortland, editor extraordinaire—you have the patience of a saint, God bless you.

To my agent, Faith O'Grady, I'm scattered and you're coping, to you and all at Lisa Richards I say thank you.

And finally to the people of Kenmare, thank you.

Apart from the Crowd

Chapter One

Only Twenty Miles

It was a rainy afternoon in South Kerry—driving rain reminiscent of the opening credits of a Hollywood action or end-of-the-world movie, and, if given to fantasy, one might expect a muscular, sinewy and scantily dressed male to power through the deluge with a damp and distressed girl in his arms and a gun in his back pocket. What he would do with the girl or the gun, and what the girl and gun would have to do with the rain, would be left up to the imagination of the fantasist. Still, we can all agree that there really is nothing like the image of a wet man with a purpose to brighten up an otherwise boring indoor day.

Mary sat on her window seat and pulled the curtains back to watch water hit water and slide from the decks of the boats bobbing fiercely by the pier. Mr. Monkels, her large golden Labrador, lay with his head on her lap. He was peeved because rain meant no walk and he loved his walks, despite the fact that his advanced years meant that they were little more than a series of rests. Mary smiled at her hefty old friend.

"It's not the end of the world, Mr. Monkels—there's always tomorrow."

Mr. Monkels remaining unimpressed. He sighed and this sigh turned to a grunt, which was then followed by a low wheezing sound that often made Mary wonder whether he had a form of dog asthma. Then again, as his age in dog years was the equivalent to eighty-one, it was a frigging miracle he could breathe unaided, never mind take a walk. Mary stroked his left ear, which although deaf still retained sensitivity to touch—as opposed to his right ear, which although in perfect working order was partly missing following a nasty fishing accident seventeen years before.

Mr. Monkels had been a present from Mary's father to mark her twelfth year. He was only ten weeks old at the time of the accident and running madly around the deck of her uncle's boat while she concentrated on taking a black-and-white photo of a dead mackerel. Her cousin Ivan was practicing casting off. Accidentally and inexplicably, the hook had found itself imbedded in Mr. Monkels's ear. Unaware, Ivan cast off. Predictably, Mr. Monkels yelped so that Mary raised her head in time to see her puppy sail through the air like a furry big-eyed missile. Ivan managed to shout out "Jesus on a jet ski! Watch him go!" before the pup plummeted paws first and with a mighty splash into the water. He rose to the surface quickly, splashing and barking. After quickly commenting on the dog's grace and agility and under threat of a battering, Ivan rescued him soon after. Unfortunately, a large part of his ear was to be what Ivan would later term "a casualty of the sea."

Now she stroked his good ear, smiling at the memory of her puppy wagging his tail despite his near-death experience. She had thought back then that her animal either possessed Herculean bravery or was Daffy Duck stupid and, as it turned out, he was a little of both. She lost herself in his big brown cloudy eyes for a minute or two. His nose was dryer than she'd like. She picked up his head in her hands and slowly moved it onto a waiting pillow. Mr. Monkels moaned a little and briefly she wondered if, in promising her dog a tomorrow, she'd led him up the proverbial garden path.

The cottage was old and quaint, well insulated and warm, with a curious homely smell of many years of log fires and home cooking. This had been her primary reasoning behind purchasing the place. She liked the feel of it. The kitchen was an extension refurbished two years previously to suit Mary's taste and yet in keeping with the old-world feel of the place. She liked pottery and had indulged herself in various lamps, vases, plates and cups in the past few years. Once, she'd made the mistake of admitting to enjoying the feel of a heavy cup and the look of a round-based lamp to her best friend, Penny, who called her a total tosser before wondering aloud as to who the hell admits to liking the feel of a heavy cup or the look of a round-based lamp. Her friend had a point and Mary didn't mention her proclivity for pottery in those terms again.

The walls were painted a deep purple but the color was only partially visible under the multitude of black-framed photographs which lined her walls. As a teenager she had been consumed by photography, taking workshops after school and saving for a decent camera and darkroom equipment. Initially, she had shown a flair for black-and-white shots, managing to inject mystique and a certain beauty into even the most mundane of subjects. She discovered her love of portraits in her late teens and hounded her friends for their faces, managing to capture their essence in expression and time despite their annoyance. It was her son who had later inspired color with his jet-black hair, his pink cheeks, red full lips, his chubby white hands and his blue, blue eyes. A boy like Ben just didn't belong in black and white. Her sitting room had a gallery feel to it; ghosts of a different time leaped from every wall. Scattered photos of the objects and the people in her life living and dead surrounded her on all sides. One photo, the one above the clock, was of the dead mackerel she had photographed the day Mr. Monkels enacted his convincing impression of a torpedo—its shiny skin shining in the sun and its black eye staring somehow managed to either captivate or disgust the most casual observer. Ivan had often described the feeling it instilled as being "outright weird," while her neighbor Mossy had excitedly described it as "pure evidence of transcendence" without ever explaining why. Another photo of a black cart laden with freshly cut white lilies spoke of the plainest beauty—but mostly she liked it because it reminded her of the day that she and Robert, her first and arguably only dalliance with love, had gate-crashed a Gypsy funeral to get drunk on generosity and free beer. Her favorite photo, and for no real reason, was of a crystal bowl in a window streaming light. These images were interspersed with those of family and friends. Her father bent forward in deep concentration, head in hand, glasses at the tip of his nose and paper in hand. Her Auntie Sheila, apron on, hair pinned back, left hand in her pocket, right hand stirring a stew, and a grin on her face which suggested she'd just heard a dirty joke. Her cousin Ivan, tanned, lean and boyish in shorts and an old fishing cap, casting off. Her old boyfriend Robert with his shining black hair and big eyes smiling, linking Ivan, who was pulling her friend Penny's blond hair, and Adam, Penny's giant footballer boyfriend, laughing with his head held back. These were only some of the photos she surrounded herself with. She liked to be able to look upon her wall and see someone she loved. She found it comforting.

Of course, her son had a wall all to himself. It wasn't shrinelike, indicating an unhealthy reverence or fascination. They didn't stand out, instead they belonged, as though the wall's sole purpose had always been to house them. And so the visitor was treated to a gallery of her son's laughter, his tears, his tantrums, his joy and sadness, all captured in twelve 8 X 10 photos which represented five years of life.

Although there were only two bedrooms, Mary didn't need any more. She lived alone and had done so for five years. She turned to look at her son staring down at her from the wall and holding on to a squiggling Mr. Monkels. She smiled at him, now dead as long as he lived, he in turn smiling back at her, locked in time, forever a five-year-old, and forever smiling.

She checked the time and this revealed her hair dye had been in for well over half an hour. The dye was organic and smelled like shit in sunshine, and she wasn't sure if it was its strength or the onset of glaucoma that was bringing tears to Mr. Monkels's right eye. She checked her roots in the mirror and, upon confirming that they were sufficiently red, made her way upstairs to wash the color away. Later, she combed it out in front of her bathroom mirror before slapping moisturizer on her face and attempting to rub away the black rings around her eyes, with little or no success. *Oh great, I look like a red-haired panda. Not exactly the look I was going for.* She had been dying her hair red since the age of fifteen and, of those around her, very few remembered her natural mousy brown color and, although her hair color was fire-engine fake, it set off her pale skin and emerald eyes even when they were tired and betrayed her twenty-nine years.

She emptied the fridge of the food that had gone off during the four days she had been sequestered in her room, having endured a particularly nasty migraine. The rain continued to pour down from an open sky, rattling her windows before hitting the ground. The rain always reminded her of Ben but for no particular reason; it's not like he had really liked the rain or that they had shared any great memories that featured rain. It was possible that it was just those lazy indoor days that allowed her the time to remember him. Maybe it was the sound—as though the world was weeping or the way it crept down her window like tears. She walked into her sitting room with the intention of playing some music, but instead found herself staring at a framed black-and-white photo on the corner wall of Robert, then a sixteen-year-old boy, standing by a lake holding up a large fish, grinning widely and with eyes so much like his son's. She viewed this boy and felt more like his mother than his teenage girlfriend. She often wondered what he would be like if he had lived past seventeen but had long ago resigned herself to the fact that she would never know.

Cheer up, Panda Face! she thought, upon catching a glimpse of herself in the mirror.

"There is nothing quite as aging as morbidness," she said aloud and with a smile.

Mr. Monkels groaned in agreement. She laughed a little and put on the Scissor Sisters. "After all, Mr. M, no one does happy like homos!" She chuckled at her own joke but her dog didn't share either her sense of humor or her taste in music, because his reaction was to bury his head under his considerably large-sized paws, reminding her that she needed to get his nails clipped.

She boiled the kettle to make a pot of tea and pulled out the biscuit tin. It was definitely a day for tea and biscuits. Ivan had dropped off a DVD earlier, and, having spent the previous four days in a darkened bedroom, she was looking forward to settling down to a pleasant evening in front of the TV. But first she'd empty the washing machine, despite encroaching exhaustion.

★ ★ ★

It was a cold and crisp March morning in upstate New York. Sam stood in the center of the room taking one long last look at the white walls, white painted wooden floor and white sheets covering a white bed complete with white blankets. Coincidentally, on this day the small cubed window looked out onto a white sky. The painting above the bed was of a white cumulus cloud with the merest hint of a deep blue sky in the background. Sam moved to sit on his white wicker chair so as to stare at the deviant color, pondering silently whether or not it symbolized his possible future—like, for instance, blue skies ahead. Then again, a blue sky suggested a brightness that would be a large leap from the pile of shit from which he'd emerged. So instead and momentarily, he decided that it was more likely to be representative of that glimmer of hope those around him had often talked about. Although, and most likely, it meant nothing, the person who had bought the picture having never discussed its intent with the individual who hung it, who was most likely a workman with no interest in the musings of an addled brain. This deliberation was concluded with the notion that after two months in rehab, he had definitely experienced way too much therapy.

He turned his attention to his brown, battered and empty suitcase, opened out on and in contrast to his pristine bed, reminding him of the imperfect world outside. *I'm never going to make it.*

* * *

Eight weeks previously and the first time he'd awoken in this ridiculously white room, he had briefly believed himself to be dead. A lifelong atheist, his strongly held belief in nothing lapsed momentarily and he waited for the appearance of God, Saint Peter, Beelzebub or his long-gone Granny Baskin. The arrival of a large hulking gravel-voiced black man had come as a slight shock, his not having expected God, Saint Peter, Beelzebub or his long-gone Granny Baskin to manifest as an NBA basketball player. *Holy shit!* Then through his haze he heard the clicking sound of the door locking, and once the function of focus was achieved, he saw the NBA player crossing his arms and surveying the mess that lay twisted in front of him. And suddenly he knew exactly where he was. *Ah crap!* Death would have been the preferred choice. Then again, it would appear that cruelly the choice had not been his to make.

And so began his new life, one filled with vomit and excrement, crying and swearing, pleading and blackmail. The level of pain the body could feel as the heroin battled losing its grip was a shock. Childbirth couldn't be worse, of that he was sure, describing it to the NBA player as fucking torture in a whimpering, simpering tone that was unrecognizable even to himself. The hallucinations had been a welcome distraction, even the ones that freaked him out, like when he was sure that his own left arm had morphed into Cher and he'd chipped a knuckle driving her into the wall in an attempt to get her to stop singing "Just Like Jessie James."

"Holy fuck, I've just killed Cher!" Sam said in alarm.

"No, but you've made shit out of your hand," Danziger replied from a faraway place.

"Sonny's going to kill me," Sam said, shaking his head, and Danziger sighed.

"Let's just try to dial down the crazy," he instructed while tucking Sam into his bed like a father would a tired son.

The image of Danziger in a tutu was interesting, especially as he had flippers instead of feet.

"You're sure you're not wearing a tutu?" he asked.

"No, man, no tutu," Danziger sighed.

"If you say so, but your flippers are really fucked up," Sam said, gazing intently at Danziger's feet.

"Yeah, well, they're not alone." Danziger grinned. *The kid has imagination. I'll give him that.*

★ ★ ★

Sam would have thought that after all this time he'd be sick to death of all this white, but he wasn't. He would have believed that he'd crave some color, but he didn't. Originally desperate to leave, now he knew he could happily remain in his white cube forever, warm and safe, with no possibility of life interrupting. Yesterday he was calm, but today fear hung over him like an invisible lead coat—his knees threatening to buckle.

Danziger, the NBA basketball player, in reality a male nurse in his early fifties, entered from the hall and tapped the inside of the door to signal his arrival.

"Today's the day." He grinned.

Sam just stared at his empty case, unsure how to respond, having lost all energy to pretend that going home was a choice he'd been given to make. Silence was best. Danziger had seen it all before, both of them were aware of that fact, and this knowledge weighed heavily in the air. Danziger sat on Sam's white bed.

"I know it's hard." He spoke as softly as a man who smoked forty cigarettes a day could.

"I know you know," Sam replied despondently.

"You're reliving your auspicious entrance into this fine facility?" Danziger said with mock gravitas betrayed by a grin.

"Yeah," Sam admitted. "I thought I'd died."

Danziger laughed at the memory of Sam screaming and begging his forgiveness for the actions of the white man.

"What?" Sam asked, smiling at his nurse's hearty chuckle.

"Anyone ever mention that you scream like a little girl?" he laughed, and Sam pretended to reach over to punch him.

They both sat silently, Danziger allowing Sam to acknowledge the road ending.

"Everyone feels scared, son," Danziger reminded him after a long few minutes. He knew that Sam liked it when he called him son.

"I know that too," Sam said with a smile that stubbornly refused to reach his eyes.

"Wow! You know a lot for an asshole."

Sam laughed and nodded because he was right on both counts and they slipped into a comfortable silence.

★ ★ ★

Mary hadn't slept well the previous night, having been woken by a strange dream in which she had seen a teenage boy with a hood pulled tight and covering his face. He was running and she could feel his heart beat so hard that her own began battering against her chest wall. She heard his feet pounding the street and watched him turn in time to witness those that followed emerge around a corner. His feet moved faster and faster but his steps seemed to be shorter and shorter until he was running in place. She woke with a start, damp and heart still racing. *Morphine hangover,* she thought, and it made sense, her having been on two injections a day for four days running.

A shower and a glass of water later, and having gargled with mouthwash, she returned to her bed accompanied by a terrible uneasy feeling which guaranteed that she would lie awake and wondering. She often had "feelings" and sometimes they had forecast something terrible, but mostly they came to nothing much. She wondered about her cryptic dream. Around three thirty, weary and yet alert, she wondered if it foretold something bad like the time she dreamed Tina Murphy The Hill was trapped inside a large angry-looking egg. At the time she had dismissed it as nothing more than her own propensity for weirdness—however, the following week Tina Murphy The Hill collapsed at Weight Watchers and a day later had a ruptured ovary removed. Or, indeed, the time she saw Jimmy Jaw frantically searching for something in what appeared to be a large medical waste bin. Later that week he lost his little finger in a freak sawing accident. Not to mention awaking to the image of Sheena Shaw's cat Johnson on a flying carpet passing through clouds in the company of a sickly miniature pig, only to hear the very next day that he had been found throwing up bacon. The cat survived his encounter with food poisoning but Sheena's six-month-old carpet was described as smelling to high heaven and required replacing. She began listing some of the endless possibilities. Was the hooded boy a metaphor for a death? *Poor Mr. Monkels!* Worrying about Mr. Monkels took her to approximately three fifty, at which time, having registered that the link between a hooded boy and an ancient dog was tenuous, she switched her concern to whether or not it in some way signified Penny's disastrous love life? Then again, this disaster was ongoing. *That could explain the running. Poor Penny!* Then again, the kid was definitely a boy and not a girl, and, after all, Penny's love life might not have been the stuff of fairy tales but at least she had one. It was just after four fifteen when she began contemplating why she was alone. *Am I frigid? No, I like to get laid just as much as the next person. It's very relaxing. Am I scared? Yes? No? Maybe. OK, this is getting too heavy. Change the subject. Am I a lunatic? Has grief driven me to the precipice of sanity?* She smiled because in her head she was humming the tune to "She's a Maniac." And although her ramblings distracted her, they didn't seem to have an effect on her elevated pulse or awful sense of dread, so she refocused, concentrating on other concerns. Her dad had just had his heart checked and he was healthier than a fourteen-year-old. Ivan seemed happy and healthy; then again, he was still adjusting to life post a nasty separation. It had been over a year and he hadn't even attempted to find himself a girlfriend. It seemed a great waste to Mary as her cousin was kind, loving and not an ugly man. At around five she vowed to watch over him, knowing that Ivan wasn't built to be alone. At six she was still uneasy. Maybe the cause of her upset was the rain which had started to fall just after she had woken from the dream. The pier had flooded the year before and some of the cottages were badly damaged. She had miraculously escaped for no other reason than sheer luck and there was no way she would be lucky twice. It was a frigging miracle she'd been lucky once. Maybe it was the fear of flooding that was niggling deep down. *Yeah, it must be that.*

Despite her outward appearance, which suggested a calm and cool nature to those who loved her and possibly an impenetrable and cold one to those who didn't, Mary often worried about things that other people didn't. She would often daydream about terrible events that she would undoubtedly survive while those around would fall. The end of the world was her recurring nightmare; she'd be left to stand in the center of the universe alone, with nothing but thousands and thousands of miles of bodies and destruction enclosing her. She wasn't depressive or paranoid; she didn't suffer from any kind of insanity, morbidness or disturbing psychology. She was just aware that bad things happened and that they could happen to her. She didn't have the comfort of viewing death and disaster as some faraway notion to be tut-tutted about before being skipped over in favor of a conversation about shoes. It was a long-held belief by not only Mary but by many of the townspeople of Kenmare that she was a curse to those who loved her. She had long ago become used to being referred to as "Mary of the Sorrows." Of course, mostly it was a name intended to be used behind her back as opposed to her face, but sometimes an individual slipped, and more often than not she responded to the truncated version: "Mary of the . . ."

The name was born because people around her died. Her mother, her boyfriend and son couldn't survive her and she had long ago accepted her place in this world, which would be forever apart from the crowd. Her father had often attempted to dispel her theory by using his own survival as an example for the defense. She would smile at her dear old dad and make a joke so that he'd laugh and not worry about her and her fears. But it didn't help that she would most likely survive him too, and one day he would be a picture she would become lost in on a rainy day.

Mary put a neatly folded basket full of clean clothes under the stairs, having conceded a four-day headache culminating in a sleepless night meant she was just too jaded to iron. The phone rang in the distance and for a second she considered ignoring it, but curiosity was her vice.

"Hello?" she inquired, her high pitch suggesting she was slightly harassed.

"Jesus, have you seen the rain?" It was Penny.

"Yeah," she agreed, relieved to hear her friend's voice. "Mr. Monkels is like a pig." She laughed.

"Mr. Monkels smells like a pig," Penny retorted, and Mary laughed because she was right—when that dog farted it brought tears to the human eye.

"Are you better?" Penny asked.

"Yeah," Mary agreed.

"No blind spots, facial paralysis or partial blindness?" Penny said airily.

"Nope, I'm back in black." Mary laughed.

"Excellent," her friend noted. "Why don't we celebrate and head over to Killarney and see a movie?"

Mary looked out the window again. "It's horrible out there. I was planning on a night in with a DVD, the rain at the window, dog on my lap and a pot of tea by my elbow."

Penny was disgusted as she had her heart set on the new George Clooney film. "I swear, you're such an old lady, Mary. How the hell are you ever going to meet someone if your idea of a great night is sitting in with a dog?"

"Oh, and going to the Killarney Cineplex is a great way to meet men?" Mary countered, grinning at the absurdity. "Besides, there's a lot to be said for staying in," she continued while attempting to remove a chocolate stain from her cardigan, armed with only saliva and her thumb. While doing so she realized that wearing a cardigan gave Penny's previous statement some credence so she took it off. She might be unwilling to look for love in a Cineplex but she wasn't inclined to turn into Miss Marple either.

"Why don't you come over?" she asked.

"Hmmm, let me see," Penny wondered aloud. "George Clooney or you and a dog?"

"What's the movie?" Mary asked, merely to satisfy curiosity.

"Who cares? I just want to look at something pretty," Penny answered, true to form.

"And I'm supposed to be the sad one!" Mary laughed, shaking her head to suggest a mock despair.

"Yeah, well, 'Penny of the Sorrows' doesn't have the same ring to it. Besides, there's nothing sad about wanting to watch that sexy bastard get up to a few tricks."

"I used to love him in *ER*. He was so great with kids." Mary's voice suggested she was far away.

"Yeah, that's what's so appealing!" Penny said, laughing.

Silence followed as an impasse had been reached. Mary was desperate to stay within her four walls and Penny desperate to break free of hers.

"Come on, I have both a deep need to be shallow and a desperate need of distraction. If you drive I can have a drink," Penny pleaded.

Mary thought about it for a second before mumbling, "You always need distracting."

Penny would have pushed but she knew how Mary felt about crossing the mountain in the rain, and she was also mindful that, despite Mary's advice to the contrary, her head possibly felt like it had just been kicked.

"I have a bottle of wine in the fridge," Mary said, knowing that it would be the deciding factor on whether her friend would choose her over a movie star.

"All right," Penny conceded. "What's the DVD?"

Mary grabbed the video box on the coffee table while looking over to where Mr. Monkels now sat with his paws pressed against the window, much like a prisoner would hold on to bars.

"*What's Eating Gilbert Grape,*" Mary said, reading the label.

"What's eating what?"

"It's directed by Lasse Hallström." Mary continued to read, deep down knowing her friend hadn't a clue or a care as to who Lasse Hallström was.

"What?"

"He directed *Once Around.*" She read on.

Penny remained unimpressed.

"Which was a Sundance favorite apparently," Mary continued pathetically.

"Sundance means worthy and worthy means complete crap." Penny had an ability to inject disdain into her tone that was quite theatrical.

Mary smiled. "Yeah, well, this one mentions nothing about Sundance, it's about . . ." She read on silently and decided against going with the blurb.

Penny was busy weighing up her options. "The eating movie directed by a man who sounds like a weather system or George Clooney?" It was an unfair contest, but then again she didn't feel like facing the mountain alone and she had to get out of the house. Still, she needed more information before fully committing to a night in—after all, she could always go to the pub.

Mary hadn't noticed the actors' names and, when she at last copped them, she knew the deal was sealed.

"Hah!" she noted triumphantly. "Starring Johnny Depp and Leonardo DiCaprio!" She could hear Penny stand up.

"Open the wine, I'm on my way."

Chapter Two

Leaving the Womb

Danziger should have been off the night that they had brought Sam in. He'd swapped shifts so he could take his kid down to New York City to check out a college the following week. It had been a pretty slow night with most of his charges with heads out of the toilet and in therapy. He was due a newbie. However, Sam's admittance had been hastily set up, the waiting list bypassed, suggesting that this one had not only money but power, or at least those around him did. He often hated the "Richie Riches" as he called them, believing them to be bigger assholes than the poor bums on the street, and usually he was right. He was called to help the paramedics transfer Sam from the bus which had transferred him from the ER and the people who had miraculously managed to revive him. His girlfriend had found him flat on the bathroom floor with a broken needle in his arm and dried foam sealing blue lips. Now she was entrusting the folks at Rebirth to save him. She wasn't in the bus but, although she wasn't allowed entry to the facility, she had followed in her limo. She stood out, with oversized sunglasses and a scarf covering her hair, giving her an air of mystery patented long ago by a deceased fifties movie star. Danziger hadn't recognized her when she approached to say good-bye to her lover, passed out and laboring to breathe. He wasn't much of a pop-rock fan. Her beauty was inescapable though, and he'd pitied her when some paranoid prick in a suit had insisted she return to the car, not allowing her the time to kiss the poor half-dead bastard good-bye. She was hustled into the limo and he, the stiff with the heartbeat, was rolled into what Danziger liked to describe as the womb. He watched the bus pull out of the yard and followed Sam inside.

From the tomb to the womb, buddy. This is your second chance. Don't mess it up.

Sam would miss Danziger, despite initially and while under the influence having thought the man to be an evil twisted bastard bent on destroying him. In his sobriety he had come to rely on him for his strength, wisdom and kindness. It was Danziger who had watched over him while he shook so violently that his teeth began to hurt, Danziger who had guided his head over the toilet while he purged the sins of his body and soul. Danziger who had whispered comfort and insight into his ear while he lay on the floor aching, his bones screaming, his muscles tight, stomach in a ball, ears and head on fire. And Danziger who had held him when he wept like a schoolgirl. Now it was Danziger saying good-bye. *I don't want to go back there.* He thought about home and panic began to swirl inside of him.

"Are you still with me, buddy?" he heard Danziger ask

in muffled tone, and his response, a lie, came in the form of a nod.

If I go home I won't make it. If I go home I'll be chasing the dragon before the end of the week. If I go home I'll let them all down.

"What are you thinking?" Danziger inquired.

"I'm thinking I can't go home," Sam admitted, attempting to regain control over the panic which was gathering alarming momentum.

"So don't," Danziger said.

"You're kidding me," Sam replied.

"If it makes you sick, walk away," Danziger warned.

"It's that easy?" Sam asked in a tone which suggested he was not prepared to believe the answer.

"Did you ever listen in therapy?" Danziger asked, betraying a certain bewilderment.

"Mostly I tried not to," Sam mumbled, and Danziger shook his head while fingering his furrowed brow and sighing.

"Listen to me," he warned in the voice he used when he wasn't playing. "If your job, your family, your girlfriend, your friends, your goddamn pet triggers you into hitting the gravy—you leave."

"And go where?" Sam asked, battling a combination of fear and frustration.

"You're a rich guy. You could go anywhere or do anything," Danziger said, without a hint of pity because there were a lot of people a hell of a lot worse off than Sam. "So your life sucks. Change it."

Although Irish Catholic by birth, Sam hadn't ever really believed in an all-seeing, all-caring, all-damning God.

As a kid he'd tried to make sense of it all but the guilt was tiresome and the priest's bullshit never really rang true. Science made sense, deity didn't.

Once his body was cleansed of narcotics, therapy was obligatory. His shrink was a surprise—a bearded white guy in his early forties who favored wearing jeans and old T-shirts featuring seventies bands like The Sex Pistols, Blondie and The Ramones. He only responded when called by his nickname, "Phones." It became obvious early into their first session that his approach to his patients would be as diverse as his appearance.

"So, Sam, you like to get fucked up?" He smiled at Sam, who at that point was still suffering from a slight tremor.

Sam had offered a feeble smile, not sure if Phones was an actual person or if he was still hallucinating.

Phones smiled. "Yeah, withdrawal's a bitch."

It helped that the staff at Rebrith were all survivors of one addiction or another. They didn't have to tell their stories—they just empathized, listened and offered whatever advice they could, usually practical stuff like tricks to avoid slipping back into old habits.

It was during one of his sessions with Phones—sessions that Sam, despite his sincere distaste for therapy, had to admit he sometimes enjoyed—that his own death came up. The conversation started with both men debating as to whether or not Sid Vicious would have lived if he hadn't fallen in love with Nancy Spungen. Phones felt he would have had a chance but Sam was adamant he was a dead man long before he met her.

"She introduced him to heroin," Phones reminded him.

"If it hadn't been her it would have been someone else," Sam noted, nodding his head as though agreeing with himself.

Phones smiled. "So you're saying he was always looking to die?"

Sam thought about it for a moment. "Yeah, I suppose I am."

"Like you?" Phones asked.

Sam laughed and raised his hands in the air. "But I'm still here."

"But you did die."

Sam looked at Phones in disbelief. "Bullshit."

Phones picked up his medical notes. "It says here you left this world for just over three minutes."

Sam was unable to speak. Instead he shook his head from side to side.

"Flatlined." Phones drew an invisible line with his finger.

"Jesus," Sam heard himself say, and felt a headache come on.

"You're an insanely lucky man, Sammy." Phones smiled. "Most people don't survive, and those that do can suffer from any number of brain injuries. Someone was looking out for you, man."

Sam couldn't speak after that. He wanted to go back to his room.

Once inside his bed he covered his head and his eyes leaked and his nose ran and all the while he lay still and numb. *Somebody looking out for me. Bullshit!* And it was while hiding under his duvet he concluded that his leaning toward atheism had been well founded. This theory was fortified by the fact that he had died and there was nothing. He hadn't heard angels sing, nor was he drawn to any bright and overpowering light. He heard no voice whispering in his ear. He hadn't felt a mighty hand resting on his shoulder. Neither, and happily, had he been engulfed in hellfire, nor was his mind dissolved by torment. Brimstone hadn't fallen from a red sky like hot arrows searching for the target that was his sinning soul. The devil in drag was nowhere to be seen and he certainly wasn't being poked in his rear by a mighty pointed stick, contrary to a promise made long ago by Mrs. Potter, his first and only Sunday school teacher.

It would appear that the mighty Danziger was the closest Sam would ever come to knowing a God.

He had waited a few days before discussing his death with his new friend and it seemed shocking to Danziger that Sam, having touched death, had never once considered prayer. Sam had tried to warn him that his belief in the Lord was unfounded but Danziger laughed him off and told him it was cool, Jesus would wait for him. Sam hoped that Jesus had a magazine because he'd be waiting a long time. Danziger had grinned and patted him on the back.

"You'll find your way." He had smiled as though he knew something that Sam didn't.

And now Sam was leaving, supposedly to find his way in a new world of sobriety and cold reality, and he'd miss their political, biblical and social debates. He'd miss their games of poker and Danziger's chuckle. As much as he had enjoyed his sessions with Phones, and despite them both sharing a love of music, he hadn't connected to his shrink the way he had to his nurse. This was possibly because Phones asked too many questions.

"Why?"

"What happened, man?"

"Where did it all go wrong?"

"What are you hiding from?"

"What are you scared of?"

"Why do you hate yourself?"

These questions were impossible for Sam to answer because to do so would be to admit and face up to what had happened to him so long ago and to the terrible thing he had done so recently and he could never do that.

Danziger didn't ask questions and, because of that fact, although he too would never know the answers to many of the questions Phones posed, he had a better sense of Sam, the man. Sam's exit now looming, Danziger wasn't sure he was ready to leave or that he'd ever be ready.

Sam looked up at his guide.

"I won't go back to that life," he said confidently.

"And you're not staying here," Danziger responded predictably.

Sam focused on the blue background that rested behind the white clouds looming over Danziger's head. He remembered what his Granny Baskin used to say: *Life is as simple or as hard as you make it.* He hoped that one of his favorite people hadn't been full of shit. Danziger sat silently, examining his nicotine-stained hands. Sam smiled. His guide was never still—like a bored teenager he would constantly tap tables or crack knuckles. It often appeared as though he was counting his fingers to assure himself that he retained all ten. Sam often pondered whether the man was afraid of losing a digit or growing another one. It was obviously a nervous thing and he considered: now that he was straight would he start to count and crack his fingers too? He was determined not to as it was the only thing about the old sage that bothered him. Out of nowhere, Sam laughed a little, and Danziger shifted his gaze from his yellowed hand to Sam, wide-eyed.

"You're right," Sam said, and he felt the black cloud dissipating. "I can go anywhere. Better still, I know exactly where I'm going."

Danziger smiled to himself because, despite his initial concerns, he liked Sam. He didn't always like the people he helped but it helped him when he did. Liking someone made him better at his job and that made him feel good. Junkies like Sam reminded him that his job was worthwhile. *Whatever you do, just don't mess it up, kid.*

★ ★ ★

Mary had hung up the phone smiling and poured herself another cup of tea. She sat dunking a biscuit and waiting for her friend to arrive. The rain continued to beat against the window, much to Mr. Monkels's utter disgust. She got up to change the music. Although earlier the Scissor Sisters had been a welcome lift, in the interim she had reverted to an old favorite, and if Penny arrived to Radiohead, who she unfairly considered to be doom-ridden dickheads, she would turn around and leave. Mr. Monkels favored Eminem but Mary was definitely too tired to be sworn at. Unfortunately for Mr. Monkels, she rarely was in the humor for that. She decided on Simon & Garfunkel as they had the ability to complement her contemplative mood while still retaining a whimsicality which she felt would belie a creeping melancholy.

"What the hell is bothering me?" she asked her dog before skipping to "Scarborough Fair," and Mr. Monkels wheezed in protest, clearly annoyed that nothing appeared to be going his way. This wheeze turned into an odd splutter followed by a series of sneezes culminating in drool which Mr. Monkels shook off himself and onto her upholstery. Mary made a silent promise to change her vet. Her eyes rested again on the picture of Ben and Mr. Monkels basking in sunshine. It made her smile. Mr. Monkels never wheezed in those days. Outside, she could hear a car. Mr. Monkels stood to attention but she just ignored it. It was way too soon to be Penny.

★ ★ ★

Penny pulled a bottle of wine from her rack, reminding herself to replenish the dwindling supply. She was pulling on her coat when the phone rang and, thinking it was Mary attempting to put in a postmigraine chocolate order, she picked it up.

"Penn." It was Adam.

Oh God, no—go away, her mind begged.

"What do you want?" she asked, coldly pissed off that he'd caught her off guard.

"You," he said, and she could sense his sheepish grin and she wanted to punch his face in.

"Is that what you told your wife?" she asked, her voice dripping in sarcasm and with just a hint of bitterness.

"Don't," he sighed, and she wanted to cry.

She remained silent. There was nothing left to say.

26

He'd said it all the night before. He had to end it. He could never leave his wife. And in truth she had known this. She knew that although she loved him—and she truly did—he wasn't hers. He had three kids and ran his wife's father's business. He belonged to his wife. She'd earned him—at least that's how he'd put it the previous night when he'd broken off their affair one last time. It didn't matter that he was her first love or that she was his passion. It didn't matter that they had loved one another for over half their lives. It didn't matter that he had married his wife on the rebound. It didn't matter that he didn't love the woman. It didn't even matter that they had turned into some soap-opera cliché. He was married to someone else and that meant that she was leftovers and destined to remain on the periphery, fated to hide in the shadow of another woman's marriage. But no more. She was well and truly sick of it.

"You were right to end it. I don't want to be alone anymore, Adam," she sighed, tears tumbling again much to her chagrin.

"I don't want that for you either, I . . . I . . ." He didn't know what to say because there was nothing to say.

She could hear him breaking down, and instead of punching him she wanted to hug him but she couldn't. She was determined to be strong.

"I have to go," she said.

"Don't," he begged.

She hung up and sank to her floor, crying for the fifth time that day. She was going to cancel the stupid DVD evening but then she was terrified that Adam would turn up at her door, and if he did she would most certainly let him in and once he was inside she wouldn't be able to say no. But first she would have a drink, just to settle her nerves.

★ ★ ★

Afternoon had passed into late evening and then on to night. The town was silent, with few venturing out. Penny drove past the pubs, restaurants and shops, all painted brightly and featuring window boxes with their colorful contents absorbing the falling water greedily. She had stopped crying, instead allowing the rain which coursed down her glass windshield to speak for her. Sinéad O'Connor's rendition of "Nothing Compares to You" had been playing on the radio and she'd broken a fingernail in her hasty attempt to change the channel. Still, it was all fine now. She would go to Mary's and they'd watch a DVD and she'd talk about rubbish and forget about the sad sorry pathetic mess that was her world. Although she had often worried that her friend had abandoned the pursuit of love, it was days like these that made her question whether or not she was right. She wouldn't admit it though, not yet. After all, she might be heartbroken but she still had some hope.

★ ★ ★

At the window Mr. Monkels stood up and barked his version of hello to Mossy Leary from number 3, who had stopped to help Penny, who was battling to open her umbrella despite only having to walk ten paces from her car to the door. Mossy was in his late thirties with long dark hair forever in a ponytail. He was skinnier than Kate Moss and had large saucer eyes which Penny often joked made him

look like a cartoon character. He was a part-time fisherman, part-time housepainter, part-time sculptor and full-
time stoner. Mary opened the door and waved at Mossy,
who gave her the thumbs-up before heading off toward
town on a quest for a few free pints. She smiled at her
friend, who was cursing the retarded umbrella while attempting to shield her entire head with her left hand.

★ ★ ★

Danziger sat quietly flexing his fingers, appearing to be
deep in thought. He wanted his new friend to go out into
the world and survive it. He didn't have fancy dreams for
him, he was certainly too old to believe in happily ever
after, but he knew that survival was achievable. He knew
this because he had done it himself. He watched Sam stare
out into the white sky.

"It's a big world out there," Danziger commented.

Sam looked over at him and nodded in agreement. It
was a big world, bigger than him, Danziger and the white
room, bigger than upstate New York, New York City, the
United States, and he didn't have to go back there if he
really didn't want to. He stood up and opened his white
wardrobe, revealing his few dark clothes, and began packing. Danziger nodded, patted him on the back and left him
to it.

Sam made it to the front door of the clinic by himself.
He was rolled in and he was glad that they weren't going
to have to drag him out.

Danziger was waiting for him outside on the veranda.
He was smoking.

"You should give that up. Those things will kill you,"

Sam said in jest, something he only recently had relearned to do, and Danziger grinned.

"Tell you what," he replied. "You stay clean for five years and I will."

Sam laughed and guaranteed that he had himself a deal.

"You sure about that?" Danziger asked.

"Yeah," Sam said, unsure.

"Then you gotta offload those demons, man. You don't and you won't make it one year."

Sam nodded his head to signal he was listening. He looked beyond his smoking friend to the chauffeur standing by the black limousine, waiting to take him home, and suppressed the urge to run.

When there was nothing left to say the two men hugged, not like brothers or a father and son, but like fellow survivors.

"I'm glad I met you," Sam said.

"Right back at you," Danziger replied.

Sam smiled at him before getting into the car. *That's because you don't know me,* he thought. They waved at one another as the car pulled away, Sam's stomach and heart pulling in different directions and Danziger knowing as much. The car disappeared and Danziger sat on the white veranda and lit another cigarette.

Chapter Three

Beginning of the End

Mary woke to the sound of Penny's knock. She checked her watch, which revealed that it had been hours since her friend had agreed to come over. She answered the door. "I thought you were on your way?"

"I'm here, am I not?" Penny asked with a playful grin.

"You live ten minutes and not six hours away." Mary smiled, pleased to have slept.

"Sorry." Penny pushed past her. "I got held up." She didn't elaborate and Mary wasn't one to push.

Ever the gracious host, Mary poured a glass of white wine from a bottle she had chilling in the fridge. Penny drank, then swiftly ended Simon & Garfunkel's ode to the sound of silence which had been on repeat most of the evening.

"What's wrong?" she asked.

"Nothing?" Mary pretended.

"Are you maudlin?" Penny narrowed her eyes to view

her friend, adopting the stance of an intimidating inter-
rogator.

"No," Mary lied.

"Liar," Penny sighed. "Still, at least it's not Radiohead. I
swear I'd have left."

Mary smiled. "I'm fine." She topped up Penny's glass.

"Good, 'cause I cannot do depressing tonight," Penny
said, slumping in the chair. She crinkled her nose as Mary
disappeared into the kitchen. "What's that smell?"

"Shit in Sunshine," Mary said, returning and handing
Penny a plate of brown bread and smoked salmon. She
mouthed the word *shit* as opposed to saying it aloud. Mary
had stopped swearing when she became a mother and had
never got out of the habit.

"Dying your hair?"

Mary nodded.

"Nice job," Penny congratulated while putting her feet
up on the sofa and making herself comfortable, with the
brown bread and salmon on her lap.

Mary disappeared into the kitchen again.

"Hey!" Penny shouted.

"Yeah?"

"Mossy mentioned that Lucy Thomas was in next door
earlier."

Mary came back and placed some chili nuts on the
table. "Oh, yeah?" she said, betraying her concern.

Penny knew her too well to be fooled by her non-
chalance. "I wonder if you're due a new neighbor?" She
smiled as she sipped from her glass and began to read the
blurb on the back of the DVD.

Meanwhile, Mary struggled with the curtains. "No

32

way," she mumbled more to herself than her friend. "She's probably just checking the house for flooding."

Penny was grinning at her annoyance. "She's come all the way from Mallow to check for flooding—yeah, that must be it," she noted sarcastically.

Mary called her a frigger before looking out at a boat, which had docked earlier that week, slapping against the pier wall. The skies were further darkening. She turned to her friend.

"What's it like in town?"

"Wet, windy, ghostly." Penny was reading the back of the DVD with an expression of confusion crossing her face. She looked at Mary and then back to the blurb. " 'A prisoner of his dysfunctional family's broken dreams in tiny Endora, IA, Gilbert (Depp)'—I love him!—'serves as breadwinner and caretaker for his mother and siblings following his father's suicide and his older brother's defection. Momma (Darlene Cates)'—who's she?—'is a morbidly obese shut-in'—Oh my God!—'who hasn't left the house in seven years; her children include retarded Arnie . . .' Wait a minute—DiCaprio is retarded? You are taking the piss!"

Mary couldn't help but enjoy Penny's disgust. "Ivan said that it was funny, in parts," she said, attempting to placate her.

"Funny? Yeah, it really sounds hilarious!" And then it dawned on Penny. "Jesus, it was filmed in 1993! DiCaprio's retarded and his balls hadn't even dropped! What am I supposed to do with this?" She was holding the DVD in the air like a demonstrator in a supermarket.

"I don't know—what would you have done with it if

33

DiCaprio *wasn't* retarded and his balls *had* dropped?" Mary grinned.

"Good point," Penny agreed. "Still, this does not sound remotely shallow." She sighed, resting the DVD on the coffee table.

"Are you OK?" Mary asked, concerned. Penny did seem OK, but then Penny was a master in the art of masking. Mary had often thought what a great actor she would have made, but Penny had joined an acting class one summer and hated it, calling those around her a bunch of jumped-up talent-free tossers before walking out in what could only be described as a grand exit. Penny was smiling but Mary could sense a problem. *Maybe the dream was about Penny.*

"I'm fine. It's just the endless rain," Penny lied. She wasn't ready to admit that she and Adam had ended their relationship, primarily because she wanted to forget but also because she wasn't sure that either of them would be able to stick to their guns. After all, they had broken up many times before. "Just put the film on and pass the bottle." She grinned.

Mary was suspicious but she didn't say anything. When Penny was ready to share her problem, she'd be there to listen. Mary knew what it was like to have people stick their noses in and it wasn't good. Instead, she smiled at her friend and her friend smiled back, both content in the knowledge that Mary would ignore the problem as long as Penny needed her to.

★ ★ ★

Mia had been up since 4:00 AM. It was now after 6:00 PM and Sam had left rehab eight hours ago. She surveyed the living room in Sam's apartment, viewing the paintings he had on the wall, all dark colors, all with a certain bleakness. She hadn't noticed that before. She looked at his famous CD collection on shelves, which took up the entire opposing wall, filled ceiling to floor with all the classics. He could always pick a tune, she could say that for him. There was a guitar placed on a stand in the corner. It was a 1954 Gibson J-50 and one of Scotty Moore's. She smiled, remembering their first date. He had spent the whole evening talking about the stupid guitar. He had spoken with such passion that she burned for him. He had been passionate once. He was a big Elvis fan and to have Scotty Moore's guitar really meant something. She noticed that now his once-prized possession was dressed in a thick layer of dust and wondered if it still meant something. He could play too although he would never play for her. It was odd looking at it hidden and untouched in the corner. She wondered if it was just his way to neglect the things he loved.

She turned her attention to the girl serving snacks to the invited guests. She yearned for something to eat but at first light she would be back on set, making a video with an up-and-coming rapper she had recorded guest vocals for a few months previously. Predictably, it was a bikini shot, so she sipped on her water and watched the door. She wished her lead guitarist, Danny, was here but he had flat out refused, due to him and the rest of her band having long ago decided that her boyfriend was a waste of space. Still, it would have been nice to have his strength, as over the past months his was the strength she had come to rely upon. She had begged but it seemed that for some reason Danny had taken Sam's failings personally and, while she could normally rely on his being pliable, this once he would not budge.

Leland approached. "So the wanderer returns." He smiled at her.

Fuck you! Mia thought. "Yes, indeed he does." She returned his fake smile.

"It must have been hard on you for all this time." He said, looking straight at her as though he could see right through her.

She detested the invasion but fought the desire to avert her eyes. *It would have been a hell of a lot easier if you'd let me have some time off to care for him, you bloated bastard!* Her smile increased. "It was never that bad, Leland—besides, in case you've forgotten, I was on tour all of last year so I pretty much missed most of it." She took a drink and wished it was booze.

Damn shame that tour didn't translate into record sales, Leland thought. "We both know it's been going on a lot longer than that," he said, patting her arm, and she pulled away ever so slightly while holding her smile.

The forced falsity was beginning to get on Mia's nerves. Her hate was palpable; Leland was no fool, nor was Mia any sort of actress.

This was annoying to Leland as she should have been grateful that he hadn't dropped her. Still, he wasn't going to get into that right now.

"Well, we're all happy he's back to himself. He gave us a scare. Sam's been in the record business for a long time now and he's certainly made a huge contribution to our success. He's always had an eye for talent—after all, he discovered you. Of course, he makes mistakes too." He fell silent, awaiting her response.

She didn't have one. He held his grin and she knew what he was thinking: *What do you say to that?*

In response she flashed her most alluring smoky-eyed smile. *Please go crawl under a rock and die!* she thought to herself as they continued to grin at one another, each determined to win their little pissing contest.

"And as for you, I'm sure that the next album will do better than the last." He smiled, holding up his glass so that she could toast with him.

What an asshole! she contemplated, clinking his glass before walking away. One of the English kids from the stupid new boy band Sam would be handling was watching her and waiting to make his move. He'd been gorging himself on free beer and, at no more than twenty and pretty as a little boy cheerleader, he fancied his chances.

"Hey, gorgeous!" was his opening line.

"Hey, kid!" she said, attempting to put him in his place.

"Kid." He nodded. "I like that. I like that a lot." He was grinning as though she had made a joke as opposed to pointing out a fact.

She attempted to walk on. He stopped her by putting his hand flat on her stomach. "Unbelievable." He grinned. "My hand on Mia Johnson's abs. Nice one!" His nodding increased and it was making him appear like a fool.

"You're the guitar player, right?" she asked.

"And backing vocals," he said, straightening in a peacock-proud manner.

"Some advice," she said, leaning toward his ear tantalizingly.

He leaned forward to receive her words of wisdom.

"Take your hand off me or it'll be some time before you play again." She smiled and nodded at him pleasantly.

He looked from her face to where his hand rested and it appeared that for a moment he was considering whether or not the trade-off was worth it. He then removed it slowly, allowing her to pass by before watching her leave with a sigh.

His friend, the lead vocalist and less attractive, sidled up to his bandmate. "Sweet shit, Derek, you just touched a goddess!"

The kid grinned. "And with the same hand I wank with, Lucian." He looked at his own hand with a certain kind of awe before repeating, "The hand I wank with." Then they high-fived before going about the serious business of finding snacks.

Mia walked through the room full of strangers and into the kitchen. The waitresses were busy. She went to the fridge and poured herself some water.

"I can do that for you, madam," a waitress said from behind her.

"No, it's all right," she said. *It's not like I've anything better to do.*

★ ★ ★

Having insisted on a number of detours, Sam arrived at his apartment block after six.

The car had come equipped with a phone and laptop and old habits ensured it had become his office before he

was halfway down the Rebirth's long and winding drive-
way. He surfed the net and made an international call. By
the time he reached home, his plan of escape was coming
together nicely.

His chauffeur held open the door that led Sam out
onto the street. He looked around at the passing cars,
upward to the movement in the never-ending windows
that inhabited the dusky sky and on to the lights that
shone brightly, filling the evening with blinding color.
People moved past him. He stood still, his heart beating in time with their footsteps. He listened hard and
could hear their rhythm but the beat was interrupted
by Ricky.

"How you doin', Mr. Sullivan?" He was smiling but
Sam knew that Ricky couldn't be happy to see him.

"Good. Thanks, Ricky." He started to walk into the
building with Ricky following, carrying his suitcase.

"So how long has it been?" Ricky asked pleasantly.

"Eight weeks," Sam answered, still walking.

"Wow, time flies!" Ricky noted as they both moved to
enter the lift.

"I can take it from here," Sam said, reclaiming his suitcase
while at the same time pulling out a roll of twenty-dollar
bills from his pocket and handing them to his doorman.
"That's for you. I'm, ah, sorry about being such an asshole
over the years." He was unable to look his doorman in the
eye.

Ricky looked at the roll in his hand. *Holy shit, there must
be at least two hundred bucks here!* He had to make sure Sam
hadn't made a mistake like old lady Winters in D5. "This
is for me?" he asked.

"You deserve it," Sam confirmed, remembering to add, "Have a nice evening," for the first time in a while.

"Thank you, sir." Ricky responded with the respect and gratitude that only money could buy.

Ricky got out of the lift, leaving Sam alone and surrounded by mirrors. Sam closed his eyes, still unable to look at himself. He didn't mind that he'd just tipped Ricky over two hundred dollars. He deserved it, especially after that time he had vomited on him. He really should have tipped him that night but he was too busy dropping his pants to moon old lady Winters in D5. It was hard to return to the building where he had almost died, and it was harder to return to the building where he had embarrassed himself over and over again, so much so that the committee had tried to oust him on a number of occasions. His connections were powerful enough to ensure that was never going to happen and so in response many had sold up and left. His past behavior was inescapable and his cohabitants and the doormen had put up with a lot of his crap for a lot of years and it would take a hell of a lot more than two hundred bucks and minor pleasantries for anyone to forget. It was just another reason why he could never stay here. He walked to his apartment and stood outside for just a second but long enough to hear the muffled sounds that signified a party. *Damn it, Mia. I just want to be alone.* He took his key from the inside of his jacket and held it in his hand, battling the urge to run.

★ ★ ★

They were halfway through the film and Penny was finishing off the bottle of wine. Mary seemed to be enjoying the sad tale. Crispin Glover as the undertaker made her laugh out loud and Darlene Cates instilled in her a deep need to emit the sound "Aaah!" a lot. It would appear that she was very much alone in her opinion with Penny mumbling the words "Kill me!" a number of times while downing her wine and playing with a broken fingernail.

"If I didn't know that DiCaprio was an actor I'd really think that he was retarded," said Mary. "He really pulled it off. Don't you think he really comes off as retarded?"

"Yeah, it's great," Penny sighed.

"Like the Down syndrome kid, you know the one on that TV show with the blond girl who was in *Romeo and Juliet* with DiCaprio. What's his name?"

"Oh, Corky," Penny said, perking up.

"Yeah, Corky. He was great."

"Yeah," Penny nodded, "he was but you're thinking of the wrong blonde."

"Who am I thinking of?"

"You're thinking of the brown-haired girl who had the HIV boyfriend. She went blond and joined the cast of *ER* where she was stabbed to death."

"So who's Juliet?"

"She was the redhead with the homeless gay friend and the song-writing slacker boyfriend. It was a completely different show."

"Wow," Mary concluded, "every day is a school day."

"It certainly is," Penny agreed, looking for the bottle opener. Once located, she opened a second bottle and poured a tall glass.

Meanwhile, on screen, the retarded DiCaprio was being

left to freeze to death in a cold bath overnight, forgotten by Depp, his horny brother.

"Kill me!" Penny repeated.

"We can turn it off," Mary offered, desperately battling the urge to cry for the child, shaking and blue-lipped, on screen.

"No. It's fine. Seriously it's not that bad," Penny conceded, but then Depp ended his affair with the married Mary Steenburgen and Penny broke down, weeping openly.

"Do you need a break?" Mary asked, and Penny nodded her head in agreement while tears coursed down her face.

"OK." Mary switched off the TV.

Penny wiped her eyes, mumbling something about how pathetic she was being.

"Do you want some coffee?" Mary asked.

"No. I'll finish my wine."

"Do you want a hug?"

"That would be lovely."

They hugged.

"I'm such a sap," Penny said, and Mary nodded. "But, Mare?" she asked, becoming serious.

"Yeah?" Mary answered, pulling away while Penny composed herself.

"Do you think it's better to be alone?" Penny asked.

"No." Mary shook her head. "But possibly safer."

Penny nodded. "Yeah, I suppose you're right."

"So you're fine?" Mary asked with a raised eyebrow while Penny blew her nose.

"I'll be fine." She smiled.

42

Mary leaned over and kissed her friend's forehead to comfort her, much like she used to comfort her son. "Yes, you will," she said. *Once a mother, always a mother.*

Penny was too drunk to drive home. Mary fixed up the spare bedroom when the film finally ended. Penny's problem had become obvious to Mary when she began sobbing. Penny wasn't usually a crier, not like Mary, for whom hiding emotion was a constant battle. Mary wasn't sure if her friend had ended her affair with the only man she ever loved and she didn't know how desperately heartbroken she was. But having said that, Mary had often admitted that she didn't know much when it came to love. Penny had thought about saying something halfway through her second bottle of wine but then she reconsidered, not feeling strong enough to share. Mary didn't really have a clue what it was like to feel anything other than ambivalence toward the men that had crossed her path since Robert had died. She had little understanding of Penny's kind of heartbreak.

And yet Penny believed that she understood the reasoning behind Mary's lethargy toward love. After all, to her mind Robert had been Mary's first and only love. He was one she couldn't forget, the one who tied her up in knots even now as she faced her thirties. Mary's first love had died, leaving her a son who had followed his dad. Of course, Penny thought that Mary couldn't let herself fall in love, or know love; love had only brought her pain and suffering. But then Penny's view of Mary's pain was simplistic. Penny was a die-hard romantic. She liked to think that Robert was the Romeo to Mary's Juliet. In reality, Mary's reasons for being alone were far more mundane than that.

Mary tucked Penny in that night while Penny, in her drunken mind, made a silent pact to be more like her friend. To this end she vowed to close off, to shut out the world and all its rubbish. It occurred to her that maybe then she'd have half a chance at being happy.

Mary stood at the bedroom door watching Penny, who began to stir. "You need to go to the loo again, don't you?" Mary smiled down at her drooling friend, wondering what the hell was going through her mind.

"I cannnn go myssselff," Penny slurred despite her attempts to conceal her verbal inadequacies.

"I know," Mary said, hoisting her from her bed.

And as they walked to the bathroom arm in arm, Penny asked her friend why life was so hard.

"Because God is a spoiled child and this world is just a game he plays to amuse himself."

"We're prawns," Penny agreed.

"Pawns," Mary corrected.

"That's what I said—prawns."

Mary helped her to sit on the loo, Penny's pants around her ankles, not shy—after all, they had been sharing toilet stalls since they were in their early teens.

"Mare?"

"Yeah."

"He loves me."

"I know," Mary agreed, steadying her friend on the toilet seat. She might not have been sure what was going on inside her friend's head but she knew she was suffering. She'd watched her suffer for years, the victim of love.

Penny and Adam had first fallen for one another aged fourteen, and six months before Mary and Robert had

44

become an official couple. Back then, everything was possible, and love, as rich and fulfilling as it was, was deemed to be puppylike. Deep down they all knew that there would be life after their pubescent passion. It was a pity for Robert that he wouldn't live past secondary school and it was a pity for Adam that Penny would move on to a college in Dublin to study journalism while he stayed at home and worked in his dad's restaurant business. After her first year, she had decided her life lay elsewhere. She yearned for city life and he was a content country boy. Initially, he felt left behind, but he was also young and as keen as she was to explore other loves. Besides, he never wanted to be anything other than a restaurateur and there was no better place than Kenmare for that. It was a beautiful place to live, and profitable. The father of the woman who would later be his wife was a millionaire from Holland and had spotted the town's potential on a visit to the place in the late eighties. He had invested in a small hotel resting by the sea on the outskirts of the town and, while Penny worked as a journalist in Dublin, her first love found a substitute and a new life as husband, father and hotel manager of a quaint manor house. It was just a shame for Penny that the reality of city living didn't meet the fantasy, worse still that no other man could replace Adam in her heart. She had believed that love would come again but it didn't and, having lost a love that was once so full, she was left empty and rattled. As for Adam, it was a shame that in losing Penny he lost his belief in romance. Maybe it was that loss that ensured that he would rush into a relationship of convenience. But the greatest calamity was that in the end, when Penny came home, it was too late.

As for Mary, well, she suffered the loss of her first love, showing great strength, and her shock pregnancy was deemed a miracle despite the Church frowning on unmarried mothers. Even the parish priest agreed the child was meant to be, despite her youth and the lack of a wedding ring on her finger. Then again, less than six years later when her son was so cruelly taken, that same priest would have probably deemed her baby's death as some sort of moral lesson. Not that any priests dared to call upon her with their views, not after she punched the archbishop straight in the face less than a month after her child's demise.

Mary settled Penny back in bed, ensuring the blankets hugged her chin. Penny was out of it.

"It will be OK," Mary whispered. "Whatever's going on, you'll get over it."

"I won'tttt," Penny slurred, surprisingly half awake.

"You will," Mary told her drunken friend.

"I ssshouldn't have come back!"

"Don't be silly!"

"I don't want to end up like you," Penny mumbled, surprisingly clearly despite her encroaching stupor.

Mary stood up. Hurt, she backed away. "No. I suppose you don't," she said, before closing the door.

Penny moaned, too drunk to respond. She would have been sorry to have elicited such a response from Mary if she had remembered what she had said.

Mary left, returning to her own room, upset that her friend would hurt her but knowing that she was drunk and, more importantly, had a point. Mary hadn't had a relationship with a man since her son died over five years before. Before that there were a few but none of them lasted longer than a few months. She pulled on her T-shirt and crawled into bed.

Mr. Monkels resented having to move aside to allow her access before stretching out on his side of the bed and deep down she knew it was ridiculous that her dog had a side of the bed but he did. Penny was passed out next door while for hours Mary lay, still anxious and awake. *What the hell is wrong with me?* Mr. Monkels was wheezing beside her but the rain had stopped, which was good. *No need for sandbags.* When she looked out her window the water seemed calm. The boat no longer slapped against the pier wall. Still, her eyes refused to close.

Chapter Four

Say Hello, Say Good-bye

Mia sat on an armchair watching the door, avoiding eye contact with her unwanted guests and attempting to become invisible. She was surrounded by Sam's A and R team, the company directors, the entire creative staff and stylist team, his PA, a few notable recording producers and the members of the stupid English boy band ironically named Detox. She started to sweat. *What if he doesn't come home? I'll look a fool.* He had promised her, but then he had broken promises before. *No, this is different. He's clean now and everything's going to change. Everything is going to be better,* she told herself, hoping it was true. She was hungry and battling that familiar pain in her gut. *Please come home!* she prayed as the others talked and laughed around her.

★ ★ ★

It took a few minutes but eventually Sam put the key in the door. *You can do it*, he told himself before entering to meet a wall of applause. He stood rooted to the door frame, shaken by his large audience. *Oh shit, I can't do this!* The panic felt a little like stage fright but far more terrifying. Mia launched herself from where she was sitting into his arms, hugging him close while whispering into his ear, "Thank God! It's so good to have you home and back where you belong."

He held on to her as a matter of necessity, his knees once again threatening to buckle. Then the sea of familiar faces descended upon him, all talking and wishing him good health and continued good fortune. Within five minutes he was in a corner sipping from a glass of Perrier water with a dash of lime and looking into his boss's face as the man talked about Detox's bright future and the role Sam had to play in it as though he wasn't a heroin addict and hadn't just emerged from rehab. *Mia is right. He is a bloated bastard.*

"They'll be ready to release their first single in a matter of weeks," Leland said.

Sam nodded. "That's good," he muttered, not really giving a rat's ass. As green as they were, he was sure the kids would make money, despite the fact that he couldn't stand the crap they were churning out. *When exactly did I sell out?*

"You've got that look," Leland noted, encouraged.

"What look?" Sam enquired.

"The look that tells me you're already on top of things," he boomed, clapping Sam on the back.

Sam shook his head and smiled at him much as his girlfriend had earlier, the only difference being that, unlike Mia, Sam was a born liar, and despite his hatred for his boss Leland was fooled into believing that Sam loved and respected him. Furthermore, Leland believed that although his brightest star had fallen he would rise again. Leland was about to be very disappointed. Sam knew that Leland was not the kind of guy that responded to negativity. It was positive or it wasn't discussed and that way he avoided any kind of reality from permeating his kingdom made up of cash, blood, sweat and sellouts.

"Testing has been very positive—the college kids loved them," Sam said before stopping to sip from his glass, his mouth dry and head hurting.

"Of course they did, son, just like you said they would." Leland laughed.

Sam never liked it when Leland called him son but he smiled at the old man anyway. *Old habits die hard*.

It was night and the gray New York sky had faded to black. Sam liked the night—black was a fine canvas on which to splay the city lights. They danced while he sat on a cold chair on the balcony, unwittingly playing with his hands in a manner not too distant from Danziger's. Mia joined him, sitting on the arm of the chair. She put her arm around his shoulder like an old friend. He looked at her and smiled.

"They're all gone," she said, returning his smile, happy to admit that she was as relieved as he was. "You can come back inside, it's safe," she added playfully in a tone both gentle and warm.

He nodded and for the first time he realized that he had missed her. It was just a shame that it wasn't in the way she wanted him to. *Why not?* he wondered. She was beautiful, talented and independently wealthy—she was a rock star, for Christ's sake, with millions of fans and the better part of the world at her feet. He marveled at what she was doing with him. Why she had remained in his life was a mystery—after all, for a long time now he had been nothing more than a sick junkie whose idea of a slow night was injecting heroin in his own toilet. He'd been a total asshole. When he was high he would embarrass her and when he was low he would abuse her, and yet this woman, who could have almost any man she wanted, still wanted him. He wondered how she could do that to herself and why she would accept his never-ending shit and then it dawned on him: when he found her she was broken. *Have I helped fix her only to go and break her again?* He felt sick because of the way he had treated her, but mostly because she had done everything to save him and, despite this, he was about to leave her. And in his mind he acknowledged that what he would miss most wasn't her caramel skin, her big brown eyes or her even teeth or perfect face and body—instead he would miss her friendship and kindness.

Mia looked out over the city lights. Sam's silence frightened her. She wanted him to hold her close and tell her that he was sorry and he loved her and that they were going to live happily ever after—but sitting there she guessed that it might never happen. Sam wasn't the kind of guy that shared his feelings. Sam was a man's man, at least that's what she told herself. She wasn't stupid, she was just hopeful. The first time she'd seen him he was so beautiful, but more than that she'd fallen in love madly and deeply and for a while it had seemed that he had felt the same way. But then most of us know that lust has a way of confusing even the coldest heart and lust never lasts—no matter how skinny you are, how pert your tits or tight your ass, and no matter how beautiful your face or full your lips, lust is always satiated—it's just a matter of time. In truth it was likely that she had loved while he had simply conquered. He'd tried to love her but he'd failed.

She wouldn't give up though—instead, she fought back tears. Sam, lost in his own private world, didn't notice. She squeezed his hand and walked inside, leaving him to be dazzled by the city lights. She cried until empty and then fell asleep alone, exhausted by her life, exhausted by the pressure of living up to the perception of who she was, exhausted by the disappointment that who she was would most likely never be enough, exhausted by success and failure. Her love life was in tatters along with her heart and her career was on a knife's edge. That bloated bastard was right—she needed the next album to work. Her last one had been a flop both critically and commercially. Her first album had sold six million. She had been huge, a megastar, everything that she had always wanted to be. All the hard work had paid off. The world was at her feet but it appeared that her elevated position had destroyed her creativity; her hunger satisfied meant she had little to say; excessive time had been spent trying to look good for the glossy magazines, too much time had been spent talking about her life, her opinions, her ambition, her dreams, too many parties and being seen. Good producers do not a good album make. Good songs make a good album and in her second album the songs just weren't that good. *Why?* she had wondered at the time. It took time to work that one out but that's what's so odd about life—it was only at her lowest point, with her record company threatening to drop her, her boyfriend a heroin addict and another rock princess sitting on her throne, that she rediscovered song, music and what had once really mattered. This album would be a success. It had to be, because if it wasn't she would lose everything she didn't want. She had resigned herself a long time ago to the fact that the glitzy lifestyle that had once appeared to be the Holy Grail was nothing more than a Brothers Grimm fairy tale, but that was OK because when she stood on a stage and sang all the pain went away.

Sam went inside when it got so cold he could feel pain. He looked at Mia asleep in his bed and wondered what she dreamed of. He knew that whatever it was, it wasn't something that he could ever truly share. He was incapable of that. It was possible that he was even incapable of love. He didn't dwell on it though because he wasn't strong enough to face that particular type of despair. He wasn't tired. He was awake for the first time in a long time. He was awake and alone, alone in a room with a woman who loved him, and he wondered how he was going to tell her he was leaving. He got into bed and Mia curled into him. He held her and closed his eyes, afraid she would wake and require his attention. He had hated himself for so long and knew that he couldn't go back to that. He wanted to be free. Free of Mia, free from the endless bands, their managers, record producers, pushy journalists, stylists, radio jocks, that next big act, the next big track and counting the cash. He wanted to be free of himself entirely, and maybe in doing so he could be free of the memory of what he had done. He would leave and wasn't sure if he would ever come back. Although they had let him down and disowned him, he wondered if he should visit his parents to let them know that he was OK. His mother would be happy to see that he had made it out of rehab clean and looking surprisingly healthy for a junkie. His dad would remind her that her son had let her down many times before, and warn her not to have too much faith that the waster they had raised would amount to anything other than a thorn in their side. But deep down Sam knew that his dad would be hopeful that his son would prove him wrong this time. Two months ago he would have said fuck 'em and not bothered with the hassle, but now things were different. He needed to be a man he could be proud of. He needed to tell them that. He didn't expect anything. He didn't really want anything. He didn't even know if he could forgive them. All he wanted to do was say good-bye. He could hear Mia's stomach rumble as she slept and it induced further guilt. *God, I wish she would eat.*

★ ★ ★

Despite another night with little or no sleep, Mary was the first in the house to wake. She showered and dressed while Penny and Mr. Monkels still slept on. She laid out the dog's breakfast and started to cook something up for Penny. She broke some eggs and the doorbell rang. She allowed them to sizzle in the pan while she opened the door. Jerry Letter grinned at her. "Soft day," he said, handing her two bills from his postbag.

"Coffee?"

"No. I'm running a bit late and I promised Maura I'd take her to Killarney to get her ingrown toenail sorted out."

"Too much information, Jerry!" Mary sighed.

"You think that's bad, you should see her arse!" He winked at her and laughed at himself, revealing his familiar gummy smile. "So I hear Lucy was in next door last night?"

Mary grinned. "You don't miss a trick."

"Well?"

"Well, what?"

"So you're getting a new neighbor?"

"You tell me." She smiled.

"I hear it's Friday," he said, winking.

Ivan walked up behind him. "Jerry!" He clapped the postman on the back.

"Ivan," Jerry said. "That was a fair old game on Saturday. Damn near close to losing."

Ivan laughed and nodded. "Ah sure, almost losing is better than almost winning."

He passed Mary, who waved at Jerry, already halfway down the road. She closed the door and faced her cousin, who was making his way into her kitchen.

"Just in time for breakfast. Jesus, I'm a mighty man for timing!" He handed her his newspaper and sat down.

"I watched the film," she noted while breaking more eggs.

"So, did you cry?" he inquired, making coffee.

"No." She grinned. Ivan knew her better than anyone including Penny.

"Liar." He smiled. "You cried when a Fraggle stole the Gorgs' tomato in *Fraggle Rock*!" He laughed at the memory.

"OK, Ivan, we both know that the tomato was Junior

Gorg's only friend. Not to mention the fact that I was a child."

"You were sixteen," he said, making himself comfortable."

"All right, I might have squeezed out a tear or two but Penny did most of the crying."

"Penny was here?" he asked curiously.

"Still is. Why?"

"It's over with Adam."

"I guessed," she said, nodding. "How is he?"

"Devastated but it's for the best—he has a wife and kids. How's Penn?"

Mary sighed. "Not really talking. She got drunk and went to bed."

Ivan nodded. "It's for the best," he repeated.

"Yeah, I know."

Penny appeared in the doorway, hung over, with her head in her hands. "And just when you think things can't get any worse you succumb to the hangover from a place they call hell." She smiled at Mary and Ivan.

Mary automatically went to her medicine press and handed her friend two painkillers while Ivan poured her a glass of water.

"You know?" she asked Ivan.

"I do."

She looked at Mary. "Did I tell you?" she asked, embarrassed by the gap in her memory.

"Not in so many words." Mary smiled. "I'm sorry, Penn," she said, serving eggs.

"Thanks," Penny said, welling up.

Ivan hugged her. "It's for the best," he reiterated.

56

They sat down together, Mary and Ivan eating eggs and Penny chasing hers around her plate.

"So what's the situation with next door?" Ivan asked his cousin.

"New neighbors?" Penny asked, attempting to perk up.

"Friday," Mary said. "Three days and counting."

Ivan smiled, knowing his cousin hated the idea of being bothered and secretly hoping that whoever moved next door would do just that.

"Stop grinning!" She shook her fork at him.

"Let's hope they're interesting," Penny sighed.

"Well, just as long as they can speak English," Ivan noted, winking at Penny.

"Jesus, there is nothing worse than having to deal with people through sign language and a shagging phrase book!" she said, returning Ivan's wink.

"Oh sweet God!" Mary moaned while Ivan and Penny grinned at one another.

Chapter Five

The New Neighbor

Four days had passed since Sam emerged from rehab and made a call which would arguably and hopefully change the course of his life. It had been a long flight, New York to Dublin, followed by another shorter and more uncomfortable flight, Dublin to Farranfore, followed by a forty-six-kilometer drive to Kenmare.

The man at Avis had given him a map, which would take him onto the Cork road rather than over the mountain pass.

"Safer," he advised. "The mountain on a night like this is a killer, especially for you tourists. Sure you're not able for it at all!" he chuckled.

Sam just said thanks and left. He should have asked some questions because a mixture of confusion, exhaustion and a bad map meant he ended up on the mountain. The rain continued and the road was slowly turning into a stream. He crawled but the water was rising and the large potholes and dips in the road were getting more and more waterlogged and dangerous. The locals were obviously all using the Cork road because he was alone.

Despite all the negatives and narrowly escaping flooding his engine numerous times, he couldn't help but stop and absorb the surrounding bleak and desperate beauty. He had never really been a picture-postcard kind of person, never having stopped to take in his surroundings. He couldn't remember ever before being touched by a beautiful beach or a field of flowers but, on this rainy cold and miserable evening, he looked out onto the jagged gray rock looming over the winding road which weaved through drenched and dripping woods, and it captured him.

Having said that, after two hours wading through potholes the scenery was getting old.

When he arrived into the town it was after seven and the rain kept coming down. It was a small black and white signpost that revealed he had reached his destination and he sighed with genuine relief. The cliff-top twists and turns had been an unexpected challenge and having nearly come off the mountain a few times he felt like he'd survived nature's gauntlet. The town opened up before him and even through the dull heavy endless drizzle its quaint charm, colored walls, rock and gray jagged stone captivated him. Despite his exhaustion and because he had no idea where he was going he circled the town twice, driving slowly so as to soak it all in. Staring out of his car window through tired eyes, he viewed the large windows, revealing warmth inside with candles placed on tables, the distant flicker of log fires in open bars, restaurants with low lighting, a chef and waitress sitting opposite one another in the window, a bottle of wine between them. He reached the top of the town for the second time and flagged down the only man on the street before handing him the address on a page printed from the internet and asking for his help. The stranger grinned widely, revealing gums, and before Sam knew it was sitting in the car beside him.

"You're nearly there now—I'll take a ride with you. I've a boat to check on," he said, grinning, revealing a large gap in his top teeth. He put his hand out. "Jerry Letter."

"Sam Sullivan," he replied, shaking the man's hand.

"Then we're both Sullivans!" the gummy man replied.

"I thought you said your name was Letter?" Sam said, confused.

"I did and it is and it isn't," he answered, laughing at the American.

"OK," Sam agreed, and began driving in the direction that Jerry was pointing to.

Jerry laughed to himself. He liked Americans. They were a lot better to banter with than the Germans. Germans didn't ever seem to have much time for Jerry.

"I'm the postman," he said after a second or two.

"Excuse me?"

"Jerry Letter." He was nodding. "I'm the postman."

"Oh. OK. That should make sense." Sam smiled at the nodding stranger.

"Ah but it does. You see, you and me, we are not the only Sullivans in this town. There's plenty more. In fact, the place is full of us, and as for first names you couldn't throw a pint in any direction without hitting a Jerry, a John, a Jimmy, a Robert, a Peter, a Frank or a Francie. So you see, to tell one Jerry Sullivan from another, we just call each

other by what we do or what we wear or what we're into."
He winked and Sam laughed.

"Take the right," Jerry nodded.

Sam took the right and looked to his left at the boats
wrestling with the high tide. Hills rose behind the water,
the heather casting a purple hue on the sky which rested
on dark blue water, and to his right he saw a line of little
cottages built out of rock, standing firm against the battering wind.

"That's you." Jerry pointed.

Sam stopped the car directly in front of the cottage.

"Looks good," Sam said, supremely pleased to have finally arrived.

"It may well look good but the place has been empty
for a year. I hope to Christ she's not damp."

Before Sam could respond Jerry was helping him remove his bags from the trunk and waiting for him to locate the house keys.

Once inside, Jerry took a good look around the place.

"She seems fine. Lucy's been taking good care of her."

Sam just shook his head for, as entertaining as Jerry Letter was, he wanted him gone. Jerry was no fool, and once
his American friend was settled and he'd ascertained the
man was a New Yorker, unmarried, some sort of executive,
and had traveled alone, he took his leave.

"Well, we'll see each other around, Uncle Sam." He
chuckled to himself, tipped his hat and walked out into
the rain, as relaxed as though it was a fine day, leaving Sam
scratching his head.

Holy shit, that guy should work for the CIA!

Without even assimilating the interior of his new home

he walked straight up the stairs, stripped off and got into the large brass bed waiting to envelop him. His head hit the pillow and he disappeared and even the distant rain beating against the window couldn't wake him.

He wouldn't wake that morning either, despite the sun breaking through the clouds and glinting on his windowpane. He slept on as the chirping birds taunted a very desperate Mr. Monkels, who barked as he attempted to run up and down the back garden while they perched on their feeding table comfortably snacking, savvy enough to know that unless the mutt grew wings he was no threat. Sam would spend his first full day in a foreign country asleep and, as a lifelong insomniac, he'd have thought the event not possible. He did wake once or twice during the next day but just long enough to remember where he was and that he was free.

While asleep Sam didn't have to think or worry about all the commotion he'd left behind. The past four days since his release had been eventful. On Day One he had planned his escape hastily and from the back of a limo. Day Two had been spent with Leland shouting in his office, pointing his finger and actually spitting as he roared about his protégé's ingratitude, disloyalty and betrayal.

"What the hell are we supposed to do with those goddamn British pretty boys?" he had screamed, referring to their latest signing, his neck reddening and vein pulsing.

"You do what you do best, Leland, you promote them," Sam had responded as calmly as someone being spat on could.

"You're not leaving!" Leland had threatened.

62

"Yes, Leland, I am," Sam had responded, steadfast despite his mentor's menacing demeanor.

"If I had known that you were just going to disappear, I'd have left you to rot!" Leland admitted through gritted teeth once he'd realized that Sam was not going to be intimidated.

"I'm glad you didn't then. By the way, did I thank you for picking up the bill?"

Leland just glowered.

Sam turned to leave.

"You'll never work in this business again!" Leland warned predictably.

"I hope not." Sam smiled. "See you around, Leland." He closed the door behind him and a part of him soared.

Walking through the office floor, he felt like Jerry Maguire without the embarrassing fall, stolen fish, or a girl called Dorothy—still, his head was held as high and his dream for a different kind of future as real. Those around him had said hasty good-byes, not really caring about him, no more than he cared about them. He took the lift to the lobby and saluted the latest doorman and promised he'd never enter that particular building again.

The saliva shower aside, his second day out of rehab had been a good one.

On Day Three he visited his mother despite his reservations and the barring order. She had cried when she saw him, pulling him in from the street quickly so the neighbors wouldn't see. His dad was out like he knew he would be. She'd brushed the hair from his face and sighed.

"You look good for a corpse," she said, attempting to grin.

"I'm OK now, Mom," he soothed.

"It's over?" she asked, hopeful.

"I promise." Then he whispered silently to himself, begging himself not to mess up.

His mom sobbed while making coffee and he looked around the kitchen he hadn't seen in over a year since he was last caught shooting up in his brother's bedroom on Christmas Day. That was the same day that he had punched his dad, breaking his nose, called his mother a whore and re-fused to leave until his brother threatened to call the police.

"I'm sorry, Mom," he said, biting back the emotion that as a man he'd been taught to conceal.

She held on to his hand across the counter. "I'm just glad you're back," she said, tears tumbling.

"I won't let you down again," he promised.

"You said that before."

"This time is different. I've left work."

"You have?" She was comforted by the thought. Al-though deep down she knew his job was only one of his problems. *I know I let you down, son. Way back then when you really needed me. I know I let you down.*

"I'm leaving."

"Where are you going?"

"Ireland." He had almost laughed.

His mom was taken aback. "Ireland," she'd repeated, shocked.

"I always promised Gran I'd go. So I'm going."

"Wow!" was all she could say. Still, she was beaming. Having never gone to her mother's homeland, she was happy that her son would visit the place that her mom had loved. "When?"

"Tomorrow morning."

"And your dad?"

"Tell him I'm sorry about his nose. Tell him I'm well and it's going to be OK."

"You're so sure." She smiled.

"I am," he agreed, lying.

"You were always your grandmother's favorite," said his mother, admitting what Sam had always known. "She'd be proud."

Sam had no doubt but that, if she had been alive, she would have kicked his ass. Still, he was glad he'd seen his mom and, as hard as it was when she hugged him, he hugged her back despite the residual resentment he held against her. Phones had been right when he had simply advised: "Whatever it is, just let it go, man!" and he desperately wanted to.

Later that night he had dinner with Mia in her favorite restaurant. As soon as he had extended the invitation, she knew he was ending their relationship, yet she agreed that he should pick her up at eight. Due to some technical problems the video shoot had run on and she had just spent her fourth day on set dancing for seven hours straight. Her ankle needed to be strapped and she'd have to take painkillers for a bad back. She left the studio and took the set beautician with her to ensure that her hair and makeup would be perfect. If she was going to be dumped by the love of her life, then at least she was going to look good while he was doing it.

Sam arrived outside her building at eight sharp. Building security escorted her to the limo. Sam kissed her on the cheek and they sat in silence until they reached the restaurant. Outside, paparazzi bulbs flashed as she made her exit from the car, careful to ensure they didn't get a shot of between her legs. Sam walked in ahead, knowing that they were only interested in a name. She duly walked behind, feeling like a lamb being led to slaughter, not that she would betray her angst. She was used to facing the flashes alone, so what was different about tonight? And so she turned it on. She smiled and paraded, winked and waved, and when they'd got what they were looking for she joined Sam, who was ready to order. They discussed the problems with the shoot, the recording of her third album and the inevitable tour, but he waited until they had ordered coffee instead of dessert to really talk.

"I have to leave," he said simply.

She nodded and asked him to pass the milk.

"Did you hear what I said?" he'd asked, slightly taken aback.

"You're leaving."

"You're not surprised."

"Well, if you're going to break up with Leland the day before you break up with me, what do you expect?" she asked, even-toned.

"I didn't think," he admitted.

"You never do." She forced a smile and waved at a fellow limelighter who was passing, reeking of Dior so that they would be forced to smell her long after she had left.

"I'm sorry," he apologized for the umpteenth time that day.

"You are," she agreed. She was playing it tough but the façade was fading. "So are we really over?"

"I don't know," he said, unable to be honest with either of them.

"You don't know?" she repeated, tears welling and all pretense finished with.

"I just need time," he said, and now she was crying openly.

"It's not over?" she begged. *Please don't leave me!*

"No, it's not." He backed down. *Coward!* "Do you want to go home?" he asked, concerned that people would notice her unraveling.

"Yes," she said. *Hold it together,* she begged herself.

"Waiter!"

And suddenly she completely broke down, despite being in public and in a place where every waiter was on the 'razzis' payroll. Her loud sobbing was deeply disturbing to Sam because the very reason he'd taken her there was to avoid this kind of scene.

Mia couldn't help it because, as bad as he was, she couldn't bear to lose him. The waiter dropped the bill and grinned widely, knowing he was going to earn himself some extra cash that night. She attempted to compose herself and Sam told her how amazing she was and how talented she was, how beautiful, how graceful, how elegant. He sounded like a fan.

"You know, you're incredible," he concluded.

"And yet you're leaving."

"I have to."

She snorted, her pain turning to anger. "So take me with you," she demanded while picking up her purse.

"I can't," he admitted, and watched her bottom lip tremble.

"So then take me home," she said, standing up. Her makeup was halfway down her face.

"Do you want to clean your face?" he asked, aware that every cameraman in Manhattan would be outside waiting.

"No," she said, striding toward the door. "It doesn't matter."

He followed her out, but this time, when the bulbs flashed into her bleary teary eyes, he stood right beside her as the vultures descended.

Chapter Six

New Town, New Man?

The rain had stopped, the sky was a bright blue, and Mary was at work for eleven o'clock. She sat up at the bar while her dad poured a coffee. Pierre the French chef breezed past and grunted hello. Mary gave him the finger.

"Oh yes, Marie, so very sexy of you!"

"I do try to please, Pierre." She grinned at her humor-challenged friend.

"Yes, well, try harder!" He gave her a poke and her dad laughed.

Pierre was soon safely ensconced in the back kitchen blasting out MC Solaar. Mary's dad sighed heavily to illustrate his distaste for French rap, which was one step too far up the musical ladder for him. She grinned at her dad's despair; she actually liked Solaar, not that she would have admitted it to Pierre.

Her dad pulled up a stool.

"So I hear he's American." He smiled.

She returned her father's smile. "Who's American?"

"Your new neighbor," her father stated with authority.

"How the hell . . . ?" She didn't bother finishing her sentence, being used to the idea that very little happened in Kenmare without her father hearing about it.

He tapped his head. "I know things," he said, nodding, before tapping his nose.

"Have you met him?"

"No," she sighed.

"He has money," he said, viewing her from the corner of his eye.

"Really," she said in a tone that suggested disinterest.

"Unmarried." He winked. She ignored him. "He's alone."

"Aren't we all?" she said, becoming irritated.

"So it's all to play for," he added smugly.

"So how do you know so much about this American?" she asked, ignoring what she would later describe to Penny as his bullshit, ensuring as was her habit that the *shit* was silent.

"Mattie Moore was in first thing this morning. It seems Jerry Letter took a lift with the American last night. Mattie says he was quiet enough."

"Jerry or the American?" She grinned before getting up to wash her cup, in doing so turning her back on him to signify that the conversation was nearing its end.

"You know well enough," her dad laughed. "Jerry will lead the rosary at his own funeral." He was resigned to his daughter's ways and yet secretly wished she showed some interest in anything other than work and that feckin' dribbling dog.

★ ★ ★

Lunchtime was hectic. They ran out of leeks, Jessie having forgotten to reorder them. Mrs. Lennon waited fifteen minutes for an omelette before receiving one smothered in tomatoes which she'd specifically asked them to omit due to an allergy that made her head swell to the size of a small country. Fiona, their latest part-timer, dropped a tray full of monkfish on the floor, causing near hysteria in Pierre. Pierre tore a strip off Fiona, who in turn proceeded to burst into tears before running out of the kitchen mumbling something about the money not being worth it.

Jessie then shouted at Pierre when he even attempted to give her shit about the leeks—as a fifty-year-old married mother of four she wasn't about to have some jumped-up tourist tell her what was what.

"I forgot the leeks, so I forgot them! Live with it!" she roared to a cowering Pierre.

"Jessie, he didn't mean anything," said Mary, acting as peacemaker for the second time that day.

"Marie, she can't forget—the ticks are there to show her!" He directed his argument at Mary, knowing that Jessie would have given him a kick.

"Is he calling me thick?" Jessie asked, knowing well he was referring to the ingredients tick-box which was designed especially so that she wouldn't forget key ingredients such as leeks.

Mary was getting annoyed. "Jessie, get a grip."

Jessie backed down. Pierre looked Jessie up and down as though he was victorious. Mary walked out before they could start another argument.

It was shaping up to be one of those days. Her dad wasn't much help, having abandoned his post in favor of joining his friends Patty Winslow and Con Moriarty, who had received his starter with his main course. After eating there for twenty-five years he wasn't that pushed and was happy to have the starter as a side order, noting that maybe he could start a trend. Patty was reading aloud about an incident in the English House of Lords and was fervent and clearly annoyed, judging from her banging her fist on the table every few minutes and mumbling about "injustice." Although Patty had retired to Kenmare and had been living there fifteen years and in that time had never returned to her hometown of Kent, she only ever read the English papers, following English politics with ferocity, and had BBC before anyone else in town. Mary's dad, Jack, and Con were far too busy enjoying their old friend's frustration and rising her every chance they got to notice or indeed care about the chaos around them.

★ ★ ★

It was after seven when Mary got home, glad that she wasn't working the bar that night and praying that she might at last get some sleep. There was a red flashy sports car parked outside. This irked her for no particular reason other than it being a reminder of an unwanted neighbor. Although the rain had finally stopped it was cold, so she lit a fire and looked through her music collection, searching for something she could disappear into. Nirvana seemed to suit her frustration. She lined up their albums. She'd start with the MTV unplugged session before moving on to *Nevermind* followed by *In Utero*. Happy with her decision, she turned the sound up so that she could hear it in the kitchen. She was cooking when unbeknownst to her the doorbell rang. Cobain was singing loudly about a dirty bird and she was absorbed in his melody while chopping onions. It was Mr. Monkels's bark and his slow but steady pacing to and from the door that alerted her to a visitor. She sighed, wishing whoever it was would go away.

Penny stood outside, shivering and jumping on the spot.

"Hey, you," Mary greeted when she opened the door, happy it was Penny, knowing that being with Penn was as easy as being alone.

"Can I come in?" Penny asked as though she needed to before following Mary to the kitchen. "You're cooking?" she said, stating the obvious before grabbing a beer from the fridge.

"Shepherd's pie—are you hungry?"

"No food. I'm on Day Five of the heartbreak diet and I must admit I'm really starting to see some results." Penny pulled at her clothes while attempting to smile before sipping from the can.

Mary laughed because she found her friend amusing even in crisis. She continued to cook. They talked about their days. Mary filled Penny in on the histrionics in the bar and Penny told Mary about her trip to Tralee to report on a local man who had won millions on the Euro Lottery. Penny had sunk three cans by the time dinner was ready to be served. Mary tried to insist that she eat by putting a plate of food in front of her. Penny was too afraid to go home in case Adam would be there waiting. She wondered aloud if she should go away for a week or two but then

Mary pointed out that she'd done that before in an attempt to end their affair and it hadn't worked. In fact, as soon as she was home he turned up at her door and she was right back where she started except for a tan. She was subdued over dinner and Mary knew what was going through her friend's mind. They'd been down this road too many times for her not to. So they sat and, while Mary ate, Penny drank and Kurt Cobain beseeched someone unknown to rape him.

Penny looked toward the stereo. "Rape me?" she repeated. "Bloody weirdo!"

"I think it's a metaphor for self-loathing," Mary noted.

"How is it that I'm the one who went to Trinity and yet you're the one full of shit?" Penny asked, grinning.

Mary laughed. "It is a mystery." She was glad that Penny had come over.

Just then Mr. Monkels began to bark and head-butt the window.

"Who the hell is that?" Mary wondered.

Penny sat up, alarmed that Adam might have followed her to her friend's home. Mary, reading her mind, assured her it wasn't Adam's style. Still, she was prepared to give him a piece of her mind if he had followed Penny. It just wasn't fair.

Penny stayed in the kitchen while Mary made her way to the door.

"There's no one there," Mary called out.

"Are you sure?"

"All clear!" She knew it just wouldn't be like Adam to follow Penny, as much as she knew he would want to. *Poor Adam, he really did make a mess of everything.*

74

★ ★ ★

Sam had woken just after 7:00 PM. He was hungry but not enough to get dressed and venture into the town. There was no food in the house and he knew that he would never make it to morning. He went to the car to find his cell phone. The glass-butting dog at the window had barked, panted and slobbered some sort of welcome. He wondered if he should introduce himself to the occupants of the house and maybe he could get a local takeaway menu from them but he decided against it. He was in a robe, after all, and besides, he wasn't hungry enough for introductions. Upstairs he took a long hot shower before pulling on a pair of jeans and a plain T-shirt and making his way back downstairs and into his living room.

As he looked around the alien environment, his new world started to sink in for the first time. The cottage was cute. The kitchen could stand to be bigger but still the sitting room had great character with its wide fireplace made out of gray jagged rock, blackened by many log fires. A ridiculously comfortable soft sofa was positioned directly in front of it and to his left a large window looked out at the gray hills and black sea. *Funny, the hills were a kind of purple and the sea was definitely navy last night.* It was then he noticed that this place came without a TV. *Weird.* The shelf under the coffee table contained a number of books. He sank into the sofa and began leafing through them. Robert Ludlum's *The Bourne Identity. Saw the movie and the miniseries. Matt Damon did a fine job. I never did like Richard Chamberlain.* His mind rambled on in that vein, debating internally as to which book he'd lose himself in. *Birdsong* maybe, although war was depressing and, seeing as he was alone in a foreign nation, having just come off heroin, he thought it might be wiser to choose something more uplifting. He picked up a rather thick book entitled *The Deptford Trilogy* by Robertson Davies. *Hmmm, three for the price of one.* The blurb was interesting: myth, magic, saints, Satan, illusion, reality—it all sounded like his past year. He decided, in the absence of a TV, he would dedicate himself to reading his first book since high school. But before that he would have to satiate the appetite that had returned halfway through his marathon shower. After searching the house for leaflets on local delivery places and coming up empty-handed he felt there was no choice but to venture next door.

★ ★ ★

Mary was sitting on the sofa. Mr. Monkels was sprawled at her feet on his bed in front of the fire. She was drinking a glass of wine Penny had insisted she indulge in, having located a stray bottle of red under the stairs once she'd consumed all the beer. Penny was sitting in the window nursing her own drink, watching the white streetlights dance on the black water and absentmindedly swirling the contents of her glass. Nirvana had been replaced by James Taylor, and the girls were adrift in worlds of their own. It was Penny's voice that broke the mood.

"There's a man out there," Penny said, suddenly alert and peering through the curtain. "It must be your neighbor. It looks like he's going to his car."

"Fascinating," Mary said, having no more interest in the stranger than her sleeping dog.

"Oh my God!" Penny said before letting go of the curtain, sinking to the floor and ducking down by the window seat. "He's coming to the door and he's a total ride!"

Mary laughed, thinking Penny was messing around, but then the doorbell rang and for some reason her heart skipped and she felt like a bold child on the verge of being caught.

"Get off the stupid floor," she whispered to Penny who was still on the floor.

Penny stood up slowly before slinking across the room to stand in the doorway between the kitchen and sitting room.

Mary viewed the front door, feeling a little panic. This man was only her neighbor twenty-four hours and already he was knocking on her door. *Knickers!* The knock came again so Mary opened it. Penny sighed. It was audible. She couldn't believe it—her best friend's neighbor was a Calvin Klein billboard underwear model, a box-office-breaking movie star, a chiseled god with pretty hair surrounding a beautiful face. Mary heard her friend's expulsion of air despite her heart beating in her ear. She didn't share her friend's view—instead, she saw a bloody annoyance. But there was something about him that even his pretty face couldn't distract from. It made her anxious and yet she couldn't put her finger on why. The beautiful man spoke.

"Hi. I'm Sam Sullivan." He smiled.

"OK," she responded. She didn't mean to sound rude but OK was all she could muster.

He put out his hand. "From next door."

She smiled politely. "Hi." She nodded, shaking his hand awkwardly, wishing he'd leave. She let the door open out so that her old friend could say hello to her new neighbor, but she wasn't asking him in.

"I was just looking for a menu for a place that delivers," he said hopefully, realizing that his neighbor wasn't necessarily as welcoming as they'd mentioned in the Aer Lingus brochure.

Penny laughed in the background. "Nowhere delivers." She smiled.

"You're kidding," he said, looking over Mary's shoulder.

Penny shook her head, smiling coyly with one leg resting behind the other and one arm hanging casually like she was a teenager on dope or attempting an impression of Bono singing "Maggie's Farm" at Self Aid.

"OK, I didn't see that coming," he noted, disturbed by this news.

"You can eat here," Penny offered. "We have loads. Don't we, Mare?" She moved toward him and put out her hand so that he could shake it. "I'm Penny Walsh"—she smiled her most winsome smile—"and this is my friend Mary Mackey. She's friendlier than she first appears. She'd love you to stay."

Mary smiled through gritted teeth at the stranger while silently wishing a nasty case of the clap on her friend.

"Of course," she sighed, nodding.

"No, thanks. I'm really tired and not much company," he said truthfully. Sam was no more interested in making new friends than his reluctant neighbor.

Mary felt bad, knowing her own reservation was obvious. "I could pack it up. It's still hot and you could drop the plate back tomorrow," she said, backing away from the door. "Just leave it outside, it's fine."

Sam was now starving and the smell of cooking was killing him. "That would be great, thanks."

Penny flirted with the American. This flirtation was born from a need to escape heartache rather than actual desire, and yet if someone had mentioned the name Adam it might have taken a moment or two to register. Mary plated the remaining food and checked the fridge for some sort of dessert. She had a cheesecake but it had been there since the previous Tuesday. She checked the date.

"What's today's date?" she called out.

"The nineteenth," Sam offered while battling Mr. Monkels, who seemed to be fascinated with his balls, while Penny laughed and pointed the fact out, much to Sam's embarrassment.

Mary screamed irately at Mr. Monkels from the kitchen and sulking he took to his bed in front of the fire, groaning like a cheeky teenager.

She emerged from the kitchen with the food steaming and plated. He thanked her; she told him it wasn't a problem with her hand on the open door. He left and she closed the door quickly.

Penny was in the background shaking her head.

"Don't shake your head," Mary warned.

"He might be the prettiest man I've ever seen, in real life. Maybe even a little too pretty. I didn't have time to make up my mind." Penny was feeling a little put out that her friend had done everything bar push him out the door. She plonked down onto the window seat, flicking at the curtain, attempting to catch one last glimpse, but he was gone.

Mary remained silent, the American already past tense.

How could I forget? she asked herself. *How is it possible that I could forget? How could I not know what date it was?*

Penny was still talking but her voice seemed far away. No wonder she couldn't sleep. The past week was starting to make sense. She needed to be alone. She got up.

"I'm taking you home," Mary said.

"What?" Penny replied, busily swirling her wine.

"I'm tired," Mary lied.

"OK, but I can drive myself." Penny got up, but after four beers and half a bottle of wine she wasn't going to be allowed to drive anywhere.

★ ★ ★

Mary dropped Penny off at her house on the hill overlooking a sweeping valley littered with sheep, interspersed with the odd cow and spotted with clusters of wildflowers. The flowers couldn't be seen by night but a hint of perfume could still be smelled in the air. The neighbors next door were having a party and the music wafted into her garden. Mary drove off, leaving Penny alone in darkness except for the small lantern lights leading the way to her door.

She had the key in the door when Adam called out to her. She braced herself before turning.

"What are you doing here?" she asked with a voice that suggested a sinking heart.

"I'm not here, I'm next door—Neil asked us." He pointed toward her neighbor's home.

"Alina's with you?" She almost cried.

"No, she's with her dad in Cork. He's not well." He approached, his hands in his pockets. "I wouldn't have come but I just wanted to see you."

"We're not getting back together," she warned.

"I know." He made it to the steps. "We're leaving." He couldn't look at her.

"I don't understand?" Her voice shook, suggesting she did.

"Alina knows."

"What does she know?"

"She knows about us."

Penny's legs felt like they would fail her. "Five years we've been together. We finish and now she knows?" She couldn't believe it.

"She found out a week ago. It's why I had to end it."

It didn't make any sense. "Why didn't you tell me?"

"She didn't want me to." His eyes rested on his feet.

"She didn't want you to?" Penny repeated, the combination of confusion and abandonment becoming a little too much.

"She wants us to start afresh. There's a business opportunity in Cork. Her dad's there and she has some friends."

"She didn't *want* you to!" Penny repeated bitterly.

"Did you hear what I said? I'm moving to Cork!"

"You hate Cork." She heard herself sounding childish.

"It's not a choice. She's going to take the kids. If we don't make a go of it, she says, she's going back to Holland. I can't lose my kids. I'm so sorry."

"You're so weak," Penny said with a trace of anger.

"Yes, I am."

"You make me weak," she admitted, softening.

"I'm sorry."

"It's really over."

81

"Yes, it is," he said, battling rising emotion.

Oh God. She closed her eyes. Sinéad O'Connor's version of Elton John's "Sacrifice" played around them; Penny just couldn't seem to escape Sinéad lately.

And suddenly they were dancing, holding on tight under a half moon, around and around in circles signifying their relationship to date, both afraid to let go, both willing the song to continue while silently their insides tore.

The song did end and Adam reluctantly returned to the party, leaving Penny to get into her bed with a bottle of vodka.

★ ★ ★

It was after midnight when Mary found herself in the forest and in the part she rarely visited. Just once a year, on the nineteenth of March, and that was enough. She'd brought a teddy, one she'd picked up two weeks previously and before she'd allowed herself to lose track of time. She carried Ben's favorite cloth and a flashlight so as to navigate her way through the darkness. The tree stood tall and strong, aside from its broken limb, which had been amputated long ago. She took out the cloth and began to wipe the plaque bearing the name of her son, denoting the place he had died but, more important, the place where he had last lived, laughing on the makeshift swing. A swing that every child in town had swung on at one time or another, until that day, March 19, 1999, when the limb gave way, catapulting her baby high into the air before gravity pulled him back to earth and, cruelly, in such a way that he'd land on his neck, snapping it instantly. She laid the teddy by the flowers her father had laid earlier that day. *At least he could rely on you, Dad.* She touched the clean plaque tenderly before looking around to ensure she was alone. It was cold enough for the mud beneath her to crystallize and she could see her breath forming a trail in the night air. She stood with a hand up each opposite sleeve and shivering despite her many layers of clothing. She exhaled much like a smoker would after taking a sustained drag from a cigarette.

"I can't believe it's been six years," she said before sighing.

"It only seems like yesterday," came a whispered reply from the darkness.

Mary peed herself a little. "Hello?" she asked in a voice that suggested a mild hysteria.

"Is that you, Mary?"

The voice was muffled but more distinct and coming from behind her. She turned quickly and pointed her flashlight in a take-charge-while-shitting-it manner that reminded her of Dana Scully in *The X Files* circa 1993 before she lost the weight and was still a skeptic. This memory was fleeting, so concentrated was she on the voice that had come from a bush.

"Hello?" she said again, scanning the foliage with her searchlight, which was of little use because, for some reason unknown, her eyes were closed.

"Mary, girl, I think if you don't help me up I might freeze to death." The voice was suddenly familiar.

"Tom?" Mary queried.

"I can't get up," he said from the ditch that hid itself behind a large rhododendron.

Mary parted the bush to reveal Tom on his back attempting to scramble up, much like an upturned turtle, and too drunk to negotiate his way onto his feet. She pulled him free of the narrow ditch which had seemed to encase him and sat him up.

"Jesus, Tom, you nearly killed me with the fright!"

"Sorry, pet," he said sheepishly. "I just thought I'd call upon our boy on the way home and mistook that bush for a chair and the rest as they say is history." His skin was frozen to the touch.

"How long have you been out here?" she asked, worried that her son's grandfather would fall victim to pneumonia.

"Not long," he said, patting her shoulder.

"I'll take you home," she said gently.

"In a minute," he said.

"OK." She nodded.

She'd always been fond of her boyfriend's father and he and his wife had always been good to her and Ben. For a while they had even felt like family, but then, when Ben died, Tom's wife, Monica, couldn't stand to stay in the town that had robbed her of so much. They had moved to Spain, where they spent most of their time, only visiting Kenmare once or twice a year. It had been five years since they had moved and in that time Mary and her child's grandparents had drifted apart.

Tom wasn't a drinker. In fact, he had been a Pioneer of Total Abstinence up until Robert had died. After that he took a drink each year to mark his memory, and when Ben joined Robert he did the same. So twice a year Tom drank, and even then he could only manage three pints before becoming helpless.

He stood in front of the plaque, with his hands knotted in prayer and swimming in drunken emotion. Mary stood back and allowed him his moment.

"Mary," he said, swaying.

"Tom," she responded gently.

"Do you think he ever looks down?" he asked with eyes brimming.

"I know he does," she said kindly.

"You do?" he said, suddenly perking up.

"They all do," she said, taking him by the arm and guiding him down the path that would lead him home.

"Do you really believe that?"

"I do," she told him honestly.

"Do you see them?" he asked conspiratorially, being aware of her cryptic visions.

"No," she admitted, "but sometimes I feel them around me."

He nearly stumbled on a root but she caught him in time and straightened him.

"I don't," he confessed, and a tear escaped. "I'd love to." His voice shook. "One last time—just to see them both one last time." He sighed and attempted to collect himself.

"You'll see them again." She smiled sadly. "I know they're waiting."

He wiped a tear from her cheek. She hadn't even noticed that she was crying. "You know, some say you're a bit of a weird one," he said, smiling at her, "but I've always thought that you were lovely, just lovely."

She laughed at Tom's honesty.

He squeezed her arm and they walked on together.

It hadn't been the visit she'd expected; it had been nicer than that.

★ ★ ★

As for Sam, he enjoyed the late meal given to him by his reluctant neighbor and then, by the light of a log fire and a small reading lamp, he opened the book that led him to a place called Deptford. There he'd bask in magic, murder and intrigue and he wouldn't have to think about the mess he'd made of his life. He wouldn't worry about the people he'd stomped on or the lives he'd had a hand in ruining. Most important, sitting in the half-light lost in another man's world, he wouldn't have to address what he'd done and why he'd done it. He could pretend that his life to date had been one long accident and that he was better now. The ghosts that once haunted him were silenced, at least for the time being.

Chapter Seven

Looking Down

It had been a very long and hard night and, if Mary was right and those that had left this world behind sometimes looked down from the skies above, it must have seemed that respite was necessary. From a distance these five souls would have seemed pretty wretched in their own quiet way, each battling something invisible, afraid to share in weakness and desperate to hide all that was unwell. Looking down, it would most likely be sad to see the children they once were versus the adults that they had become.

Sam, the American boy who was once so full of promise now hiding terrible secrets that would hold him hostage, clean or not. Penny, the girl forever alone dressed in vomit, hugging a bottle instead of the man she lost to unfulfilled ambition. Ivan, the cheeky chap, a father of two at twenty-four and so terribly alone in his thirties. Adam, the boy who had dreamed of being a hero only to go and mess it all up. And Mary, in hindsight born unlucky, once luminous but now dulled by pain.

★ ★ ★

In this world, Mary had been tested more than most, born to a dead mother and her father wailing and traumatized. He didn't pick her up for six months but once he did she was held and loved like any other child by a doting father. And although her mother's absence was felt, it was mostly in her teenage years, and to be fair her Auntie Sheila was always on hand to provide the necessary and perfunctory feminine influence. Auntie Sheila was her father's brother's wife and Ivan's mother.

Mary's teenage life was promising. She had a father who was wrapped around her little finger. She had a best friend in Penny, who shared her life within a boarding school in Dublin. And when she came home, she had her older cousin, Ivan, waiting with all his attractive friends lined up to hang out with the two glamorous girls who schooled in the capital. She was popular, attractive, quick-witted, curious and infectiously giddy. She loved photography, was a dab hand with a paintbrush and was intelligent too, winning praise in most subjects. It was thought that she could be anything she wanted to be once her mind was set. And at sixteen her mind was set: she would move to New York City and become a photojournalist. She would study photography and imaging at NYU, using the money her mother's family had left her to pay for her dream. In the meantime, she would give her heart to Robert Casey, which she did the first time he smiled at her. She was fourteen then but they didn't date until six months later at a party in her cousin's house. He had guided her into the toilet under the stairs. They had made out under a blue light on a white porcelain toilet while inhaling lavender. Meatloaf was playing in the background and a queue formed outside, with teenagers banging on the door pleading for the sake of their bladders. A little over a year later they lost their virginity to one another on a patch of grass under a summer moon where the forest met the water, lapping gently as they experimented with rubber. When she left for school their teenage hearts would break and promises would be made. When she'd return they'd make up for lost time, both desperately in love, and the education system and world against them ensuring a lasting burning fervor. Mary was passionate then. She was wild and free, believing the world to be some sort of giant playpen.

She had just turned seventeen when she discovered her pregnancy, taking the test in the girl's communal toilet with shaking hands, an uncooperative bladder and three minutes of concentrated prayer resulting in a positive.

"Oh bollocks!"

And panic ensued. She knew exactly the moment of conception. It was the night she'd spent in the boathouse, having snuck past her friends standing around the flames of a barbecue and chatting loudly over her favorite band Take That singing "Pray."

"Damn you, Take That!"

Alone, they hadn't wasted time; their hurry was enough to ensure that the prophylactic was not properly positioned. It came away easily but this wasn't noticed until it was too late. They had discussed the morning-after pill but after debate they agreed that the risk of exposure through visiting a local GP was greater than the threat of reproduction. This proved to be a mistake.

It was two weeks before Easter. Penny was stuck in school, working on a project she had been avoiding for far too long. Mary returned home alone. Robert picked her up at the Killarney station, proud of his newly acquired learner's license.

She broke the news on the mountain. He had stopped the car and pulled in dangerously close to the cliffside. His face had changed colors and his relaxed demeanor had metamorphosed into something twisted. Their conversation quickly descended into screaming and shouting, and he had taken off his safety belt so that he could face her. He also had plans—he was set to be an engineer—and they both acknowledged their perfectly planned futures were in terrible jeopardy. After a while, their desperate debate in deadlock, he decided to start up the car. Without thinking, he rammed the car into first gear, needing to get back onto the road, drive fast, whatever—he just needed to clear his head. As he put his foot down on the accelerator, the car bolted forward and he drove straight over the mountain.

If you asked Mary about the accident she wouldn't remember anything after the argument, but those looking down could tell you every terrible moment. Mary heard Robert roar and saw him turn the wheel in midair. She felt the terrible drop as the car was plummeting. She watched the glass in front of her shatter as her boyfriend sailed through it, leaving her alone to face the ground below. She braced herself to smash and die. *Oh Dad, I'm so sorry!* And then for her there was nothing. A busload of German tourists had witnessed their fall and, in a world before the mobile telephone, the bus driver radioed the depot and they had informed the police and ambulance. One of the tourists, a doctor, had insisted on being winched down with a climbing rope to where the boy lay broken, the other tourists and bus driver holding the rope, praying they wouldn't let him fall and wondering where in the hell the rescue team was. The boy was dead; the girl was too far down into the gorge and his rope too short. His fellow holidaymakers wanted to pull him up and away from the deceased teenager but he insisted on staying with the boy until the ambulance sirens could be heard in the distance.

Mary was cut out of the car that had become her co-coon, with both legs broken when gravity had ensured that they rose in time to batter against the dashboard. They said it was a miracle that she had emerged at all. Her left arm had shattered against the windscreen but it was Robert grazing the side of her head at 200 miles per hour that had induced coma. The car should have crumbled and she should have been dead, but the frame had somehow managed to sustain the impact and, when the rescue team made it down the mountain, they found her asleep but alive. Later in the hospital her father discovered that not only had his daughter survived against all odds but, unbelievably, so had his surprise grandchild. As Robert's mother roared and screamed in the background and his father pleaded with the doctor to turn back time, Mary's dad held her hand and prayed that she would survive her shock pregnancy unlike her mother before her.

"I don't care. Do you hear me, love? It doesn't matter. You're not in trouble. Just survive. And when you wake up we'll take care of this baby together. Don't you leave me now." He patted her hand as though to comfort her, attempting to hide the crack in his voice and glad she didn't have to witness his eyes leaking. "Don't you leave me now."

She didn't wake for three months. Some had given up hope that she would be anything other than an incubator for her baby, but her dad was sure his daughter would return to him and Penny was sure too, knowing that Mary hadn't survived merely to sleep. She would come back, and her best friend spent as much time as was possible sitting by her side, gossiping and playing her favorite music.

"Music will bring her back," she had told Mary's father while filling the room with CDs.

She gave him a schedule of songs for morning, afternoon and evening listening, divided into weekdays and weekends. She made it clear that it was important he adhere to the schedule as per the list, as Mary would not stand for a weekday song at the weekend or indeed a morning song in the evening. Paul Simon's "50 Ways to Leave Your Lover" was a weekday song, preferably to be played in the morning—afternoon would be pushing it and it most definitely was not to be played in the evening. Leonard Cohen's "Everybody Knows" was another weekday song, but this was deemed appropriate for evening, not morning or afternoon. Prince's "Little Red Corvette" was a weekend evening song, but late afternoon would be OK—so she'd noted in the margin that it should not be played before 4:00 PM. And so she went on until Mary's poor dad was fully appraised and therefore entrusted with this weighty task when Penny was forced to return to school in Dublin

so as to complete her Leaving Cert. When she was gone
Ivan picked up the slack. Every day after school he'd visit
and talk to and read to Mary so that her father could go to
the canteen or take a shower or drink a fortifying coffee.
Every day her tummy grew under a hospital blanket and
Robert's parents would call to visit with the part of their
son that wasn't buried in their family grave and they'd
speak in whispers and Robert's mother would cry and his
dad would insist on shaking Mary's dad's hand.

★ ★ ★

She came back one Tuesday on a warm June day. It was
around half past five. Ivan was reading aloud from *The Lord
of the Rings*. And Van Morrison's "And It Stoned Me" was
playing on CD. Her hand had jerked. He ignored it at first
as spasms were not unusual. However, it moved again. Her
fingers appeared to be searching as opposed to twitching
randomly. Slowly he lowered his book and followed her
hand, then her eye flickered and blinked and at the same
time her mouth opened and breath escaped. He froze and
her eyes opened—slowly as though coming unstuck.

"Mary?"

"Iv . . . zan," she responded hoarsely, her mouth and
throat like sandpaper.

"Oh Jesus on a jet ski! You're back!" He jumped up and
ran out of the room, leaving her alone to wonder what the
hell was going on.

She could hear him screaming, hailing her return in
the corridor, and it wasn't long before a team of doctors
accompanied by her teary father revealed how long she
had been lost, that Robert had perished, her Leaving Cert

exams had been missed and she was just shy of six months pregnant and soon to be a mother. Lying there surrounded by strange and harried faces while looking down at her swollen self, with her boyfriend dead, her own limbs unco-operative, and slurred speech braying in her addled brain—lying there disorientated and yet painfully aware that the girl who had got into her boyfriend's car would never emerge—through the haze of this new reality, her mind settled on Van Morrison's familiar beat. And he spoke of water and prayed it wouldn't rain all day.

★ ★ ★

For Sam, in contrast to his new neighbor, his entrance to this world was a joyful one. He was born to a tired but grateful mother and a proud cigar-toting father, his older brother then a toddler inquisitive and desperate to stroke his tiny face. His early memories were full of train sets, a mother's perfume, a father's laughter, a brother's teasing, but it was his granny who took up most of his brain space, she being the one who raised both boys while their mother worked in her husband's Manhattan restaurant. Sam's days would be spent accompanying his gran to the local gro-cery stores, where she'd barter with old friends and catch up on gossip while making the men laugh with her flir-tatious quick wit and the women smile at her kindness. Granny Baskin had moved in with her daughter and son-in-law a year before the birth of her favorite grandchild and just after her own husband had quietly died while sit-ting on a steel girder 1,300 feet from the ground. Granny had often talked of Sam's grandfather and the day the sky took him from her. She wasn't bitter—he was in his late sixties, which to some would be considered young, but to Granny Baskin it was long enough for a man such as her husband to be grounded. "He was never meant for this earth," she'd say, and smile. "His head and heart were always skyward." And she'd look up toward the heavens and wink as though he was watching. Most afternoons she'd collect Sam and his brother, Jonah, from school and take them to the park so that she could catch up with her old friends playing chess and telling stories while the birds fed on the scraps they sprinkled about themselves. Jonah would run off with some boys and play football or basketball with any ball he could find, and in the event a ball was not to be found he would run as though he was chasing something invisible. Granny Baskin would laugh and wink at Sam, who preferred sitting by her side listening to a group of old immigrants reminisce about their homelands, comparing stories of the plight of the old world, each one bettering the other one's tale of woe. Sam had thought it odd how they could tell such sad stories and yet laugh and joke so easily and Granny had counseled that time was a great healer. He was six at the time so he really didn't have a clue what she was talking about, but when she said it she gave him that smile that came with a twinkling eye and pushed a hard-boiled sweet into his hand so he would remember it. Mr. Grabowski and Mr. DiRisio would often fight for the old woman's attention and even a six-year-old could work out that his granny was as sassy as she was old, just like wrinkled-faced Mrs. Gillespie always said.

It was his grandmother who encouraged his love of Irish music, sharing with him her taste for the Clancy Brothers, the Chieftains and the Dubliners. Luke Kelly made her cry but her tears were always accompanied by a smile. She introduced Sam to all kinds of music—jazz, blues, bluegrass, rock, pop and the only artist they ever disagreed about: Neil Diamond. She bought Sam his first guitar, telling him that once he'd learn to play he would never again be lonely. She saw it in him first, that singularity which would polarize him for his peers. Normal little kids didn't hang out so willingly with their grandmothers. He was an old soul content to remain friendless. His parents weren't worried that he wasn't a great mixer. All kids were different and he'd grow out of it. Teachers felt that he was merely a shy sort and agreed it was most likely a phase. Granny Baskin knew better. Her grandson's eyes betrayed a certain melancholy which was something that, as an Irish emigrant, she was more than equipped to recognize. He wouldn't fit in with the crowd and there was a chance he would not fit in at all.

"Who were you before—a warrior or the wounded, my sweet boy?" She'd ruffle his hair and he would smile at her as though he knew the answer but dare not share it.

Sam had started out in the world as a gawky creature, too skinny for the large and piercing facial features that seemed to dwarf his minuscule neck. The kids at school made fun of his square jaw, often referring to him as "Desperate Sam the Pie-eating Man." It hadn't bothered him, at least not at first. He was too busy locked in his own thoughts and playing riffs in his head while others around him talked nonsense just to hear themselves speak. But as the years passed the noise grew louder and their contempt became harder to ignore. He often wondered why they couldn't just leave him be. But jealous souls demand to be heard and his ambivalence taunted them as surely as their bullying haunted him. He was in his midteens when he started to fill out. His features no longer overtook his face. His blond hair was shaped into a crew cut by the local barber, his gran smiling at the result, ruffling his freshly waxed mane.

"As handsome as your grandfather in his day," she'd said in a whisper, and taking his hand, she admitted he'd had a rocky start but that she always knew there was a heart-breaker in there somewhere.

The girls in school noticed too and now, instead of being weird, suddenly he was considered deep. He instantly rec-ognized these hypocrites for who they were and retreated further into himself, distrustful of his newfound popularity and cursing his appearance for drawing unwanted atten-tion. Instead of hanging with the guys, getting drunk and exploring girls, he preferred to hide for hours in his room, playing his guitar and losing himself in melody, playing from his heart, a heart full of all kinds of music. His gran would enter his room with tea, shaking her head and hips; he'd grin when she'd twirl around without spilling a drop of liquid or allowing a biscuit to slip from its plate.

"You'll be a star someday," she'd say proudly.

He'd shake his head, embarrassed to be seen to agree with her theory, but deep down he prayed that he would reach the dizzying heights his loving gran had dreamed of. Playing guitar was the only time he felt like he was honest with the world.

It was just after his sixteenth birthday when his gran keeled over in the kitchen, taking a pot of mercifully cold tomato soup to the ground with her. She woke up a day later, the left side of her face sliding toward her shoulder as though trying to rest upon it, her speech impaired and an arm and leg now useless. He sat with her and talked while she stared blankly at the ceiling, one eye blinking. It was only when he began playing his guitar that a tear escaped and he knew she was still with him.

His parents flew into action. First a bed was placed downstairs in the unused drawing room, then a hired nurse and a physiotherapist were organized who would call three times a week. But Granny wasn't improving at home, not the way the professionals had thought that she should. After six months Granny Baskin was moved to a hospital that specialized in stroke victim aftercare. It was Sam who helped his mother to wheel her to the car. She hung loosely around him while his mother removed the chair from beneath her. His strong arms maneuvered her into the front seat, stopping only to smooth down her skirt when it attempted to ride up her leg, negating a further assault on her dignity. His mother was busy attempting to fit the chair into the trunk, cursing silently when she scratched the paintwork.

It was then, while his mother cursed the trunk, that his granny leaned forward, almost flopping, and her mouth attempting a sideways grin. "Don't let the bastards get you down!" she managed through her mangled voice. It had been the first real sentence she'd attempted since the stroke. With her good arm she ruffled his hair and he could have sworn the twinkle that had vacated her eye all those months ago returned, if only for a brief moment and just for him. His mother drove away and he sat and rocked on the stairs that led to his bedroom and the world that his old gran had helped him create, and the pain of his loss engulfed him, tearing his insides out. The fear of what lay ahead of her burned his chest wall as surely as a hot plate would burn a naked hand. Her absence in his life and the fear for her future threatened his very sanity, but the worst of it was his own impotency. He couldn't break her out and take her away to a better place. He couldn't tend to her. He couldn't save her. She had given him everything and he had let her down. He cursed himself and his inadequacy. He hurt himself punching his fist against the hard wood banister that didn't even budge, further highlighting his failure. And so on the day his grandmother was taken to a home, Sam sat with head in bleeding hands, sobbing and wondering if he'd survive his miserable life without her understanding, and worse still, would she survive hers without him.

One year later Sam's granny was dead and he mourned her a second time, but, since the time she had left his home, life had moved on and although he missed her, he was used to missing her as he had really lost her a year and a half before on the day of her stroke. He'd also managed to find himself a girlfriend. Hilarie was a strange-looking punk with green hair, a pierced nose and cherub tits that could even make a top with a picture of dog shit look good. She was an outsider like him. They met when he auditioned for a garage band. She was the only girl. The other guys were noncommittal but she wanted him from the moment he walked through the door. Luckily she had the deciding vote. She liked it that he was insular, choosing to speak only when necessary. It made a nice change from the shit she had to listen to from the other guys. She also liked it that he didn't come on to her every chance he got, especially reveling in the idea that she would most definitely have to make the first move. She waited until the night of their first gig when even her solitary new bandmate had reached a level of exhilaration that opened him up ever so slightly. She spotted the chink and before he knew it he was leaning against a tiled toilet wall, with a bass player on her knees sucking so hard his knees threatened to give way. Afterward, when she kissed him, he could taste himself. Although he missed his gran and sometimes still ached for her understanding, it could have been OK. He had a small window of opportunity to become a person deemed to be normal, but then the bullying started again. This time it was different and more menacing. In the end it only took one night to destroy any chance he had of ever being OK again.

★ ★ ★

Ivan was a funny fish, at least that's what his mother always said. He loved the sea, learning to swim as soon as he was dropped in water, and he spent his childhood and early teens sitting at the end of a fishing rod, pondering his existence while awaiting the tug of the pole. His brothers, Séamus, Barry and Fintan, were more interested in sport—Fintan and Séamus being the footballers and Barry an avid hurler, ensuring he would lose most of his own teeth by the age of eighteen. His parents paid for caps while cursing the cost of dentistry and as a result Barry had what his twin would describe as a movie star mouth. Throughout their childhood, Ivan's brothers would win the medals but Ivan would bring home the tea. He was born relaxed and never changed. No terrible twos. No challenging teenage years. He just got on with it and, as long as he could fish for a few hours a day, he was as content as an old man sitting out on a warm day. He was always popular with the girls even when they were kids and supposed to dislike the opposite sex. The fact that he was one year older than his cousin Mary never seemed to affect their relationship; from bassinette to adulthood they were drawn to one another. He found himself having more in common with her than he did with his older brothers. His mother had deliberately left a five-year gap between the twins and her second pregnancy, despite what the church thought. Unfortunately for her, the contraceptive method that had worked so beautifully for the five years preceding Ivan's birth failed miserably in the months after and Fintan was conceived all too quickly. Ivan was the archetypal middle child, happy to blend in and doing so wherever he went. He experienced his first love at twelve with a fair-haired, blue-eyed whippet of a thing called Noreen. They kissed behind the dressing rooms in the football field, holding their lips together until he counted to sixty. Once their lips parted, she ran off, and after that she wouldn't talk to him, but the memory of her lips against his ensured he wouldn't be behind the door about discovering someone else. He lost his virginity at fifteen, which was young in the eighties, and to a seventeen-year-old at an Irish college. He hadn't learned much Irish but to be fair to his parents, as far as he was concerned, the three weeks he spent shagging on an island off Cork was money well spent.

When he wasn't breaking hearts, he was hanging out with his cousin. She was the only girl he ever shared his thoughts with. She felt like part of him and he had never believed he'd experienced something unless he shared it with her. Luckily for her, she wasn't one for embarrassment, so when he had described his first sexual experience it was without reservation and Mary, mesmerized, made mental notes for when she dared adventure as her cousin had.

It was when Ivan nearly lost his best friend and confidante that he'd reevaluated the world around him. He didn't bother with his Leaving Cert, which, despite the year he had on Mary, he was due to take at the same time. He didn't need it anyway, not for what he wanted to do with his life. His parents attempted to put up a battle, but with their niece in a coma and their son as stubborn as he was calm, they were forced to surrender. So while the rest of his classmates studied, Ivan sat by his cousin's bed day and night, sharing sentry duty with his broken uncle. He philosophized, whispering old sayings and reciting her favorite song lyrics into her ear. He also read to her the books he thought she would like and that he'd research during the few hours he'd leave her. The fact that she was pregnant came as a horrible surprise and he'd blamed himself, his fanciful stories leading her to follow him toward sexual experience. He wondered if the baby that had survived tumbling down a mountain would suck the life out of its mother in order to live. If so he would despise that child for stealing away his best friend. Every now and then he would close his eyes and in his head he would see her eyes open and he would watch a grin spread across her face. She'd taunt him and his ways while smiling and resting in his company. But then he'd reopen his eyes and she would be lying where he'd left her, still and vacant, his stomach knotting and guts twisting.

The baby surviving had been the first miracle. Mary waking had been the second. The fact that she'd survived without brain damage, the third and final. Her skull was weakened and headaches would haunt her for all her days, but medication would keep them mostly at bay and she would be back to herself soon enough. There would be a wheelchair and physiotherapy and a wig to hide the hair loss as a consequence of the operation she had undergone to insert a metal plate into her skull. The baby would grow inside her and Ivan would be there by her side through it all and yet they would never speak of his best friend's death or her miracle child. That part of her was closed. Deep down, Ivan knew she'd come back to them, and every time he made her laugh he knew he was one step closer.

It was during this time that he first fell in love with Norma. She was a quiet town girl as bookish as she was pretty. She would ask after his cousin and talk about treatments that she had read about. She planned on studying medicine and he was falling in love with her. Mary was out of the rehabilitation hospital one month when they announced their engagement and Norma's pregnancy. Their child was less than one when Ivan first left his hometown for a faraway oil rig that would earn him enough money to support his family, leaving his new wife behind with the baby. She never did become a doctor and it would be too late before her husband would realize that his wife had felt so desperately cheated.

★ ★ ★

And then there was Penny—poor Penny—daughter to two solicitors and an only child. Her conception was deemed a mistake as children were never part of her parents' agenda. They weren't bad people, at least not that she knew of. Mostly they weren't around. Their house was a base rather than a home. Both parents worked mostly in Cork, staying in their apartment there, only popping back to the base on the weekend. Their child would be taken care of by a series of live-in nannies until she was old enough to be sent to boarding school.

"If it's good enough for royalty, it's good enough for you, darling!" her mother would say, smiling.

Mary had plonked herself beside Penny on that first train journey, heading toward their new life in Dublin. They didn't really know each other as they had attended different primary schools, but her face was familiar as any face would be growing up in a small town. Penny had been sad but Mary was at ease and excited at the prospect of a new school and a new world, and by the time they had reached Dublin she had managed to infuse that excitement into her new best friend. Penny and Mary were kindred spirits from the start. Mary may have been the child that the townspeople pitied—she was the one they whispered about as she passed, her dead mother never far behind— but it was Penny who suffered from the most terrible rejection and Mary understood that. She may not have had a mother but at least she had a father, which was more than poor Penny had. From the day she sat down beside Penny, Mary did everything to guarantee that she wouldn't have to feel lonely again, including introducing Penny to one of her cousin's best friends, Adam. Mary swore he was perfect for her. She was right: Adam and Penny were inseparable from the start. Still, when Mary nearly died, Penny thought she might just die along with her. She returned to an empty house and spoke with Adam on the phone. He told her that her best friend might not live through the night. He was desperate to be with her but his parents wouldn't let him leave the house, not after his friend had plunged to his death, leaving his half-dead girlfriend with child. That night alone in her big empty house, she opened her parents' drinks cabinet and poured herself a whiskey. When she'd finished it, she poured herself a second and a third. After her fourth she passed out on the sofa, waking up the next afternoon still alone.

The first time she'd seen her friend lying in stasis, she waited until they were alone before stroking her bandaged head.

"You better not leave me!"

She wasn't allowed to stay away from school, it being her Leaving Cert year, so instead she was forced back to studying for a degree she didn't want. Luckily for her she was as smart as she was lonely and, despite the fact that she had spent four months without opening a book, she would breeze through college just like her parents had before her. She wasn't there the day that Mary woke but Adam called her and she cried down the phone. She wasn't allowed home until the weekend, four days after her best friend came back. Penny had entered the room and Mary had burst into tears, and Penny's heart had soared because she was so happy to be recognized. To celebrate, that night she and Adam drank three bottles of her mother's Christmas stash of wine. Penny might not have known the drama that Mary had experienced, but she knew emptiness, and no matter how hard she tried she was never going to fill it up.

★ ★ ★

Adam was the kind of kid that was never going to set the intellectual world on fire, but put him in a field with any kind of ball or stick and it was like watching genius. He loved his sports and really was a much more suitable friend for Ivan's brothers than the sport-shunning Ivan. But there was something about Ivan that drew Adam from the first day. He liked his calmness and admired his simplicity. Ivan didn't care about appearance and Adam enjoyed his friend's lack of ego—being surrounded by sportsmen's egos most days, he found his friend's easy way relaxed him. If Ivan was the easygoing one and Robert the adventurous one, Adam was the funny one. He could make anyone laugh, even the sternest of his teachers, ensuring he would often talk his way out of trouble. Of course, his abilities on the field ensured a place on the Kerry youth team and with this came a hint of celebrity, and the fact that he could pick up a cup and make a joke in front of a local TV crew and half of Kerry further endeared him to the hearts of the small town. But his heart belonged only to Penny and it always had.

A long time before the day his friend introduced them he had watched a young girl with the prettiest blue shoes sit on an opposite wall. It was the wall that separated the primary school from the roadside. The school was empty, the bell having rung long before, and the children's exodus was only an echo in time, but there she sat alone with bowed head, staring at her pretty blue shoes. He hid behind a bush that separated his friend's father's land from the roadside that lay between him and the mysterious lonely girl. He had been making his way home across the fields when he caught sight of her. He was eleven and stopped in his tracks. Although for the longest time he couldn't see her face, her pretty blond hair shone in the evening sun. When she eventually did raise her cherubic face, he was reminded of an angel in the prayer book his mother had often made him read. He scrambled to hide in the growth in case she caught sight of him, feeling ashamed of his voyeurism, but she was somewhere else, squinting at the sun.

The teacher came out looking at her watch. "Well, Penny, there's no answer at home," she said, failing to disguise her annoyance.

"I'll be OK," Penny said. "You can go. I'm sure someone will be here soon." Her voice was full of sadness, the kind of sadness that only kids can convey. Adam heard it but her teacher didn't.

"This is the second time this week, not to mention three times last week," the teacher said. "This is not a babysitting service."

"I'll be fine," Penny said.

"I cannot leave you here," the teacher said. "I'll try your neighbor." She sighed.

Adam watched the woman leave the girl called Penny on her own and he watched the fat tears roll from Penny's eyes. *Don't cry,* he thought. Her head once more was bowed and he watched as the tears hit her pretty blue shoes. *Please don't cry.* Every minute she sat there alone and in tears seemed like an eternity and each moment a lifetime. He was too scared to move, although he wanted to place his arm around her shoulder, so he just sat in the grass, pretending he was beside her and willing her to be

OK. Penny dried her eyes before her teacher returned to advise her that her neighbor was on her way. Twenty minutes later a car pulled up beside Penny, who automatically jumped from the wall and silently crept into the car. The teacher spoke with Penny's neighbor in hushed tones and both were shaking their heads, neither hiding their disgust. Penny stared straight ahead and he wondered what she was thinking and if he'd see her again.

Adam too was an only child but he, unlike Penny, was smothered by his parents' love. His every whim and wish was catered to and it was a testament to all concerned that he didn't end up being a spoiled brat. There was a kindness in him instilling in him a deep desire to please. He saw the joy his very being brought to his parents and it inspired him to at the very least attempt to bring it into the lives of those around him. He'd score a goal or a point or throw a basket or make someone laugh. Pleasing people came easily. He was no pushover though. He was a winner, and all winners share a common trait in that they have the ability to put themselves over others when it really matters. That's where he and his friend Ivan differed, but it was a trait he shared with Robert. The first time Adam dressed up for Halloween he was Superman, the next year he was Spider-Man, the year after that he was Batman. Batman lasted three years running because his outfit was way cooler than that of the tights-wearing Superman/Spider-Man. At twelve he had fancied himself as some kind of hero like Westley in *The Princess Bride*, which was his favorite film, although if his friends had asked he would have told them it was the Rambo *First Blood*. But consumed by football, hurling, basketball, movies, Nintendo, music, friends and

family, and unlike the hero, Westley, he had yet to find his
true love, Buttercup, until that day when he saw Penny
crying on her school wall.

I'll save you.

Summer came quickly after that day and the girl he
would watch sitting on a wall sometimes for five minutes
and sometimes for an hour vanished. He didn't know that
her mother's mother had a house in France which she was
sent to every summer, so he watched for her around town
but she had disappeared as though she had been a dream
or a figure of fantasy. He prayed that they would end up
attending the same secondary school, but that September
he was bitterly disappointed. Three months later and out of
nowhere and like a miracle, Adam was formally introduced
to Penny by his friend Ivan's cousin Mary. The boys had
been sitting on a bench in the woods smoking cigarettes
and drinking Cokes when Mary appeared with Penny in
tow. Ivan was preoccupied by the news that his favorite
chocolate bar was being taken off the market. Robert had
a thing for Mary, but he was still with Shauna Ryan at the
time. He was busy flirting with Mary anyway and Adam
was gone, lost to the girl who reminded him of Buttercup in *The Princess Bride*. Ivan wanted to go to play video
games in the chipper and Robert had to meet Shauna,
but Adam was going nowhere. Mary had laughed at him
because apparently his mouth was open, but Penny had
smiled. Mary tagged along with Ivan, leaving Adam to
walk Penny home, talking about everything and anything
along the way. He made her laugh easily and her eyes lit up
and her hands fluttered nervously around her neck. Later
that night they sat on her wall and at last he got to put his

arm around her. When he was leaving they kissed and for both it was a first. *My Buttercup.* The trouble is, Westley married Buttercup and not a Dutchman's daughter.

★ ★ ★

Sam had taken his book to bed, falling asleep book in hand sometime after two. Around the same time Mary emerged from the woods, frozen both inside and out. Mr. Monkels had forgone his usual fourteen-hour sleep; instead, he was standing at attention by the door ready to welcome her home as if to remind her that, despite all that she had lost, she still had him. She turned to straighten the picture of her son holding Mr. Monkels on a better day. *Goodnight, baby boy, your mammy loves you.* She rubbed Mr. Monkels's tired kind face and, head bowed, he followed her upstairs. She undressed quietly and fell into bed, drained dry and exhaustion taking hold. At last sleep was inescapable.

★ ★ ★

As Mary lost consciousness, Penny continued to slug from her tumbler of vodka while flicking TV stations, propped up by pillows, feigning interest in reruns of bad sitcoms just so she could finish the bottle. Breaking up with Adam was hard enough but losing him to Cork City was unbearable. She forwent a mixer in favor of the purity required to block out her misery as quickly as possible. It flowed down the back of her throat like water, the lining happily unaffected by what should have been spluttering-inducing heat. She wasn't about to lose a drop and she didn't cry. Instead, she lost herself to the bottom of the bottle, waiting to pass out. It was after three when the glass fell from her hand and her head lolled forward, so that when she vomited it was messy but safe.

* * *

Ivan was restless. He wasn't used to being uneasy; it clashed with his character. He was worried about his kids—a phone call earlier had left him feeling perturbed as his son, ten and usually a smart-ass, was subdued and his daughter, seven and a chatterbox, was quiet and hesitant. His ex-wife had attempted to allay his concerns, noting that they were kids and being moody was part of the deal, but on reflection she too had sounded off form. He wondered if she was stressed but then again five days out of any given month she would suffer from severe PMS, during which time she could take a man's head off if she had a mind to. It was hard to forget that the slightest infraction would induce a tear tantrum that had to be seen to be believed. Ivan would often scratch his head in awe at the woman he married dancing around the kitchen in temper until sanity returned and with it a sense of humor. He had casually glanced at his wall calendar during their brief stilted conversation and surmised that, if the pattern remained unchanged, she should have another good week of sense in her. He knew she didn't really like talking with him. He could hear it in her voice. She was friendly and polite but it was obvious she was glad to have escaped. Although in the end, after a nasty patch, their parting was amicable enough, she couldn't hide her disinterest in him, the man she used to love—always so quick to get him off the phone. He missed his kids even if they were moody and in truth he missed his wife even if she had run off with some English tourist, taking his whole life with her. He was never one for television; instead, he listened to the ticking of an old clock.

★ ★ ★

And Adam returned to an empty house in time to take a phone call from his frosty wife. The phone rang and silence ensued because there was nothing left to say and he wished it would all end. His head hurt, being so full of obligation and desire, love and hate, bitterness and regret. His head hurt because this winner was in a no-win situation. His children or his lover—with no room for maneuver he had to do the right thing, which meant him losing everything. He looked around the home he had built and loved. He would miss his home, he would miss Kenmare and his parents and his friends, but mostly he would miss the girl in the blue shoes that stole his heart at twelve, and when he fell asleep he dreamed of her.

★ ★ ★

At various times and under different circumstances sleep came to Mary, Sam, Penny, Ivan and Adam that night. They would sleep peacefully and as they slept it's possible that those above took pity, for despite their problems, ghosts and guilt, they would visit a faraway and tranquil place, and although their visit would only last those few hours and their sanctuary would be quickly forgotten, that night's sleep would sustain each one of them even if it was only for a while.

Chapter Eight

Meeting the People

Sam woke early. He was hungry, having merely staved off starvation by feeding on his reticent neighbor's scraps. Yet he was slow to leave his new home to venture forth into the town he had traveled so far to explore. He picked up the book that had fallen to the floor just as he had fallen asleep. His intention was to read a few pages only but inadvertently, and despite his hunger, he lost himself in another man's imagination. It wasn't unusual that he found himself comfortable in make-believe. Some would say, as a seasoned heroin user, he was well accustomed to fantasy.

★ ★ ★

Next door, considering the previous night's heartache, it was surprising that Mary's morning had started off so full of promise. She had woken from a blissful sleep. The anniversary of her son's death was now thankfully behind her and the giant invisible weight had lifted from her mind. Strangely, she felt bright, breezy and full of vigor. She'd even danced in the shower while Dolly Parton belted out "Nine to Five" and Mr. Monkels head-butted the glass door. Dolly Parton was one of his favorites although her bluegrass stuff made him whine a little.

Mary didn't have to be in the bar until midday so she pottered around the house. She cleaned the kitchen, drank coffee and spoke with Penny on the phone.

Penny told her about Adam's first bombshell.

"She knows?" said Mary, aghast.

"I still don't know how she found out. Still, after five years, I suppose it was about time."

"It's a miracle you got away with it for so long. God help her."

"God help her?" Penny repeated in disbelief.

"He did marry her, Penny," Mary said with a sigh.

"Yes, he did."

"Finding out your husband has been having an affair must be a nightmare," Mary added.

"To be honest, I always thought that she knew, at least on some level," Penny said, sighing.

She had felt that was the case for years. She had no relationship with her lover's wife. Any social interaction was awkward and neither female could bring themselves to look the other in the eye. It was bigger than jealousy, between a man's first love and his wife.

"Well, that's something you're never going to know. Just be glad she's not on your doorstep causing murder," Mary said, relieved that Penny's adversary had such dignity in the face of her husband's betrayal.

"Why would she? She's won. They're moving to Cork," Penny said, injecting anger into her voice.

"What?" Mary cried out, and a part of her immediately began to fret. She really did hate change.

"The hotel is going up for sale. She's already found a house she likes, the stupid bitch." Penny's voice was tired. She knew it wasn't her lover's wife who was at fault and, in fairness, if it had been the other way around, she knew well she wouldn't have handled the situation as deftly as her nemesis.

"He's leaving us? Unbelievable!" Mary uttered, screwing up her face, something she did when she was puzzled, distressed or embarrassed. In this case her wrinkled forehead indicated her distress.

"At least we got to dance one last dance." Penny allowed a fat tear to escape.

Mary could almost hear it course down her face. "I'm so sorry, Penn."

"You'll miss him too," Penny offered kindly and she was right.

Mary would miss him. They had all been friends for so long.

"Why don't you come into the bar tonight?" said Mary.

Penny wasn't sure, saying she wasn't feeling so well. "I'll probably stay in and keep my head down."

"Well, the offer is there if you change your mind."

"Cheers, Mare!"

Mary hung up the phone and felt sad for Penny and Adam and sad for herself. She would miss her friend. Adam was the impulsive to Ivan's dependable. He was funny too, but not like Ivan, who was funny in turn of phrase and mostly without intent. Adam was sharp and often the center of attention. Born with charm, that's how her dad had described him once. Her dad was right, he was charming, but he was also terribly unhappy and she worried for him. Moving to Cork was possibly the worst plan ever. She knew he wouldn't want to leave his home, his friends and most of all Penny, the girl he had fallen in love with while she sat on a wall. *Oh my God, is Adam the boy in the hood?* Poor Penny and poor Adam. Of course, they were in the wrong—Adam's wife was the victim in all of this. But Adam's wife wasn't her friend. Mary had thought about the sad situation while hanging the washing, accompanied by Aretha Franklin belting out "Do Right Woman, Do Right Man" from her new neighbor's second-floor open window.

Later she sent a text to Adam, asking to meet during her break. He responded instantly, agreeing to rendezvous at seven.

★ ★ ★

Another hour passed and, despite the fact that he was surely about to discover who it was that killed Boy Staunton, the sincerity with which Sam's insides burned proved too great to ignore. He released his grip and put the book onto his side locker after carefully marking his place on the page. He then pressed STOP, and once Aretha was hushed he made his way toward the shower. He washed and shaved in mere minutes. Once dressed and having grabbed his neighbor's dish, he exited his new home.

★ ★ ★

Mary found her jacket and grabbed her handbag, signaling to Mr. Monkels that it was time for a furry kiss. He walked in step. She opened the French doors leading to the back garden.

"In or out, Mr. M?" she asked, looking down while he looked up.

He took a step outside and faced her.

She bent down. "Good choice." Then she kissed his furry face, rubbing her cheek against his before he turned toward the bird table to resume a battle he had begun earlier that morning.

Breezily, she made her way to her front door.

★ ★ ★

Sam's intention was to leave the bowl outside Mary's front door as directed the previous night. He certainly wasn't in the mood to be scowled at. The sky was a bright vibrant blue and the day was unexpectedly sunny, in contrast to the rain which had washed him into this small curious place. The light danced on the water—now a clear color approaching a light blue or a deep green, depending on which angle it was viewed from. He inhaled without thought. Sea air filled his lungs, clearing his tired mind. Overhead a seagull squawked a greeting. Either that or he was being told to ef off by a bird. He grinned to himself. If it had flown in from New York Harbor the sentiment was definitely the latter. He opened the gate signifying his neighbor's boundary, pushing it slowly, attempting to negate the squeaking sound he had encountered the previous night, afraid that it might herald his presence. He popped the bowl down on the step and turned away but only for a second—enough time for it to dawn on him that a bowl on the middle of a step could easily be stood on, prompting the necessity for a visit to an emergency room. This was definitely not the impression he wished to make. He bent down to retrieve the bowl with a view to putting it beside the step and next to the large flowerpot which housed a hardy-looking red-leafed plant and a deep-blue pottery hedgehog. It was the hedgehog that caught his eye, delaying him from standing upright.

He didn't hear the door open and his neighbor didn't see the man stooped over her front-door step.

That is how she managed to walk straight into him—his face imbedding itself in her crotch—unbalancing him. Her initial shock gave way to absolute horror when he chose to grab on to her arse. Beating him about the head with a handbag was her only option and she did so with gusto. A strange man with his face in your crotch will provoke that kind of reaction in a woman and, if she was honest, with each blow she felt a little tension escape.

Still, in Sam's defense, he hadn't planned the assault and her handbag had buckles.

"Get off, you frigging perv!" she roared while slapping him silly with her bag.

"Your bowl!" he begged, pointing with one hand while the other rose to protect his face.

She managed to look behind her while still reaching her target with something approaching expert precision. She gave him one last smack before conceding and for him the onslaught ended as quickly as it had begun.

Unfortunately, it was that last smack that drew blood.

"Ahhhhhhhhh!" he cried out, holding his eye.

Mary took a moment to survey the damage she'd inflicted. "Oh!" she exclaimed, her face screwing up, like a little kid who knew she'd just done something bad. *Frigging buckle.*

"Oh God, what is it?" Sam inquired urgently because like most men any minor injury was tantamount to this world's end.

"Your eye is bleeding. It must have caught on the buckle." Helpfully, she raised the bag in the air to demonstrate the part of her weapon which had inflicted maximum injury.

Sam took his hand off his face and she was right—it was red, his blood pooling in his palm. He heard her sigh. It was a frustrated sigh. She really did have a nerve.

For Mary's part, obviously, she was embarrassed at having gone one step too far, and yet his reaction to a tiny cut was extremely amusing, even endearing.

"I have a first-aid kit," she offered while managing to hold in a further sigh.

He would have told her to shove her kit, but seeing his own spilled blood made him feel a little faint. He had always been a little squeamish around blood, which proved to be a handicap when he was a heroin addict. Of course, the promise of liquid Nirvana had enabled him to get over it but, now clean, his weak stomach and wobbling legs had made a surprising return.

Unsteadily, he followed her inside, and she indicated for him to sit at her kitchen table. He sat and closed his eyes with his hand tight against the cut just over his eye. He could hear her shoving pots and pans about and then she was standing over him, her crotch at a happy distance.

When she began to tend to him she was reminded of her little boy and it made her smile.

He could have sworn that she was grinning but nothing was funny so he dismissed it as some residual paranoia.

"You have to move your hand," she advised.

Eyes closed, he was almost sure he could hear a grin in her voice. He was slow to comply.

"It's a tiny cut. You're not going to lose an eye here."

Easy for you to say, you bag-wielding lunatic! He lowered his hand and his good eye opened in time to see her approach him with a little bud covered in liquid.

She held his head, arching it back. "This will sting a little," she warned, and he braced himself.

It wasn't that bad. She was surprisingly gentle. Using another bud, she applied antiseptic cream, and then before he knew it a small plaster covered an even smaller cut.

"There, all done!" she said before packing away her first-aid kit.

"I guess I should thank you," Sam said, still a little shocked at sustaining a head injury so quickly into his trip. It wasn't hard to detect a hint of sarcasm in his voice.

"Don't bother," she said, brushing herself down.

He got up, sensing that she wanted him gone—he was only too happy to oblige.

"Sorry," he heard himself mumble while walking quickly to the door.

She followed and once outside she attempted to reciprocate his apology, conceding that it had all been a misunderstanding and that in all probability he was not a pervert. Still, it was clear to him she was not entirely convinced.

In fact, he was so desperate to prove his innocence that she almost felt sorry for him—still, she wasn't about to let him know that. She'd known way too many foreign neighbors—the best of friends one day and the next gone forever. She didn't need the hassle so she allowed him to think that she wasn't absolutely convinced of his virtue. *That should keep him at bay.* She was getting into her car when he realized that she would know where he could get a decent lunch. She rolled down the window to respond to his query.

"Everywhere is good," she noted before driving off. Obviously, she could have mentioned her place, but that would be like an invitation to some sort of neighborly relationship.

"Everywhere is good," he repeated, wishing he'd left the stupid bowl where it was. "Thanks a lot, lady."

Sam decided to walk. He reckoned town was ten minutes by foot and, as he was still a little light-headed, he deemed it better not to risk driving. This concern was interesting coming from a man who one night six months previously had driven from Boston to New York having pushed five hundred bucks of heroin into his system that day. He was halfway to town when the realization struck that he actually cared about his welfare and this reminded him that he had indeed come a long way. *I hope it lasts.* He reached the top of the town and looked down at the sloping street that led to a steeple signaling God's empty house. The sky resting above was a deeper navy than the one over the water and yet it seemed as bright. Stratus clouds seemed to pass quickly above him, making their way toward the sea. The street was busy with cars beeping and people waving as they made their way in and out of the colorful shops.

★ ★ ★

While Sam sauntered through his new world, half a street away Mary parked in her father's yard and entered the kitchen to be met by Pierre, who was in foul form, having borne the brunt of Jessie's frustration.

"Oh, that woman!" was his greeting to Mary, and Jessie wasn't far behind.

"I heard that," she noted with her face a ball of anger. "Arse-crack!" she roared, following him to the storeroom at full speed. Despite her advancing years and conservative appearance suggesting decorum, "arse-crack" was a term that Jessie used at least three times a day.

Mary made her way into the dining room. Her dad popped his head up behind the bar.

"Have they been like this long?" she asked, laughing.

"All morning—they're like feckin' caricatures," he sighed, not so entertained. Then he asked kindly, "Are you OK?"

"Thanks for the flowers, Dad. He would have liked them." She smiled, signaling that she wasn't going to cry.

"You're both welcome." He patted his daughter's back. They had both been through hell over the years but he knew that as long as she was OK he would be.

The place was busy enough and within seconds of her arrival Ivan was sitting up at the bar ordering his usual seafood salad.

"Don't you ever want to eat something else?" Mary asked, laughing at her cousin and his rituals.

"No," he said plainly. "What about you? I hear you're meeting Adam for a drink. Is there something I should know?" He was chuckling.

"Shut up." She grinned before becoming serious. "I can't believe he's leaving."

"I'll believe it when I see it," he said, playing with the redundant menu.

"Penny says he's definitely going. He's got a job managing some restaurant in Cork and they're selling the hotel."

"I'll believe it when I see it," he repeated, frowning.

★ ★ ★

Sam was too hungry to survey the many restaurants on offer, instead he planned to eat in the first place he found. He didn't have to walk too far. The menu was plastered on the front door and it looked good. Better still, the aroma coming from inside could only be described as mouthwatering. The place looked real homey—pottery and luscious plants filling the window and ornate furniture bedecking the large entrance. Once inside he wasn't disappointed. Faces and events from another era lined the walls, intermingled with a smattering of small canvas paintings. The dark wooden tables and red velvet sofas suggested warmth and, even on a bright day, the burning candles didn't seem out of place. He melted into his chair, having already decided to start with the crab salad and to follow with the house omelette. Someone had left a newspaper on the seat. He began to read local Irish news, which turned out to be not so much local as international and much of it criticizing the Iraq war. He put the paper down just in time to see his neighbor and basher behind the little bar.

"You're kidding me," he mumbled.

"Crap!" Suddenly Mary disappeared.

Ivan bent over the bar and looked down at her crouching.

"What are you doing?" he asked, intrigued at his cousin on her knees biting her nails.

"Frigging American," she mumbled. "Of all the frigging places. I have to go." She popped up again and disappeared into the kitchen. Ivan looked around and spotted the blond pretty boy. *Interesting.*

Ivan refilled his coffee before he made his way toward Sam's booth.

"Excuse me?" Ivan said, moving in beside Sam. "You're on your own?"

"Yeah," Sam agreed while wondering whether he could still make a break for it without being noticed.

"Not from around here?" Ivan noted in a tone that didn't make it clear to Sam as to whether the guy was talking to himself or asking a question.

"New York," he ventured.

"Ah," Ivan nodded, "you're the new fella by the pier. Sam Sullivan."

"Yeah." Sam shook his head, amazed.

Ivan laughed. "I bumped into Mossy first thing."

Sam shook his head. "I don't know Mossy."

Ivan grinned. "You will."

"Man, this is a small town," Sam said, shaking his head and grinning.

"You've no idea," Ivan agreed, returning Sam's grin.

A fat woman in her fifties took their orders. To say she wasn't in a good humor was an understatement. When Ivan made a joke she smacked him over the head with her order book. Ivan had laughed but Sam remained sober, unwilling to risk further injury at the hands of another crazy Kerry woman.

Over lunch they conversed easily. Sam liked Ivan mostly because he was easygoing and not intrusive. The guy was more interested in talking about fish than asking probing questions. He found himself relaxing despite the fact that it was obvious that Mary had seen him and was steering well clear. The crab salad was to die for and Ivan had gone to great lengths to explain why and Sam found himself laughing.

"I'm talking about fish too much," Ivan admitted sheepishly.

"You really are, man," Sam admitted while enjoying himself.

Ivan liked the American too. He wouldn't have stayed on for a pint with him if he hadn't.

★ ★ ★

Meanwhile, Mary made herself busy chopping onions in the kitchen in an attempt to avoid any interaction with her neighbor. If he hadn't asked her to recommend a place to eat and if she hadn't been so dismissive, she wouldn't have felt the need to hide. She should have volunteered her own establishment, and seeing as she'd drawn blood the offer of a free lunch was possibly the least she could do. *Of all the frigging places.*

Jessie questioned her motives for remaining within the confines of the kitchen. "I chop. You lord it over everyone. What's changed?" she asked insultingly. Pierre laughed despite himself, signaling that he agreed with his enemy's interpretation of the situation.

"I'm hiding," Mary admitted, and Jessie was suddenly interested.

"From who?" she asked while making her way to the door of the kitchen.

"Jessie!" Mary called out.

Jessie didn't even have to open the kitchen door before she copped it. "It's the American," she noted triumphantly.

Mary was impressed. "How did you know?" she asked despite herself.

"He looks like an arse-crack. Why wouldn't you hide?"

"No, he's not," Mary answered before she gave her statement thought.

Jessie's eyebrows rose. "Really?" she noted, and looked toward Pierre, who grinned.

"Ah, *chérie,* you like him, no?"

"What?" Mary asked, alarmed. "Don't be ridiculous."

The enemies had converged, nodding at one another, enjoying her moment of torment.

" 'Arse-crack' is a disgusting term, that's all I'm saying," she said while chopping into her eighth red onion.

★ ★ ★

It was over the third pint that Ivan offered to take Sam out in the boat with him. Sam was enthralled with the idea of fishing so Ivan promised to take him out the next day, adding that as it was Sunday he was obligated to eat with his family so it would have to be late afternoon. Sam could see no problem with fishing in the afternoon and reflected that it would give him time to finish his book. He then insisted that his new friend allow him to pay for his food in thanks.

He made his way home, feeling a little dizzy but full and happy. He also felt a little guilty. Drinking three pints was as close as he'd got to oblivion since rehab. He wasn't an alcoholic so it was not like having a drink was totally against the rules. *But does it make me want to get high? No. Definitely no. OK, this is cool. I'm just a little happy. I'm fine. Everything is fine.* This was a relief and yet he would have to keep an eye on himself. He wasn't strong enough yet and he knew that he was still on a precipice and the slightest ill wind could knock him off.

Chapter Nine

Past and Present

It was the third time in six months that Penny had been awakened by the smell of her own vomit but, too hung-over to distinguish smell, she remained unaware of her sensory alarm until she looked in her bathroom mirror and, in doing so, realized the extent of the previous night's debauchery. *Oh sweet God!* Disgusted by her gluttony, she had stripped off and got into the shower. The water was pounding against her skull, which felt as fragile as her mother's ugly fine bone china. Her legs felt weak and were shaking under the weight of her delicate yet surprisingly heavy head. She leaned against the wall and found herself sliding toward the shower tray. She didn't attempt to stop herself from crumpling; instead, she sat with her knees under her chin and her hands cupping her head to protect it from the water tumbling down.

She took painkillers with a pint of chilled water and made coffee while two DJs bantered about Madonna and her latest religion. She imbibed three espressos before opening her email. She answered some of her editor's queries and typed a redraft of her lottery story and by mid-morning her limbs had stopped shaking.

When Mary called her on the phone she cried, which was something she had promised herself she wouldn't do. She declined Mary's offer to come over, telling herself that like any wounded animal she needed to be alone. That wasn't the truth. She hated being alone but deep down she knew that she couldn't get through the next few days exchanging pleasantries and girl talk. It was then she acknowledged that, as soon as she had finished a telephone interview at three, she would open a bottle of vodka and, when that bottle was gone and depending on how she felt, she might break out another one and she didn't need any witnesses. After that, she promised herself, tomorrow or the next day she'd emerge from the haze and everything would be fine.

★ ★ ★

Ivan always woke in time to witness sunrise. In spring and summer he would enjoy it from his veranda, drinking hot coffee while the birds sang from the branches of the many trees that lined the boundaries of his property. In autumn and winter he would be already on his boat by the time the sun came up. Whatever the season, he would be on the deck of his boat in time to enjoy five hours of good fishing before heading into town for his lunch. Ivan was a creature of habit, so much so that many townspeople had commented that they could set their watch by him.

He spent his afternoons at home locked in his study,

reading magazines on stocks and commodities or online share trading. He was never going to be the cause of Donald Trump losing a night's sleep but he was smart enough to know when to buy and sell. He enjoyed risk but was never seduced by it. Sometimes his judgment let him down, but those occasions were rare. Ivan was no mathematician but he was a pretty good economist.

It was curious that he had deviated from his routine and it was possibly curiosity that had driven him to do so, but, whatever it was, he had thoroughly enjoyed drinking a few pints with the American. It had been a nice break from the mundane and it was even nicer to remain outside his home in the afternoon, even if it was only for a few hours.

Ivan's large house was a symbol of success to the on-looker, but his many empty rooms only reminded him of his failure. When he had uttered the words "I do" and "forever," he had meant it, and foolishly he had believed his wife when she repeated them. Years later when she came home one night out of the blue, battling tears so as to make an announcement, he had been shocked to his very core. In the weeks following her desertion he was numb, but at least she and his children, whom she had packed bags for and left with the very night she'd dictated their split, were still in Kenmare. It was her second announcement, the one in which she spoke of their planned departure and their new lives beginning somewhere in England, that had reawakened him, and as surely as if she had poured petrol on fire it ignited in him a fierce anger. It was then he considered fighting her for custody of their children. His fury simmered and his wounded heart bled and this pain was compounded by the terrible embarrassment he endured at his most private business being the talk of the town. He consulted a solicitor and incredibly was told that his rights were secondary to his wife's. He had argued that she was the adulterer, the homewrecker, the assassin and that it was she who had killed their family. In fairness there were plenty around him who weren't shy about pointing that out and if necessary would stand in a court to swear to it. He argued that he had been a good provider, a good husband, he'd never strayed despite opportunity. He would never have strayed. He had loved his wife and he adored his children. He would never have risked them. He asked why he should be the victim. He asked why he should lose everything. His solicitor had no answers and despite this negativity Ivan was determined to fight for his kids. Then one day, having witnessed his daughter's confusion and tears, it dawned on him that this was about his kids and their life and his love of them and not about the woman who abandoned him. His kids needed her, and despite her failings as a wife she was a good mother and the prevailing force in their children's lives. He couldn't rob them of her as she had robbed them of him. He could never have forced his children into battle merely to meet his own needs. When he finally admitted to himself that he would lose them, he had quietly fallen apart.

Earlier that morning and while alone on his boat, he found himself reflecting on the day that he had driven his children to the airport and out of his life. This was possibly brought on by his nephew's anniversary. He remembered that, following their mother and her lover in the car ahead, they had cried all the way. Neither had wanted to move away from their dad, their friends and their entire lives, but dutifully he told them to be brave and to enjoy the adventure and that their home would always be waiting. Everything inside of him had threatened to snap, but he held on tight to reason and reminded his children that he loved them. He told them to think of the UK as boarding school, as they would spend all their holidays with him at home. When they walked through the gates he battled so hard not to cry, knowing a father's tears could scar a child. The ball that formed in his chest surely threatened blood flow and he had wondered if his heart would fail in a Departures lounge. He wept all the way home, having to stop the car a number of times on the road simply because he couldn't see the road through his tears. When he eventually made it back, he hibernated in his soulless home, choosing to spend his days dressed in an ill-fitting tracksuit, holed up watching daytime TV with the phone in his hand. He was like that for two weeks.

At the end of the second week it had been Mary who'd sorted him out. She had let herself in with his spare key and, ignoring his protest, she cleaned the pigsty that his home had become while cooking up a spicy lamb stew, which was his favorite of her dishes. He showered and shaved but only after she threatened him with a kitchen knife. He joined her at the freshly laid table, silent and distant. She consoled and he scooped up his spicy meal from a large bowl and attempted to eat while she talked to him about all the things that he could do with his kids when he saw them.

"Remember when Chris was a baby?" she asked.

"It seems like a lifetime ago," he mumbled.

"Nah, not so long." She remembered. "You were abroad working for a lot of that."

"Don't remind me," he said with his hands cupping his ears.

"Did he forget you then?"

"No."

"No," she agreed. "He used to sit on the doorstep waiting for you to come home." She smiled at the memory. "You are their dad. You're the one they love. So miss them while they are out of sight but remember it's not forever. You will see them again."

Suddenly, he became embarrassed. "I'm sorry. I know it's not the same as losing Ben," he said, and she shook her head sadly.

"This isn't about me," she replied. "Not everything that happens has to be measured against losing Ben. You have a right to your pain. I just want to make sure that it doesn't swallow you up."

He reached across the table and took her hand in his. "What would I do without you, cousin?" he asked.

"What would I do without you, cousin?" she responded.

"Life goes on," he sighed.

"And the only choice we have is how we want to live it," she replied.

Mary had brought one of Pierre's cheesecakes and they had enjoyed it with a glass of sweet white wine.

★ ★ ★

At first Ivan's kids had groused and griped about their new life. Friends, school, teachers, money, boys, girls and their mother were all bashed. They turned grumbling into an art form. He would spend hours on the phone attending to their petulance. Their problems were not so different from the ones they left behind, and with time new friends came into their lives and they became accustomed to their environment and intermittently he'd receive some positive information about a friend or an outing or something happening in school. They had settled in as he knew they would and Kent was not as far away as he'd first thought. Kerry airport was only half an hour down the road and there were cheap flights going in and out of all three London airports every day of the week. The flight was less than an hour. When he actually thought about it and investigated the number of flights available, the traveling distance between his children's new home and each London airport, Gatwick being the closest, he worked out that it would take longer for them to travel home from Dublin than Kent and that made him feel a lot better.

And just when he'd relaxed something changed and his kids stopped talking to him. No more whinging and whining, no more bitching and moaning. No more stories of friends or outings or anything. The conversations had become stilted and strange and again he worried that he was losing them but then something in the back of his mind was telling him that it might be worse than that. . . .

After his few pints with the American he didn't feel like going home; instead, he returned to his boat with a view to tidying. The evening sky contained a hint of purple and the weather was mild enough for it to be warm in a jacket while sitting on the deck. He located a beer in the fridge and, instead of getting busy working, he got busy sitting and sipping while watching the dark waters lap and comfortably resting on the undulation. Ivan was most content on the deck of his boat and especially while tapping his foot to The Waterboys. They were singing "Fisherman's Blues" from an old CD player he'd fitted in the cabin. Ivan liked to think he inspired the song. He'd met and had pints with the lads a few times when they'd played in Kenmare, so his theory was at the very least plausible.

While the rest of the world busied itself, he sat in contemplation. He was glad to see that the previous morning's cloud had passed and that his cousin was in a lighter humor. He had realized the date and its meaning, which is why he'd checked in on her the previous morning, but he would never mention it. Being there for her was enough and in fairness she always made a lovely breakfast. Her reaction to Sam had struck him as odd. Mary was not inclined to fluster easily if at all. Then again she often behaved peculiarly around the time of Ben's anniversary and to be fair the American seemed like a really nice fella and he looked forward to introducing the city boy to the sea.

★ ★ ★

It was just after seven when Mary made her way into The Horseshoe Bar. Adam was sitting at a table, picking at a bowl of mussels and sipping on a pint. The bar waitress saluted Mary and made some joke about her being the competition. Adam stood and they hugged before taking their seats.

"You've had some week." Mary wasn't one for beating around the bush.

"I've had better." Adam was a bush-beater.

"So you're really leaving?"

"Yeah, you know I wouldn't put Penn through it if I wasn't."

Mary raised her eyebrows. "You've put her through everything else."

Adam nodded to concede his friend had made a good point. He loved Penny too much to cause her intentional pain, but pain caused, whether intentional or not, is still pain. It was such a pity he didn't love his own wife.

"You're in a pretty terrible fix," she sighed.

"I am," he agreed, "but it's no different from the fix I've been in for years."

"Yeah, it is. You won't have Penny," Mary said, and instantly she regretted it. "I'm sorry. I shouldn't have said that."

"Why not? It's true." He took a drink.

"Cork is only sixty miles away," Mary noted, attempting to compensate for her previous comment.

"Cork is a lifetime away," he said while attempting a grin.

Mary ordered a gin and tonic and he ordered another pint, and then he explained how his wife had finally worked out that her husband was having an affair and how she had threatened to take his kids to the Netherlands and how he had to make it work. He had no choice. Not after he'd witnessed what losing his kids had done to Ivan. Mary squeezed his hand, understanding his desperation as, given the choice, she would have traded anything or anyone for her own child. She had often theorized that people waste so much time seeking out the love of their lives in the belief their greatest love will come in the shape of a partner, when the truth is that for most of us the real loves of our lives are our children—and everyone else is dispensable. Once when Ben was still a toddler she had used this theory to explain her lethargy about seeking companionship and now years later Adam and Penny were proving her theory had legs.

Adam's wife had gone to Cork to set up home but her spies were everywhere. When Peggy Dawson passed by she leaned in to say hello to Adam, but the manner in which she looked Mary up and down, accompanied by a deep line-furrowing frown, suggested that what she really meant was: "Your card is marked." Mary wanted to point out that she wasn't Penny but then realized that, as she was Penny's closest friend, Adam was deemed to be fraternizing with the enemy. He was nice as pie to Peggy and even managed to make his wife's friend laugh despite herself. Mary also made an effort to smile at the local gossip and harridan who had often described her as the Angel of Death. When Peggy had passed, Adam smiled and apologized graciously, admitting his bad behavior had ensured he was being closely monitored. Peggy continued to eyeball them until they finished their drinks and left.

Adam wanted her to go to McCarthy's for another but she needed to get back behind the bar, and he asked her if she wanted company and, since Penny had decided to stay at home, she agreed. He sat up at the bar and she poured him a drink while he looked through the available CDs as she'd promised him the music would be of his choice. Jack was tired and she had assured him that she was OK on her own, and that besides Adam had offered to step into the breach if necessary. Jack didn't need to be told twice.

Adam picked Damien Rice's O and handed it to her.

"Again?" she asked, hand on hip.

"What do you mean 'again'?" Adam asked with mock horror.

"I swear to God you're turning into Ivan," she said, shaking her head.

"Ivan has eaten the same salad for fifteen years. I've requested this record three times," he laughed.

"Yeah, well, it's a slippery slope." She grinned.

Once the CD was playing, Adam settled on his bar stool while Mary wiped down the counter in front of him.

"Is she drinking?" he asked out of nowhere. An explanation as to whom he was referring was unnecessary.

"A few bottles of wine last week but I think she's OK."

"You sure?"

"No, but she's favoring staying at home rather than going to the pub so that's good." She smiled. "Last week was the first time I've seen Penny drunk in an age and, let's face it, she'd just been dumped."

Adam nodded guiltily. "OK."

"She will be as soon as you leave," Mary couldn't stop herself from saying.

"You're a coldhearted bitch," he said, shaking his head.

"And you're a cheating bastard." Mary retorted.

"I'm really going to miss you," he said.

"I'm really going to miss you too."

Interrupted conversation followed as they talked about this and that while she served drinks and swapped pleasantries with fellow locals. Adam told her about the restaurant he'd secured a management position in, and the legal wrangling involved in selling the hotel, and the place his wife had found for them to live. It wasn't all that bad, he had noted. The restaurant was an award winner and there were some excellent schools, but then he would always find the positive in even the worst of situations. Mary had told him about her dreadful neighbor and was pleased when he'd enjoyed her terrible embarrassment and the subsequent tourist-bashing incident.

It was after ten when Tin Fitz and Roy Rice plonked themselves on the bar stools either side of Adam.

"Adam," Tin said.

"Tin," Adam responded.

Tin nodded his head and sniffed. "Caught rotten."

"I suppose so," Adam agreed.

"You'll have a drink," Rice said, and Adam nodded.

Rice ordered three pints from Mary and within moments the three men were immersed in a conversation about Kerry's chances of winning the All Ireland Hurling Final.

A few hours later, when last orders were finally served, Mary joined the three lads at the counter.

"Mary, have you decided to marry me yet?" Tin asked, grinning.

"I hadn't heard you'd divorced," she said, putting her drink on the counter.

"I haven't but I've a big bed," he laughed, nodding. "I'm sure Nora would make room."

"That's some image," Rice laughed.

"I've always believed two wives were better than one," Tin said, and he nudged Adam. "It would sort out a lot of hassles."

Adam smirked but refused to be drawn.

"What's that called?" Tin said to Rice.

"Polygamy," Rice said before draining his drink.

"How you fixed for a bit of polygamy?" Tin winked at Mary.

"I'd rather gnaw through my own foot, thanks, Tin," Mary said, smiling.

Adam and Rice laughed while Tin shook his head. "All right—if you feel that strongly I'll get rid of Nora."

Later, when the bar was cleared out, Adam and Mary sat drinking coffee and reminiscing.

"Remember the night on the boat?" he asked.

They had been on the boat hundreds of times but she knew the night he was referring to immediately. Of course she remembered.

"It was the stillest night. The water was like glass. I still can't believe Uncle Pete didn't catch us or that we didn't crash," she said, grinning.

"Crash? Ivan could drive that thing in his sleep even at sixteen!" Adam was laughing. "Penny and I were hot and heavy that night."

"I threw a bottle of water on you to cool you down." She grinned.

"And night swimming!" he lamented.

She smiled widely at the memory of her first induction to skinny-dipping. Ivan had been embarrassed to take off his trunks in front of his cousin, but then he was seeing a girl called Bridget and she was definitely one to see in the nip so he had conceded, based on a borderline system. Then, under the cover of darkness, the six of them spread out with only the moonlight to guide them to their partner.

"Robert was the first to jump in," Adam sighed, re-membering his long-dead friend.

"Robert was always the first," Mary said, remembering her first love with all the warmth a fond memory relived could bring.

"He wanted to be an engineer," Adam reminded her.

Mary nodded in agreement. "Yeah, and he also wanted to play guitar for Bon Jovi." They had both laughed, re-membering their friend's youthful passions.

"Do you miss him?" he asked.

Mary was taken aback by his query. "Not really," she answered honestly. "Mostly, he's a stranger, a kid I knew a long time ago, but then on nights like this one when we talk and reminisce I do, but it's fleeting and not real. We were just teenagers finding our way—it's highly likely that we wouldn't be together now even if he was alive."

"Like me and Penny," he said sadly.

"No," she admitted, "not at all like you and Penny."

"How long will it take her to forget me?" he asked, looking into the dregs of his mug.

"A long time," Mary answered.

"It's killing me," he admitted.

"I know," she responded simply. There was nothing else to say.

★ ★ ★

Mary got home just after one. Mr. Monkels was extremely put out by the fact that he had been outside for the entire evening, despite the fact that he had been well fed and there was a shed with a deluxe quilted dog bed at the end of the garden. He articulated his feelings by employing

141

various forms of sustained groaning. He was not impressed with his owner's timekeeping and was determined to ensure she was not unaware of his disgust. Mary gave him a bar of chocolate just to shut him up. Obviously, this was the act of a bad mother, dogs being intolerant of chocolate, but he really loved it and she only gave it out on either a very special occasion or as a response to guilt.

The light was on next door and when she went into her back garden to retrieve Mr. Monkels's bowl, she could hear Billie Holiday singing in her neighbor's kitchen. She had stopped to enjoy "April in Paris" while inside, her dog's mouth opened into a moan, silenced by glass.

And next door Sam was sitting book in hand, having resumed his journey to Deptford and beyond. He didn't worry about the cut above his eye or ponder his new life in a small South Kerry town. He didn't worry about those he'd left behind. He didn't think about anything, even managing to drown out Billie Holiday reminiscing about a spring day in the French capital. By 1:00 AM he had long ago left Kenmare.

Chapter Ten

Sunday Bloody Sunday

It was Sunday and Ivan was having dinner with his parents and his twin brothers, Séamus and Barry, Séamus's wife, Vicky, their four-year-old twin girls, Beth and Bonnie, Barry's boyfriend, Steven, and their puppy, Pluto. Ivan had become slowly accustomed to attending his mother's lunches alone. He still found it hard. The friendly noise made it harder to go home to silence. He missed the familiar sounds of a full house and envied his older brother but, having said that, it was obvious that Séamus was at the end of his tether.

"Beth! Bonnie! Leave the dog alone!" Séamus shouted. Neither Beth nor Bonnie seemed to hear their father, so busy were they trying to capture Pluto, who had managed to squeeze himself behind the TV.

Steven was beside himself, calling out to his pet. "Pluto! Pluto! Daddy's here!"

The girls, like scavengers, were reaching in as far as their little arms allowed them and Pluto was squealing, waiting for his daddy to save the day. Steven, in his haste to attend to his baby, tripped over one of the girls' Disney Princesses, nearly knocking himself out on the edge of the coffee table. Barry, seeing his partner crumpled on the floor, dropped his cup of hot coffee and then slipped on it in his haste to attend to his beloved boyfriend. Séamus helped his brother up while still roaring at the girls, who didn't seem to notice either accident, still determined to catch the dog, who was now whining softly. Ivan attended to Steven while his mother attended to Barry. Séamus stormed out of the room with a little girl under each arm, calling out to his wife, who roared that she was in the bathroom. Well used to blocking sound, Ivan's father snoozed in the chair.

Later at the dinner table Steven insisted on eating lunch with Pluto in a little doggy knapsack attached to his chest. Pluto slept, exhausted after battle, and so the family was spared Steven sharing his meal with his pet. Bonnie and Beth were also strapped into their chairs, both a little too old for high chairs and yet a little too hyperactive for seating without strapping. Séamus and Barry talked about the Cork versus Kerry game. Steven, Ivan's mother, and Vicky complained to one another about the price of cashmere and discussed Greece and its virtue as an all-round holiday destination. Bonnie and Beth threw food at each other while Ivan and his dad sat silently enjoying their meals.

Ivan's mother had always known Barry was a little different from her other sons, and even his love of football hadn't encouraged her to look forward to grandchildren. Her first indication that he might not marry was when he was four. She would often find him asleep in her wardrobe with a face full of lipstick and wrapped up in one of her dresses. At six he broke his leg while walking in a pair of her heels. His dad took him to the emergency room and told the doctor that he had fallen from a tree, but Barry had cheerfully corrected him. During his teenage years he threw himself into sport and his mother worried that he was doing so as a means of escaping himself. His brothers, Séamus, Ivan and even her youngest, Fintan, were all sluts, each week a different girl, but not Barry. His father pretended that this was because he was an overachiever, studious and a consummate sportsman, but she knew deep down that her husband knew better. She wasn't sure how to tackle her son's ambiguous sexuality, but after long consideration she thought it best to allow him to discover himself. So she sat back and waited, all the while ensuring that he knew that he lived in a house of tolerance and acceptance. Barry came out at a Sunday dinner during his last year in college. His mother was relieved and kissed her son, ruffled his hair and told him his boyfriends would always be welcome in her house. His father was a little pale and yet resigned—after all, his wife had been preparing him for this day for many years. He put his arm around his son, patted him on the back and said: "Never mind, son." Ivan and Fintan didn't seem to care either way. Ivan was preoccupied as to how to tell his parents that he'd got his girlfriend pregnant and Fintan was working out how to dump his latest girlfriend, who was a great kisser but also had a flatulence problem.

Séamus had been the most put out about his twin brother's revelation. Barry had joked that his twin's storming out of the kitchen had something to do with him

thinking that maybe Barry had tried to have his way with
him in the womb but he assured everyone that he was not
into incest. His mother had attempted to laugh before asking him to follow his brother and to have a quiet word. It
turned out that Séamus was upset because what had been
so obvious to his mother had not been obvious to him.
He had always thought they were close and had a special
bond. He thought he knew all there was to know about
his twin and suddenly Barry was a stranger. After that, their
relationship had changed a little. They used to refer to each
other as twins, now it was merely brothers.

Over the years, Sunday dinner had been the place
where most revelations took place. Barry's coming out;
Ivan's impending fatherhood a mere two Sundays later.
Ivan had not been met with the same understanding as his
brother—in fact, his mother had threatened to have him
shot and his father had to hold her back while shouting
at his son to run for it. A few months later it was Ivan and
Norma's engagement, a much more sedate affair and met
with congratulations and champagne—initially, his mother
had worried that he was moving too fast, but by dessert
Norma had won her over. A few years later Séamus's engagement to Vicky became yet another announcement
over Sunday dinner. Later their pregnancy and a month
after that the fact that they were having twins. Ivan's wife's
infidelity was imparted over a salmon starter, the separation a few Sundays later. Fintan's decision to move to New
Zealand to start a bungee-jumping business had been the
last Sunday revelation.

But on this Sunday, aside from Barry and Séamus nearly
knocking themselves out, the twins being terrors and

Pluto's nervous disposition, all was going quite well. That is until Ivan's mother advised them that she had an announcement. Everyone fell silent. After all, the news could be good or bad. They braced themselves.

"I'm pregnant," she said.

Barry nearly choked, Ivan went red and Séamus stood up. Vicky looked confused and Steven seemed impressed.

Ivan's mother laughed and his dad joined in.

"Only joking."

Séamus sat down. "Very funny, Mother. You nearly gave me a heart attack."

Her face changed a little.

"It's funny you should say that." She wasn't joking anymore. She squeezed her husband's arm. "Your father had a mild heart attack last Monday." She smiled at her kids. They all stared back blankly.

"Everything's fine, they only kept him for two nights in Cork. He'll have to go back for tests and maybe a little operation. It's nothing serious but of course he'll have to change his diet." She looked over at her husband. "His cholesterol is off the chart but I won't go into that." She stopped talking and smiled at him, and he in turn grinned sheepishly at her before extending the smile to his kids, who remained blank. Steven was shifting in his seat, appearing to become slightly embarrassed.

After a moment Barry spoke. "Dad had a heart attack."

"Yes," his mother confirmed.

"And you didn't think to call any one of us?"

"No," she confirmed.

"I cannot believe—"

Barry's father put his hand up immediately, silencing

him. "I told your mother not to say anything. I didn't want a fuss. It wasn't serious—I was never at death's door. The only reason we are telling you is that I may have a genetic heart condition." He stopped talking as though he'd said enough.

His kids and their partners stared at him, waiting for the punch line. He picked up his fork and resumed eating.

Their mother took control. "It involves thickening of the valves. A good diet can be preventative but you should all get checked out. You are young men so it shouldn't be a problem but it's better to know." She sat back in her chair.

Vicky looked at her husband with concern. Steven looked at Barry with the same concern. Even the twins were silenced. Ivan looked at his plate. His mother leaned over and squeezed his hand.

"It's going to be fine," she said to the table.

Afterward the others had made their way into the sitting room. Ivan insisted on helping his mother in the kitchen. She allowed him, knowing that he hated sitting in the crowded sitting room alone to be reminded of the family that had left him. Halfway through drying up, he sat up on the counter and looked at his mother.

"Wow, a separation and a possible heart condition all in the space of a year. I must be on a roll."

She laughed. "Don't be ridiculous!" She scrubbed hardened potato from a sudsy plate.

"What do you mean?"

"You're not going to have a heart problem," she advised confidently. "You and Fintan take after me; it's Barry and Séamus that won't be able to eat a fry for the next forty years."

Ivan laughed out loud—he couldn't help it. His mother was not a doctor and yet he knew that if she said he had nothing to worry about, he had nothing to worry about.

"Thanks, Mom," he said, leaping off the counter like a teenager. He leaned over and gave her a kiss on the cheek.

"You'll get checked though?" she asked, and he nodded.

He walked to the door.

"Tell me this," she said, "who's your new lunch mate?"

He was confused.

"The American," she said.

"Oh, Sam!"

"Tell my niece her Aunt Sheila likes the cut of her new neighbor!" She winked as she said it.

Ivan grinned. "Will do."

"And tell her to come and visit and sure if she likes she can bring him along."

Ivan left the room laughing.

★ ★ ★

By five he was on the water and in the company of the American the whole town seemed to be talking about. Sam wasn't much of a fisherman but he was a quick study and Ivan enjoyed guiding him. The sea was crystal clear and the mackerel were biting too so it was shaping up to be a pleasant evening. They had been fishing for over an hour when Sam broached Ivan about his standoffish neighbor and commented on her unfavorably. Ivan had let him speak, allowing him to indulge in his distaste before mentioning that the woman he was dismissing was his own cousin and best friend.

149

"You're kidding me?" Sam said.

"I'm not," Ivan replied.

Obviously, Sam felt like an ass, but Ivan had laughed heartily, thoroughly enjoying his new friend's discomfort. It was then he had offered him two pieces of valuable information. One: a warning never to speak ill of a local unless he was absolutely sure there was no connection between the person to be spoken of and the person being spoken to. In a small town, he had pointed out, this would be difficult. And two: a reason behind why his cousin and Sam's cold neighbor was the way she was.

Ivan spoke of how he'd watched Mary beat the unbeatable, surviving a devastating crash to go on to give birth to her dead boyfriend's son whom she would shelve all her ambition to raise. Sam had briefly thought his neighbor's story had a relatively happy ending although he hadn't seen the kid, but that wasn't unusual—he'd only been in Kenmare a few days and in New York he had neighbors he wouldn't see for months. Ivan reminded him he was no longer in New York and then he told him about the place where his neighbor's little boy had died. The tale was devastating. A beautiful child broken and a mother's screams. She had held him in her arms knowing that death was instant and that no doctor could bring him back to her. Others stood around silently bearing witness to her agony while clinging to their own children, covering their small faces from horror while rooted to the spot. The doctor had attempted resuscitation but it was redundant, and all who observed the boy's dangling neck knew as much. Ivan was a storyteller with the ability to tell a tale so as to transport the listener to another time and place. Sam felt a lump in his throat but was confident that Ivan hadn't even noticed, locked instead in his own terrible memory. Ivan confided that his cousin had almost disappeared after that day. Sam sat quietly, feeling pretty guilty for judging the poor unfortunate woman.

Ivan was silent for a while and Sam didn't know what to say so he concentrated on the water. After a few minutes of silence, the pole bobbed and then he felt strain. Ivan smiled, returning to the present in time to help the American hook the smallest fish he'd seen in a long while. They both had laughed before throwing it back in. Then they talked about other subjects, sharing a flask of coffee and shooting the breeze about nothing in particular.

But Sam wanted to hear more about Mary and about what happened in the aftermath of such terrible tragedy. Ivan had been kind about Sam's query. It was obviously a painful subject but he didn't seem to mind returning to it.

"Well, we thought we'd lost her," he said, scratching out the sea salt lodged in his hair. "We thought, *There's no coming back now.*" He nodded his head, affirming it. "Her mother she could get over, sure she'd never known anything different. Robert, well, he was just a boy—'twas hard on us all but we knew she'd recover all the same. But after Ben 'twas different and no one was sure if she'd ever be right again."

"But she was," Sam found himself interjecting.

His new friend smiled. "After time, a long time, she came back to us," he said, nodding.

"But not the same?"

"No," Ivan noted a little sadly, "not the same." He put down his pole to pour some more coffee into his cup.

"How long has it been?" Sam found himself asking.

"Six years this week."

"Holy shit!" Sam breathed.

"Yeah." Ivan nodded. "It's always a bad time for her but it's over now and summer is around the corner."

Sam felt like an even bigger asshole for scrounging food from a grieving woman, but then his pole bobbed, the line tightened and so did his grip. This would not be a small fish.

Later that evening when Ivan had docked the boat outside Sam's, Sam had wandered past it and made his way to the wood and walked until he came across the plaque that bore his next-door neighbor's child's name, under which lay a sodden teddy bear and flowers which were beginning to wilt. He had no idea as to why he felt it necessary to sit by a stranger's memorial, but then recently he hadn't much reason for anything.

★ ★ ★

Ivan had gone home that night and phoned his kids. Chris was out playing soccer with some new pals but Justine was there and she seemed to be in a lighter humor than when last they spoke.

"How's school?" he began predictably.

"Jenny Thompson's dog got run over!" She seemed quiet but excited.

"Oh, I'm sorry to hear that," he said, choosing to ignore his daughter's glee.

"I'm not!" she replied adamantly.

"You're not?"

"No." She remained firm.

"Why not?"

"The first time I went to her house he bit me and anyway he only broke a leg!" She spoke quite victoriously, as though she'd been waiting for the dog to receive his comeuppance.

"Fair enough so," Ivan conceded.

"He has a cast and everything."

"Yeah."

"It's funny."

He could hear the smile in her voice.

"How's Chris?"

"He's a pain."

Ivan laughed.

"Mom wants to talk to you," she said with a sigh.

"I love you, Justy," he said quietly.

"Love you too, Dad."

He waited for her to pass the phone to her mother.

"Dad?"

"Yes, love."

"I can't wait to see you."

Before he could answer she had passed the phone.

"Ivan."

"Norma."

"Look, I was thinking that maybe you could take the kids for the Easter holiday." She began rustling papers.

"I'd love to have them," he said without having to think.

"Good."

"Doing anything nice?" he asked.

His question came as a surprise—normally they restricted their conversation to the subject of the children only. It caught her off guard.

"No, Des and I just need some time alone," she admitted.

"Oh." He regretted asking. "Well, I can't wait," he added with genuine delight.

"OK then."

"Right then," he responded before putting down the phone.

His kids were coming for an unexpected visit in less than a month. He thought about painting their rooms but then decided against it. Justy feared change almost as much as her Auntie Mary and indeed himself.

★ ★ ★

Sam made his way from the wood in time to bump into Mary, who was coming home from the pub. Sunday nights were always quiet and her father was happy enough to close on his own.

Sam was trying to open his wooden gate as she got out of her car. The damn thing seemed wedged shut and refused to budge. He shook it and shook it, cursing under his breath.

"You have to kick it," she said.

"Kick it?" he replied in slight disbelief.

"It probably swelled in the rain."

"Swelled," he repeated, but she was bored with conversation so she put her handbag on her car and gave her neighbor's gate a good boot. It swung open. She picked up her bag and walked into her own garden.

"Thanks," he said.

She responded by putting her key in the door.

"I said thanks." He wasn't used to being ignored and didn't like it.

"I heard you," she replied.

"So say 'You're welcome,'" he ordered, and the pity he had felt for her earlier had all but disappeared. Nothing excused bad manners.

"You're welcome," she said in a tone that suggested amusement before closing her door.

"Did that kill you?" he mumbled, putting the key in his own door.

Chapter Eleven

All Is Forgiven, Brinkerhoffs

A red sun rose in the dusky evening sky. Sam walked through the wood, eyes north, watching color seep. The various shades of this small town had fascinated him during his two weeks in residence. This evening he was taking another walk through the wood, a little conservation area that nestled between the golf course and the river. This place, the place with the Gaelic name he couldn't even attempt to pronounce, was filled with trees, swamp and river. It had the smallest hills to climb so as to overlook the water closeted by ancient trees. This place now full of wooden benches, a bat sanctuary, leafy trails and scampering teenage would-be lovers, this place where his impolite neighbor's child last lived, was by coincidence the place that his gran had talked of most. Before the days of conservation, wooden benches and a bat sanctuary, this was the place where she had been a girl full of romantic dreams for a bright future anywhere but in a small, depressed town in

South Kerry. This was the place where she would lie on her back and count the stars and pray that someday she would cross them to reach the place that would be her destiny. Even as a child, his gran knew she would not rest in this beautiful little town that she was so desperate to leave and yet in some small way would mourn all her days.

"Torn between two lovers!" she'd laugh. "Ireland versus America"—her smile would fade just a little—"heart versus head." There was nothing in Kenmare for his gran in the early thirties. The war had scarred the whole country and there was little opportunity, especially for a woman who didn't believe in being matched for the sake of it. Her mother had despaired of her but she was the apple of her father's eye. Her five brothers treated her like the princess they felt she was destined to be. Her mother found a man to take her but she stood firm, not willing to compromise in a time when compromise was the way of life. Maybe it was her feisty nature that turned her mother against her, but it was that same nature that ensured support from her doting father and admiration from her equally stubborn brothers. And when her mother attempted to force her daughter's hand, it was the men in her life who had constructed her escape. Her father could have put his foot down and ended the matter but he knew that, married or not, his daughter wanted more from life. She was desperate to taste the New World and he was desperate to give her all she wanted. Something inside told him his beloved girl belonged to another place so he drove her to the boat and sobbed as he handed over the money he and his sons had worked so hard for, to secure her emancipation. It was her father who had held her close while the whistle blew insistently, willing them to part. He pushed the money they had gathered into her hand.

"It's up to you now, girleen," he'd said with a voice choked and eyes brimming. "We can't help you when you're gone. America is so far away."

She wiped the tears from his eyes. "I'll always be in here, Daddy," she said, laying her hand on his chest so that he could hold it there. "You tell the boys that I won't let you all down." She was crying because she knew she might not see her dear old dad again. The American Wake, that's what they used to call the party often held before a family member moved to the States. It was a wake because the distance meant that they might not ever be seen again. Emigration was tantamount to death. Sam's grandmother didn't have an American Wake and her mother didn't ever get to say good-bye to her daughter. In hindsight her father would have possibly admitted this was a mistake, as his wife was never the same again after her only daughter had deserted. The boys hadn't made a fuss either; each one had packed a small token in her bag and kissed her good-bye on the day that she thought she was accompanying her dad on a job. She only realized she was leaving on the docks, when he'd handed her a bag filled with her clothes and her brothers' gifts of good-bye.

"I love you, Daddy."

"I love you, *mo chuisle*." And with that he turned and walked away, never looking back at the daughter he was destined never to see again.

Sam's gran would often talk to him about finding herself alone on a boat to America with the price of the ticket paid and enough money to last a week or two. She would speak of the fright of it all and that first night desperately seasick deep within the bowels of a large ship, lying on hard wood, rocking from side to side, without a soul to comfort her. But then she'd smile and tell him that she need not have concerned herself with the fear of facing the New World alone because the third day into her boat trip she met the man she would marry. Together they would get off the boat and together they would forge a new life better than the one they'd left behind.

When Sam was dragged to the premiere of *Titanic,* he had smiled at the story that seemed somewhat familiar— aside from the treacherous fiancé, the large jewel and the sinking ship. His gran loved to talk about how she had fallen for his grandfather over a game of cards and one too many whiskeys. She'd spoken of home too, lamenting its beauty and the love of those she'd left behind. She never let go even as an old woman. The small town was still her identity, despite it being as foreign to her on the day she died as America had been the day she stepped off the boat as a teenager in love.

Sam looked around at the old trees, all witness to his grandmother's youth. The grass, the sky, the water that lapped against the rocks all renewed themselves, but the trees held time and one of them a message from the grave. And now here was her grandson, a New Yorker through and through, tramping through her old sanctuary looking for that one tree in a million, the one that bore her carving. She had only mentioned her dalliance with vandalism once. She had smiled while reflecting on her life and the hopes she had always insisted had come true. She told him about the tree in the wood where she'd sit to pass away the time in her own head and how she had one day spent hours carving into it.

"I left my mark," she had said, smiling. Sam hadn't understood what this meant at the time but now, an adult in Kenmare and with time on his hands, he was determined to find the tree his gran had marked. Unfortunately, this entailed a lot more work than he had first anticipated because for a small wood there were a hell of a lot of trees. Still, he was as determined to find her there as she had been to leave.

While surveying trees he had time to contemplate his short time in Kenmare. Since the incident with the swollen gate, he had tried to keep out of his rude neighbor's way, but fate had acted against him. It seemed like every time he'd opened his front door she was there in her garden, coming in or going out, or on the pier with her dog or getting into her car. When he ventured into his back garden to hang clothes she'd make her way into her own garden with a similar intention and just a wall away. They'd attempt to ignore one another, which was uncomfortable due to proximity. He didn't enjoy awkwardness and with each encounter he'd curse coincidence, and yet he would have been lying if he said that he didn't miss her face on the rare day he didn't catch a glimpse of her. When he thought of her past he felt sorry for her, but this feeling ended each time he laid eyes on her. She just didn't seem like a victim and, besides, it was difficult to feel for someone who so obviously didn't like him. Sam was not used to this. Of course, there were a hell of a lot of people in the business who disliked, even hated him but they had good reason. This woman had disliked him on sight but that was OK. He didn't need some stranger's approval—he had enough crap to deal with. He had his recovery to focus on, so screw her. If she ignored him, he ignored her. If she sighed loudly at the sight of him, he sighed even more loudly. If she made a face, he met her face and raised her snarl. Their annoyance had become a game and it was getting old.

Besides, now he had his little project to keep his mind active. He tied a small red band around a branch of the last tree he had surveyed. This would signal where his search would next begin. It was getting late and he had promised Ivan he'd help him move furniture.

★ ★ ★

Adam's wife and children had driven out from Kenmare, leaving him to finish off packing their worldly goods before he would follow them on the long road away from his home. Ivan had attempted to keep things light and Adam endeavored to maintain a brave face. Sam had just kept his head down, conscious that he was assisting a new friend in saying good-bye to an old one. It was on their last trip and while carrying a particularly ornate and heavy mahogany desk that he and Ivan had emerged into the evening light to be confronted with Adam and Penny wrapped up in one another, kissing deeply and tears flowing. Sam was acutely embarrassed at accidentally witnessing their private moment, not to mention a little confused, having waved off the man's wife less than an hour before. He and Ivan immediately rested the desk on the ground before making their way back inside, unseen by the parting lovers. Ivan made tea, knowing that theirs would be a long good-bye.

Sam sat looking around Adam's empty home, and although he felt sorry for him and his predicament he was also a little jealous, jealous that he had never felt as strongly about anyone as the man outside, quietly desperate in his lover's arms.

Mary had turned up just in time to say good-bye to her old friend and to put an arm around a very distraught Penny. Adam put his car into gear and, with one last look back at the love of his life flanked by his two best friends, he drove away. Sam stood back, watching them all from the doorway, but it was Mary that captivated him—her tenderness and strength and the way she held her grieving friend, kissing her tenderly on the top of her head. He found himself thinking that she would have been a beautiful mother. *Damn shame she's such a bitch.* Ivan had suggested they all go and get something to eat and, despite himself, Sam hoped that Mary would agree. But Penny was too distressed so Mary took her home, with Sam watching her drive away, one hand on the steering wheel and the other stroking her sobbing friend's hanging head. She hadn't looked him in the eye once.

★ ★ ★

Penny stood under a shower while Mary surveyed the contents of her fridge. The ingredients were sparse and yet, when Penny emerged in a toweling robe, miraculously a Spanish omelette awaited her.

She attempted a smile. "I can always rely on you to cook in a crisis."

"Just eat," Mary scolded. "When's the last time you ate a decent meal anyway?"

"Now," Penny said before shoving egg into her mouth.

Mary worried about the amount of vodka in the fridge but said nothing. Penny always liked to have a stash in case of a party and she often threw parties, mostly after the pub. Mary guessed she wouldn't be throwing one of those for a while, so with that in mind she made a mental note to throw some of the vodka down the sink as soon as Penny's back was turned. *Just in case. She probably won't even notice.*

Penny was silent.

"What can I do?" Mary asked.

"Nothing."

"What are you thinking?"

Penny sighed loudly.

"Honestly?" Mary urged.

"I thought he'd pick me," she admitted. "I know he has kids, but when it came down to it, I really thought he'd pick me!" Tears rolled down her face and her nose began to run, forcing her to sniff.

"I'm so sorry, Penn."

"I know I'm selfish," Penny said, wiping her nose with her hand.

"You're human."

"I wanted Adam to abandon his children."

They sat in silence, Penny's distaste for herself hanging in the air.

"Penn, I don't give a frig about any of that. I think you're it."

Penny looked at Mary. "You think I'm it?" she said with an emerging smile.

Mary nodded. "I do."

"What? Are you sixteen?"

"No. I just look sixteen," Mary grinned.

After that Penny said that she felt better. Mary insisted on washing up and mopping the floor, having decided that Penny was too traumatized to engage in such menial tasks. Penny attempted to argue but Mary was in her in-charge mode so she sat with her coffee while Mary cleaned.

"So what's the story on the American?" Penny asked while stirring her coffee.

"He's everywhere," Mary sighed. "Every time I turn around there he is with a stupid face on him. The other week he actually pulled me up on my manners."

"He did not!" said Penny, amused.

"He did. And I wouldn't mind, I'd helped him with his stupid gate. I never thought I'd say this but I miss the Brinkerhoffs. At least they knew how to keep to themselves."

"The Brinkerhoffs were wanted by Interpol," Penny said with a slight smile and annoyingly still stirring her coffee.

"And now he's Ivan's new best friend. Three lunches last week, two nights in the pub and clay pigeon shooting last Sunday." She shook her head. "It's unbelievable."

"Ivan's lonely," Penny commented quietly.

"So he should get himself a girlfriend," Mary said.

Penny scoffed. "Yeah, right, because that's so easy. And what's your big problem with the American anyway? He seems nice enough. He helped out today."

"That's exactly what I'm talking about, Penn. Four life-time friends saying an emotional good-bye to one another and there he is. Mr. In-Town-a-Wet-Day-Tourist stuck in the middle of it."

Penny smiled. "This is not you. What's going on with you?"

"I don't know," Mary answered honestly. "There's just something about him. I can't put my finger on but I don't like it."

"Oh, are you being the all-seeing psychic again?" Penny laughed, having never really bought into her friend's abilities. "He's not featuring in any dreams, is he?"

"No." Mary smiled. "I don't know what it is, but sometimes when I look into his eyes I want to cry."

"Weird," Penny said, banging the spoon off the side of the mug.

"I mean, what do we know about him anyway? He could be a psycho killer."

"Psycho killers don't usually look like movie stars," Penny said, having returned to stirring her coffee.

"I don't know—Ted Bundy wasn't bad."

Penny grinned to herself. "He was the one with the gold VW Beetle?"

Mary nodded.

"Yeah, OK, he was all right. Not worth dying for all the same."

"My point exactly," Mary agreed, before taking Penny's spoon out of her coffee and throwing it into the sink. "It's stirred."

Penny was glad that her friend had stayed, and idle chat had helped lighten her mood for a while at least, but by the time Mary left Penny was happy to see her go. She waved her off and closed the door.

She went to the fridge and pulled out a bottle of vodka. She thought about it for a moment before putting it back.

She had promised herself she would take it easy, so instead she reached for a bottle of white wine. She spent a minute or two looking for the bottle opener, which stubbornly refused to be found. *Fuck it,* she thought. She opened the fridge and grabbed the bottle of vodka. *Fate has spoken.*

Once seated, she poured a tall glass, took her first sip and sighed before switching on the TV. *I could have sworn this bottle was more than half full.*

★ ★ ★

Mary parked the car outside her house, content that she had left Penny in lighter spirits than she had found her. The blue sky was fading to light purple and the water was still and reflecting the two upturned half-moons of the imposing bridge under which the River Roughty joined with the Sheen. Once inside, she made her way to the backyard, to alert Mr. Monkels to her homecoming. Usually he would sense her from halfway down the road or else he'd hear the car engine—either way he'd be sitting at the glass patio door panting hello. He wasn't at the door. Instead, he was lying flat out on the ground in front of the shed and half concealed by an untamed bush.

"Mr. Monkels!" she called out. "Mr. Monkels?"

She picked up her pace and her heart started to beat in time with her feet. She bent down to him and it was clear that he was breathing but he wouldn't budge. She stroked him and he whined a little.

"OK, buddy," she said calmly, "everything's going to be OK." She tried to lift him but he groaned and she knew he was too heavy to carry without fear of her dropping him. She could hear that the American was in because the sound of gospel queen Mavis Staples was leaking from his kitchen. *What is it with that man and gospel?* She wasn't going to ask him for help so instead she ran to number 3 and hoped against hope that Mossy was there. He opened the door with hands caked in clay and a joint hanging from his lips.

"Mary of the Sorrows, always a sight for sore eyes," he said, wiping his hands with a tea towel. He seemed completely unaware that he had referred to her by her nickname.

"I need your help," she said, despite the fact that, judging by the size of his pupils and him dropping the tea towel twice between his door and the center of his sitting room, she was in no doubt that he was pretty stoned.

He stood over a table which housed a piece he was working on.

"What do you think?" he asked.

It looks like a brown banana—that or a piece of . . . "Lovely," she said. "There's something wrong with Mr. Monkels. Can you help me get him into the car?"

"Oh, sorry, Mare, I can't," he said, shaking his head.

"What?" she replied, not sure she'd heard him correctly.

"I'm out of my mind," he giggled. "Seriously, I've got this new stuff and it's off the wall but really getting the inspiration juices flowing."

She took a second look at the piece of crap on the table. "Yeah." She nodded. "Thanks anyway."

"Ask the American," Mossy advised her. "He seems like a very accommodating fella."

She was stuck. Mrs. Foley in number 5 had difficulty

carrying a cup of tea, never mind a large dog, and she couldn't waste any more time. So she knocked on her new neighbor's door.

He opened it moments later and just in time to hear her exhale.

"Can I help you?" he asked, appearing nonchalant.

"I'd really appreciate if you could," she responded, careful to mind her manners. *I don't have time for a hissy fit.*

"What is it?" he asked, delighting in this unexpected power.

"My dog. He's not well. I need help lifting him to the car."

"Oh," he said without a hint of his previous smugness, "sure." He felt a little bit like an asshole.

He followed her to her back garden and to where her dog lay panting. He seemed bigger when lying out flat—in fact, he seemed a lot bigger and heavier. Sam's back already ached from carrying heavy furniture earlier that day but he could see the genuine concern on his neighbor's face.

"OK, how do you want to do this?"

"Mr. Monkels, we're going to lift you now," she said to the dog before nodding to Sam. "You take the end," she instructed.

Sam squatted down. Mary placed her hands under the dog's upper body and Sam did likewise under his hindquarters.

"OK on three," she said. "One—two—*three!*" They both proceeded to lift.

It was at this moment that something in Sam's back clicked out of place. He froze. "Holy shit!" he uttered, and

Mary was immediately alarmed because the look on his face suggested something terrible. "What?"

"My back! My back!"

"What's wrong with it?" she cried, and still they were holding the dog between them. "Oh my God!" she said, noticing the guy's face becoming ashen. "OK, put Mr. Monkels down," she ordered as calmly as possible.

"I can't."

"What?"

"I can't move. I think it's locked!" He was becoming more alarmed.

"Knickers!" she said quietly before composing herself. "OK, I know what to do. Don't move. Just stay calm. I am going to lower the dog onto the ground headfirst. Do not move."

"You don't have to keep saying don't move. I *can't* move."

"Don't get snippy," she warned.

"Snippy?" he inquired a little shrilly as she lowered the dog so that his head lay on the ground while his hindquarters remained raised and in Sam's custody. "Holy shit, the pain!"

Mary stood beside Sam and leaned in, placing her hands beside his under the dog.

"Let go!" she ordered.

He did and she lowered the dog until he was once again lying on the ground. She stood up while he remained bent forward.

"I'm going to die," he mumbled, and with those words and in a manner not too distant from that of Lazarus, Mr. Monkels rose to his feet and shook himself off before pottering into the sitting room, jumping onto the window seat and making himself comfortable as though he had not a care in the world, and all the while Mavis Staples sang "Oh Happy Day."

"Am I fucking dreaming?" Sam asked earnestly while bent over and facing the ground.

Chapter Twelve

Back to Back

Mary managed to negotiate her injured neighbor into her house before putting in a call to her doctor. Unfortunately for both of them, Sam was unable to do anything other than lean over her kitchen table.

"I'll make you some tea," she said, screwing up her face in sympathy with Sam's obvious pain and stalling for time, wondering how long it would take for the doctor to arrive.

"No. I'm good," he said with a hint of sarcasm.

She couldn't really hold it against him—the man had just sustained his second injury at her hands.

"OK. Can I get you anything at all?" She knew she sounded stupid.

"No. I'll just wait for the doctor," he said through gritted teeth.

"OK." She nodded. "Good idea." She wasn't sure what to do next. "Would you like to be alone?" She was embarrassed by the manner in which she was handling the whole incident.

"That would be great," he suggested with yet again a hint of sarcasm.

I thought Americans didn't do sarcasm. "OK." She left the kitchen, closing the door behind her.

Sam released his exasperation by sighing heavily, but regretted it because the breath traveling through his body increased his pain tenfold.

Dr. Macken arrived within half an hour.

"Hello, my dear," he said in his usual happy-go-lucky manner despite the alarm Mary had injected into her voice over the phone. "You look well," he added, fixing his comb-over.

"He's in here," she said, in no mood for pleasantries.

He followed her into the kitchen, to where Sam remained in the unfortunate position in which she'd left him.

"Oh dear," Dr. Macken said. However, the sentiment was lost under his chuckle. "That does not look good."

Sam did not respond but Mary could see he wasn't happy.

Dr. Macken put his bag on the table beside Sam. "A cup of tea would be lovely, Mary," he said before rubbing his hands together.

Sam's face fell and Mary heard him mumble, "You're kidding me."

Suddenly, she wanted to laugh, but she suppressed the urge. She turned her back on the disgruntled patient and her GP.

"Now this may hurt but bear with me," Dr. Macken instructed.

Mary gulped while filling the kettle.

Sam braced himself. "Holy shit!" he cried out.

"Hmmm," Dr. Macken mumbled.

"Ho-ho-ho-lee shsh-it!" Sam called out again.

Mary switched on the kettle and bit her knuckle in the absence of something productive to do.

"Ever slipped a disc before?" Dr. Macken asked.

"No," Sam said, perturbed by the question.

"Well, son, it looks like you could have slipped a disc." He went to his bag. "Now if you're lucky it could just be a serious muscle spasm."

The kettle whistled to suggest the water was boiled.

"Milk, no sugar, Mary," said Dr. Macken. "Now I'm going to give you something to relax the muscles and then I'm going to prescribe painkillers."

He walked into the sitting room and Mary followed him with his tea.

"We're going to need a fairly hard mattress. You'll have to move the sofa but he'll be fine here for a few days," he said, taking his tea from Mary.

"Excuse me?" she asked, alarmed.

"What?" Sam shouted from the kitchen before crying out a little.

"Well, you'll hardly send him in next door," the doctor observed.

"Why not? That's where he lives," she whispered urgently.

"I'm not staying here!" Sam shouted.

"He can't be left on his own, Mary girl, and besides, you have a downstairs bathroom."

Mary silently cursed her extension.

"I am not staying here!" Sam shouted again, despite the pain shouting caused in his lower back.

"Do you have a suitable mattress?" Dr. Macken asked, ignoring all objections.

Mary sighed and rolled her eyes, much like she did every time he pretended to knock on her head before making some annoying comment alluding to her having a metal plate.

★ ★ ★

Sam was being assisted into the sitting room by Dr. Macken while Mary wrestled the mattress from the spare room down the stairs.

Dr. Macken looked at her. "Oh, that will do nicely!"

Sam was a whiter shade of pale. Dr. Macken resumed a conversation with his patient that Mary had not been a party to. "You either take the muscle relaxant or you end up in this particularly amusing stance the rest of your days."

"Not until you tell me what's in it."

"Is there something in your medical history you would like to share with me?" Dr. Macken asked.

"No," Sam replied.

"And you're not allergic to anything?"

"No," Sam confirmed.

"Then take the pill."

The doctor held the glass of water in front of his face and he swallowed the tablet and drank until the glass was empty.

"Good," Dr. Macken said.

He helped Mary move the sofa, and when the mattress was dressed he reintroduced Sam to the art of lying down, ably assisted by his unwilling aide, Mary, who was charged with providing cushions to prop up the patient's knees.

"As he loosens up slowly, take away the cushions," the doctor ordered Mary.

She responded with a heavy sigh. Sam covered his face with his hands and inhaled deeply.

"Well, I can see this little sleepover is going to go beautifully," Dr. Macken laughed while patting his comb-over before pretending to knock on Mary's head. "Hah, Robocop, I'd say it's a match made in heaven!"

Mary rolled her eyes. Dr. Macken ignored her and turned to Sam.

"It's a wonder she can't pick up a few more channels on that thing," he said, pointing to her head while she pursed her lips so as to prevent herself telling her doctor to ef off. Sam chuckled a little. Dr. Macken softened. "Still, it's a wonder she's with us at all!" He smiled at one of his most miraculous and tough patients before becoming serious. "Any headaches since I last saw you?"

"No," Mary responded, embarrassed by his questions in front of a stranger.

"You're due a scan," he reminded her.

"I know."

"I'll make the appointment," he said, picking up his bag.

"OK." She walked toward the door. Thankfully he followed her.

"I'm giving you a prescription for painkillers."

Sam called from the floor. "What's in them?"

Dr. Macken laughed. "Don't worry, just a little opioid—they won't kill you."

He probably thinks I'm being one of those health freaks he reads about, thought Sam, *the kind of guy who dates in oxygen bars and whose idea for a great weekend involves a colonic.*

Of course, he couldn't be more wrong. Sam knew that he couldn't touch an opioid, not if he didn't want to end up an addict again and right back where he started. This meant that he was going to be in pain without the possibility of relief. *I'm on the fucking precipice.*

★ ★ ★

On the morning following Adam's exit from Kenmare something clicked in Penny and she emerged from her booze-laced cocoon. She had been drinking for three weeks straight and, like a reluctant genie, it took courage to emerge from the bottle. She had hidden away and licked her wounds and her friends had given her the space to do so, knowing that Penny liked to do things her way. But they were unaware as to what exactly her way entailed.

She had spent the greater part of her day cleaning herself and then her house until she felt that there was no visible trace of her transgression. Her clean start was tiring work but it kept her mind off the fact that Adam was gone. She'd avoided Mary's five calls, needing time and space. Later she packed her car boot with empty bottles and drove to the recycling center. It was late evening so she hadn't anticipated meeting anyone. Unfortunately, she was halfway through unloading when she spotted one of her lover's wife's more vocal friends, Bridget Browne.

"That must have been some party," the ally of her nemesis sneered.

"You've no idea," Penny said, her face threatening to break under the strain of her fake smile.

"You have a thick neck!" her opponent spat out as she passed so close they almost touched.

Penny turned quickly to face her but Bridget walked on. "Excuse me?" She didn't need to take this crap from a woman who was once one of the town's biggest sluts.

Bridget turned back to look Penny up and down with contempt. "You heard, you callous bitch!"

"Hey, Bridget, guess what?" Penny asked cheerfully.

"What?" she responded through gritted teeth.

"Your husband recently fathered a child in Sneem." She watched Bridget's face fall. "Is that callous enough for you?" she asked in a tone laced with arsenic.

Bridget was momentarily stunned, shock robbing her of any expression. Penny immediately realized the depths to which she had unnecessarily sunk. She might have even apologized but the moment passed and Bridget's initial numbness was subsiding in favor of a mounting anger.

"What did you say?" she screamed, outraged.

A little panicked, Penny shut her boot, still half full of bottles, and walked around to the driver's seat.

"What did you say, you bitch?" Bridget was now thundering.

Penny opened the car door quickly, knowing that her enemy was on her way to give her a possibly well-deserved punch in the face.

She locked the doors just in time and backed out of the

recycling center with a screaming and red-faced Bridget pounding the roof of her car.

Once she'd made her getaway she broke into laughter born from a mild hysteria and tears quickly followed. *Oh God, what did I just do?* Revealing a husband's secret love child was brutally petty and maybe even a little despicable. An internal debate followed in which she reasoned that, although she had done something terrible, Bridget was a horrible human being who had often reveled in the misery of others. She silently accused Bridget of being the kind of person who liked to lord it over others and one only too happy to judge all and sundry. She still felt a little sick so she reasoned that Bridget and her husband had been known as the town sluts for years. It was bound to come out sooner or later. By the time she'd driven halfway home, she'd decided that Bridget deserved it.

The truth was, she didn't deserve it, and if Penny hadn't been bitter, brokenhearted and hungover she would never have so willingly and viciously torn apart any person, even one of Bridget Browne's disposition. She dried her eyes and decided to forget her vitriolic verbal assault by buying a bottle of her favorite red wine—after all, she may have been off the hard stuff but wine never hurt anybody.

★ ★ ★

Penny had decided to throw herself back into work and by coincidence the next morning the Cork correspondent was forced to take a sudden leave of absence. She had a fluff piece about an obese cow in North Kerry and was covering the opening of a restaurant in Dingle, but despite time constraints and impending deadlines she readily agreed to cover his story. She briefly worried that the decision to help out a colleague was based on Cork being Adam's new home. But then she concluded that it most certainly was not. She reminded herself that Adam had made his decision. Furthermore, he hadn't even told her where he would be working, nor had he whispered his address, but then she didn't want to know. That ship had sailed and she was moving on, except of course that she wasn't moving on—instead she was drowning in its wake. The emptiness made her insides ache, but she wasn't about to ask Mary or Ivan for information on Adam's exact coordinates because then they would know that in her heart she was desperate to see him, despite the fact that she had almost convinced herself that she definitely wasn't. She was not going to appear like a lovesick moron for anyone. She'd let herself down enough over the years, never mind turning into a part-time stalker. If he'd wanted to see her he would have called and he hadn't, not that she was waiting for him to call. In fact, she probably wouldn't have taken the call, so determined was she to start afresh.

However, upon arriving in Cork City she did find that she had a desire to walk around and explore it more than she had in previous years. She might have even walked around the city center for a few hours paying particular attention to the restaurants, peering at the menus stuck to the windows and accidentally catching glimpses of front-of-house staff members, none of whom were Adam. Then again she'd always been a fan of restaurants and Cork was full of very reputable eateries. Late afternoon and after a long walk, she arrived at her destination. The piece she had been asked to write was a story about a young Cork woman, Lacey Doyle, who'd traveled to an exotic location only to become a bomb victim, returning home minus two legs. Despite her horrific loss she'd been deemed lucky, as her best friend standing less than ten feet away could only be identified by DNA. Notwithstanding the sad demise of a young girl in a faraway country, the crux of Penny's story lay in the revelatory if not magical new limbs that her friend's supporters had paid for. It was all very complicated and Penny wasn't sure how these artificial limbs were different from any others, but Lacey was only too happy to demonstrate. The limbs were state of the art in a weird kind of futuristic way. There was no attempt by the manufacturers to create the illusion of real legs. The girl's skin met metal and at the end of metal was a shoe but she didn't seem to care, which was a little weird since soon it would be summer. She spoke a lot about their flexibility and was happy to demonstrate. Every time she exposed her stumps Penny felt a little sick.

"It's horrible, isn't it?" Lacey asked happily.

"No," Penny lied, "it's fine," and she attempted to smile.

"My legs were ripped off—it's OK to feel a little repulsed." Lacey laughed at a pale Penny.

"OK," Penny conceded, "I do feel a little sick."

Lacey smiled. "I couldn't look down for six months," she admitted.

"What changed?" Penny asked.

"I got bored looking up." Lacey laughed and Penny joined in.

"I don't know how you get over something like that," said Penny. In truth, she was a lot more interested in the woman who'd lost her legs than the revolutionary limbs.

"You don't," Lacey said, "you just get on with things. You either do that or you rot. And of course there was George."

"George?" Penny asked, intrigued.

"My boyfriend. Well, actually, he's my fiancé—we got engaged last month."

Penny's mouth almost fell open.

"You're surprised anyone would marry me?" Lacey said astutely.

"No," Penny lied, horrified that her disbelief was apparent.

"I was surprised too," Lacey confirmed. "It took me a year to let him touch me, never mind anything else."

Penny wasn't sure she wanted to hear any more—the idea of stumpy sex was a little much.

"Sex was a nightmare at first," Lacey said, "but it got better." She nodded. "And now it's good."

Penny was glad she was sitting down as her own legs were feeling a little shaky.

"You're sickened again, aren't you?" Lacey asked.

Penny nodded. "Yes, but it's not what you think."

"What then?" Lacey asked.

"I look at you and I'm jealous."

"You're jealous?" Lacey queried suspiciously.

"Pathetic, isn't it?" Penny asked.

"A little bit. Can I ask why?"

"You're not alone," she said, and a tear escaped. She

couldn't believe she was crying in front of a girl who'd lost both her legs but she was and the legless girl comforted her.

★ ★ ★

Having burst into tears in front of an interviewee, it occurred to Penny that she might be having a breakdown. She couldn't face driving home so she booked into a hotel and headed for the bar, where she sat directly in front of the barman and ordered a vodka on the rocks.

"Tough day?" he asked.

"I met a bomb victim without legs who is happier than me," she said silently, raising her glass before drinking deeply.

"Jaysus, your life must really suck then," he said, grinning.

"What part of Dublin are you from?" she asked robotically.

"What part do you want me to be from?" he retorted, winking.

"A part that answers direct questions with direct answers," she responded before draining her glass.

He laughed. "Crumlin."

She nodded.

"You want another?"

She nodded.

"What about you? Where are you from?" He handed her another vodka.

"Nowhere," she said.

"You're homeless then?"

"Home is where the heart is," she responded with a bitter laugh.

"And where's your heart?"

"Lost." She raised her hands in the air before drinking her vodka down in one.

"Women! Does the drama ever end?" he sighed, shaking his head from side to side.

"You tell me," she said with a hint of a grin.

The bar was quiet so he had little to do but flirt with her so she stayed there drinking vodka after vodka talking with the barman from Dublin. When he got off his shift she led him up to her room.

"I'm married," he said.

"So was my boyfriend," she noted before she closed the door behind them.

★ ★ ★

The next morning she awoke alone and with bruises on her arms and thighs from rough sex. The room was a state as a result of Penny and a stranger taking out their frustration on one another. She had a bruise on her hip from where he'd slammed her against the dresser and her leg was scraped although she couldn't remember why. He would have been marked too and she wondered how he'd explain it to his poor wife or if he'd even bother. Her neck was sore from when he held her against the wardrobe until she felt she couldn't breathe, then again she'd kicked him onto the ground and when she was on top she bit him hard. Her nipples were raw and when she went to the loo she bled a little and felt a little sick inside. After a cleansing shower she decided not to drink alone anymore. It would be best to only drink in the presence of friends, that way she wouldn't find herself overindulging until she was sick or prostituting herself. *Jesus, what was last night about?* It was a good plan. She had made a mistake but she was OK and wouldn't put herself in that position again. *Easy. No problem.*

Chapter Thirteen

Knowing Me, Knowing You

Ivan was late but only by half an hour. Sam hadn't noticed, having disappeared into his own thoughts, ably accompanied by Roberta Flack's melodic melancholy. Ivan's knock broke the spell, returning him to earth and to Mary's floor.

Mary came out of her kitchen with a tea towel in hand to answer the door.

Ivan looked at his new friend lying on a mattress on the floor.

"Well?" he asked.

"Agony," Sam said simply.

Ivan shook his head. "Four days later. I'm telling you the Bone Man will sort it in five minutes."

Sam sighed. "So you keep saying."

"Well, if a thing is worth repeating it's worth repeating," Ivan said, chuckling softly to himself while getting comfortable on the sofa before looking down upon his friend.

"What do you think, Mary?" Sam asked, having established a kind of rapport with his host over the previous ninety-six hours.

"I don't know," she said. Ivan gave her a dirty look. "I don't know," she repeated to her cousin with hands in the air.

"What about Tommy the Coat?" he asked.

"What about Tommy the Coat?" she replied.

"He was on his back for four months. One trip to the Bone Man and he was up and dancing a jig three days later."

She shrugged her shoulders. "I don't know. The doctor said it could be a disc and a disc isn't bone."

Sam nodded to agree with his neighbor.

Ivan raised his hands in exasperation. "Bone Man is just his name. He deals in back problems—all back problems!"

"I'll think about it," said Sam.

Mary went back into the kitchen to finish dinner while Ivan nipped to the loo, leaving Sam alone.

The front door must have been on the latch because it opened on Penny's push. She closed the door behind her and it seemed like she had walked past Sam without noticing him—that is, until she called out to Mary.

"Mare, there appears to be an American on your floor!" She looked down and winked at Sam as Mary came into the room.

"Where have you been?" Mary asked, ignoring the matter of her new lodger.

"Cork," Penny said.

"Cork?" Mary repeated in alarm.

"No, not with Adam. I was working."

Ivan emerged from the toilet. "Hey, Penn, where've you been?"

"Cork." She smiled.

"Cork!" he said in alarm.

"I was working!"

"OK." He nodded. "Good."

"Are you hungry?" Mary asked.

"Starving," Penny said, realizing that it had been a while since she'd eaten an actual meal.

After that Mary returned to the kitchen and Ivan and Penny sat on the sofa with Sam at their feet. Ivan appraised Penny on the details of Sam's accident. Penny suggested he see the Bone Man.

"Hah! I told you!" Ivan said, vindicated.

"Who's this?" Penny asked, referring to the music.

"Roberta Flack."

"Nice." Ivan nodded.

"You had your music brought in from next door?" said Penny.

"Sure. I'm going through a phase."

"Wow!" Penny laughed. "Mary won't like that."

"What do you mean?" he asked.

"Well, she's really funny about music," Penny said, and Ivan nodded.

"I don't understand," said Sam.

"She has a band or a sound or a song for every mood, emotion or event in her life. You could say that she lives her life to a soundtrack and now you are here and messing that soundtrack up." She was laughing.

"You're kidding me?"

Penny and Ivan both shook their heads.

"Unusual," he mumbled to himself.

They all ate dinner in the sitting room so as not to leave the patient alone. Mary cut up his food. She helped him onto his side and positioned cushions to support him as he ate the meal. She placed a straw in his drink and pushed it toward him. Once he was sorted, she sat down in the armchair opposite her friends, who were staring from the sofa. Both Ivan and Penny noted the significant shift in Sam and Mary's relationship with some interest. Of necessity he relied on her, but more important he appeared comfortable in her care and she tended to him deftly, knowing exactly what to do.

"What?" she asked of her friends, who were both slightly agape.

"Nothing," they said together.

"Do you want to change the music?" Sam asked out of nowhere.

"No, it's fine," Mary said, unsure as to why he was asking, since he had completely taken over her CD player and had been listening to nothing but American black women since he'd arrived.

"Are you sure?" he asked.

"I like it," she replied.

"OK."

Penny and Ivan laughed.

"We mentioned your analnality regarding music," Penny admitted.

"*Analnality* isn't a word," said Mary.

"Well, it should be," said Ivan.

"I'm not anal," she argued.

"Hah!" Ivan said, snorting.

188

Penny laughed and pointed to her. "When Mary listens to Radiohead?"

Ivan answered, "She's sad."

"When Mary listens to Dolly?"

Ivan answered, "Happy."

"And when Mary listens to Nirvana?"

Ivan answered, "Frustrated." He winked and Penny stuck out her tongue at a mortified Mary.

"Wow!" Sam said. "The wall between us is pretty thin and she listens to Nirvana a lot."

Ivan and Penny both laughed and Mary bit her lip in silent outrage.

Penny and Ivan left together. As Ivan put on his coat, Mary asked him about his ex-wife. He told her that she seemed fine. Mary nodded but she seemed unsatisfied by his answer. She smiled at him to hide her concern but he knew her expressions better than anyone.

"Is there something wrong?" he asked.

"No," she lied.

He crossed his arms and waited for the truth.

"I mean I don't know," she admitted, screwing up her face.

"What did you see?" he asked, a little alarmed.

"Oh, for God's sake!" Penny mumbled, frustrated by their insistence in believing in the unbelievable.

"It's nothing," Mary said, embarrassed by Penny's indifference to and Sam's ignorance on the subject of her dubious psychic abilities.

"Mary!" Ivan said. He had always believed in her ability and deep down he was worried that something was not right with his ex-wife.

"OK," she sighed. "I saw her calling for you." She had mumbled so as to encourage him to lower his voice. It didn't work.

"Calling for me?" he questioned, a little confused.

"That's it," she mumbled, "she was calling out for you."

"How?"

"What?" She was wishing the conversation would end.

"Oh, for God's sake!" Penny repeated. "Was she calling out in a Heathcliff-it's-me-Cathy kind of way or in a kids-come-in-for-your-dinner way?"

"Oh," Mary nodded, "neither. I don't know."

"Was it real?" he asked.

"I don't know," she admitted.

Penny snorted. "I wish you'd stop wrecking your head with all of this stuff," she said to Mary.

Sam lay on the ground wondering what the hell was going on.

Penny pushed Ivan out the door.

"I'll give her a call tomorrow," he said before adding with a grin, "Tonight I'm on a date."

Penny and Mary stopped in their tracks.

"A date?" Mary quizzed, her raised voice betraying astonishment.

"Ah yeah," Sam remembered aloud, "good luck with that, man."

Mary looked from Ivan to her uninvited guest with raised eyebrows to match her voice.

Ivan laughed. "Sam will fill you in." He winked and closed the door behind himself and Penny.

Mary looked at Sam, wondering what in the name of knickers was going on.

Sam, a practical stranger, filled Mary in on her close
family member's exploits in McCarthy's bar the previous
week. They had been having a few pints and a girl whose
name Sam didn't have the good grace to remember had
sidled up to them. She had sat beside Sam and asked him
to a party. He explained to Mary that he had declined the
invite, unnecessarily adding that he didn't have any interest
in parties.

At this point Mary interrupted to clarify that the
woman Ivan was dating had originally asked Sam out. He
considered this for a moment before conceding with a
nod. Mary screwed up her face to suggest certain distaste at
her cousin opting for sloppy seconds. Sam laughed as her
distaste showed. He explained that when it was his turn
to go to the bar, her cousin and the girl whose name he
couldn't remember had struck up a conversation and had
got along so well that by the time he returned with drinks
they'd forgotten that he was even in the room. She viewed
him skeptically and he assured her it was true. She wondered how it was possible that a week had passed without
her cousin confiding in her, and in her mind she acknowledged that his omission was made all the more grievous by
her uninvited guest's obvious delight in knowing something about her cousin that she didn't.

But of course Sam was delighted. The look of horror
on her face was comical.

After that she was quiet. She cleaned the kitchen while
he flicked channels, bored by TV but too tired to read.

During Sam's short sojourn he had noticed that Mary
followed a series of routines. For instance, in the evening
she cooked she ate she washed she dried she brushed the

floor she emptied the bin before making tea, and while the kettle boiled she covered the leftover food in cellophane and put it in the fridge. It was always in that order and in truth it was a pretty innocuous thing to notice, but noticing the innocuous was one of the things that had once made Sam great at his job. She wasn't a clean freak but she liked everything to have its place, possibly to a pathological degree. If he put his book down for over five minutes, it mysteriously appeared in the magazine rack which considerately she'd left close enough for him to reach. The second he dropped the remote, it found its way onto the left-hand side of the coffee table on the TV guide, which was placed so that the edge of the guide met the edge of the coffee table. *Weird.* Her CD collection, which was vast and too far away in the corner of the room for him to actually see, appeared to be alphabetized, and a CD was only out of its case when playing. Her friends were right—behind her calm exterior she was anal—but it wasn't overt and it appeared possible that she didn't even realize it. She was also painfully honest in both word and deed. When he smelled she told him. When she promised that she'd close her eyes while helping him to wash, she didn't open them once even when she somehow managed to swallow suds. He had guessed that she'd given up any attempt at lying years before as her expressive face would have given her away every time. In that way she was nothing like him.

Every night before she went to bed she fixed one of the photos on the wall. It was the one closest to the door of her son and the damn dog. She didn't ever straighten any other photo, just that one, and it was always the last thing she did before turning out the light and leaving him with just the glow of the television as per his request.

She had noticed a lot about him too. He didn't like questions, but then again neither did she, so that was OK. Still, he could sidestep an uncomfortable or uninvited query as well as or better than a seasoned politician, while she was forced to resort to rudeness. This fact irked her. He liked American soul, R & B and gospel singers, but then again she knew that already. When he laughed, she noticed, his nose crinkled and his jaw stuck out, which he unconsciously covered with his fist as though he was concealing a cough, and in that moment the darkness lifted from his eyes, if only briefly.

He could play the guitar too. On the first day Sam lay on her floor Jerry Letter arrived with a package, which turned out to be a very valuable guitar which he'd had shipped from the U.S. She had helped him to sit up if only for a few minutes so that he could hold it and examine it for damage. When he told her it had been Scotty Moore's she was impressed and he was in turn impressed that she knew who Scotty Moore was. This pissed her off and she wasn't happy until he apologized for presuming her ignorant. He had proved himself stubborn as he only got around to asking for help when he was desperate for the loo and unable to travel the distance unaided. He laid the guitar on his chest and strummed and, although he messed up a lot and cursed under his breath, she enjoyed listening to him, and as he was loosening up he improved each time he picked it up. She noticed he was what her father would describe as eagle-eyed. It was annoying when he pointed out her foibles, which she had no idea were so many, but it was also interesting if not a little disturbing having a mirror put up to her face. She liked that his body felt relaxed in her care. She liked that he didn't pander to her past. If he thought badly of her he said it, while most people tiptoed around her afraid of breaking the shell she'd coated herself in.

"Why do you work in a bar?" he'd asked out of the blue that very morning.

"Because I do," she answered, yawning and stroking her morning mug of coffee.

"You're better than that," he said, as though he was interviewing her for a job as opposed to taking up half her floor.

"Excuse me?" she'd said, annoyed at his arrogance.

"It probably made sense once. But not anymore." He looked at the wall that housed the pictures of her son before returning to meet her widened eyes. "Those photos you took are truly beautiful. Trust me—I have an eye."

"You'll have a black eye if you don't shut up," she said, getting up and striding to the kitchen.

"I was only saying!" he called out.

"Yeah, well, nobody asked you," she said before slamming the kitchen door behind her.

Of course, once seated behind her kitchen table she started to think about what he had said. She had tried not to, even singing "Ring of Fire" in her head to escape his unsolicited reasoning, but she couldn't because he was right— why after six years was she tending bar when she had once and long ago been so full of ambition? Ben had stopped her from becoming the photographer she had always dreamed of becoming but what was stopping her now?

Despite his demeanor and possibly because of it, it was nice for Mary to have someone to take care of.

And it was nice for Sam, the guy who had painted himself invulnerable to the whole world for so long while silently destroying himself—yeah, it was nice for him to be taken care of. Like Danziger, Mary was stronger than he was, and it felt weird being there but strangely it also felt a little good, even if he thought about the pain pills he hoarded under his mattress a little too much and even if the stupid dog and cause of his predicament attempted to sit on him at least twice a day.

★ ★ ★

That night Ivan shared his first official date with Sienna. They had agreed to meet for dinner at Packie's because that was Ivan's favorite restaurant and, being a creature of habit, when he ate out his order never deviated: a herb potato pancake followed by a medium to rare steak with the softest sweetest carrots in the world accompanied by creamy colcannon with caramelized onions on the side. He wasn't a dessert man so that was never a factor in his choosing. The other places, as good as they were, could not offer him the same menu—not exactly anyway—so when he'd asked her to Packie's he hoped to God she liked it.

When Sienna said she was happy to allow him to pick the wine, he panicked a little as he was not a wine connoisseur and to order the house wine would seem cheap. So he deferred the choice to his helpful seventeen-year-old waitress.

They sat together in warm low lighting, surrounded by

well-dressed people speaking lowly and intimately. They ate slowly and drank at their leisure, concentrating their energy on conversation of which neither was short.

Sienna had been living in Kenmare for six months. She was working on Reception in the Sheen Falls Hotel, having worked in a number of five-star hotels before it. She was used to the trappings of wealth yet it was apparent that in her free time she had little time for the frivolity of luxury. Sienna had flaming red hair much like his cousin Mary's; she had brown soulful eyes and a heart-shaped face. When they stood he had to look down. She was five six to his six four and a hippie at heart. Beads were threaded into her hair and she sat comfortably in a dress that flowed from as opposed to clung to her body. On her right hand she wore two rings, on her left she wore three, one being a tiny claddagh ring on her baby finger. They were all silver—she admitted she had little time for gold. She was two years younger than him and had never been married. Her one serious relationship had lasted four years. He had left her on August 6, 1999—it was her birthday and she had not heard from or seen him since. She liked animals but didn't own one. She came to Kenmare because her flatmate in Adare was annoying. She knew of Ivan's past, and although she sympathized she didn't make a fuss or make him feel like the asshole whose wife had left him. She liked it when he talked with passion about fish. Her own father was a fisherman in Galway Bay and she'd spent many a summer gutting fish on his boat. If this didn't seem too good to be true, she loved The Waterboys. When she laughed it came from her belly and by the end of their evening together he was desperate to shag her. They were the last to leave. Ivan thanked the seventeen-year-old for picking a feckin' nice wine and she in turn thanked him for a large tip.

He walked Sienna home through the busy town. Spring had arrived and with it the bars, restaurants and streets were repopulating. The stars rested over the mountain which lay ahead, and when he put his arm around her she rested her hand in his pocket. When they reached her apartment they kissed at her doorway. She was soft and he could taste the wine. She asked him inside and internally he leapt for joy. *Please God, let me have sex!*

★ ★ ★

Penny made her way to Mickey Ned's. The bar was busy and she waved at Tin and his wife before passing them in favor of Josie and Jamie, the beautiful black-haired Casey sisters, who were both once Kerry Roses in The Rose of Tralee beauty pageant and who had both gone on to become bored housewives of very wealthy men in Kilkenny and Tipperary, respectively. They waved madly, delighted that someone slightly less tedious than their present company had entered. Penny grinned and approached while signaling her drink order to Donny the barman. He knew exactly what she wanted—the same as always, vodka on the rocks. Josie and Jamie both hugged her at once and told her how great she looked. Jamie managed to squeeze the bruise on her arm and Josie rubbed against the really sore one on her hip. She grinned through the discomfort and welcomed the girls home while nodding at their husbands, who were deep in conversation about the new iPhone. The girls and Penny moved away from their en-

197

grossed spouses and found seats near the corner of the bar. The girls were grinning insanely.

"So you've heard I'm an adulterer?" Penny said, matching their grins so as to disguise her humiliation.

"Technically, he's the adulterer," Josie said.

"You're the coveter," said Jamie.

"And yes—" Josie said excitedly.

"—we can't believe it!" finished Jamie, shaking her head.

"Maire McGowen said it's been going on in secret for years," said Josie, shaking her head like her sister before her.

"I don't know how you did it," Jamie said in awe. "I mean, nobody can keep a secret in this town."

"Yeah, well, I'm the Inspector Clouseau of sluts," Penny said, grinning at her own joke. The sisters didn't get it. "I wore disguises," she qualified.

They both laughed but she could tell they didn't understand the reference.

"You're filthy," Josie laughed.

"You've no idea," Penny said before taking a drink.

"You and Adam," Jamie said, nodding. "Even if we didn't know you were actually doing it, there was always something there."

Suddenly, Penny felt like crying. Jamie, quick to spot her discomfort, ordered her another drink and Donny was quick to return with it.

"Is he gone for good?" Jamie asked.

Penny sighed and nodded. "I believe he is."

"You're better off without him," Josie said.

"I'm really sorry," said Jamie.

"Thanks," Penny replied, "me too."

After that the girls spoke of their kids and how their husbands played golf too much and when they weren't playing golf they were working, and when they weren't working they were watching sports, and when they weren't watching sports they swore they were just sitting there flicking channels as though brain-dead. The kids didn't get a look in as far as they were concerned and yet when they did the smallest thing the kids considered them bloody heroes. Jamie was remodeling the house and builders were now her new nightmare. Josie was taking yoga lessons and felt her periods had become heavier since she'd started. Still, she was sticking to it because it was nice to get out on a Tuesday morning and her thighs felt firmer. Penny made jokes and they laughed and told her that she had always been a scream. All the while they drank and neither sister noticed that their friend was imbibing three drinks to their one so delighted were they to offload their crap and so happy that she could make jokes so funny as to lift them from their perceived misery.

"Josie?" Penny leaned in with drink in hand.

"Yes," Josie laughed in anticipation of her wit.

"I know your husband's a dick but look at it from my point of view," she drawled.

"And what's that?" Josie played along.

"Men are like parking spaces, the best ones are always taken and the rest are handicapped."

The girls laughed along and Penny silently gave thanks for the existence of the joke email. Afterward the girls asked her for her news, and aside from the scandal she didn't have any news and for a journalist that was pretty sad. She could have talked about work but why bother—they could read that and anyway it wasn't hers, it was someone else's. Instead, she stuck to making them laugh and drinking.

"So is there anyone in here you're interested in?" Josie asked Penny while surveying the room.

"Now, are you looking for me or for you?" Penny queried with a grin.

"Ah, stop it!" Josie said. "For you, of course—still, the one in red with the black-and-gray-speckled hair, the sharp jaw and the dick the size of a large foot toward your left looks interesting."

Penny and Jamie both shot their head toward the man in question. "I believe that's his hand rather than his foot in his pants," Penny noted while squinting to negate double vision.

"Oh my God!" Jamie snorted so much so that Bacardi Breezer dribbled from her delicate nose.

"As I said before, the best ones are taken and the rest are handicapped." Penny smirked.

The two girls became teary with laughter while she called for more drinks.

Chapter Fourteen

A Diamond Day

The next morning Mary woke up around seven. She was meeting her dad at the bar at eight. She showered quickly and fed Mr. Monkels, who was sleepier than usual. He followed his food into the back, ate it and flopped back into sleep. Sam was sound asleep so she closed the door to the kitchen and quietly ironed a shirt while eating a slice of toast. She drank her coffee in the car.

Her dad was standing outside the bar. He waved and got in. They hugged.

"Morning, Dad."

"Morning, love."

They drove to the graveyard in silence. Once they'd arrived Mary lifted the large bouquet of her mother's favorite flowers from the back seat.

Her dad smiled. "The bouquet seems to get bigger every year," he remarked.

Mary smiled and inhaled the lilies. They walked together in through the little iron gate, which brought them to the grassy hill laden with planted colorful graves. Like most inhabitants of Kenmare the dead also overlooked the water. They walked through the narrow passageways, making their way to the family plot. The sky was white and the water glistened as though fresh from a diamond downpour. Mary held on to her dad so they didn't trip over the rocks which peered intermittently through the hardened mud pathway. Once they arrived at the grave they began their yearly ritual. Mary laid the flowers on her mother's grave, her father blessed himself. They would then stand in silence for approximately five minutes, although on a rainy day this would be cut to between two and three minutes on account of Mary's dad being susceptible to bronchitis. At the end of this silence, Jack would signal it was time to say good-bye. Mary would lean down and place a black marble stone on the white marble gravestone to signify the passage of another year. Then her father would blow his wife a kiss.

"She turned out all right, love," he'd say to the gravestone. "You'd be proud of her." Then he'd take his daughter's hand and they'd walk back to the car.

Years before, when Mary was a child, her father decided that to avoid his daughter enduring the pain of her mother's anniversary on the same day as her own birth he would have to separate them. Of course, it would be impossible to change the past. He felt it would be wrong to change the child's birthday to a different date and obviously he wouldn't be able to change the date of his wife's death either. The only answer was to change the day he remembered her so that's what he did. Every year on his wife's birthday he and his daughter would lay flowers and remember her. Mary's birthday would then be for Mary alone. That way the dead could rest and the living could get on with it. And early on he decided that because his daughter had been robbed of her mother he would ensure that on the day of his wife's birthday they would spend the entire day together, and during that day he would tell Mary something she didn't know about her mother. It had been a great idea and over the years it had worked very well, especially when she was a teenager. If she was going through an awkward phase he could pick a memory of his wife that would speak to her even if he couldn't. Of course, as the years passed it was harder to pick a memory he hadn't already shared. Sometimes during the year he might think of something and write it down in preparation but mostly he'd then go and lose it as he was never known for his organizational skills.

They drove to the Silver Strand and took a walk on the beach. A man was throwing a stick to his dog, who was pretending she hadn't noticed, preferring instead to rub her face in the sand. They didn't talk on the beach; instead, they both listened to the wind and the waves hit rock and the birds screech at one another, taking turns to nosedive into the waiting water. The dog barked in the distance and the man yelled, "Fetch!" Mary smiled at her dad as they walked arm in arm and, although he returned her smile, he was far away in a place where he wasn't with his daughter but with his wife and they were courting.

Back then, when he was a boy and she was only a girl, they'd walk the strand and she'd talk to him about her latest craze. One week she'd be into knitting and she'd

arrive with a woolly sweater full of holes and ten different stories surrounding the making of the garment. The
next week she'd be an avid swimmer, swimming day and
night for the entire week, regaling him with accounts of
the benefits of the breast stroke and the highs and lows
that came with it. Then swimming would get lonely so
she'd move on to Irish dancing, which was very social and
she was quite good at it. Then one of the girls came on to
her and, being polite, she had agreed to go to *The Sound
of Music* with her—so of course she could never be seen
in that particular dancing hall again, especially as the girl
had waited for her for approximately four hours outside a
cinema one Tuesday.

She used to make him laugh and he liked that she was
flighty and never dull; he also liked that she was always
moving on, but it didn't go unnoticed that the only thing
that she did not move on from was him. Their walks on the
beach were his favorite memory of her. It was then, when
she was outdoors with the wind in her face and through
her hair, that she would entertain him with her whole self,
exposed and excited, expressing every thought about herself and others, dreams and reality, habits and doubts, plans
and obstacles. It was on the beach with her hair wild that
she was most alive. And while he walked with his daughter,
his wife's voice was calling to him from inside his head.

"Jack, put it on!" she said, and he could see her holding
the oversized knitted sweater and grinning.

"I don't even know if I can," he replied, trying to work
out the neck from the sleeve.

She laughed. "Sure the way you're built it won't make
a difference."

He put on the sweater, which gaped at the neck and met his knees, with a hole in the side. He stuck his hand into the hole.

She took his hand out and placed his arm at his side, covering the hole. "There now, you can't see a thing wrong with it."

He looked at her with laughter. "You want me to keep my hand by my side for the rest of all time?"

"I do."

"And what if I need to use this arm?" he queried her grinning face.

"Now, Jack, I have no doubt that whatever it is that needs doing, as a man of industry you will find a way." She laughed at his grin and he pledged that for her love he would find a way.

Later behind the dunes she had stripped him of his new sweater and they had fooled around until interrupted by an old man and his wife tut-tutting and warning them of the wrath of the local parish priest.

Jack laughed to himself and Mary squeezed his arm, bringing him back to the present.

"What are you thinking about?" she asked.

"Your mother," he admitted.

She smiled.

"You look so like her," he reminded her.

"I know I do, Dad."

"And you're as bold as her," he laughed.

"Maybe once," she said.

They walked on in silence, each smiling at different memories.

Later they ate lunch in a small restaurant in the middle

of nowhere. Each year they would find a new place to lunch so as to keep the day fresh. The food was good, and as Mary was driving, her dad allowed himself a Guinness, which was rich and creamy. He held it up.

"Now that's a good Guinness." He admired it as an antique dealer would admire a rare teapot.

After they had consumed two bowls of steaming beef stew, he placed a small wrapped box on the table.

"That's for you," he said.

"Dad!"

"It's not from me, it's from your mother," he told her, bowing his head in her memory.

Mary nodded and opened the gift. It was a solitary diamond on a short gold chain.

"Dad, this is beautiful!" She was shocked and delighted.

"It was your mother's engagement ring—I had it melted down," he admitted as though a little sad and happy all at the same time.

"Why now?"

"Well, initially I thought to myself, if a young man ever asked for your hand in marriage and he was a little stuck, I could slip him the ring."

"Father!" Her outrage was pretense.

"And anyway no one ever did because they weren't given a chance to, and time is pushing on so I thought 'twould be nice to see that diamond worn once again and sooner rather than later."

"So you've given up on me?" she asked, grinning.

He shared in her grin. "No. I wouldn't say I've given up, but I wouldn't say that I was holding my breath either!"

She looked at her new diamond necklace. "Thanks, Dad," she said, hugging him.

Mary and Jack arrived home around six. Pierre and Jessie had been handling the bar alone all day and both Mary and her father were surprised to find them laughing together in the kitchen. Jack, having been the greatest victim of their ongoing dispute, had to ensure this was not a momentary cease-fire.

"You're friends?" he asked tentatively.

Jessie looked at Pierre and nodded to indicate he could speak for them both.

"We are." Pierre bowed.

"Oh well, isn't this just the greatest day"—Jack grinned widely—"and thank the Lord above for it."

Pierre and Jessie shared a smile and Pierre mumbled something about God having nothing to do with it and Jessie nodded her agreement. Mary looked both of them up and down, her eyes narrowed.

"Yes, Marie?" Pierre quizzed.

"Am I ever to know how this amnesty occurred?" she asked, knowing the answer.

"Of course, dear," Jessie told her, "when your father sells this place to me for four pence."

Pierre laughed.

Mary's dad entered the kitchen with a bottle of his favorite wine and poured four glasses.

"Here's to the team back together again! And may whatever it was that was driving us apart be no more! Here's to a bicker-free future!" He raised his glass, as did Pierre, Jessie and Mary. Of course, in that room at that moment, Mary's dad was the only person who wasn't aware how the argument between Pierre and Jessie had started, but then again it didn't matter, some sort of peace had been reached. It would seem that all they had needed was some time alone to work it all out. Mary did wonder what had been said to bring about peace and in particular how she could find out what had been said. After they had enjoyed a second toast to Mary's long-departed mother, Pierre and Jessie left, leaving Mary and her dad to tend the bar.

Fresh from a glass of wine and wearing her mother's diamond, Mary was in high spirits. Penny arrived shortly thereafter with news of Ivan's second date with Sienna. She had accidentally encountered them while lunching in The Horseshoe. She described the woman and Mary knew instantly who she was talking about.

"We use the same hair dye," Mary said.

"What?" Penny queried.

"We had words in the chemist over the last box of dye about three months ago," Mary admitted.

"Words," Penny pondered.

"And a slight tug-of-war," Mary admitted.

"Who won?" Penny wondered.

"She did," Mary said, raising her eyes to heaven. "I called her a pushy cow," she mumbled. "Of all the people!"

Penny laughed.

After that Penny stayed for a drink before promising to check in on Sam. Mary was worried about having left him alone for the entire day. Ivan was supposed to have checked in on him but now in light of his new romance she was afraid that he had forgotten. Penny left soon after and made her way up the street, but before she reached the top of the town another bar lured her in. She intended to stay for only one, but then Jerry Letter bought her a drink to demonstrate that despite his own clean record he was not one to sit in judgment of others, and Pierre, still celebrating the end of his row with Jessie, was only too happy to include the partying Penny in his round. Five rounds later Penny remembered the American on the floor. *Oh Christ.* She slipped away unnoticed. She was halfway down the hill and toward the pier when the oxygen kicked in and she felt kind of dizzy and a little sick. She sat on a wall for a minute or two and concentrated on sobering up. She got up and pushed herself down the road, zigzagging all the way, and by the time she reached the house she had convinced herself that she had recovered enough to pull off the appearance of sobriety. She opened the house with the spare key Mary had left under the hedgehog in the pot beside the door. Sam was playing his guitar but stopped when he saw her.

"Still alive then?" she joked in a manner approaching a slur.

"I'm fine," he replied, a little confused. "Where's Mary?"

"Working," Penny said before burping. "She asked me to check on you."

"As I said . . ." He was uncomfortable in her presence.

She was so drunk she was sloppy and she was coming too close. He was afraid she'd fall on him.

"You eaten?" she asked, realizing she herself hadn't eaten since lunch.

"Ivan brought me something."

"Oh, good old Ivan! Even in the afterglow of a long-awaited shag he remembers those less fortunate!" She grinned while feeling for the sofa so that she could plonk herself on it. "Always thinking of others!" She looked down at him as she perched precariously on the edge of the sofa, and laughed. "You look so helpless." Her grin turned into a yawn. "Maybe I should come down there."

Sam panicked. "I don't think that would be a good idea." He was praying Mary would come home.

"I promise I won't hurt you," she laughed before leering, "You're so beautiful." She sighed. "I bet you get that all the time"—she nodded to herself—"but she won't notice," she mumbled, "she'll never notice, no matter how pretty you are." She laughed to herself in a manner that encouraged Sam to worry for her sanity.

He remained silent, not wishing to engage her despite his outrage. *She won't notice me. Who? Mary? Why should I care? I don't want her to notice me. I'm on the fucking floor, for Christ's sake.*

Suddenly, Penny was on her knees leaning over him, and her hand was reaching to stroke his face. Painfully aware of his vulnerability, he pushed her away so that she fell back. She giggled and attempted to get back to her feet.

"I think you need to stop drinking," he said. "It doesn't seem to suit you."

She appeared to sober up momentarily and hurt was evident, but suddenly her face changed color and her hand rose to her mouth.

Oh my God, thought Sam, *I'm going to be vomited on.*

She got up quickly, the necessity to puke sobering her long enough to make a direct path to the downstairs loo. Once she'd finished evacuating the meager contents of her stomach, she stood and flushed. Minutes later she wiped

her face and emerged as though nothing unusual had occurred.

"You seem fine so I'll leave you to it."

She exited before he could answer.

★ ★ ★

Sam must have fallen asleep after that. He didn't hear Mary
come in after midnight and she was careful to be quiet.

She had come to notice that Sam's sleeping patterns
were as erratic as her own. He spent much of his nights
awake staring blankly at the TV, while upstairs she tossed
and turned before taking the book from under her bed
and losing herself for a while.

She had also noticed that he was not taking his prescribed medication. This medication was never going to
be the difference between him recuperating or not, but she
wondered why he chose to hide his pain medication under
his mattress rather than take it or indeed simply refuse it.
She had found his stash, having taken the opportunity to
change his bedding while he was in the loo, but had failed
to give in to her desperate curiosity. She didn't need to
open any can of worms—life was hard enough.

It had been a long day and tonight she fell asleep instantly.

★ ★ ★

Mary was standing on an empty urban street. A red light
glowed above her head and it was reflected in the rain-
water pooling by the grate by the side of the road. She
was wondering what she was doing there—that is, until
the familiar teenage boy with a hood pulled tight cov-

ering his face came around the corner. He was running just like before and she could feel his heart beat so hard that her own soon followed. He turned in time to see the boys following. She called out to him but he couldn't hear her. She ran out into the road with her hands up to stop the boys but they ran through her. She turned to watch them as one of the boys grabbed at the hooded boy before pushing him to the ground. She watched helplessly as the blows rained down. The gang divided up. Three of them kicked and punched him while he attempted to protect his hooded head from their feet and fists. A large boy built like a bear loomed in the middle distance. He was holding an empty glass vodka bottle as though it was a tennis racket and was jumping up and down screaming out that it was his turn. The other boy was leaning against a car watching the boy being beaten, and it was obvious that he was the violent rabble's leader. She couldn't help but notice that he was surrounded by darkness. He turned away from the beating to watch the large boy built like a bear dance with the bottle. His slashlike mouth bled into a grin and he called out to the other three boys, who were busy kicking. She heard him laugh and saw him point at the bear with the bottle.

"Look, Topher's excited!" he sneered.

She looked around and found the street to be otherwise empty. *Somebody please come. Somebody save him.* She ran down the street and saw a man and woman, and she willed them to turn onto the street to where the boy was being attacked, but they got into a car and drove away. *Oh God!* She ran back in time to see the gang leader's mouth move and she heard him direct the other boys.

"Give Topher a go."

The boy-bear called Topher moved in and the other boys made way, leaving the hooded boy on the ground exposed and too badly beaten to run. She felt his broken knuckles clutching at his hidden face and his body curl into the fetal position so as to protect his balls from the oncoming onslaught before she woke with a start.

She was shaking. Her heart continued to race along with her pulse. Her hair was damp and she felt a migraine coming on. She could hear the TV murmur faintly through the floor. She needed to take a pill but she kept the bottle in one of the kitchen cupboards. She put on her long cardigan, the one that made her feel like Miss Marple, and made her way downstairs.

Sam looked up from the floor.

"Are you OK?" he asked, concerned.

"Just a touch of a headache, that's all," she said, passing into the kitchen.

"You look like you've seen a ghost," he remarked, noticing how pale she was even in the half-light.

She returned with a glass of water and a pill, which she popped into her mouth and swallowed as she passed him.

"Stay!" he called out painfully, bored of his own company.

His invite stopped her in her tracks.

"After all, we're both awake," he added, and she nodded in agreement, knowing that sleep would not come easy.

She sat on the sofa and he lowered the TV further.

"Are you getting a migraine?" he asked as though intimate with her medical file.

"I think I've caught it in time."

"You're shaking," he pointed out. "What's wrong?" He knew it was more than a headache.

"It was just a nightmare," she admitted, and without warning her eyes filled with fat tears threatening to tumble. *Oh my God, I am mortified. Do not cry!* she warned herself, but despite her inner cautioning, a rogue tear rolled toward her chin. *Knickers!*

"It must have been a bad one," he commented, surprised by the tear.

She nodded. "It was."

"You want to share it?"

"No," she said, wiping her eye.

"I have nightmares too," he said with unexpected honesty. "A lot. I guess that's why I have trouble sleeping. It's hard to sleep when you're scared to."

Mary was as taken aback by his candor as he had been by her tears.

"It seemed so real," she said.

"Like one of your visions?" he asked, and she eyed him suspiciously. "Ivan told me."

"No, usually they are pretty surreal."

"Like the cat on the flying mat?" he said with a smile.

"Yeah." She laughed before becoming serious. "This was like a movie and somehow I found myself in the frame." She rubbed her forehead.

"But it's just a nightmare, right?"

"I don't know. I've had it before. It was exactly the same except this time I got to see a little more. It's never happened like that before. Maybe it was a dream but there's something not right." He was silent and she spied him from the corner of her eye. "You don't believe it could be anything other than a dream, do you?"

"It's nothing personal, I just don't believe in much," he admitted.

"That's OK." She grinned. "Penny thinks I'm a basket case—maybe she's right."

Later, Sam thought about mentioning the state Penny had been in earlier that night but then he thought better of it. After all, it was none of his business.

After that Mary made some warm milk and they chatted freely. Sam admired her diamond necklace and she told him about her day spent remembering her mother. She shared some of the tales of her mother that her father had shared with her and he spoke of his grandmother. In the telling, he inadvertently revealed his nerdy origins.

"I can't see it," she laughed.

"Well, trust me. My teenage years were a nightmare."

"You're not alone." She smiled.

"Oh shit, sorry."

"Don't be." She smiled. "It was pretty good up to the coma, dead boyfriend and freak pregnancy."

He laughed and she stood up.

"I should get back to bed. I'm in the bar first thing and you have a full day on the floor ahead of you."

"Actually, I'm booked in with the Bone Man. Ivan set it up earlier."

"Good for you," she said, smiling.

"You think it's the right thing?" he asked, betraying a little panic.

"You've got nothing to lose."

"Well, except for the ability to walk, not much."

215

"You'll be fine," she soothed.

"Thanks for taking care of me."

"You're welcome," she said with a warmth that was new to him. She briefly stopped to straighten the picture of the boy and the dog by the door before making her way up the stairs and back to her bed.

Chapter Fifteen

Rear Window, Hard Ground

Although Sam was capable of straightening and with great difficulty assuming the seated position, the pain that followed was excruciating, so much so it brought tears to his eyes. Mary wanted to insist he take his pain medication but she thought better of it. Sam had seriously considered taking it but then he, being more informed than his neighbor, also thought better of it.

Ivan tried to take his friend's mind from his discomfort with what his own mother would often describe as idle chatter. His description of Sienna's performance in bed took them to the other side of Killarney.

"Jesus, she's a wonder!"

Sam laughed despite the pain.

"I tell you my balls could have been on fire and my wife wouldn't have licked them." He continued happily.

Sam wondered what woman in her right mind would lick balls that were alight but let the analogy rest.

Ivan was busy rubbing his nose on his sleeve. "Jesus, she's a wonder!" he repeated. "And as for positions!" He slapped the wheel of the car. "Jesus, the woman must come from circus folk!"

"I'm happy for you." Sam grinned. "She sounds like she could be the one."

"I tell you, it's a wonder I don't have to visit with the Bone Man myself!" Ivan turned off for the long and winding road that seemed too narrow for their car, not to mind the oncoming one, but well used to such roads he carried on unconcerned and unabated.

Later and while they were still on the tiny road, now lined with looming trees so dense they stole the daylight, Sam asked Ivan about whether or not he had called his wife.

"This morning."

"And?" Sam asked, curious as to whether Mary's vague premonition had any merit.

"And"—Ivan sniffed—"she told me I had some ego for an eejit."

Sam laughed.

"Apparently, I'd be the last person in hell she'd call out for," he said, wrangling with the glove box looking for tissues. "Feckin' hay fever," he mumbled.

"So Mary was wrong?"

"She is not," Ivan said, blowing his nose with a tiny sheet of balled tissue.

"You still think your wife wants you?"

"Oh, I know she doesn't want me, but she might need me because there is something wrong. I know that much."

"So what are you going to do?"

"Well, I'm going to wait until the kids come for Easter and I'm going to ask them," he said in a matter-of-fact manner before turning down into a farmyard and noting: "We're here."

Sam couldn't conceal his concerns when it emerged the Bone Man was in actual fact a farmer and his surgery was a table in the back of a hay barn. But Ivan swore by him and Sam was only hours away from submitting to the painkillers prescribed by the GP—or at the very least smoking the cannabis Mossy had so generously offered when he had called in to apologize to Mary for being too off his head to help with the stupid dog. Sam knew he couldn't risk imbibing any drug, prescribed or not, despite the temptation. He figured he couldn't get much worse off, although that thought changed on meeting the Bone Guy, who had hands the size of shovels, wild curly hair and a big beard. He reminded Sam of one of those crazy homeless guys in New York. He did what he was told though because the guy was six eight and almost as wide. In the end it only took a moment. He heard a loud click and felt an excruciating pain that lasted only one second, and then the relief took over and the effect was much like heroin.

★ ★ ★

Sam wasn't dancing a jig like Tommy the Coat but he was home and back in his own bed that night, and although he was happy to return to isolation he found himself missing Mary moving around. In the absence of the TV he had become accustomed to vegetating in front of, he turned his full attention to the guitar he had previously only tinkered with. It had been odd that he had been so comfortable playing in front of Mary. His ex-girlfriend had begged him to play many times but he had refused. Then again she was a world-renowned recording star and Mary tended bar, so he guessed it was most likely something to do with that. He didn't have anything to prove to Mary and, even if he felt he did, she wouldn't have given a shit anyway.

And yet he felt good when she had stopped to listen to his version of Bonnie Raitt's "I Can't Make You Love Me." It had been shoddy but she hadn't noticed or maybe she just hadn't cared either way. It was nice. When Jerry Letter had knocked on the door with Sam's prize possession carefully boxed, her emancipation only reliant upon a signature, it had been a good day despite his unfortunate circumstances. Once the front door was closed he was desperate to set about freeing her with a ferocity that matched that of a zealous child on Christmas morning. However, he was forced to leave the unveiling to Mary. And, once the guitar was unveiled, he stopped to take in breath as though seeing her with new eyes and a new appreciation.

"Hello, Glory!" he'd sighed.

"It has a name?" Mary laughed.

He grinned, not caring that she thought him stupid—a hero of his once named that guitar and that was good enough for him. And now, alone in his own home and fabulously free from pain, he took Glory out and held her on his lap, his right hand sliding up and down her neck, his left cupping her body. Before his time on Mary's floor he hadn't played guitar in years; in fact, he'd only ever played this particular guitar once before, on the night it was presented to him by Leland when his first signed act for Seminy Records went platinum. He took her home and alone he tinkered, but he was drunk, and she was the original Scotty Moore Gibson ES-295, so he'd thought better of it. When sober he found the guitar embarrassed him. As much as he loved her and the idea of her, he had a deep-rooted fear that he wasn't worthy to play her. She was used to being played by one of the all-time greats and he had long ago proved that he was mediocre at best. And so Glory's new owner retired her and Scotty Moore's Gibson was designated to becoming a museum piece, an expensive part of a businessman's décor.

Alone and lost in a distant memory, he held her for five minutes before he strummed. Her strings needed tuning. He didn't have a tuner so he set about doing it by ear. This took a few hours, but when he'd finished he knew that she was perfect. He always did have an ear. Once she was tuned, he placed his fingers on the desired chords, and after a moment or two he began strumming lightly and the guitar sang "Hotel California," one of his gran's favorite tracks. He followed up with "Life in the Fast Lane," forgetting the mid-8 but returning to it after the second verse. He played it again right through three or four times until it flowed and his hand became less stiff. The Kinks were next—working out "Louie Louie" took him to teatime. He stopped to boil an egg and fry up some French toast, then he resumed, playing Steely Dan, the Grateful Dead, a little Floyd and of course he couldn't resist Led Zeppelin. It was after ten when he put her down and exhausted took to his bed, and still his mind was full, buzzing with something he had long ago forgotten about. Sam's gospel phase was over.

★ ★ ★

Music had mattered to him once, long before he'd been disappointed one too many times. His first band, Diesel, featuring Hilarie the dick-licking bass player, had lasted a mere six months. They broke up when the drummer broke his leg in a car crash and Hilarie decided she wanted to be a nurse. Sam had also been hospitalized at that time but for different reasons. His bones hadn't broken like his friend the drummer but his injury would take the rest of his life to heal. He had also moved schools that year and spent his last year of high school as a stranger and self-imposed recluse. He didn't bother with college but, desperate to leave home, he found himself a job in a music shop and rented a box room in a box-sized apartment which he shared with a lesbian couple, Ronnie and Sue. It was Ronnie who introduced him to the bass player in the band Limbs, which was an all-guy unit made up of three art school dropouts, Fred, Paulie and Dave. They used to joke about it, saying they were missing a limb like it was funny, but he guessed at twenty-two and high it pretty much was. The music was serious though. Fred was the bass player and lead vocalist—he had a set of pipes on him. Paulie was the drummer, and what he lacked in talent he made up for in raw energy and enthusiasm. Dave on guitar was the quiet one and the main songwriter. They wanted a second guitar player and Sam fitted the bill. As the new addition, he would have been designated "the pretty one," but this title was used only once by Paulie and not again after Dave and Fred had to pull Sam off their terrified drummer. He sustained a black eye and a fat lip, and although Sam apologized for a seemingly unprovoked attack a few days later, he didn't explain to his new bandmates why he tore into Paulie the way that he did. Suffice it to say, he was never called pretty by those guys again.

Sam was desperate to be in a successful band and he knew with the right songs these guys could go all the way. Dave's songs were shit so he hoped that after an apprenticeship he could introduce a few of his own, and maybe then they could rocket and he'd no longer be just window dressing. It didn't work out like that though. Dave was prickly and, although Sam's songs were infinitely better, Dave was boss. It was his band and Sam could fuck off if he thought he was coming in to take over. So he did fuck off. Instead of trying to hook up with another band he auditioned for his own. That's how he met Sophia Sheffer, the rocker chick with the big hair, hips and voice. He knew instantly that she was the one. He also knew that she was into him and he slept with her that first night, sealing their newly formed partnership. He wrote the songs and although she worked on some of the melodies, mostly they were his. She wrote the lyrics because she insisted that they had to mean something to her. He didn't mind because she wasn't bad and it felt right that she should sing about chick stuff. He definitely couldn't write chick stuff. He plugged them as "The Carpenters of the Late Eighties." Of course, they sounded nothing like the Carpenters, and the comparison merely suggested that they were a male and female act. Unlike the Carpenters, their songs were hardcore rock anthems which they considered to be an antidote to Karen and Richard's squeaky-clean soft pop rock. Also they weren't related, which was good because they had sex at any given opportunity. It wasn't love and Sophia understood the concept of opportunistic fucking—after all, she was a rocker. They worked well together; he secured them paid gigs early on and free recording time, finding that he could schmooze with the best of them. She was serious about improving vocally, became stronger with each passing day and was dedicated to working on her image. They had uncomplicated sex most evenings and neither batted an eye when the other slept with someone else. He acted as manager and found that for some reason doors were quick to open. Maybe it had something to do with him flirting with the PA to every record-company executive in New York and maybe not, but their demos were always heard.

Sam was always working. When they weren't gigging, they were writing. When they weren't writing, they were practicing. When they weren't practicing, he was networking. They'd been together nearly two years when the buzz around them started to happen; vocally Sophia really had found her niche—one critic describing her voice as being husky, dark, warm, sexy and pitch-perfect. The music was strong too, reminiscent of Janis Joplin's raw iron but also hinting at what would later become grunge. But then music is all about timing—what's hot today is not tomorrow—and it turned out that Sam's burning pain-soaked anthems were a little ahead of their time. The world was still into metal-inspired rock and roll in the hay. In 1988 the masses craved tight-pants-wearing big-dick rock gods singing about sex and how they were going to get it. The charts were dominated by bands like Guns N' Roses, teasing the girls and instructing the guys with "Patience," and, on the other side, U2's spiritually laced emotive yearning was at its peak—*The Joshua Tree* had delivered America a newfound church: the Church of Bono. Record companies with little imagination were looking for the next U2 and the next GN'R. Sam and Sophia didn't fit the bill but Sophia alone—well, she had a voice that could raise the roof just like Axel and Bono and all those guys but she was different because she was a girl. Better than that, she was a girl with balls, and Max Westler, the hottest A-and-R guy on the East Coast, had wondered the first time he'd seen them play how much better this girl would be with a shit-kicking band around her. He'd sat back and watched her own the stage, analyzing her dirty against her guitar player's pretty. He had liked the songs but the songs were the guy's and he was a complication. Besides, he *had* songs—great writers, great producers, great players were all available to him and all he had to do was get rid of the blond kid.

It turned out it wasn't at all hard to get Sophia to abandon Sam—after all, they had no allegiance to one another, not sexually and certainly not emotionally, and hey, business is business, after all. Just as they had a chance to get somewhere, she walked and his faith walked with her.

"Please don't do this," he had begged.

"It's done," she responded without being able to look him in the face.

"Please." He was on his knees.

She shook her head from side to side and sighed before biting her lip. "You're a good player, Sam, but we both know that you're never going to be great." She still couldn't meet his eyes.

"I'll work harder," he pleaded.

"Max is right—talent like yours is . . . well, you're expendable. I'm sorry." She paused and added, "This is my shot and I can't blow it on some guy I probably won't even remember in ten years."

Sam was crying when she left. He was on his knees and crying and he hated himself for it but he hated her more. Her desertion and her reasoning had hit him hard, knocking his confidence so much that he retired his guitar and swore he'd never trust anyone again, nor would he ever again show weakness. He meant it and was blessed or cursed with great resolve.

During his time with Sophia he had realized something interesting about himself. He realized he was an intuitive businessman and, better than that, he had been born with the gift of spotting talent. He could walk into any club in New York and put money on the bands that would make it versus the bands that wouldn't. And in truth, if he had been that guy Max, he would have done the same thing because Sophia was better off without him. Still, he despised her for doing to him what he knew, given the chance, he would have done to her and he was determined that she would pay. Within weeks he'd picked himself up and made a decision. He was never going to be the next Santana, but as sure as shit he was going to be the next Clive Davis, the next greatest music executive in America. He'd never again be expendable. He would be the best at his chosen profession, and if being the best meant being a complete fucking asshole like that guy Westler, then so be it.

Fate must have taken him in hand because one week later he bumped into the most beautiful blue-eyed blonde, called Frankie. Mesmerized by her unaffected beauty, he offered to replace the coffee she'd just spilled all over him, and after half an hour she had made the decision to dump her boyfriend of three months. On their second official date Frankie mentioned that she was the daughter of Joe Merrigan, head of New Moon Records. Sam couldn't believe his luck and believed his encounter with Frankie was destiny. It was six weeks before he met Joe over dinner in his mansion, his daughter on one side and his beautiful ex-showgirl wife on the other. Joe conducted the meal like it was an interview and Sam, ever prepared, came through with flying colors. Afterward, when the girls were making drinks, Joe spoke to Sam in hushed tones, telling dirty jokes which he described as his weakness and not tolerated by his reformed wife and their squeaky-clean daughter. Sam indulged the old man by responding appropriately and telling him a few of his own. Joe smacked him on the back while laughing hard and Sam knew he wouldn't have to wait long. When he wasn't brownnosing Frankie's father or having polite sex with his sensitive daughter, he was trawling clubs looking for that next big act. He narrowed it down to six bands early on, following them night after night and gig after gig, narrowing them down further and further until four months into his relationship with Frankie he'd found The Deadbeats, his first great act.

He'd phoned her dad in his office at around noon. He told him that he'd discovered a great band and respectfully asked if he would attend their gig later that night. Joe had laughed, saying he had young guys who did that, but Sam was insistent. Joe broke and met Sam after eight in a small club in Hoboken. The band played and Joe's initial bemusement slowly turned to interest and after their fourth song he was hooked. Sam, having cultivated a relationship with the band over months, introduced Joe to The Deadbeats and as instructed they sucked ass. Joe was really impressed with their knowledge of his medium-sized company and of its many quality acts. He was especially impressed with their lack of ego and commitment to the process of making music—something that Sam had spent most of the day indoctrinating them in. Later in an all-night diner over pancakes, Joe offered Sam his first job in A and R. He started the next day and at first he worked under a gay guy called George Le Forge, a coiffeur turned A and R in the late sixties merely due to a chance encounter with Misty Day, a buxom blues singer he introduced to Arista Records. She went on to sell eight million records before dying of a coke overdose in the early eighties, while he had found another metal outfit who was doing nicely for Blue Moon. Sam guessed that George had just been lucky, having only discovered two acts in ten years, while he was planning on discovering one a year. Within six months Sam controlled The Deadbeats and George was back doing hair. After successfully signing another two million-dollar acts he migrated to RCA America, leaving Frankie and Joe both devastated. Frankie lost the man she thought would marry her and Joe a natural son-in-law and heir. Sam felt a clean break was best. As much as he liked Frankie, she had turned out to be a little too fragile for his taste, and besides, he had enough of his own shit to deal with. He didn't love her and so he reasoned that he was doing the right thing. So he didn't look back, not even when Frankie ended up in the hospital, having starved for six weeks. A year later and with two more massive acts tearing apart the charts, he had gained a reputation of having the Midas touch and being a hardcore asshole. After successfully taking over Max Westler's job and axing Sophia's band, Demonic, explaining to both of them that unfortunately in the current climate they were both expendable, he left RCA America to head up A and R in Seminy Records. Leland had made an offer that he couldn't refuse. Seminy was a hot new label nipping at the heels of the establishment.

At twenty-six years of age Sam was one of the biggest players on the American music scene. He was sitting on top of the world and deep inside he knew that for him the only way was down.

* * *

Sam had managed to navigate his way through eight weeks of rehab without really examining who he was and how he came to be, and yet while alone and playing guitar it was all he could do. He had been such an asshole and for so long. He never wanted to be. He just wanted to succeed so that maybe the pain would go away. He believed that if he was the best then nothing could touch him—at least that's what he'd hoped for. He was wrong, of course. The gold records, the penthouse, the limos, the sexy girlfriend, the money, the suits, the great restaurants, the cool clubs, the awards—none of it made any difference and, in the moment he realized he couldn't escape himself, he lost himself.

Sam played his guitar for two days straight, until his hand became so stiff he found it difficult to hold a fork. He hadn't seen Mary in those two days but she had ensured that he had left her home with enough food to last him a week. He was looking forward to seeing her again. She had been such a surprise to him. The nights he'd spent on her floor had been illuminating. His once-frosty neighbor was warm and natural, not like most of the women he'd known, who were mostly too busy holding in their stomachs to be able to engage. She engaged, looking straight through his eyes and into his soul. He knew that he would have to be careful as it would be difficult to hide anything from her.

Chapter Sixteen

Every Day Is Like Sunday

Ivan woke with his seven-year-old daughter sitting on his chest. He opened one eye playfully then closed it before opening the other. She giggled. He raised his arms and she held on to them, then he lifted his legs and her feet met his and suddenly she was suspended in the air screaming and laughing. He dropped her on the bed and she giggled and curled up. "Happy Easter, Dad!"

"Happy Easter, Justy!" He smiled. "Where's your brother?"

"Down by the water."

Chris, a ten-year-old who could pass for thirteen, loved the water just like his dad. Ivan knew his son missed it and pitied him.

"Eggs?" he queried.

"An omelette with mushrooms, ham, cheese and Granny Sheila's brown bread," Justine demanded.

"You don't ask for much!" Ivan noted, ruffling her hair,

happy that he'd stocked up and could fulfill her wish list.

Sitting in the kitchen, she happily chatted about her Granny Sheila and her twin cousins and Auntie Mary, who'd promised to take her to Killarney to buy something pretty. Ivan attempted to question her about her new world but she remained closed off.

"Is everything OK with your mother?" he'd asked eventually.

She shrugged her shoulders and pretended to smile.

"Justine. Answer me. Is everything OK?"

She looked a little nervous, playing with the sugar bowl, and he could have sworn a tear sprang into her eye.

Chris opened the back door and came in rubbing his hands together. "I could smell that omelette from forty paces!" he said gleefully.

Justine laughed at her brother and Ivan winked at his son, happy his children were in his company and temporarily forgetting his concerns. After all, it was Easter Sunday, and for the first time ever his mother had excused her children from their obligatory Sunday meal in favor of Ivan hosting a family barbecue to welcome his children home.

In truth, Ivan had missed out on the majority of his kids' lives. It wasn't just his wife's defection. A house and lifestyle like Ivan's didn't come from a fisherman's pay packet. As a teenager, when he had discovered Norma's pregnancy, he had two choices: the first was to be poor and a full-time father and the second was to train as a commercial diver, work in Saudi Arabia and make a mint. He'd already completed advanced diving courses during summers while his brothers played with footballs and hurleys. Of course, the reality meant leaving his young family for an oil rig off the Red Sea coast and working in dangerous and deadly conditions—but the pay met the danger, and if they were to have any kind of life, it was a risk worth taking. And so he left his new wife and his baby boy to live on an oil rig. He worked on that rig for four years straight, only returning when his nephew died on a swing, having missed most of his existence and shocked into ensuring he wouldn't miss the lives of his own children. He came home, bought a large house, a small boat, a number of properties in Cork and a few stocks and shares. He'd made it and initially his wife seemed happy. After years of sustaining family life alone, her husband had returned. It should have been good. It wasn't. They were strangers, both having grown up apart. Their breakup was always going to be only a matter of time but he hung on to the love they once shared, desperate not to lose the kids he'd just regained.

Sam had been surprised that his relaxed friend had once been a risk-taking daredevil, but to Ivan commercial diving had only ever been a job. Of course, he'd be lying if he didn't admit it was an adrenaline-charged and exciting way to earn a living—life-threatening activity usually is—but he didn't miss it. Diving was always a means to an end. He was always apart from those adrenaline junkies around him. He just liked to fish, and diving for a few years and making the right investments would ensure that he could do just that for the rest of his days.

It was just a damn shame he lost his family in the process.

★ ★ ★

Penny sat in her living room with music blaring. If she was more like Mary it would have been cohesive with her mood, but she wasn't Mary—so, despite her desperation, Britney belted out "Hit Me Baby One More Time" while Penny slugged on the end of a bottle of white wine. Red would have left telltale marks whereas white, while not being her favorite tipple, didn't betray her.

She had attempted to get out of attending Ivan's barbecue to no avail. Ivan wasn't taking no for an answer. He was in the mood for celebration and he felt it was as good a day as any for his friends to really get to know his new girlfriend. This had made Penny a little sick. The cause of her illness was jealousy, a very unattractive quality that Penny often battled.

But, in fact, her main reason for attempting to escape Ivan's party had less to do with his new girlfriend and more to do with Mary bringing Sam. She had avoided the American since her drunken attempted pass of which she was so monumentally embarrassed that it had caused her great despair. She had felt cheap and dirty and exposed. He had rejected her and had looked upon her with a kind of horror reserved for circus freaks. Through his eyes she had transmogrified. The next morning she had woken hating herself, but within hours and in the company of a stiff drink she had mentally dumped her self-loathing onto Sam. After all, who the hell did he think he was? If Adam hadn't abandoned her, she wouldn't have even looked at the stupid American twice. He did fancy himself. It was then she decided he was an arsehole and a jumped-up arsehole at that. She didn't want to see him. She couldn't stand having to make polite conversation with him. She couldn't believe he and Mary had become friends over the past number of weeks. It was as though they had become close to spite her. Just when she needed her best friend most, some stranger rolled into town and stole her away. It didn't help that she would be attending the event alone yet again.

She finished the dregs of the bottle. It was the least she deserved.

★ ★ ★

Mary and Sam were up early so as to fit in a few hours' tree tagging before heading to Ivan's. It had been the third afternoon in a row that Mary had joined her neighbor in his quest to find his grandmother's message.

Sam had initially been reluctant to share his pastime with his neighbor but, when he discovered that half the town was surmising that he had some form of tree-tagging autism, he explained himself to Mary.

Mary had grinned at him.

"What?" he'd asked, expecting sarcasm.

"Nothing," she said, smiling.

He was freaked by her inane grinning.

"It's nice, that's all. I hope you find her."

"She's dead. I'm not looking for her."

"Whatever," she said, laughing.

He wasn't sure when she asked him if it would be all right if she and Mr. Monkels joined him on his quest, but she was convincing, mentioning the valuable time he'd lost while lying on her floor.

It turned out to work very well. They talked and Mr. Monkels groaned and halfway through that first day, when

Sam pointed to light streaming through a parting in a cloud, Mary took out her camera and took her first photograph in six years.

It was Sam's turn to be smug.

"What?" she asked.

"You took what I said to heart," he said, pleased with himself.

"No I didn't," she lied.

"Yeah, you did," he laughed, so she pushed him.

After that she took a lot of photos. One was of Mr. Monkels resting at the base of a tree, another of Sam running his hand over bark, another of him hiding his face from her incessant clicking. A bird swooping low over still water was her favorite, at least that's what she would tell people—in actuality it was one of Sam giving her the finger. Afterward he'd helped her change her spare room into a dark room.

"Haven't you heard of digital?" he asked while gaff-taping blackened cardboard to the window.

"One step at a time," she said with a smile, grappling with the old thick black velvet curtains that her Auntie Sheila had made for her long ago.

Now the weather was getting warmer. Today Mr. Monkels had refused to budge when Mary had attempted to attach him to his lead. Instead, he lay inside her glass door soaking up the heat of daylight against glass. Mary and Sam only had a couple of hours before they were going to help Ivan prepare for his guests.

Mary wished Sam a Happy Easter and she laughed at his grunted response. She teased him about attending a service and he reiterated that he didn't do Mass.

"Me either."

"But you believe in God," he said in a tone which suggested he thought she was crazy.

"Yeah."

"I don't get it." He took her hand so as to help her up a grassy verge.

"What's to get?" she asked, amused.

"With the way things have gone for you, if you believe in a God it must have crossed your mind that he might have it in for you."

Mary laughed. He was right—there was a time when she believed that the Almighty was an arsehole but that had changed one day.

She said, "A very wise woman told me once that the world doesn't revolve around me."

He smiled at her and nodded.

"She said that those who had gone on before had merely followed their own path as opposed to being a casualty on mine." She shrugged her shoulders. "We're all just visiting this world. Some stay longer than others, that's all."

"I really hope for your sake you're not going to be disappointed."

"About what?"

"What if I told you that I had died?"

"You died?" she asked with one eyebrow cocked.

"It was only minutes but long enough for me to know there's nothing." He was puzzled when she smiled.

"Ask me about what I remember during my coma," she said.

"What do you remember?" he asked, playing along.

"Nothing," she said, shrugging again, "absolutely nothing."

"So?"

"So it doesn't mean there wasn't anything going on."

"It's totally different," he sighed.

"No it's not."

"I just don't get why you would believe," he mumbled.

"Because if I didn't I'd lose my mind." He nodded because that answer made sense to him.

Later, while they were making their way home, Mary returned to the subject of Sam's death.

"So are you ever going to tell me about what happened to you?"

"Maybe someday," he said, quite alarmed that he had become so carried away as to impart that much.

"It would be easier to get a straight answer from James Bond," she noted, and he glanced toward the floor.

"I'm sorry. I don't like talking about the past."

"I understand. Some join the foreign legion and some come to Kenmare."

He nodded and laughed. And it occurred to him that one of the things he liked most about Mary was that, although she didn't know much about where he'd come from or what he did or even the terrible mistakes that he'd made, she did know him. She knew him better than anyone.

It was after three when they arrived. Auntie Sheila and Mary's dad were vying for control of the grill. Mary kissed them both. Her dad shook Sam's hand and her aunt winked at him and told him that if her niece didn't have such a good left hook she'd steal him away for herself.

"We're just friends," Mary told her for the fifth time.

"Yeah, that's what they always say and then someone gets pregnant." Her aunt laughed and nudged her brother, who laughed along with her.

"We're really just friends," Sam clarified before Ivan called him over to join in a game of football that he was having with his son and his eldest brother, Séamus, who was running with abandon around the garden having the time of his life without his wife and twin girls. As luck would have it, one of the girls had been struck down with chicken pox earlier in the week. Séamus had never had chicken pox and, while they waited to see if the dreaded spots would appear in her twin sister, the doctor had advised it better that Séamus stay out of harm's way until the impending threat had passed. To this end he had moved in with his parents and he was determined to make the most of his limited freedom.

Mary made her way over to Penny, who was sitting at one of the garden tables toasting with Steven and Barry.

Steven jumped up to greet her. "Mary, you look like a diva."

"Isn't that your way of calling me a bitch?" she asked.

"No, it's his way of telling you to take it easy on the hair dye," Barry said. "Or are you trying out for the Pussycat Dolls?"

Mary gave him a dig as Penny threw her head back, laughing.

"And you've competition," Steven said, throwing his eyes in the direction of Sienna and a blond friend helping her carry condiments.

"Two redheads but who is the reddest head of them all?" Steven said in his movie-trailer-guy voice.

Mary looked at Penny. "You told them about the hair-dye incident."

"We heard it was more like a pushing, bitch-slapping affair." Barry smirked.

Mary moaned. "Who's the blonde?" she asked, looking over at Sienna's friend.

"Her name is Flory." Steven grinned. "As in Floor E."

"You're messing," Mary said, but her cousin Barry and his boyfriend, Steven, shook their heads to signal that, no, they were not messing.

"And here is the best bit," Barry added. "The lovely Sienna has brought her along as a potential date for your new neighbor."

Penny started to laugh and that struck Mary as being unkind although she wasn't sure why.

"Well, I wish her the best of luck," Mary said before Steven stood up and took her by the arm so that they could walk to the makeshift bar together.

"Don't worry, she hasn't a patch on you," he whispered.

"We're just friends," she sighed.

This friendship had been decided over the course of a meal in a local restaurant which had been made uncomfortable by the hovering waitress, Minnie Morrow, who had insisted on offering the new couple a free bottle of wine. Mary had attempted to explain that her neighbor was merely thanking her for taking care of him during his convalescence to which Minnie had commented that she bet she had before leaning in to the American and whispering that if it didn't work with Mary of the Sorrows he would know where to find her.

In the wake of Minnie's embarrassing assumption, Mary had felt it necessary to define their burgeoning relationship.

"Don't worry, I'm not looking for a relationship," she had said.

"Right back at ya," he replied.

"I knew that. I just didn't want you to think that I was sitting here with any expectations. I'm happy as I am."

"Me too," he had said, smiling, before raising a glass to toast. "Here's to friendship!"

"Friendship," she'd agreed happily.

Mary made peace with Sienna over a hot dog. They had grinned sheepishly at one another and Mary had told her how happy she was making Ivan. It was true. Ivan was happy as a playful puppy. He'd lost more than his family when his wife walked out—he'd lost his confidence—and Sienna had restored it and Mary would be forever grateful to her. Ivan had put his arm around his favorite cousin and toasted his friends and family while Justine sat on her grandmother's knee and Chris sneaked a sip from his uncle's beer. Penny spent the night with Steven and Barry, maintaining her distance from her best friend. Mary cornered her when she was pouring vodka for herself at the bar.

"Hey, stranger!"

"Hey, yourself!"

"You've been keeping to yourself."

"I know," Penny admitted, "I've just been really busy."

"Maybe I could call up in the morning—I'll bring breakfast," Mary volunteered.

Penny looked over her shoulder at Sam, who was talking with the blonde. "Great."

Mary had watched Penny from a distance and had noticed she was never without a drink. But it was a party. She silently vowed to keep a closer eye on her.

"You're OK, aren't you?" she asked.

"I'm fine," Penny said. "You want a drink?"

Mary nodded and Penny poured her a drink and they sat together.

Penny looked back toward Sam and Flory. "I don't trust him," she said out of nowhere.

"Who?" Mary asked.

"Sam."

"Why?"

"I don't know. Why did you dislike him at first sight?"

"I didn't know him."

"Aren't you a great believer in gut feelings?"

"And don't you think my gut feelings are a load of crap?" Mary retaliated with laughter, attempting to defuse a potentially uncomfortable conversation.

Penny let it go—after all, she'd made her point. She wasn't sure what her point was. All she knew was that she didn't want to be around Sam, not after what had happened. He was an arsehole. She hoped he liked the blonde with the stupid name so that she'd get her best friend back.

"Do you think he likes her?" Penny asked, watching Sam talk with Flory.

"I don't know. Maybe."

Later, when night had fallen and Ivan's garden was lit up from his porch to the sea, when Justy was asleep on her grandfather's knee and Chris was in the den watching a DVD with his friend who was sleeping over, the party continued on.

Denis and his band, a Dubliners tribute band called The Pale Pretenders, arrived a little after nine. The first time Mary had slept with Denis she'd mentioned the fact that their name was pretty bloody stupid. He insisted on explaining the origins of the name so as to change her mind.

"You see, they are The Dubliners, meaning they are from Dublin. Dublin is also known as The Pale. We are not The Dubliners, but we do play the music of The Dubliners, so we are The Pale Pretenders."

"I get the reference and it's still rubbish."

"Fair enough," he'd acquiesced. "Any chance of a shag?"

He was the most relaxed man she'd ever met. Then again he, like her neighbor Mossy, smoked hash the way others smoked cigarettes, which pretty much explained his permanently numbed state. Initially, although instantly attracted, she had thought him to be one of life's losers, which hadn't bothered her at all. His grubby appearance suggested this and his lackadaisical approach to his life almost confirmed it, but that was before she became aware of his past. He intrigued her with his sharp green eyes, his matted hair and the clothes that were ten years old while he owned half of Kildare. Later she would discover that he had bought his first property at sixteen, his second at seventeen, and while she was night swimming and getting herself pregnant he was building an empire. At twenty-six he got bored and learned how to play the guitar. He was always a fan of traditional music and especially The Dubliners, so by the age of thirty-two he was a bona fide Traveling Wilbury, touring wherever the music took him.

243

She had liked him instantly, especially as he was only in town for one night every few months—it was his distance more than anything that really appealed.

Now he smiled at her, bringing her back to the present. She nodded as he made his way over to the area that would become his stage. The fiddle player, Dillon, and the kid who sang with the voice that belonged to an old man followed him.

"Howya, Mary."

"Good, Dillon. You?"

"Just like jam." He grinned.

She had no idea what *jam* meant but guessed that it was good as he looked pretty happy.

"Good for you." She smiled, and he laughed because he liked it when a crease developed above her eye suggesting a mild confusion.

Mary brought Denis a drink as they were setting up.

"It's nice of you to do this," she said. "I didn't know Ivan had asked."

"We were in Tralee last night. It was no problem."

She nodded and smiled. It had been four months since they'd seen one another.

"So are we on tonight?" he asked with a wink.

"You don't waste time," she responded, swirling the contents of her glass.

"I think Jesus would be sad if I did."

She laughed. "I'm sorry—it's not a good night."

"No harm in asking." He grinned and he sat with Dillon and the boy, and suddenly there was live music and dancing.

Sam had viewed the guy talking with Mary from a distance. He looked like a hippie with dreads and was wearing a sweater two sizes too big. There was a hole in the arm that hung over his hand; this hole housed his thumb, which bore a thick silver ring. He was tall, well built and his face was chiseled like rock. His eyes were a piercing green, and when he introduced their first song his voice was like gravel, briefly reminding Sam of Danziger. The guy beside him with the fiddle was smaller and rounder and the hair on his head had long ago absconded. What he had lost on his head he made up for on his face with a gray speckled beard so long it sat on his chest. The third guy and singer, in contrast, looked like a kid in a suit—short hair and rosy cheeks with freckles. The kid was engaging—close your eyes and it was Luke Kelly back from the dead—but as engaging as he was, Sam kept returning to the hippie with the face like rock that spent his time staring at Mary.

Penny sneaked off to skinny-dip with Steven and Barry. She listened to the live band lying on her back in the water while Steven and Barry, drunker than they'd been in a long time, frolicked as only men can, each pushing the other underwater and taking turns to give chase.

Sam danced with Flory, who was possibly the most insistent woman he'd ever met. He had been polite all night as the woman clearly had issues with men. She had cried three times and every time he'd attempted to escape she'd grabbed his hand and wouldn't let go. Mary had kept her distance, and when he'd attempted to catch her eye she'd merely smiled before looking away. Everyone else was having a good time. Meanwhile, he was at a parallel party listening to the problems of a disturbed woman. Mary was sitting with her uncle, who was caressing the hair of his sleeping grandchild while he complained that his wife re-fused to feed him properly.

"Who in the name of God in heaven eats whole grains?" he asked.

Mary laughed at her uncle's lament for sausages, bacon and butter.

Séamus was up dancing on his own with his shoes off and his trousers turned up. "God help him," his father said.

Mary looked at her cousin and then back to her uncle.

"Twins will do that to a man," he said, nodding.

She looked past him toward the band, catching Denis's eye, and past Denis to where Sam was kissing Flory. She turned away and got up, deciding she needed a drink. She met her dad at the bar.

"A good night," he said, pouring her a drink.

"Yeah."

"You're OK?"

"I'm great."

He nodded. "Right so." He left her to it.

Mary put her drink down and made the decision to go home.

Chapter Seventeen

A Kiss Is Just a Kiss

The pounding rain woke Sam sometime after five in the morning. He was thirsty and needed the loo. After emptying an alarmingly extended bladder he made his way downstairs. He opened the fridge and took out a bottle. He was pouring water into a glass when he noticed that Mary's back doors were open. When he looked over the wall he could see the rain pooling on her kitchen floor and drenching her drapes. It was a marvel to him how in the matter of a few hours the weather had changed from a glorious spring night to a winter deluge. The lights were out and he was sure she wasn't awake, let alone up and about. He had seen her leave Ivan's party much earlier, just after he had pried the insane blonde off him. He hadn't had a chance to say good-bye. She was gone before he could speak with her. He had considered that she had seen the kiss and, aware that from a distance his innocence would be indecipherable, it concerned him. He knew that they were just friends and yet he didn't want her to think that he had kissed another woman. It would have been fine if in fact that is what he had done, but it wasn't. Returning from his concerns and back to the moment, he realized that it was very unlike Mary to leave her back doors wide open and considering the hour and the fact that her wooden floor would suffer from his inaction, he made his way toward her garden.

"Mary?" he called, but there was no answer. "Mary!" he repeated a little louder and still nothing. He was getting soaked. The moss-ridden rock wall separating the two houses was slippery not to mention sharp. Concerned for his weakened back, he decided against making an attempt at any kind of leap. Instead, he brought a chair out of his kitchen and stood on it, then maneuvered himself carefully over the wall, dropping down loudly on the other side. For some reason he felt like a criminal—his heart was beating way too rapidly to be good for him.

He took a deep breath before entering the kitchen gingerly. He immediately noticed a heavy vase overturned and cracked on the floor, and as he ventured farther inside he noticed that the place was a mess—in fact, the closer he looked the more apparent it became that he might be interrupting a burglary. A book of menus which had obviously been laid out on the table was now spilled across the floor along with CDs out of their cases. It was the CDs out of their cases that caused him the most concern. *She never leaves CDs out of their cases.* He listened carefully, attempting to hear something above his own heartbeat. He picked up an ornate heavy wrought-iron poker from beside the fire and as he stood up he heard a thud coming from upstairs.

He had no choice but to hold his weapon tight and run toward the stairs to save his neighbor from an invisible intruder.

★ ★ ★

It was after five when Mary emerged from the bathroom and made her way into her bedroom. Just as she was closing the door she heard a noise coming from downstairs. She listened intently, interrupted only by Mr. Monkels's thud when he fell off the end of the bed. He didn't even wake up—instead he rolled onto his belly and wheezed lowly. She had been extremely worried that her dog had been the victim of an epileptic seizure on the night that Sam had hurt his back. However, her vet had disagreed, and despite scrutiny he had not displayed symptoms since. She viewed her sleeping dog intently for a moment or two before hearing another sound. She grabbed the hardback book she'd been attempting to read and made her way down the stairs. They met halfway, both with their weapons held high.

"Sam?" Mary whispered.

"Mary? Are you all right?"

"I'm fine. What's wrong?" She lowered her hardback book before hurriedly pushing him down the stairs.

Once inside the kitchen, he answered.

"This is what's wrong!" He swept the room with his hand.

"So I left a mess."

"Exactly. You don't leave messes."

"Well, I did tonight."

"And what about the doors?"

"I forgot the doors," she admitted, picking up the vase before moving to close the French doors and standing in the pool of water. "Knickers!" she said under her breath before reaching for the mop.

Absentmindedly, Sam sat.

Mary raised her eyebrows. *He has a neck. One minute kissing the blonde and the next sitting in my kitchen.* Mary had convinced herself on her journey home that she didn't care about the kissing incident.

"Do you often leave your back doors open?" he queried in an attempt to have a reason to remain in her presence so that he could set the record straight about his unwanted kiss.

She pushed her hair off her face. "You know well that I don't leave my back doors open." She felt the damp curtains. "Frig it! I just had those dry cleaned." She walked across the room and past Sam. Despite the damp, he smelled expensive. She suddenly became aware that she was wearing a pair of little black pajama shorts and a vest top, especially now that her nipples were sticking out like bloody spare parts. She turned her back on him and faced the kettle, wondering whether he wanted tea and how long he was planning to stay. She felt him behind her and turned to face him. His close proximity made her heart skip. He slipped his hand into hers and leaned toward her face. She looked into his eyes and it became apparent that he might be about to kiss her. The impending kiss hung in the air while internally his head battled with his heart. *Don't do it! Do it! Don't do it! Do it!*

She was paralyzed in a manner much like her dog had been two weeks before. Moments passed but they seemed like years. His face remained fixed at an intimate distance. Mary bit her lip, completely out of her depth. *Oh holy crap! Pull away, Mary! Pull away before he does something you will both regret!*

It was at that moment that Denis entered the room. His piercing eyes took Mary in while seeming to ignore Sam standing opposite her. He walked right up to them and placed his hand on her shoulder.

"Are you coming back to bed?" he asked.

Sam dropped her hand. She nodded while battling the urge to throw up.

Denis held his hand on her shoulder long enough for him to take Sam in. He put his hand out to shake Sam's. Sam reciprocated while waging an inner battle of his own.

"You're the neighbor?"

"Yes."

"I'm the casual shag," Denis noted, and Mary closed her eyes so as to escape her neighbor's expression.

"I should go." Sam turned to leave.

She walked him to the door and opened it to let him out.

"I'm really sorry," she muttered.

"Don't be," he said cheerily as though nothing had happened, but then of course nothing had happened.

He would pretend that he hadn't considered kissing her and she would pretend that she hadn't believed that he had considered kissing her. His momentary lapse in judgment would be ignored by both parties. He would pretend to be grateful for the reprieve that Denis had provided—after all, he wasn't ready for a relationship or indeed anything other

251

than friendship. She would pretend that she hadn't wished him to kiss her and that it was a good thing that Denis had been there to save the moment and their friendship. Both would determine that this friendship was all important and not worth jeopardizing.

She watched him walk out of her little front garden. Denis's two bandmates were waking from an uncomfortable sleep in the car parked out front. She motioned at them to come in for breakfast while her neighbor entered his house, closing the door behind him without looking back. She guessed he'd seen enough for one morning.

Oh my God, he thinks I'm a whore.

★ ★ ★

It was after nine and Penny was in bed and dreaming of a frog dancing a hornpipe on a blue carpet surrounded by GAA football players clicking their fingers.

Mary plonked down on her bed and she sat up still asleep.

"What? What? What is it?" she called out to the weird little frog clicking his heels.

Mary laughed and opened a bag of fresh fruit scones under her nose. "I've got raspberry jam and fresh cream in the kitchen."

Penny's eyes opened slowly. "My favorite."

Mary nodded and went to the window to open the curtains.

"You wouldn't believe the weird dream I just had." Penny yawned.

"I wouldn't believe it if it *wasn't* weird," Mary said, making her way out the door.

"What the hell are you so chipper about?" Penny grabbed her robe and followed her friend.

"I had sex last night."

"Oh my God, either pigs have taken flight or One-Dimensional Denis had his way." Penny actually took time to look out the window and up to the bright blue sky before catching up with her friend in the kitchen. "No pigs. It must be Denis."

Mary was dumping bottles of beer. "Did people come back here?" she asked, holding up an empty bottle.

"Yeah," Penny lied, not really knowing why. Still, she didn't need questions about bottles so early in the morning.

"What the hell happened to your tooth?" Mary asked, approaching her.

Penny remembered that when she returned home from the party she had needed a drink. After a few weeks of over-indulging in wine she had decided to buy beer only, thus negating her tendency to overindulge in wine. She couldn't find the bottle opener. After mere minutes of searching, she became annoyed, and annoyance turned to frustration. Eventually she did what anyone else would do: she used her teeth to get the top off the bottle. Her endeavor was successful—however, at the cost of a cap on her left molar, bought by her parents many years previously. She felt the gap in her mouth with her finger while Mary scrutinized her.

"I said: what happened to your tooth?"

"It's been loose for weeks. I must have lost it when I was asleep."

Mary surveyed her friend. "OK," she said as though she didn't believe her.

"Anyway, enough of that, so how's One-Dimensional

Denis?" Penny said, both in an attempt to distract from her lie and because she had a genuine interest in her friend's nocturnal activities.

"He is not one-dimensional."

Penny scoffed. "And?"

"And he followed me home from the party." She started to make coffee.

"And the mood just came upon you," Penny noted, shaking her head. "Well, after how many months? I suppose that kind of thing can happen."

"Ha-ha," Mary said, giving Penny the finger. She knew how Penny felt about Sam but she was desperate to talk about the possible kiss and to seek counsel as to the handling of such a delicate matter—or at the very least confirmation that ignoring it was favorable to their friendship. So she decided to test the waters.

"And do you know what else?" she asked.

"I can't wait," the gap-toothed Penny responded.

"I had a late-night caller."

"A late-night caller?"

Mary nodded.

"Go on."

"Sam."

"What did he want?" All the warmth had vacated Penny's voice. So Mary decided against confiding in her.

"He thought I was being burgled."

"What a hero!" Penny sneered.

"You really need to see a dentist." Mary advised, changing the subject, and Penny nodded.

"What am I like, Mary?" she laughed, and made a funny face exposing the gap.

Mary smiled but didn't respond. She knew her friend long enough to know that the question was rhetorical.

After breakfast they sat out on Penny's patio, each holding on to their coffees for warmth.

"I forgot Ben's anniversary," Penny admitted, staring off into the light blue sky.

"It doesn't matter. You had a lot to deal with." She wasn't lying. The anniversary had been weeks before and it hadn't even occurred to her to be annoyed that her best friend had forgotten it. Penny had enough of her own present-day problems.

"It does matter. I'm really sorry."

Mary nodded. "Sam left flowers." She hadn't intended to mention Sam again that morning, it just slipped out.

"You're joking," Penny noted in genuine wonderment. "How do you know? Did he leave a card?"

"No. Cassie Boxer saw him. She told Rita Sullivan Flowers, who mentioned it to Jessie after Mass a week after he came here."

"That's weird."

"I know you don't like him, but I really think I was wrong about him."

"It doesn't matter what any of us think," Penny said, eyeing her friend. "He's just passing through. This time next year he'll just be a memory like the Burkenheffs."

"The Brinkerhoffs," Mary mumbled.

"My point exactly," Penny noted, smiling, "and in the meantime I hope he and Flory are very happy together." She viewed Mary, who had forgotten about his little indiscretion with Flory.

What the . . . ? She returned Penny's smile before quickly changing the subject and saying in her get-ready-for-gossip voice: "Oh, you'll never guess what I heard last night."

"What?" Penny asked, gripped by the sudden prospect of scandal.

"Bridget the Bike and her husband have split up." This statement was met with silence so she continued, "Someone told her that he'd fathered that child in Sneem."

Penny inhaled.

"I know," said Mary at her friend's intake of breath.

"Bridget Browne. Oh dear God!"

"I know. Apparently, she found out weeks ago. They've been trying to work it out but . . ." Mary was shaking her head. "After all this time I wonder how she found out?"

"Well, the whole town is talking about it," Penny said defensively.

"Yeah. But I wonder if it's really true?" Mary pondered.

"Of course it's true," Penny said, betraying a little panic. "You think it's not true?"

"Well, it wouldn't be the first time a rumor was unfounded." Mary smiled.

"Well, she's left him. So it must be true."

"Maybe. Still, I feel sorry for her. She sent me a lovely card when Ben died."

Penny remained silent. She wasn't ready to admit her terrible part in the dissolution of the Brownes' marriage so, despite the awful emergence of guilt, she managed a smile before inquiring as to whether or not her friend wanted more coffee.

Later Penny was sitting in her dentist's with a gap-tooth smile and a serious hangover. Silently, while flicking through endless pages of ancient magazines, she promised not to mix her drinks anymore. It just wasn't worth it. The woman opposite smiled. She returned her smile then retracted it, conscious of the gaping hole in her mouth.

"Cap?" the woman queried.

"Yeah, a cap."

"Hmmmmm. I have false teeth myself." She loosened them in her mouth to demonstrate.

"Oh!"

"Eating a steak's a pain in the face."

"Right."

"I miss them all the same."

"Right," Penny reiterated, not sure whether the woman was referring to steak or teeth and not really caring.

The nurse called the steak-deprived woman in for consultation, leaving Penny alone. She picked up a magazine and flicked. *Boring.* She dropped it and picked up another, again boring, so she looked around for a while—this too was boring so she returned to the magazines. It was then that she picked up a gossip-ridden magazine that normally she wouldn't have dreamed of reading. She sighed as she looked at the singer, Mia Johnson, on the front page of a rag, crying. She read the article, which speculated as to why the diva was so desperate, with shaking hands—and not just because she was hung over but because in that picture behind Mia Johnson stood the ever-elusive Sam. She thought about bolting but the gap in her gob forbade anything so radical.

Once her tooth was fixed she drove straight home and went online. *Who is this man?* At last she had found a story worth reporting.

★ ★ ★

Saying good-bye to his kids was always hard, but this time Ivan didn't experience the same terrible trauma. This time he had someone standing by him as he waved his kids away and that meant something. Sienna had come to mean something. And he knew it had only been a matter of weeks and he knew that she was eight years younger, and he knew that except for Mary those around him felt him too vulnerable to be serious, but they were wrong—he had never felt stronger. He put his arm around Sienna as he watched his children disappear behind frosted glass and she snuggled in tight.

"They're nice kids," she said.

"They are, even if they were little bastards to you," he admitted with a smile. Chris had practically ignored her and Justy had followed his lead, and when they weren't ignoring her they were either viewing her suspiciously or replying to her attempts at communication sulkily and sarcastically.

"They'll get used to me," she said, laughing.

"They have plenty of time," he ventured.

"Yeah, they do."

Ivan sniffed a happy sniff and they made their way to the car park.

Chapter Eighteen

Digging for Digging's Sake

It had been two weeks since the kiss that never happened. In that time both Mary and Sam had bumped into one another and behaved politely, embarrassed and yet maintaining the facade of normality that comes with age. This polite distance was annoying to both parties, who, although unwilling to truly admit to any feelings above or beyond friendship, couldn't help but miss one another. Sam was particularly freaked and for many reasons, the first of these being his near inability to control his impulse to kiss Mary. *What the hell was that all about?* Not to mention his suffocating jealousy of Denis. *So she slept with the guy—big deal.* Her sex life, now revealed, had been a shock. Ivan had painted her as some sort of sexual recluse—he had believed her to have been celibate and all the while she was boffing some traveling musician. *People never cease to amaze.* He worried that he was attaching feelings to this woman in a bid to escape from himself. A new relationship was not advisable within the first year after rehab. *I've got enough to deal with.* But there was something else, something he wouldn't admit to—and ego related. Mary didn't pay attention to him the way other women did. Sam often observed women looking at him. It was difficult not to, they made it so obvious. Some women just stared and giggled in his general direction or raised their voices in an attempt to gain his attention. Others grabbed at him and hung themselves from him, patting his ass while making suggestions into his ear, usually while drunk and at their least attractive. Other men envied the strange effect he had on women, most especially his ability to attract the opposite sex by merely entering a room. Sadly for Sam, the endless stream of female passivity had bored him for many years. Like any man, for him the best part of that initial attraction was the hunt, but he'd had no need to hunt since his late teens. It was rare that he wasn't the most beautiful man in the room, and women were not ashamed to let him know of their interest in no uncertain terms. He wasn't stupid enough to believe that they were interested in him as a person. He had long ago come to terms with the fact that most women were far more interested in how he looked than in anything he had to say. Sam was one of the few men on earth who could identify with a Playboy model. Of course, Mia wasn't like most of the women that had crossed his path. She had seen past his face and loved him but she didn't know him, not like Mary. *But how the hell could Mary know me?* And he knew her. *I just don't know why.*

After two weeks of their pussyfooting around one another, he was relieved when she asked him to meet her for dinner and he had agreed.

Mary arrived at the restaurant early. She was a stickler

for punctuality, always overestimating the length of time it would take to get from one place to another. After years of arriving between ten to twenty minutes early, she had learned to ensure that she always carried reading material. She ordered a glass of house red from Roni Shea, who was desperate to talk about the Browne breakup.

"So you've heard nothing?" she said, eyeing Mary while tapping her pencil against her order book in a slightly menacing way.

"Nothing more than you."

"It's amazing—I mean, the child is six months old. If she was to find out, you'd think it would have been sooner," she pointed out astutely.

"Well, maybe it was the girl—what's her name?"

"Tracy Whelan, and no, it definitely wasn't Tracy. Bridget attacked her after Mass on Sunday and gave her a black eye and Lisa Harmon says she knocked out a front tooth." She was nodding animatedly, speaking in hushed tones.

"Ah well," said Mary, pretending to be bored, afraid to be caught gossiping by her neighbor.

"It all happened in Sneem. The parish priest had to pull them apart. Apparently, Tracy Whelan gave as good as she got. Of course, it's sad for the little one." Roni's voice softened as did her eyes, suggesting she truly cared.

"Yeah," Mary agreed, "the poor child."

Suddenly, Roni became awkward and businesslike as though she'd just remembered that Mary had lost her own child and despite the passage of time she was embarrassed at having been so insensitive as to bring up the subject of a child. She reddened slightly and repeated that the house red was a good choice and then made her escape, leaving Mary to once again wonder whether or not she'd ever be allowed to move on. Just then the door opened and Sam entered, washed and making an immediate impression on the women seated as well as the girl behind the counter. Mary's head was in her book. The young girl blushed and stuttered a welcome. He pointed toward Mary to suggest he'd found his date. The young girl blinked as though she found it difficult to assimilate that the living embodiment of Barbie's Ken was eating with Mary of the Sorrows. The women in the room watched him approach and Mary put down her book and smiled. He didn't lean in for a kiss and she hadn't expected him to. Despite their recent hiccup, to the outside observer they seemed easy with one another, and when Roni was apprised of the situation by the front-of-house stutterer, she made it her mission to discover the nature of their business together because they all agreed that surely to God it wasn't romantic.

After a glass of wine Mary was still not relaxed but hoping for a pleasant friendly evening. She was glad that Sam had agreed to meet her but it soon became apparent that he was feeling as tense as she was. After her initial feeling of utter humiliation, she had come to realize that it was actually a good thing that Denis had arrived in her kitchen when he did, for surely if he had not she would have jumped the man whose hand had electrified hers and whose close proximity had set some sort of fire in her, and that would have been a bad thing. It would have been bad because although to some she was odd, she wasn't blind. During the time that Sam had lived in her small town it was impossible not to notice the effect her new friend had on women and she didn't want him to mistake her for those who fell so willingly at his feet. She just wanted to know him because he was more than pretty. His eyes betrayed a troubled soul and possibly a fractured heart. Being broken, she had the ability to see it in others, despite their attempts to hide behind their various facades. She was drawn to damaged souls like a suicidal moth to a wing-burning flame. She wanted to help him. She didn't know how or why or even if she could, but something inside her told her to try. She also knew he wouldn't be around for much longer and that their time together would be short. Friendship would be enough.

"I'm glad you called," he said while glancing at the menu.

"I'm thrilled you came." She smiled and looked up at him. "Besides, I wanted to apologize."

"You have nothing to be sorry for. I'm the one who invaded your space."

"Space invader," she mumbled, and laughed nervously at her own joke.

"That was not funny," he said but his eyes betrayed his amusement.

"Frig off!"

"Can I ask you something?"

"What?"

"Well, I know what knickers are, but what in the hell is a frig?"

"Oh, it's a replacement word for *fuck*." She smiled.

He nodded. "Why not just say what you mean?"

"Well, I used to—that is, until Nora Donnelly asked my three-year-old if he wanted an ice pop and he told her to go fuck herself."

He laughed and she laughed with him.

"I stopped then and after that just never got out of the habit of avoiding words like that."

It was still awkward. They sat in silence reading their menus for a minute or two.

"You use the term 'Are you kidding me' at least once a day," Mary said out of nowhere.

"I do."

"Yip." She nodded.

"Does it bug you?" he asked.

"A little bit," she admitted.

He laughed. "I'll do my best to correct that."

"Don't." She smiled. "Nobody likes perfect."

They laughed together and any remaining ice thawed. He turned to look for the waitress, who appeared within a second of his turning. Later, over dessert, they talked about movies. Sam wasn't really into movies but it was something to talk about that deflected from his misguided past and Mary liked movies.

"Robert and I saw *St. Elmo's Fire* eight times." She smiled, remembering how they had once planned to move to America based on their love affair with that movie.

Sam was amused. "You were going to move to the States based on one movie?"

"Well, that and a photography course at NYU." She sighed. "It would have been a good course."

"You could still do it."

"Yeah, right," she scoffed. "I'd fit in beautifully."

"You would."

"I was being sarcastic."

"And I was ignoring your sarcasm."

"What about you? Why didn't you follow your dream?" she asked.

"How do you know I didn't?" he asked.

"Do you play guitar for a living?"

"No."

"Well, then?" She shrugged.

"You're so sure that's what I wanted?"

"I am."

They sat in silence for a moment.

"Sam. What did you do?"

"I told you, I was in management."

"Management of what?"

"Management of people."

"OK"—she nodded—"don't tell me. But whether you like it or not, you can't remain a mystery forever."

"Just give me some time," he said honestly.

She nodded and smiled.

Their night ended on her wall. They sat looking out onto a low tide of black water lit by sparse streetlights and uninhabited stranded boats.

"I've made so many mistakes," Sam said from nowhere, taking Mary by surprise.

"We all make mistakes."

"Not like me."

"We all make mistakes," she repeated.

He smiled at her but remained silent.

"Are you free tomorrow?" she asked.

"For what?"

She smiled. "If you can be mysterious, so can I."

He sighed and they watched the water for a while.

★ ★ ★

Penny had spent two weeks locked indoors. She was working on her own assignments, picking up the slack from the Cork correspondent and investing the rest of her time on personal research. She told Mary that she wouldn't be around for a few weeks and Mary didn't question her—after all, she was often busy. Mary must have wondered what kept her off the phone all the same. No matter how busy she had been before she had always found time for a quick chat, but even Penny could see that, over the past while, she and her best pal had been drifting. This was her own fault—after Adam had left she had pushed Mary away. She wasn't sure why and she missed her friend, but sometimes, despite her terrible loneliness, it was easier to be alone. In those two weeks she spent more time working than drinking, managing to hand in her assignments on time and with little need for correction.

Each evening she would sit at her computer spending her time on Google. It was incredible how many times Sam's name came up. It was easy to find out he was A and R. It was easy to trace the companies he'd worked for and it was easy to find out how many famous acts he'd discovered. The relationship he had with Mia was not so simple to determine. Penny knew that he was her A-and-R man, the man who had discovered her and groomed her, but looking at that picture she was sure there was more to it. But Google wasn't telling. Mia's relationship with Sam was never made public so Penny was forced to dig a little deeper. So she started at the beginning. She spoke to David the songwriter in Sam's second band, Limbs, and he filled her in on Sam's arrogance and his propensity for violence. He spilled his bitterness, deriding Sam's contempt for the band's direction. Penny would later quote him in her article and yet for the sake of credibility she chose not to mention that David Lindman, formerly of the band Limbs, was working as a distributor for a large toy company, having never actually made it in the music business.

In something approaching a miracle, Sophia Sheffer picked up the phone at the first ring. Since losing her record deal at the hands of a vindictive Sam, she had fallen on hard times. However, she was slowly recovering and recently had scored a hit with the *The Rocky Horror Show* on Broadway. The blame for her failure as a recording artist predictably lay at Sam's feet. She could have recovered her sales if given the chance—at least that's what she desperately believed. The fact that she hadn't been able to get another record deal since she had been dropped or write any good new material so as to catch the eye of an all-important hit-making producer would not be discussed. Instead, Sophia was determined that Penny would paint her as Sam Sullivan's unfortunate victim. After all, she had left him for a promising record deal and as soon as he became head of A and R at her record company she had been instantly dropped. It was an easy link to make although further research revealed that Sophia was only one of ten acts dropped that year and of those acts she had achieved the second-lowest sales. She spoke to Joe Merrigan, Sam's first A-and-R boss, and he in turn gave her his daughter Frankie's phone number. They both made compelling interviewees, Joe's disgust at his right-hand man's defection and Frankie's heartbreak still evident after so many years. The obviously fragile-minded woman's attempt at her own life would make for gripping reading. After much finagling she managed to speak to Leland on the pretext of having some information about Sam that he would find interesting.

As it turned out it was Leland who gave away Sam's relationship with Mia but only after Penny took a calculated risk.

"I think he'd really like to go back," she lied.

"I wouldn't have that junkie back if he was the last A-and-R guy left with ears," Leland drawled. Of course, he didn't mean it. Leland would have taken Sam back in an instant despite hating the asshole because Leland knew that money talked and a guy like Sam, as fucked up as he was, was money in the bank.

Junkie. He was a junkie? What kind of junkie? Play it cool. Play it cool.

"He's clean now and he misses Mia," she ventured.

"So?" Leland said.

"So I think he wants her back," Penny said as though she knew what she was talking about.

Leland laughed. "Forget it. He'll never get her back. He had four years to do the right thing. He blew it."

"You're so sure?" *Oh my God, this is gold!*

"Listen, honey, I know you're from some small town in some small country and he's your neighbor and your friend and you're trying to help 'cause you think that you know this guy, but you don't. Nobody knows him. Not Mia, not me and certainly not you."

"So he was a coke addict. All he wants is another chance." She needed to confirm what kind of junkie he was so she ventured a guess, knowing she was about to be hung up on.

"Coke," he laughed. "Is that what he told you?"

"Yeah, and I have no reason to doubt him," she said, injecting enough hurt into her voice to illicit from his ego the truth.

"Ha! Try heroin. The guy's a loser and my advice to you is to stay clear."

"So what you're telling me is that Mia Johnson had a long-term relationship with a heroin addict?" she said with glee.

"Excuse me?" he said, somewhat alarmed at the change in her tone.

"You're right, I am from a small town in a small country, but it looks like I'm going to be the one to break Mia's sordid love story. Maybe you could pass on my number just in case she wants to comment. After all, these revelations can have a life of their own. If he was a junkie, maybe she was too. Maybe she drove him to drugs, or was she the angel who saved him?"

"You're swimming out of your depth," Leland warned.

Penny laughed. "And yet I'm not the one sinking," she said before hanging up. She poured herself a glass of vodka with a shaking hand and pondered whether or not she would hear from the lady herself.

★ ★ ★

The sun was out and Sam had taken to playing his guitar in the back garden. He had woken with the idea for a melody that refused to go away, so instead of fighting it he spent the morning working out the chords, and like Sister Sledge many years before he was lost in music.

Mary popped up from behind the wall, scaring the crap out of him.

"Nice song," she said. "What is it?"

"Nothing." He laughed.

" 'Nothing.' I like it. It has a nice ring to it."

He laughed her off.

"Are you ready?" she asked. "For my surprise trip?"

He put the guitar down. "I'll meet you out front."

Once inside the car, they began a trip which took them across the bridge and eight kilometers down a narrow winding road. Once out of the car, they had to walk through a rain-soaked field of grazing cows.

She refused to give him any indication of where they were or what they were doing until they reached what could only be described as the burned-out shell of a stone hut which housed two chewing donkeys.

She stopped and took a photo.

"Well?" he said.

"This was your gran's house." She smiled.

"You're kidding me?" he said, his voice laced in awe.

"Of course, it's buggered now, but I found an old map in the library and this article about the fire. I'm sorry about that, by the way." She nudged the map into his hand.

He was still busy staring at the remnants of his grandmother's family home.

"How did you know where to look?" he asked.

"You're joking, aren't you?" she laughed. "You mentioned your gran's maiden name to Ivan, who mentioned it to me. I spoke to my dad, who spoke to Jerry Letter, whose ancient ex-neighbor Dick Dogs had known your grandmother's brother David. I researched the rest in the local library."

Sam spun much like Maria on a German mountaintop, surveying his ancestral home.

"I didn't think there would be anything left," he said.

"I was pretty surprised myself," she admitted. "And look over here!" she called while walking toward a smattering of tall trees.

He followed wide-eyed.

"Someone thought to put up a plaque. It must have been your granduncle Tim, since he was the only one to survive."

Sam read the plaque.

> AT THIS PLACE CALLED HOME,
> SIOBHÁN AND COLM BASKIN,
> MOTHER AND FATHER TO FIVE,
> REST WITH THEIR SONS
> VINCENT, JACKIE AND DAVID.
> THEY WILL BE FOREVER MISSED
> BY TIM AND LENA.

A lot of text followed but it was in Gaelic.

"Lena Baskin was my grandmother's name," he said to himself.

"So your grandmother was an unmarried mother?" Mary said in a tone that suggested she was slightly impressed. Sam seemed confused and a little horrified. "No, what do you mean?" he asked.

"Don't people change their names when they get married?" Mary replied, a little pissed that he seemed to recoil at the notion of his granny being a single mother.

"Ah." Sam nodded. "She kept her maiden name; she said it was all she had left of home." He laughed. "An unmarried mother!"

"I was an unmarried mother." Mary reminded him.

"Sorry."

"So you should be."

Sam thought it best to move on quickly. "So can you translate?" he'd asked. She smiled triumphantly.

"I can. I had to look it up. I was always rubbish at Irish." She read the transcription: " 'May God grant you always a sunbeam to warm you . . .' "

Before she knew it he joined in:

" '. . . a moonbeam to charm you, a sheltering angel so nothing can harm you, laughter to cheer you, faithful friends near you. And whenever you pray, Heaven to hear you."

He smiled. "It was a blessing my grandmother's father used to whisper to her each night before sleep." He spoke with a voice that was soft and coming from a faraway place, when he was a boy.

"A family blessing. That makes sense." She nodded as though something had clicked into place. "It's a bit of a weird prayer for the dead," she noted while taking a photograph.

"I can't believe you did this," he said, touched by all the trouble she'd gone to.

"Me either," she sighed. "Usually I'm pretty lazy."

Later, while walking to the car, he told her the story of how his great-grandparents and their three eldest sons had perished in a fire a year after his grandmother's father had waved her good-bye. Tim had returned from a dance to find his family dead and his home destroyed. He'd left the town within weeks of their funerals. It was only when he died of a bad case of pneumonia and his wife, a Cavan woman, had written to Sam's grandmother that she was informed of the demise of her entire family. It turned out that for the six years after their death and before his own he had written to her in their name, pretending that all was well.

"My God," Mary had said, a little overwhelmed, "why?"

"My grandmother used to say that her brother had thought it best to carry the pain of two."

She was silent until they got to the car. "Let's open a bottle of wine when we get home."

"You celebrating?"

"No, but I think it's only fair to raise a glass to Tim."

He nodded. "I'd like that."

Chapter Nineteen

I Hate to Say I Told You So

Ivan went straight home as Sienna had promised she'd call for a late supper at the end of her shift. The place was a mess and he wanted to ensure a certain level of respectability was achieved before her arrival. He cleaned, using the hiding and stuffing system that he had perfected as a teenager. As long as Sienna didn't attempt to open any type of cupboard, she would believe him to be a neater and therefore better soul than he actually was. He spent a maximum of two minutes dusting after banging the large rug against the back wall as opposed to vacuuming. Mrs. O'Connor of the O'Connor Murphys would be annoyed by his shoddy attempts at maintaining her high standard of cleanliness in her two-week absence. And although he would be chastised by his cleaning lady much as he had been chastised by his mother many years before, he was most definitely looking forward to her return.

He was sitting by his window, reading that day's paper while listening to Dave Fanning debate the hundred greatest rock stars on 2FM. A hot tea, an interesting article and AC/DC's "Thunderstruck" suggested a good night lay ahead. The phone rang as Brian Johnson was beginning the second verse. *Ah Christ!*

He was surprised to hear his ex-wife on the line. Her tone was decidedly frost free.

"Do you have a minute?"

"Of course," he said, a little alarmed, momentarily believing she was about to discuss his budding relationship with Sienna, and, if so, a part of his brain prepared itself to be annoyed. After all, what right had she to talk to him about his relationships?

"The kids had such a good time this Easter," she said.

Here we go. But her voice sounded more relaxed than it had in months. She almost sounded like his wife.

"Justy's cheeks are still rosy. I'd forgotten what that looked like."

He found himself smiling. "She ate me out of house and home."

"She'd live on your mother's brown bread alone," she said with warmth. "And Chris, he's been talking about that salmon he caught with you since."

"It was a big salmon."

"I'm glad you've met someone," she said out of nowhere.

"Thanks," he replied.

"I'm really sorry about everything."

"Right," he said, which was stupid, but he was unprepared for kindness.

She laughed, knowing her ex-husband well. "I wish you both the best."

"Thanks," he said, and there was something about her tone and the conversation that made him consider asking her once more whether or not there was anything wrong. But suddenly his wife's voice changed to something approaching fear.

"I have to go," she said.

"Are you OK?" he asked, but she was gone.

It was a minute before he hung up the phone. The conversation resonated as it was the first light conversation he'd had with his wife since she walked out on him, but also he'd found it a little disturbing. *What the hell is going on over there?*

Sienna arrived a little after nine. They settled together on the sofa.

"What's on?" she asked.

"Me."

"I was talking about TV," she said before blowing her nose.

"I was talking about me." Ivan laughed.

"Will you still want to be with me when the first thing you don't want to do is jump me?"

"I can't see that happening." He smiled.

Sienna belted him. "It will."

"And I will," he said, which was a smoother response than she had anticipated.

His pants were around his ankles when the phone rang again. *Ah Christ.*

★ ★ ★

The plane landed in Gatwick just after 8:00 AM. Ivan was up and out of his seat before the seat belt light flickered off. Sienna grabbed his hand and squeezed it.

"It's going to be fine," she said in an attempt to soothe him, but instead it brought tears of anger to his eyes. He held them off with a giant will and went about retrieving their hand luggage. He was exhausted, having not slept a wink since the call. Sienna insisted on driving the rental car and he relented on the basis that he didn't have time to argue. He called his daughter from the passenger seat.

"Justy, are you all right, love?"

"I'm OK, Dad."

"Where's your brother?"

"Beside me."

"Put him on the phone, love."

"Hi, Dad."

"Hi, son. Are you all right?"

"We're fine."

"Your mother?"

"They said she's sleeping. I haven't seen her but I think it's bad, Dad." His voice broke on the word *bad*.

"I'm on my way, Chris. I'm nearly there."

"OK, Dad."

He hung up the phone and looked at Sienna. "How could this happen?"

She didn't have the answer—instead, she told him to open the map so that they could take the right exit and get to the hospital as quickly as possible.

A momentary smile crossed his lips. He liked her no-nonsense approach to an emergency and would be forever

277

grateful for her help as he wasn't sure he would have coped as well alone.

They arrived at the hospital just over an hour later. Justine and Chris were in the family room, which the nurse directed him to. Sienna told him she'd get coffee and left him to visit with his traumatized children. When he entered the small room Justy was lying across the couch and asleep. Chris had his back to him, staring at something in the middle distance.

"Chris!" he whispered, and his little boy turned to him with tears streaming.

"I'm here, son," he said, hugging him tightly, "I'm here now."

His son clung to him, his face wet against Ivan's chest.

Justine woke. "Dad!" she said, rubbing her eyes.

"There she is," he said, his voice light with a hint of happy.

She smiled and Chris moved over so that she could share in their father's warmth. "I missed you, Dad. I really missed you."

"That's all over now," he replied, stroking her hair.

They were interrupted by a policeman who'd been assigned to the case. Ivan told his children to stay put and he left the room to stand in the corridor to discuss his ex-wife's domestic disturbance.

"What's happening?" Ivan asked.

"By the time we got there your ex-wife had been badly beaten. And as you know, she was unconscious. Her boyfriend was gone, but with information provided to us by your son we tracked him down to his local pub. He's in custody. Obviously, we can't hold him unless your ex-wife is willing to press charges."

"She's still my wife," Ivan mumbled.

"OK." The man nodded.

"Have you spoken to her?" Ivan asked.

"So far she's pretty uncommunicative. She's sleeping now, but when she wakes maybe you could speak with her."

Ivan sighed. He doubted that anything he had to say would assist but he promised to give it a try. The policeman walked away.

Ivan spotted Sienna sitting in a chair in the corridor drinking coffee and reading the newspaper. He waved at her and she smiled back before shooing him away. He went back into the family room to be faced with his two hungry kids. They were all in the canteen with Sienna eating chips, sausages and beans when the doctor tracked them down. Again Ivan went into the corridor to speak in hushed tones.

"Well, she's got three broken ribs, a broken arm and a cracked skull."

"Jesus Christ!" was all Ivan could bring himself to say.

"She's lucky she wasn't killed."

"I understand. Can I see her?"

"She's very upset," the doctor warned.

"I'm sure she is," Ivan noted. "I'm only here to help."

"OK. Follow me."

Despite having been apprised of her injuries, Ivan wasn't prepared for the reality. His wife's face was reminiscent of a distorted, deflating purple balloon. Her left eye was swollen shut and her lower lip was bloody and stitched. Her arm wasn't in a cast—instead, it was bandaged with metal bars piercing her skin. Her right eye was bloodshot from the little he could see of it.

He couldn't help raising his hands to his mouth.

"Oh, Norma!"

His ex-wife's right eye started to leak and he wasn't sure if it was tears or blood. She tried to talk.

"Don't speak," he said, "you don't have to say anything."

She shook her head slightly. He pulled over a chair and sat close to her bed. He held her hand. "Mary warned me. I should have come to see you for myself. I was too busy with . . ."

Norma raised her good hand and placed a finger gently to her damaged mouth. "Shh."

"I'll murder him," he promised.

"He never laid a hand on the kids," she said, her words resonating with pain both physical and mental.

"I know."

"I'm sorry," she whispered.

"I'm sorry too, love."

He stayed with her until she slept.

★ ★ ★

Ivan woke from a broken sleep at dawn. Sienna was sleeping soundly so he got up and moved across the room as quietly as was possible. He managed to make it as far as the dressing table before stubbing his toe—his yell was muted and he only hopped once.

"I'm awake," she said with eyes closed and a grin on her face.

"Sorry," he said, sitting down on the bed with his foot in his hand, "that feckin' hurt."

Sienna stretched and luxuriated in her distension like

a comfortable cat. "The bed's hard," she noted, and Ivan agreed. "Have you checked on the kids?"

He confirmed that he'd looked in on them in the room next door a number of times during the night.

"They'll be OK," she told him while hugging his waist.

"I know," he agreed, although worry continued to etch his face. "I'll have to take them home." He turned to her so that she was looking up at him.

"I know."

"I mean them all. Norma too."

"I know," she repeated.

"She can't stay here. She's got nothing here," he said by way of explanation, but Sienna didn't need an explanation and discouraged him from continuing by pressing her finger to his lips.

"You don't have to explain."

"I don't love her anymore," he said.

"Good." She grinned.

"Good," he repeated, nodding happily.

She lifted the covers. "Now get in here," she said, pointing at the bed, "and then get in here," she laughed, pointing at herself, and Ivan, despite all his problems, was only too happy to oblige.

★ ★ ★

Sienna took Ivan's shell-shocked kids to the cinema so that Ivan could visit with their mother. Norma seemed a little better than the previous day. Her lip was less swollen and her speech less impeded. She didn't seem to be in as much pain, the morphine having fully kicked in. Her mental state had improved too. She didn't appear to be constantly on the verge of tears. She'd even smiled at him, or so it appeared, but behind the swelling and stitches it was hard to tell. They had talked about how it had all started. She told him about how many times she had been beaten. She gave him reasons as to why she hadn't confided in him. He didn't understand any of the reasons given but he didn't say so because it was unnecessary and Ivan was never one to enter into an unnecessary argument. She reiterated that her boyfriend had never laid a hand on the kids. Ivan had soothed her when she became distressed while recounting her recent and most brutal experience. Later he brought in two coffees. He helped her to drink hers by holding it to the less damaged side of her mouth because her broken ribs and fractured arm prevented her from doing it for herself. She gave up after a few sips.

"Your doctor says you'll be fit to travel in a week's time. I spoke with Dr. Macken and he said he can get you into the regional in Cork for any follow-up appointments for your arm—"

She put her good arm up as though to halt him. He stopped talking.

"Dr. Macken? Ivan, I'm not going back to Ireland."

The shock on his face was clear to see.

"What made you think I would go back to Kenmare?" she asked, seemingly as shocked at his assumption as he was at her vetoing the idea of returning home.

"I don't understand," he admitted, scratching invisible sea salt from his hair.

"Ivan, I won't be going back to that house, but we are staying in the UK." She attempted to meet his eyes.

"Well, where are you going to live?" he asked, exasperated.

"That's my problem," she said.

"What?" he all but roared.

"We'll be fine," she said sternly.

"No, Norma, you won't be fine. You're in bits. You've nowhere to live. You've got some lunatic trying to kill you and you've got my kids." He was trying to be calm but his face was becoming flushed.

"I'm tired," she said when he sat down. "Please leave."

He got up from the chair. "This isn't over, Norma," he promised before leaving her to her own insane thoughts.

★ ★ ★

The kids were next door in the hotel playing with an Xbox he'd bought earlier that afternoon. Sienna sat cross-legged on the bed listening intently to his rant while also attempting to allay his increasing frustration.

"What the hell is wrong with her?" he asked.

"Just give her time," Sienna directed.

"To do what?" he shouted.

"She's had a shocking experience. You need to give her breathing space," she counseled calmly.

"I gave her breathing space and she nearly got herself killed," he said, lowering his tone in an attempt to match the frequency of his girlfriend's.

"You're not her father. You can't just drag her home."

Ivan sat down on the bed beside Sienna and took her hand.

"I know. But whatever she does," he said with great resolve, "I'm taking the kids home."

"You've spoken to your solicitor?" Sienna asked, taking him in her arms.

"In the car. They need to come home with or without their mother."

"Is that what you want? To take them without their mother?"

"Of course not. They've been through enough this year. But she's leaving me with no choice," he sighed.

"Talk to her," she advised.

"I have!" he said with frustration building once more.

"No, you haven't. You presumed she was coming home and when she told you she wasn't you went mental, and going mental is not talking."

"So what do you suggest?" he asked, burying his head in his hands.

"Look at the situation from her point of view."

"I am. She's fucked. Excuse my French. She needs to come home."

"She left her husband, her hometown, her friends and her family for someone who ended up beating her and terrorizing her kids. If it was me I would find it hard to face people." She shrugged, something he noticed she did when she was talking sense.

Ivan nodded. "You think she's afraid to come home," he mumbled, about to scratch his head.

"I think she just needs a little reassurance," Sienna said, taking his hand away from his hair.

Of course Sienna was right. Norma did want to go home. While Sienna talked with Ivan, Norma lay in a hospital bed contemplating a bleak future. There was nothing but misery for her in the UK. She had desperately wanted to go home for months but how could she? How could she return to the hometown that had watched her walk out on her husband for a man she barely knew? How could she return with her tail between her legs, beaten and broken by that same man? How could she ever walk through the streets of Kenmare with her head held high? People would say that she was selfish. People would say that she deserved what she got. People would say that she was an unfit mother to have allowed her children to be subjected to months of witnessing such violence. And all those people would be right.

Ivan took the kids with him for the evening visit. They were subdued in their mother's presence. They spoke quietly as though afraid that a loud noise would break her. They maintained a distance from the wires and protruding steel, but she smiled through the discomfort while insisting she was fine and that everything was going to be all right. Ivan sent the kids to the canteen so that they could talk, but first he offered to help his wife correct an awkwardly positioned pillow. Norma agreed to accept his assistance and was grateful. He placed his phone on her locker and just then it rang. Mary's name appeared. He silenced the call while noticing Norma's fearful expression. Ivan's phone was a link to all those who judged her.

"It was Mary. She's been worried about you," he said.

She remained silent. It was obvious she didn't believe him.

"We weren't happy, were we?" he asked.

"No," she mumbled.

"No." He nodded. "But I would have stayed with you until the end."

She sighed and raised her hand as if to defend herself.

"You were right to walk away. I'm glad you did what you did. You knew something was wrong and you were brave enough to make a change." He smiled at her widened eyes.

She wasn't expecting gratitude. Norma's eyes sprang a leak.

"Marriages break up, Norma. And no matter what is said or done, everyone knows there are two sides to the story." He tried to hold her hand but she pulled away.

"Easy for you to say. You're not the bitch who broke up her family!" Tears ran down her swollen face. "You're not the one who got what she deserved."

"You know, my father always says a small town is like a big family. It doesn't matter what you do or where you go, you are always welcome home. People still care, Norma."

She remained silent. A minute or maybe two passed, then Ivan stood and put on his jacket. He leaned down to kiss the small area of forehead which remained undamaged. Then he paused, looking down at her. "You have a lot of thinking to do," he said then, "but you need to know."

She looked at him quizzically.

"I'm taking the kids."

She nodded.

"I'm taking them home for good."

Her head stopped nodding and her eyes started filling.

"I didn't fight you before because I believed that they were best off with you. I was wrong. If you choose to stay here, you'll be alone."

Tears slid down her face but she was in no shape to

argue. "I thought it was all a little too good to be true," she mumbled.

"I meant what I said. I'm glad you left. It nearly killed me but I'm glad. This isn't about punishing you. It's about our children. Deep down you know that to be true. You've been hurt enough, Norma. You're in a terrible place but you'll make your way back, and when you do we'll be waiting."

"Don't take them, Ivan!" she begged.

"I have to," he said before turning his back on his broken wife and walking away to the sounds of her cries.

Outside he wiped away his own tears. *I'm so sorry, love.*

Chapter Twenty

Beauty and the Beast

It was a beautiful spring day. The kind of day that in-
stills a sense of well-being in even the most troubled
soul. Bright green grass surrounded healthy brown barks
and deep green leaves grew on branches that spread out
against a translucent blue sky. Light shone down on the
pretty town and with it came a kind of warmth that was
more than the effect of global warming.

Sam had started his day with a walk down by the back
of the pier. He lay on the grass and stared into the blue
sky with a light heart. He had come to love this little
place. He had come to feel a part of it. No journey would
go uninterrupted by the sounds of "Hello!" or the question "How are you?" No distance was traveled without
a beep or a wave or a hat being tipped in his direction.
He was known. He was liked. And even though he had
not made those around him aware of his past, nor was he
ever pressed for those details, he was no longer a stranger

to the people of Kenmare because for the most part they didn't really care about where he'd come from or who he used to be. They only cared about who he was in the now. Gossip mostly favors the present tense and that was something he was grateful for. He had thought about coming clean with Mary. He figured she deserved to know the truth. She knew he was hiding and he knew it was only a matter of time before his past would catch up to his present. The problem with enlightening her was a simple one. He had grown used to not hating himself and it felt good. That said, he was always on the verge of and one memory away from feeling sick inside. At home he was surrounded by those he had disappointed. They stood before him like mirrors reflecting his every fault and flaw. Here it was different, he had a clean slate. If he told Mary the truth then she would become just another mirror he'd have to escape. He didn't want that. He couldn't bear the idea of losing sight of her, and not because he was foolish enough to believe in the possibility of a soul mate. Neither was he stupid enough to think that because his skin tingled in her presence it meant anything other than physical attraction. His senses were often before heightened in the presence of a woman he wished to invade. But he would never invade Mary. Instead, he yearned to crawl inside her because someone unseen was whispering to him that in her he would find home.

★ ★ ★

It was such a beautiful spring day that Mary booked herself a facial. Spring was a time for buds, lambing, blue skies and exfoliation. She was booked in for midday. Of course she was fifteen minutes early, having miscalculated the time it would take to find parking on Main Street.

Patty Winslow was sitting by the window reading a well-worn copy of *The Canterbury Tales* while enjoying a complimentary cappuccino.

"Hello, dear," she said once she'd fixed her glasses on her nose.

"Hi, Patty." Mary smiled.

"A little restoration?" Patty suggested.

"Something like that."

Patty dropped her book before sitting back to look at Mary.

"What?" Mary asked, a little uncomfortable under scrutiny.

"You appear tired."

"I haven't been sleeping," Mary admitted.

"I haven't seen dark circles the like of that since Marianne Faithfull was a teenager in love." She smiled.

"Well, I'm afraid it's not love keeping me up all night," Mary laughed.

"And of that you are sure?"

Mary sighed. "We're just friends, Patty."

Patty laughed to herself. The Italian girl at the counter told Mary in broken English that the beautician was running a little late and asked if she would like coffee. Mary asked for a cappuccino to the Italian girl's utter disgust. She looked at her watch before shaking her head while making her way back to an unseen kitchen.

"Who is she?" Mary asked.

"Ah, the lovely Lucia!" Patty said, amused. "Yes, you see, it's after midday. Ordering what is essentially a breakfast drink upsets the poor girl's sensibilities. Italians take coffee drinking very seriously."

"Really?" Mary pondered.

"Oh yes." Patty smiled. "It really is a wonder how Italy is not now nor ever has been a superpower."

Mary laughed. She couldn't help but enjoy her upper-class British friend's acerbic wit.

Lucia arrived back with Mary's coffee. Mary introduced herself and welcomed the girl to Kenmare. Lucia melted and Mary's ignorance was immediately forgiven. "I come to learn," she said.

Mary nodded. "You're doing great."

Lucia raised an eyebrow. "Doing great?" she repeated.

" 'Well,' " Mary ventured.

"OK," said Lucia. "Yes." She smiled. "Nails?" She pointed to her own hand.

"No but thanks."

"OK," she said with a smile before walking away.

Patty grinned. "You have such a way with people."

Mary nudged her.

"So how is Ivan?" Patty asked.

"He's fine." Mary smiled. "He's great, in fact. His kids are home and, despite that, things seem to be going well with Sienna so it's all good."

Patty nodded. "Good."

"It is," Mary agreed.

"And Norma?"

"She's still in the hospital and after that he doesn't know."

"Of course she'll come home," Patty said. "Where else would she go?"

"I don't know. Either way I hope she finds some peace."

"And you, my dear?"

"And me?"

"Have you found peace?"

"I haven't given up," Mary answered with a lying smile.

"Any day now," Patty said, winking, "any day now." She patted Mary's arm. "You just be careful not to miss out. You keep eyes and heart wide open."

Enjoying Patty's honesty, Mary took a chance. "Patty?"

"Yes, dear."

"You and my dad—are you together?" she asked with a grin.

Patty smiled to herself. "If we are then I'm most certain that neither of us would ever admit to it."

"Why?" Mary asked.

"Because, my dear, mystery is half the fun."

Mary laughed.

It was then that Gemma emerged from room 1 with Penny trailing behind her. Gemma apologized to both ladies for the delay. She told Patty to make herself comfortable in room 2 while she took money from Penny. Tina would be taking care of Mary but she was just freshening up room 3. Once payment was received, Gemma scurried into room 2, where Patty now waited.

Penny sat beside Mary.

"Well?" Penny said.

"Well?" Mary smiled despite being shocked by Penny's appearance.

"Are you well?"

"I am."

"I've been so busy."

"I know."

"I've missed you." Penny smiled.

"Missed you too."

"Mary, I've been working on an article . . ." She didn't get to finish as Lucia returned, pointed at her cup and asked, "Again?"

"No," Penny admitted sheepishly. She had already indulged in four of the woman's strongest espressos in an attempt to disguise the smell of booze which had seemed so determined to seep from every pore.

Lucia left them alone.

"Are you free later?" Penny asked, having decided that the waiting area in a beauty parlor was not the ideal place to break the news she needed to break.

"Sorry," Mary said. "I'm taking Sam to visit with Dick Dogs."

Penny reeked of booze and it was there in a beautician's waiting room that Mary had to acknowledge that her friend had a drinking problem. *What now? What can I do?*

"Dick Dogs?" Penny repeated.

"He used to be friends with his grandmother's brother," Mary explained.

"Don't waste your time with him, Mary," Penny warned.

"Excuse me?"

"You don't know him," Penny said.

Tina emerged from room 3 before Mary had time to respond. She didn't say good-bye to Penny, so hurt was she by Penny's cryptic warning. Instead, she just followed Tina into the small room filled with scented candles and soft music.

Penny left immediately, knowing that Mary wouldn't be calling her and berating herself for not telling her friend why she offered such a warning. It was clear that this man had found his way through the armor that shielded Mary from most. It was clearer that in exposing Sam she was risking her friendship. She didn't want to lose Mary and yet every instinct she had told her to proceed to publish. The story was ready to go—she was just waiting on one thing. It was a long shot but still a possibility. Mia Johnson was scheduled to play in Wembley the following weekend. She then had one day off before she would play in Dublin. Penny was waiting to see if Mia would take the time to travel to a small town in Kerry to address the woman who was about to expose her errant boyfriend—or indeed face the man himself. After all, it would make an excellent ending, and if she didn't, well, then it suggested another kind of ending. Either way, it was a story worthy of the telling.

Mary needed to know who she was allowing to steal her heart. He was dangerous and hadn't the capacity to love, only to hurt. In her lifetime Mary had been through hell and high water. Penny might lose her friend through exposing Sam for the selfish weak bastard he was, but at least she would save her from grievous heartache. *She's suffered enough.*

★ ★ ★

Tina had lived in Kenmare for five years. She was a born-and-bred Dubliner and she wouldn't mind admitting to anyone who would listen that the transition from city to country was a bitch. She would never have dreamed of moving to a small town in Kerry had it not been for meeting the love of her life in The Big Tree on Gardiner Street one Saturday night before an All Ireland final. At first she couldn't understand his thick country accent and he found her flat Dublinese as difficult to navigate, but by the end of that night language had lost meaning and within five months they were engaged. She had settled in well and even she would admit that despite Kenmare being full of country folk, two of which were her very own children, and despite the fact that she had to travel to find a Next, the quality of life was far superior to the one she had left behind. And although her extended family had spent a great deal of their time slagging her off for her move, it was all she could do to keep them from visiting every chance they got. She enjoyed her job at the salon because it was a hub of activity and rarely did anything go on in the town that was not first discussed or revealed there.

While cleansing Mary's face she filled her in on her theory regarding the parentage of a local teenager's newborn.

"I didn't even know she was pregnant!"

"You and the rest of us, honey. Josie Riordan says she didn't even know herself. She went into the hospital with suspected appendix."

"No!"

"Oh, you are way behind. It's bleedin' bizarre in this day and age not to know you're pregnant and it's not like the young one is mental or anythin'."

"Maybe she was just scared to say anything," Mary surmised.

"That one? She's a cheeky mare. I don't know kids today. It wouldn't have happened in our time."

"Tina," Mary said, about to remind her that she herself had been a teenage mother.

"I know. I know. It was out before I thought. Jaysus, Mary, I'm sorry."

Mary laughed. After that Tina was silent, so busy was she massaging Mary's face and shoulders. Her embarrassment made her work harder at relaxing her client and it worked. By the time she left Mary alone with a face pack on for fifteen minutes, Mary was fast asleep.

★ ★ ★

Mary was back standing on an empty urban street. She looked up to see the same red light glowing above her head and back to the ground, where it was reflected in the rain water pooling by the grate by the side of the road. *Oh no. Not again.* The familiar teenage boy with a hood pulled tight covering his face came around the corner. *Please let me go!* He was running exactly like before and she could taste his panic. She watched him turn in time to see the boys following. *"Run!"* she screamed. *"Run!"* she roared yet knowing her calls to be redundant. She'd seen this movie before and no matter how long or hard she called, she knew the boy would be caught. *"Please don't make me watch this!"* she cried up into the night sky. *"I don't want to be here!"* She turned away when one of the gang grabbed at him. She heard the thud as the boy hit the ground. She heard him cry out as the blows connected with bone. *"I won't watch it!"* she roared to someone unseen. *"Do you hear me? I won't watch it!"* She tried to flee the scene but every corner she turned brought her back. The gang leader leaning against the car was grinning sadistically, watching his friends beat the hooded boy. Darkness seeped from his every pore much like booze from Penny's in the waiting room. She wanted to hurt him. Violence welled inside her.

"Look, Topher's excited!" he sneered.

"Oh no!" she cried.

"Give Topher a go!" the sneering Satan called out.

The boy-bear called Topher moved in and the other boys made way, leaving the hooded boy on the ground exposed and too badly beaten to run. She felt his broken knuckles clutching at his hidden face and his body curl into the fetal position so as to protect his balls from the oncoming onslaught.

I'm so sorry! she screamed out. *I'm so sorry!*

★ ★ ★

Gemma, having finished Patty's pedicure, had enough time to drink coffee and berate Tina for not getting the scoop as to whether or not Mary was getting it together with the cute American. Tina explained that she was unable to glean such information in the wake of her faux pas. Gemma laughed at her stupidity.

"Excuse me, I'm not from here. I can't remember every little bleedin' thing!" Tina snapped.

"There's definitely something," Gemma mused, ignoring her employee's outburst. "I mean, he was staying in her house for over a week."

"I heard she made him sleep on the floor," said Tina conspiratorially.

"Dr. Macken told her to!" said Gemma with amusement.

"My arse! My father has had a bad back for twenty years. I've never seen him on a floor."

"Have you seen Mary and the American tagging trees?" Gemma queried.

"That's so weird! I heard he's looking for something belonging to his granny."

"Excuse me?"

"That's the word on the street. Some say there's something buried under one of those trees."

"Jesus. It could be anything."

"I'd say it's jewelry," said Tina. "Obviously valuable or he wouldn't go to the trouble."

"And he visits that tree, the one where her little boy died. He's been seen there a number of times."

"Why would he do that?"

"I don't know. It's weird. They must be together."

"I'm not so sure—I always thought she was a lesbian."

"Sure, didn't we all? Herself and Penny made a lovely couple to most people's minds—of course, that is until we found out that the bold Penny was servicing a married man all these years!" Gemma giggled. "People never fail to entertain."

"Speaking of which, she was reeking of wine this morning," Tina commented.

"Isn't she always? Brona in the off-license maintains she's never out of the place."

It was at this point that they heard crying coming from room 3. They stared at one another, each registering the confusion that comes with unexpected sound. Gemma was the first to move toward the door with Tina following.

"Run! Run!"

"Is she saying 'run'?" Gemma asked Tina.

"Please don't make me watch this!"

"Wha' is she on?" Tina asked Gemma.

"I don't want to be here! I won't watch it. Do you hear me? I won't watch it!"

"She's crying," Gemma said with her hand on the door, opening it to reveal a sleeping Mary.

It was clear the woman was very distressed—her face was soaked in tears and her face pack ruined.

"I'm so sorry!" she screamed so loud that Tina jumped. It was at that point that Gemma gently took her client's hand and called to her softly.

"Mary! Wake up!"

"I'm so sorry!" Mary sobbed.

Tina started to cry. It really was terribly upsetting to see the woman renowned for her strength crumble.

"It's all right, Mary, come back to us," Gemma said, squeezing her hand gently.

It was then that Mary woke to find her face a mess and an audience around her.

"You gave us a fright," Gemma said, but she didn't elaborate.

"Sorry, it was just a nightmare," Mary stammered.

"Let me fix your face," Tina said, wiping away tears of her own, but Mary was too embarrassed—she just wanted to wipe the gunk away and leave. Later she would hear bits and pieces of the story as to how Mary of the Sorrows lost it in room 3.

Chapter Twenty-one

People in Glass Houses

At eighty-nine years of age, Dick Dogs was now a full-time resident of a local old folks' home, perched on a hillock overlooking a spectacular and colorful view that ironically most of the residents were unable to see.

In the wake of the embarrassment suffered in the local beauty shop and the headache brought on by the stress of being forced to relive a young man's misery, Mary had asked Ivan to accompany Sam in her place. Ivan brought a box of hard-boiled sweets which were immediately confiscated by Sheila Dubury, who wondered aloud if Ivan was intending to kill her residents. Sam had brought ice cream, which had been one of the few things his grandmother had enjoyed after her stroke. Sheila smiled at Sam because not only had he managed to present the old man with a gift that wouldn't lodge in his windpipe, but also he was a vision in jeans and a white T-shirt. Among friends she'd later compare him to Jimmy Dean in *Rebel Without a Cause* before mentioning that since Ivan had met Sienna he had definitely put on a little weight, not that she minded much. She'd always had a soft spot for Ivan, having been one of his conquests before his marriage to Norma. Dick was blind as a bat and deaf in one ear. Sheila directed Ivan to the old man's right side and Ivan reminded Dick who he was before introducing him to Sam.

"Sullivan, you say?" Dick shouted at Ivan.

"That's right," Ivan agreed.

"Which Sullivan?"

"No. He's not from around here. His granny was a Baskin."

"Ah, Lena!" he said immediately, making Sam's heart skip a little beat.

"That's right!" Sam shouted.

"Ah, Lena," he repeated, "my good friend David's sister and the best-looking girl in the town!" He smiled, revealing a mouth empty of teeth. "She was a rare one."

Sam didn't know how to respond so instead he smiled at the old man who was grinning madly at the memory of a young beauty.

"I'm glad she escaped," he said after a moment. "That fire, what a terrible thing! No one survived. My good friend David, I hope he slept through it. 'Twas a terrible thing to see." The old man had tears in his eyes. "The smell was the worst of it." He covered his nose as though he could smell it still. "I'm glad she escaped it." He paused. "They're all ghosts now. Laid to rest. They were lucky in their sleep." He laughed a little to himself.

In the end it was Sam who changed the subject and the old man was happy to talk on any number of topics.

As Ivan and Sam walked down the pathway to their cars under the watchful eye of Sheila Dubury, Sam admitted that maybe it was time he too laid his grandmother to rest. He hadn't found her inscription on the hundreds of trees he had tagged, and now under the light of a bright spring day the task seemed inane. After all, his grandmother's graffiti was the work of a bored teenager and hardly a message from a loving grandmother from the grave to her adoring grandson. Ivan had patted Sam on the back and mentioned that in all probability he had merely needed a project, before noting that it was possible that he didn't need that project anymore. Sam smiled at his astute friend and nodded his head because Ivan was right. It occurred to him that during the hours he had spent tagging trees he had given himself the space to work out many of the things that he had refused to touch in therapy. In the woods and alone he allowed his mind to wander into times gone by and when Mary had joined him in his project he had time to rediscover comfort in the company of another human being.

That afternoon, with the eyes of Sheila Dubury and the warmth of the sun on his back, he left Dick Dogs and the ghost of his grandmother in a home on a hillock sweeping toward green crystal water overlooked by a cartoon blue sky.

★ ★ ★

It had been a long day for Penny. First her awkward encounter with Mary followed by an unexpected and deeply unpleasant phone call with her editor, who had called to advise that he had sold the story on to a larger daily tabloid newspaper that would be running it the very next day.

Penny was astounded. Her editor informed her that the money they received for the story would pay her salary for the next two years and explained that they just didn't have the power to break such a story. He explained that the daily had enough contacts to check Penny's facts and the kind of legal team behind them to fight any action Mia Johnson might wish to take.

"We're just too small," he said.

"You mean we've got no balls!" she had said angrily.

"You still get credited but not as the writer."

"So I'm the source? The sellout, the fucking nark?"

"It's a tabloid story and we're not a tabloid."

"It was my story," she said, battling to hide the shake in her voice.

"Not anymore," he said before hanging up.

And there it was. Penny's pet project had blown up in her face. Not only had she not told her best friend she was working on the story, but now that story was being re-told by another writer, who no doubt would subvert every element so that all that would emerge would be poison. Penny was not Sam's biggest fan but she wasn't stupid either and, despite her inexplicable distaste for the man, her better self had ensured that the second draft of her article was injected with some balance. Now the story was out of her hands and worse she would be credited. *Oh God, Mary, please don't hate me!*

The phone rang just after 11:00 PM, waking Penny from a drunken nap, and she answered while still sleepy. The shrill voice antagonized her sore head and it took a moment to realize with whom she was speaking. Adam's wife's voice was as distinctive as was her Dutch accent.

Penny was caught off guard and yet the call had been a long time coming.

"You selfish bitch!" Alina correctly asserted.

Penny had long ago realized that putting her own needs above those of Adam's wife and children was indeed selfish and had no real answer to the accusation thrown at her.

"I'm sorry," she said with head in hands.

"You're sorry?" came her adversary's disbelieving reply.

"I am. I'm sorry that he married you when he was in love with me. I'm sorry I couldn't have loved someone else. I'm sorry that your marriage is a joke and I'm sorry that I'm alone. I'm sorry for a lot of things—for you, for your kids, for me and for him. I spend most of my time being sorry."

For a moment there was silence on the end of the line and Penny wondered whether or not her accuser would hang up.

"All you had to do was stay away," Adam's wife asserted.

"If only I could have," Penny admitted, and a succession of tears escaped and raced down her cheek.

"I hate you!" was all Alina could say.

"I hate you more," Penny replied. "And I'm sorry for that."

Then she hung up the phone and threw it against the wall while she rocked and wailed, allowing all her pent-up pain to spill out.

★ ★ ★

It wasn't her broken phone that woke Penny the very next morning. Instead, it was the incessant knocking and sustained front-doorbell ringing. She dragged herself out of her bed and toward the inescapable noise. She had barely unlatched the door when Mary stormed in past her toward her kitchen. Penny followed, mentally preparing herself for Mary's onslaught. The newspaper was balled in Mary's hand and red-ringed eyes suggested that what she had read had caused her to cry.

"I'm sorry," Penny said, putting her hands in her pockets to conceal their shaking.

"I don't understand," Mary said, eyes filling and clearly confused. "How could you? How could you not even tell me?"

"I was going to. It wasn't supposed to come out until after Mia played in Wembley next week. My editor, he sold it on. I swear I didn't know."

"You didn't know. *You* did this, Penny! *You* did this!" Mary slumped onto one of Penny's kitchen chairs.

"Have you spoken to him?"

"What would I say?" Mary asked angrily.

Penny shook her head. "I know you're angry but I didn't mean for it to happen this way. It was a good story and I am a journalist."

"That article is nothing but gossip-ridden tat. You think there's merit in destroying a person?"

"I think your friend was the one who did the destroying," Penny defended.

"Really?" Mary asked with steel in her voice.

"He's destroyed or devastated everyone he's ever known. He was a heroin addict for Jesus' sake, and frankly since he's come here he's been playing you for a fool. He's dangerous and not to be trusted."

"Why? Because he was an addict? That's rich coming from you!" Mary said, directing her freshly sprung well of anger at her best and worst friend.

"What's that supposed to mean?"

"You want to know what I mean?" Mary asked, giving Penny a way out but Penny didn't take it.

"Yeah, I want to know."

Mary went to the sitting room and came back with empty vodka bottles, placing them in front of Penny. She went to the fridge and opened it to reveal it empty of booze.

"That fridge had three bottles of white wine and at least twenty cans in it four days ago. I wonder where they went." She walked over to the bag which lay by the bin and opened the knot. White and red wine bottles and numerous cans spilled from it. "Oh, there they are!"

"How dare you!" Penny said, fighting tears.

"Is that it? How dare I? No excuses. No bullshit about an impromptu party or your editor and his wife coming to dinner or that it's been months since you've been to the bottle bank?"

"Get out!" Penny roared so loud it was possible her neighbors would hear her and wonder.

"My pleasure," Mary said, grabbing her bag.

She made it to the car before she began to cry. It was ironic that she had intended to visit her friend to attempt to address her drinking problem that very morning. Jerry Letter had stopped by just as she was making breakfast with a copy of the offending article. She had read it in disbelief. Hurt and shock had followed. Mostly, she felt bitterly let down by both Sam and Penny. Penny had borne the brunt of it, but then again, why wouldn't she? She was supposed to be Mary's best friend and not her worst enemy.

★ ★ ★

Penny was left shaking after her encounter with her best friend. She picked up the discarded crumpled-up paper and straightened it on her kitchen table. The picture was of Mia. The story was on Mia. Sam was reduced to a footnote in the story of someone far more interesting to the public. He was merely the latest crisis that Mia had to overcome: failing sales, a failing relationship with a man once her Svengali, then a junkie in her bed. A junkie who she'd saved so that he could walk away from her. How Mia had suffered! How devastated she must be! How would this affect her new album? How would it affect her sellout show in Wembley? A show that was previously canceled so that she could be by the side of her deadbeat boyfriend. Would his defection mean the end of her career was in sight or would she rise from the ashes like her aptly entitled first album, *Phoenix*?

Penny realized that the reason she hadn't lasted in the city was because she really wasn't very good at her job. She had foolishly believed that just because Sam Sullivan's life was interesting to her, it would be interesting to others. How stupid of her! Of course the story was Mia. Who the fuck was Sam Sullivan? All this time she had worried that Sam would make a fool of Mary but in the end the only fool was her. *You're such a loser.*

She cleaned up the bottles that were spilled by Mary's hand. She walked around in circles, not sure what to do or what to think. Her best friend had turned on her. Mary had been venomous. She had humiliated her and insulted her and OK she had been upset about the article, but Penny hadn't done anything to deliberately hurt Mary while Mary had sought to destroy Penny, trying to make out that she was an alcoholic, and maybe she was. She wasn't completely stupid, she knew that she drank too much, and maybe if she tried she would find it difficult to stop, but then again maybe she wouldn't. Besides, this hadn't been an intervention led by concern, it had been an attack. She wouldn't allow herself to concentrate on Mary's accusations. She wouldn't allow herself to think about them because Mary was right. She cleaned the house, even scrubbing the bathrooms in the hope that hard labor would silence her mind. *I made a mistake. I didn't mean to hurt anyone. I don't need her. I don't need anybody.*

★ ★ ★

After Mary's ugly encounter with Penny she drove first without direction but later found herself heading toward Cork. From her car she called Ivan, who was himself halfway through the article that his mother had left for him to read. Tina Turner was blasting out "Proud Mary," which complemented Mary's state of hysteria beautifully.

"Turn the music down," Ivan ordered.

She switched it off.

"You've seen it."

"A fascinating read." She laughed just enough to hint at the possibility of impending insanity.

"Are you OK?" he asked, ignoring her fake laughter.

"I really cared about him," she sighed, giving up on all pretense. "*Care*—that's a funny word. I care about Mr. Monkels."

"I don't know what to say."

"I thought I knew him. But how could I know him? I've had a longer relationship with an expensive night cream."

"It's a lot to take in but I'm not sure any of it changes who he is now."

"Yeah, maybe, but then again maybe Penny's right, maybe he's made a fool of me."

"Then he's made a fool of all of us and I don't think that's true."

"Heroin," she mumbled. "You know he told me he died once. He said he didn't see anything or believe in anything. How could he see anything when he was off his tits?"

"He came here to get better," Ivan reminded her.

"I always knew he wouldn't stay. I always knew there was something. So he gets better and me, I get worse!" She laughed but her laughter was fat with tears. "I was OK. I was content with my lot. I didn't care, I didn't want to."

"You can't go back. You've come alive again, Mary. Don't lament that," Ivan warned. "If you thank him for nothing, thank him for that."

"Heroin," she repeated in disbelief. "The article refers to him as a pathetic junkie."

There was silence on the phone for a moment while Mary absorbed this new information. "And I mean of all the frigging ex-girlfriends. What next? Demi Moore was his babysitter or Julia Roberts was his prom date?"

Ivan laughed a little but he didn't say anything. Mary

didn't need to hear the hint of excitement that his voice would betray. *Mia fucking Johnson—that lucky bastard!*

★ ★ ★

It was Ivan who was the one to break the news of his exposure to Sam. He did so over the phone in a stilted manner that suggested his own hurt and hinted at a little anger. Sam was gracious and thanked his friend for the tip-off.

"So it's true?" Ivan asked.

"It's true I was a heroin addict. It's true I've done a lot of things I'm not proud of."

"You're clean," Ivan tried to confirm for the sake of his own head.

"Yes," Sam answered robotically.

"You're not the man I've just read about."

"No. I'm not," Sam confirmed, a little relieved that his friend was giving him the benefit of the doubt.

"You should have said something."

"I needed not to be that guy for a while. Does Mary know?"

"Yes."

"She hates me," he guessed.

"I don't know."

"Where is she?"

"She's gone for a drive."

"I would have said something," Sam said, "eventually."

"I hope for your sake eventually isn't too late," Ivan noted before hanging up.

Sam sat in his sitting room in silence. The news had acted like some sort of unwanted anesthetic which crept through him so that within minutes he felt paralyzed. *It's over.*

★ ★ ★

Mary had called Adam from the road.

"I need to see you."

"OK."

"Where?"

"The Gingerbread House."

"I'll be there in an hour. Twelve."

"I'll be waiting."

Adam was waiting. He got up off his seat to greet her. They hugged and sat down opposite each other.

"I just got some coffee," he said, indicating the large cafetière in front of him. "It's still hot—I knew you of all people wouldn't be late!" He poured her a cup.

She drank gratefully.

"It's good to see you," he said, seeming genuinely pleased.

She nodded. "You too," she replied, taking his hand in hers. "How've you been?" She was concerned about her friend whose gray face betrayed his carefully constructed happy-go-lucky facade.

"I'm fine," he'd said, obviously lying.

"I've had enough crap for one day. Tell me the truth."

"Alina hates me. She's so angry all the time. I think she's planning on punishing me for the rest of my life." He dropped his head so as to hide. He took a series of deep breaths and Mary gave him the room he required to compose himself. "What about Penny?" he asked after a few minutes.

"Not good," she disclosed through gritted teeth.

312

"Drinking?"

"Heavily," she sighed.

"She'll cut back, she always cuts back."

"I think it's time we all faced the fact that Penny has a real problem."

"Jesus"—he shook his head—"everything is such a fucking mess."

For a moment Mary looked like she was about to cry.

"You know there's nothing we can do," he said with a resignation that came from a childhood spent watching his mother caretake an alcoholic grandfather.

"Right now I wonder if I even care," Mary admitted.

"I read the article. Whatever's going on, I know she didn't do it to hurt you."

"But she did," Mary said, welling up.

"It's my fault."

"You certainly didn't help." Mary said plainly.

"Good old Mary. I can always count on the truth from you. I should have been a better man. Your new friend is not the only one who has made terrible mistakes."

She nodded. "We all make mistakes," she whispered to herself.

"Do you think I should call her?" he asked, knowing it was the wrong thing to do.

"No," Mary advised, "it would only make things worse and I've already done that." She sighed.

"You made it worse?" he asked with a snort that implied that he had long ago taken full ownership of any blame to be bestowed on a third party for Penny's problem. Mary shook her head. "I was hurt and I said some things. I'm not sure there's a road back for us."

"Of course there is. She won't want to lose you."

"You think? If it comes down to me or to booze, will I win?"

He looked at her and then down into the contents of his own cup and shook his head. "Has it really got that bad?"

"I think it has," she said.

He put his hand to his forehead and began rubbing it as though trying to erase this new information.

"If things are that bad there's nothing any one of us can do. It's up to her now."

"She's too far gone."

"Then it's only a matter of time."

"Until?"

"Until she hits rock bottom," he said, biting his lower lip.

Later, over a nice lunch, they realized that they were more depressing than a Dickens novel.

Adam attempted to lighten the mood. "So you'll forgive the American his omission."

"Pretty big omission," she'd said lightheartedly. Adam could always make the worst of situations seem perfectly normal.

"You're telling me!" he laughed. "Half the town was on the phone about it before half nine this morning."

"That's comforting." She attempted a joke.

"Mia Johnson!" He inhaled.

"I was thinking about the heroin!" She laughed a little.

"Why would anyone turn to drugs with a girlfriend like Mia Johnson?"

"Do you want a slap?" she couldn't help but ask.

He laughed. "You'll forgive him." He smiled.

"You're probably right," she admitted, a little disgusted with herself.

"He's definitely given up all that crap?"

"Yeah," she answered. Having spent pretty much day and night with him for as many weeks, she knew that that particular addiction would have been impossible to hide.

"When he was staying with me I found a stash of his painkillers under the mattress. He was in agony but he wouldn't take the pills. I thought it was weird but I suppose it makes sense now."

"Did you say anything to him?"

"No. I ignored them for a while and then one day and just before he left I had the impulse to bin them so I did. I didn't say anything and he didn't ask."

"How does he feel about you?" Adam asked, happy to concentrate on someone else's pathetic love life so as to momentarily escape his own.

"I don't know," she admitted honestly. "I'm hardly Mia Shagging Johnson, am I?"

"No, you're not, but I guess he wasn't looking for Mia Shagging Johnson"—he grinned and rose an eyebrow playfully—"the lunatic!"

She remained silent.

"Do you trust him?" he asked after a moment or two had passed.

"I know he's hiding something," she said, answering and yet avoiding the question.

"You mean other than being a junkie?" Adam asked, intrigued, as he was well aware that Mary was more intuitive than most.

"Why would a man who has the music world at his

feet, millions in the bank and a rock star in his bed—why would a man like that turn to heroin?" She swished the wine at the bottom of her glass.

"Well, I don't know, Hetty Wainthropp," he laughed. "What is it they say about Rock-and-Roll excess?"

"Cocaine is excess, heroin is desperation. But then what do I know? I'm just a country bumpkin with a voice like a crow and a flat arse."

Adam laughed at his friend while remembering the rap music video he'd seen only days earlier in which Mia Johnson had revealed her fabulously curvaceous arse in a tiny pink bikini. *Jesus, Mary, I love you but she is a hard act to follow.*

Chapter Twenty-two

Facing Up to Those Who Would Look Down

Sam woke after eight. His sleep had been broken and a familiar weight had resumed its seat at the center of his chest. Before he eventually turned in for the night he had watched Mary's house with the staying power of a stalker but she had not returned home. Earlier that evening he wondered if Mr. Monkels would be OK. When he jumped the wall he found the dog asleep by the kitchen window, his bowls full of water and food. He was fine. *Good.* He had long ago forgiven the dog for his back injury—after all, it was that very injury that had really introduced him to his neighbor. Without that they might still be passing acquaintances. *Please don't hate me.* By midday he was desperate for food and having imprisoned himself for one full day he felt it was time to face his public. He showered and changed and then paced a little before finally opening his front door. He met Mossy exiting his house.

"Well, well," Mossy said, shaking his head, "you are a dark horse."

Sam didn't know what to say so he just stood there nodding uncomfortably.

"Mia Johnson." Mossy was still shaking his head. "A rock star, no less." He laughed. "Ha!" he called out as though to himself. "Mia Johnson and a side order of smack. Ha?" He laughed again at his own joke. "Jesus, boy, that stuff would kill you!" He nudged Sam and gave a little wink, before walking on giggling to himself.

OK, that was weird. Then again it was Mossy. Still, if everyone was as easy as Mossy . . . *It might be OK.* He took his time walking toward town. It was well after one when he entered the bar. It seemed to be buzzing with a little more energy than usual. However, as he materialized, the buzz subsided to a lull, which in turn descended into a stark silence. All faces faced him and it was difficult to ignore the collective inquisitive stare. His destination—a table on its own at the end of the room and near the toilets—seemed to be a million miles away but he couldn't turn back, not while the pack lay in wait. He eventually sat and took up his menu, which he quickly employed as a shield. Mary was nowhere to be seen, nor was Jack or Ivan. *Where the hell is everyone?*

Jessie emerged from the back and, with pen and notebook in hand, she strode over to take his order—as pleasant as always.

"What do you want?"

"World peace!" he said, attempting an ice-breaking joke, but she wasn't about to thaw.

"In the event that I cannot deliver on that order, is

there something you'd like off the menu?" she asked without breaking a smile.

"I'll have a coffee and a ham, cheese and onion toasted sandwich to go." His weary tone conceded defeat.

"We don't do 'to go,'" she replied haughtily.

"To stay then," he sighed.

"Fine," she agreed, striding back to base in the military manner in which she'd stridden forward.

In her absence he realized that all eyes were now averted and the buzz although hushed was returning. He wasn't close enough to hear his fellow diners' muted conversations but neither was he blind to the occasional eye being cast upon him before a mouth was cupped and a head leaned in toward a lunch companion conspiratorially.

Mary's father emerged from the kitchen with his coffee and sandwich. He took the chair opposite.

"I thought you could stand to see a friendly face," he said with a smile.

"Thanks, Jack. I appreciate that."

"You have the whole town talking," Jack said while absentmindedly cleaning the table.

"I get that."

"Ah, what harm!" He grinned wide enough to reveal a gold tooth. "Sure, wouldn't it be worse if they weren't talking?" He laughed at himself.

"Not really. No."

Jack continued to laugh. "I suppose not. Still, it's something to pass the day and after all it's only talk and not the end of the world, now is it?"

"I guess not," Sam conceded, trying hard not to sound like a teenager.

Jack nodded and got up.

"So Mary's not in today?" Sam said, hoping that any anxiety he felt was untraceable in his voice.

"She took a few days off."

In truth, he had demanded she get some rest, having been informed of his daughter's near breakdown in Gemma Gibney's beauty shop.

"Oh. OK." Sam nodded. "Thanks."

"Son?"

"Yeah?"

"She comes across as tough as old boots but she's not. She's had it hard enough."

"Yes, sir," he heard himself saying.

Jack nodded and left him to his coffee and unwanted toasted sandwich. Luckily, lunchtime for the workers was approaching an end and the place was emptying out. He was sipping his coffee when he felt someone stand over him. He turned to see a woman whose face and name he recognized but with whom he had previously had no contact. Bridget the Bike.

"Hi, I'm Bridget Browne." She held out her hand and he took it.

"Hi," he replied as they shook hands.

"Look, I just wanted to say that soon it will be somebody else's turn."

"You're so sure?" He almost laughed.

"I was the previous occupier of those boots you've just stepped into."

"Ah." He nodded, enjoying her turn of phrase despite the circumstances.

"So thanks for that." She smiled, signaling her joke.

"You're welcome."

"It'll be OK. It always is."

He nodded and she made her way to the bathroom, and when she returned he was gone.

★ ★ ★

At home that evening he attempted to watch a show from the second season of *The West Wing*. Mary had presented him with the DVD set on the day that she'd helped him shop for a TV. He was finding it difficult to concentrate. Josh had just explained the superstring theory to Leo, and Toby seemed to be losing it with CJ but none of it was filtering through the haze that separated his visual cortex from his brain stem. *The West Wing* demanded the kind of attention that Sam couldn't commit to in that moment, so he switched it off and made his way into the garden in search of mind-sweeping oxygen. He sat on a plastic chair, taking deep breaths, while focusing on the wall which separated his garden from his neighbor's.

He must have fallen asleep because the next thing he knew he was cold, he had a crick in his neck, and his watch revealed it was after ten. Mary must have returned because Mr. Monkels was in the back sniffing a bucket.

He went and knocked on her door but there was no response. He also peered through the window and called out her name. He hoped she wasn't hiding from him but feared that she might be.

He decided upon a walk to clear his head. He found her under the night sky sitting on the bench by the pier end, looking out over the water and seemingly mesmerized by a bobbing red buoy. He sat down beside her. She remained still for a few moments before conceding to switch off her Walkman and remove her earphones.

"How does it feel to be the talk of the town?" she asked, without removing her gaze from the water.

"I'm guessing you know."

"They'll get tired of it and soon enough the town spotlight will descend on somebody else," she said evenly.

"Bridget Browne was kind enough to tip me off."

"Well, she's certainly qualified to know," she said, and still her eyes were averted.

"She was kind," he heard himself mutter, and she faced him.

"Well, that's the thing about small towns. Everybody knows everybody else's business, sniggering and judgment usually follow, but when it's important all that fades away and what's left is solidarity. Maybe if you had known that, you could have trusted us."

"I shouldn't have lied."

"Everybody lies," Mary replied a little sadly.

"I should have told you about my past."

"So why didn't you?"

"I was afraid. I haven't been a decent person for such a long time." His eyes were dark and the melancholy she had seen in them that first night had returned.

"And you're a better man now?" she asked without judgment.

"I'm trying to be," he said quietly with his eyes cast downward.

"And your girlfriend?" she said after a moment of silence had passed.

His eyes locked with hers and they shared a terrible sadness.

"I didn't love her," he admitted.

She didn't respond, instead averting her eyes so as to lose herself in deep water.

After some minutes had passed she turned to face him. "I need some space," she said.

"Because of my past?"

"No, because of mine. When I'm around you I feel like I'm falling. I need to stop before I smash into the ground."

"Are you always this honest?"

"No, mostly I'm a liar just like you."

"I don't want to lose you."

"And yet you won't be staying here."

"You don't know," he mumbled.

"Yeah, I do," she said sadly before getting up.

He grabbed her hand and held on until she pulled it away slowly while holding the light of the moon in her watery eyes. He nodded his head dejectedly. It was odd that this was the first real indication either had given of any romantic hope and all at once it was over.

"I just need some time," she said before leaving him with only the bobbing red buoy for company.

She knows. She knows I'm not worth it.

★ ★ ★

On the day that the article was published about Mia Johnson, Penny began a week of self-induced oblivion. She'd requested a two-week leave of absence, and because of the fact that she rarely sought holidays, her editor and traitor

323

was happy to oblige. She'd stocked up on booze and snacks in Killarney and upon returning home she'd parked her car in her garage. Once inside, she'd pulled out the plug on her home phone, switched off her mobile, locked her doors, closed her curtains and opened the first of many bottles, thus beginning a long descent to a place that Dante would term *The Inferno*.

A few days had passed when she heard knocking on her door. She wasn't sure how long Ivan had stayed banging and calling out because she had drifted off to sleep in the middle of it all. It could have been seconds or hours; either way Penny had no intention of answering the door. *Just go away*. The second time she'd woken, the banging and shouting had disappeared. The bottle of vodka was nearly empty. She got up and went into the kitchen. She opened the fridge, which was stocked with booze, and placed the near-empty bottle inside beside a fresh one close to eggs, which she considered frying up. But then in that moment her stomach turned. She closed the fridge door but then considered her actions before reopening the fridge so as to remove the near-empty bottle. She then opened the freezer and placed it in the quick-freeze drawer. She put the timer on the oven, allowing for ten minutes. She sat on the floor and watched the oven timer count down. The buzzer sounded off. She opened the freezer and, feeling the bottle suitably cold, she opened it and downed it before laughing to herself and spluttering. *This is the life.*

Four days into her binge, she had decided to open her laptop and write down why she felt she was a drunk. Having imbibed two bottles of vodka before twelve in the day and yet feeling surprisingly lucid, it seemed like a tremendous idea. She entitled the document "Why?" She centered the question at the top of the page. She pressed the return button twice and pressed the tab button with a certain amount of conviction before beginning her first paragraph. However, the return button pressed, she was a little stumped as to where to begin so she sat and waited for a little inspiration. *Why?* She took a drink from a fresh and chilled bottle of vodka with a dash of lime, which felt tingly bitter and a little sweet. *Nice.* After a moment or two and her muse coursing down her neck, she was ready to begin. She concentrated her thoughts, flexed her fingers and wiped the residual spittle from her mouth.

She decided to entitle each paragraph and her diatribe went as follows:

Why?

Parents

My mother was on the pill ergo my conception was as a result of a nasty case of the trots. Apparently, my unlucky parents had decided against having children, even considering abortion, but then Catholic guilt set in and the fear of an angry God ensured that I would survive gestation to emerge into a world that didn't give a fuck. Were my parents cruel? Certainly not intentionally but then being cruel

requires giving attention, which is
something neither could afford. Do I
wish I was aborted? Yes. It would have
been kinder. Did my parents love me?
How could they? I was fed and clothed.
I was educated and then nothing. They
don't even know me. I don't know them.
Aren't parents supposed to know their
kids? Aren't they supposed to *care*? So
I wasn't abused. But was I neglected?
Doesn't it mean something when you feel
closer to your best friend's dad than
you do to your own? Why didn't they care?
Was it me? Why was it that when I was
born that change that occurs in everyone
else's parents didn't occur in mine?
Where is my unconditional love? How is
it that I could be so alone from such a
young age? Why didn't they love me? Why
didn't they love me? Why?

Adam

He was my world. He promised me he would
wait. He told me he loved me and I believed him. I believed him because he
did love me. It was real, it just wasn't
enough. He picked his wife over me. He
picked his kids over me. Funny how the
man I love and who loves me would choose

his children and misery over me and
my own father would choose his stupid
job. Is it me? It must be. There is an
emptiness in me that is noticeable. I
couldn't make Adam happy. Just like his
wife, I would be a letdown. That's why
he left, deep down he knows that there
is nothing to me. How could there be?
That night when we danced in the garden
and when he said good-bye, I wanted to
die. I desperately wanted to die. Why?
What is wrong with me? Why can't I get
over him? Why can't I just feel normal?
Why won't he choose me? Why won't he
choose me? Why?

Mary

She gave me hope. That first day on the
train to Dublin she sat beside me and
when she looked at me she made me feel
like I was special. Together we were
popular and she brought out all that
was good and funny in me. Her encourage-
ment ensured that I would strive to be
the entertainer. Now I am the consummate entertainer but to be that I needed
help. Why? I wanted to make her happy.
I wanted to make her laugh. And now she
judges me. She got pregnant and I was

there for her. She nearly died and I
nearly died with her. She lost her son
and disappeared but I stayed with her
because I loved her through it all. How
hard is it to stay with someone so destroyed? Fucking hard. How hard is it to
witness desperation? It's a nightmare.
Watching the person you care about utterly decimated is tantamount to feeling
a knife cutting through a bone. I didn't
desert her. Has she deserted me? Worse,
has she deserted me for some prick she
doesn't even know? The girl who was once
impenetrable now reduced to a sucker for
an asshole. Heroin is forgivable but alcohol is not? Why has she chosen him
over me? Why has she deserted me? Why?

Me

I am nothing.

After that she stopped writing. She went to the fridge
and pulled out a fresh bottle of vodka and she opened it
and drank from the neck because she was thirsty, because
she was desperate, but mostly because she wanted to van-
ish. She lost track of time as days were beginning to blend.
She ignored the doorbell. One morning she woke to find
a card on her mat. It was from Mary. She had written one
word: *Sorry.* Penny tore it up and binned it, and then she

cried until she was sure there was nothing left. A while later she began to feel hungry for something other than a bag of crisps but she didn't want to stop drinking long enough to sober up so she called a taxi to take her to a little pub that served traditional fare just outside of the town.

She found a quiet corner booth and hid there drinking while she picked at a cottage pie and its accompanying salad. It was when she got up to go to the bathroom that she saw Ivan and Sam, who had annoyingly chosen the same out-of-town sanctuary. However, she felt sure she remained unseen. She cleaned her face with cold water and cursed herself for leaving her coat in her seat. She hadn't paid either so she couldn't leave. She knew it was possible for her to return to her seat unseen but she couldn't risk then seeking the attention of the barman and she'd been waiting for him to approach her for a while. She needed another drink. *Damn it.* She emerged from the bathroom minutes after she had entered and gingerly made her way back to her seat.

The men had their backs to her and were deep in conversation. Her curious nature made her wish she was a fly on the wall. But of course she didn't really need to overhear what Sam was saying. He was probably tearing her apart and Ivan had been nodding his head so he was probably agreeing. *Bastards.* She could hear them laughing. *Were they laughing at her?* Of course they were. She heard them get up so she pressed herself into her seat and they passed her little booth without noticing her presence. *Thank God,* she thought before ordering another drink.

Much later, when the same taxi man who had dropped her off had collected her and once he'd helped her inside before leaving her to herself, she flipped open her laptop and opened up her document so as to add Ivan's name to the list of reasons she found for being a drunk.

```
Ivan

He's a backstabbing bastard.
```

She woke sometime in the afternoon one week after the article had been published. Her head hurt, her breath stank, and she was so dehydrated her skin was beginning to flake. She decided to clean up. She decided that enough was enough and that she couldn't go on the way she had been. She even accepted that she didn't want to. She even considered getting help. She poured the last of the booze stash down the drain. She showered and made herself some toast, which she barely nibbled. She opened her laptop and looked through her emails. All were work-related despite her colleagues being well aware that she was on holiday. She opened up her stupid document, the one that blamed everyone and everything for her problems.

"Stupid girl," she heard herself say, and yet she didn't delete it. She missed her friends. She missed Mary and Ivan but mostly she missed Adam. She watched an afternoon movie and moisturized, but by seven she was pacing the floor with her head in her hands and her body screaming.

★ ★ ★

While Penny spent a week drinking, Mary spent hers catching up on sleep and work. Sam played guitar, took long walks, ate late suppers in restaurants now busy with tourists. He had read, listened to music, and once he'd even sat in the large empty church soaking up the silence while sitting on hard wood and taking the time to contemplate his own Catholic upbringing. His mother was of Irish Catholic descent, his father Irish/Polish Catholic. His mother went to a Catholic girls' school and his father was taught by Christian brothers. They met at a Catholic dance aged seventeen and eighteen, respectively. They were married four years later in a big traditional Catholic wedding. He had been baptized, he'd made his Communion and was confirmed. For his first fifteen years he had sat in one of God's many houses Sunday after Sunday and yet, aside from stillness, churches or Catholicism had nothing to offer him. He looked around at stone and tile, stained glass and candles. He could smell the slight scent of incense and hear the whispered prayer of the nun who made her way past him and he left, not surprised that for him it still held nothing. The nightmares had returned and no amount of guitar playing, late suppers or even religion would make them go away.

Midweek he'd met Ivan for a pint in a small bar a few miles outside of town. Ivan had only an hour to spare as the kids had returned home with him and he didn't like leaving them with a slightly frazzled Sienna. He filled Sam in on how his ex-wife was coping and when she would be released from the hospital. They discussed her indecision as to whether or not to press charges and more importantly whether or not she would come home. Ivan was adamant that the bastard that had broken her deserved everything he got, but a part of him was afraid she would go back to him. Halfway through their pints, Ivan had mentioned another fear that he'd harbored since he'd first seen her twisted and bloody.

"You don't think he would have forced himself on her?" he'd asked, and Sam had nearly dropped his pint.

"Has she said anything?" Sam asked, recovering.

"No. And I can hardly ask her."

"I doubt it," Sam said before finishing his pint. "Just because he hits—it doesn't mean that he . . ." He didn't finish his sentence as Ivan had begun nodding his agreement halfway through it.

"You're right. But if I ever find out he did, I'll hunt him down and I'll kill him," Ivan said with conviction.

"If you find that he did, I'll be happy to help you," Sam said with a similar conviction.

"You're a good friend," Ivan had said, "for a junkie!" He laughed at his own joke.

Sam had become used to his past indiscretions being joked about and he was smart enough to know that although they joked, those around him would not tolerate his failure to remain clean. This worried him. Each night that passed made it harder, all the more so now that he was being watched.

Then they talked a little bit about the aftermath of Penny's article. The furor hadn't been quite as considerable as it could have been. To Ivan and indeed most of the townspeople the fact that Sam had cleaned up his act and continued to remain clean was an achievement meriting consideration. The man described in the newspaper was far from the man that he and his fellow townspeople had come to know, and this ensured that when judgment was passed it was in favor of their new resident, just as Mary had expected.

Ivan had been sheepish when he broached the subject of Sam's famous ex but he couldn't help himself.

"Give me something."

"Something?" Sam had queried, playing with his new friend.

"Anything at all."

"OK." Sam sat back in his chair. Then he sighed and put his hand to his chin.

"Oh, come on!"

"It will stay between you and me?" Sam asked.

"Absolutely," Ivan agreed, and yet both of them knew Ivan couldn't hold his water.

"Horror movies turn her on."

"What do you mean?"

"I mean horror gets her really hot"—Sam laughed at the memory of her jumping him midway through *Scream*— "the gorier the better."

"Really? I love horror films." Ivan seemed satisfied with the tidbit he'd been given. "One last thing," he went on after a minute spent contemplating which horror movie he'd like to have taken Mia Johnson to, given the opportunity.

"What?"

"Did you ever do J-Lo?"

Sam had laughed as Ivan drained his glass. Ivan seemed lighter and happier than before. His kids returning home had wiped the gloom from his eyes. His smile seemed warmer and his laugh was heartier. Sam was happy for his new friend. Neither party mentioned Mary and Ivan didn't mention it when he saw a disheveled Penny sneak into the booth. *It's not the time. God save her!* he thought while laughing with his American friend.

Chapter Twenty-three

My Oh Mia

It was one of those days that Ben would call a yellow day—bright and sunny enough to pass for summer. Mary had just returned from a day shift at the bar. She was busy fixing the remote controls in line with the corner of her coffee table when her doorbell rang. She wasn't expecting company. Penny hadn't spoken to her for over a week. Sam was giving her the space that she had sought. Ivan was busy with his kids. She answered it, expecting to see no one in particular.

The woman at the door was very beautiful. She also seemed familiar in some way. It only took an instant before it all clicked into place. *Frigging hell!*

"Hi. I'm Mia." The rock star put out her hand.

"Mary," she replied, suddenly embarrassed by her plain name. She took the rock star's hand and shook it.

"I was looking for Sam," Mia said, having been directed to Sam's small cottage by the helpful hotel manager.

"Oh," was all Mary managed to say without having to stop to inhale. "I'm not sure. I think he's on the water."

Mia raised her perfectly arched eyebrows. "Excuse me?"

"It's Sunday. He usually fishes with my cousin on Sundays."

"Oh," Mia sighed. "I can't imagine him fishing." She smiled and it didn't look like she intended going anywhere.

"Would you like to come in?" Mary asked tentatively, not wishing to seem too pushy to the rock star, who possibly would think she was some weirdo fan.

"Sure, I'd love to," Mia said, walking past her.

"Right then," Mary noted, closing the door and deep down freaking out a little. She turned off Alanis Morissette in case Mia had a problem with competition. Mia didn't seem to notice. Instead, she sat on the kitchen chair that Sam had occupied on the many evenings Mary had cooked for him.

Mary made a pot of coffee and placed it on the table between them.

"Nice place," Mia said, looking around.

"It's OK," Mary said, embarrassed by her humble home and for the first time.

"So you and Sam are friends?" Mia asked, gauging Mary's expression. She smiled when Mary nearly spilled the coffee she had begun to pour.

"We're giving each other a little space," Mary admitted once she had regained control of the coffeepot.

"Space?" Mia queried suspiciously.

Instantly, Mary regretted her comment. *Shut your mouth, Mary!*

"So are you here for long?" she asked as breezily as possible.

"Not really. No," Mia said, smiling. "I was surprised to discover that he was here. He never did like the country-side."

"People change."

"Not so much."

Mary wasn't enjoying her conversation with an inter-national rock star. It was uncomfortable, as though the women were in some unspoken competition. It made her edgy, especially since she felt at a certain disadvantage, being so ordinary.

"Are you hungry?" she asked, for something to say more than any desire to cater. Besides, her Aunt Sheila had often said: "When in doubt, feed someone." It made sense now, especially since Mia's stomach refused to stop gurgling.

"No, I'm fine." But then Mia's stomach grumbled again and Mary's facial expression suggested that, unlike most, she didn't have the good grace to ignore it. "Well, actually, I'm a little hungry."

"Good. Do you like fish?"

"I love fish."

"Shellfish?"

"Yes, please."

"How about a warm scallop salad with homemade dressing and a round of fresh brown bread?"

"I'm sorry—I may drool a little," Mia laughed.

Then Mary got her to work on chopping leaves for the

337

salad and it was while they were in the process of preparing dinner that both women relaxed.

"Do you like blues?" Mary asked.

"I should but I don't," Mia admitted.

Mary checked her CD player. Rufus Wainwright was loaded directly under Ms. Morissette. "Rufus Wainwright?"

"Why not?" Mia said, taking off her jacket before shaking Mary's fresh salad dressing.

They were halfway through their scallop salads when Mia broached the subject of Mary's relationship with Sam.

"I hope you don't mind me asking but are you two together?" she asked.

"Seriously, we've only ever been friends," Mary said.

"Yeah, that's what we said for the entire duration of our relationship," Mia laughed.

"He's here to get better," said Mary quickly, "nothing more."

"He got better at home."

"What about you—do you want him back?"

"Yes"—Mia nodded—"but I'm not stupid enough to think it will ever happen. He's been here months and I didn't even get a phone call. I had to find out he was here through a damn tabloid. We didn't even officially end it. He wanted to but I begged." She smiled to hide her shame. "Of course, deep down I knew it was over."

"I'm sorry."

"Don't be. He didn't love me." She shrugged. "He didn't then, he doesn't now and won't in the future. It's just like I said: people don't change that much." She placed another forkful of salad in her mouth. "God, this is amazing!"

Mary smiled.

"You're wondering what I'm doing here?" Mia asked.

"I suppose I am."

"My therapist says I need closure," Mia said between bites.

"Oh. OK," Mary laughed. *Americans!*

Their meal was eaten and they were both enjoying a glass of white wine while lying on deck chairs placed at the edge of the pier when Mary caught sight of Ivan's boat heading toward shore. Ivan caught sight of his cousin in or around the same time. He turned to his son, who was untangling a net.

"Chris, pass me the binoculars, son," he said, and Chris dutifully complied.

"Christ in a canoe! It's Mia Johnson!" Ivan called out excitedly.

Chris grabbed his father's binoculars. "Jesus!" he said under his breath.

"Don't swear!" Ivan said.

"Holy crap!" Chris was still staring at the rock star lounging beside his aunt.

"That's better." Ivan grabbed the binoculars. "Sam!"

Sam emerged from below with a flask of coffee and Justy by the hand.

"I heard you," he said with a sigh.

Ivan had the boat tied off in record time. From their chairs, Mia and Mary watched Sam and his comrades walk the length of the pier. It was evident despite his smile that Sam was feeling the pressure for although it was a warm day he was sweating excessively. Ivan on the other hand was dry as a bone and happy as a puppy, practically bounding toward the beautiful stranger so as to shake her hand and tell her how much he admired her while drinking her in. Mary wanted to slap him. Chris sat on the side of his aunt's chair so as to prevent his knees from buckling in the aftermath of Mia's cheek kiss. Justy just held Sam's hand, not really giving a crap about the beautiful woman. She liked Jamie Lynn Spears.

Sam was the last person to welcome her. It had been just over five months since he had nearly died of a heroin overdose. It had been just over three months since Sam had ended his relationship with Mia and yet, standing there on the edge of the pier and seeing her face and feeling her arms wrapped around him, it felt like an entire lifetime had passed. She was a stranger with a tight grip. He pulled away slowly, not wishing to give away any feelings that his ex-girlfriend's presence stimulated. Sam suggested taking Mia back to her hotel but Mary and Ivan insisted she stay, at least to finish her glass of wine. They made their way into the house. Ivan grabbed two more glasses and told the kids to go watch TV in the sitting room. After much moaning and serious bribing, Ivan joined Sam, Mary and Mia Johnson sitting around Mary's kitchen table sipping on white wine. He was beaming like a kid at the circus.

"Mr. Mockless?" Mia was saying, rubbing Mr. M's back.

"Monkels," Mary corrected.

"Weird name."

"Originally he was called Norman," Ivan said, still beaming.

"What changed?" Mia asked, intrigued.

"One day when my son was three years old he decided that the name Norman didn't work and 'Mr. Monkels' did." She smiled at the memory.

Ivan laughed. "The strange thing is, the dog immediately responded to it."

"It was like he'd always been Mr. Monkels," Mary added happily. "It just fit."

"It's a cool name," said Mia. "Your son has good taste. So where is he?"

"He died," Mary said.

"Oh, I'm so sorry!" Mia covered her face to hide her embarrassment.

Sam stood up. It was obvious he was uncomfortable. "We should go."

"You don't have to go," Mary said, ignoring Sam.

"No," Mia said, "Sam's right. I should go. It's been a long day." She smiled. "It was really good to meet you, Mary, and you, Ivan." She leaned over to shake his hand and he took the opportunity to kiss her cheek.

"You're a lady," he said to her, and she seemed really pleased.

Chris was too busy talking on his mobile phone telling his friends about his encounter with a rock star to take the time to say good-bye to one.

Justy waved at the window with Mr. Monkels by her side.

Mary closed the door and turned to Ivan.

"Christ on a cruise ship!" he said. "Stick a fork in me, Mare, I'm done."

She laughed at her cousin yet she would have been

341

lying if she said a part of her wasn't feeling a little jealous—not a lot jealous but definitely a little. *Frig it, why couldn't she have been a bitch?*

★ ★ ★

Mia returned to the old-world hotel that she'd booked into earlier that day. Sam had agreed to meet her there for drinks at nine. She sat by her window, looking out at the majestic grounds which led to a little gate and she wondered what lay beyond it. The suite was reminiscent of a bygone era, sumptuous and scattered with antiques and oil paintings. She hadn't expected such decadence and had prepared herself for the small town being as hick as some of those she had spent months in while touring the States. But of course that wasn't Sam's style—she was the hick one, after all. She considered spending some time in the spa, being particularly impressed with the couple's day suite offering seclusion and privacy, but then she remembered that she wouldn't be requiring a couple's day suite and there didn't seem to be a suite for one. No matter how many treatments, how beautiful the view, or how tranquil the spa pool, that empty chair would surely taunt her.

She lay on her bed for a while, opening a trouser button, having eaten too much brown bread.

She pondered Sam's welcome. He had put his arms around her and he'd smiled too, but then again falsity was his strong suit. She had felt his warmth. She sighed at the memory. He looked well and healthy. His friend Ivan seemed nice and his kids were cute. They were also a well-placed distraction. She had noticed Sam attempt to catch

Mary's eye on the pier. Mary had remained stoic and she wondered, *What is it with those two?*

It was after eight when she showered, being careful not to wet her hair, which had been styled in the UK earlier that morning. She sat at her dressing table so as to apply her makeup. The mirror was deceptively large and seemed to engulf her. *Mia, what are you really doing here?* Mia often stared at her own reflection with wonder. Not because she was intoxicated by her own beauty as others were and not because she even really saw herself as being that extraordinary. She stared at her face in the hope that it might betray her origin. Mia didn't know where her beauty came from and she never would. Declared an orphan, she'd been in the system since she'd been found sleeping in a brown box one hot morning in the car park of a Kmart in Michigan. She was of mixed race and answered to the name Lola. In the late seventies, mixed-race children had been difficult to place. Adoption agencies wanted a newborn, preferably one race, color and creed. They didn't need the headache that came with a kid whose origin was in question and who was approaching two. Throughout her childhood she had been fostered over and over and never quite found a fit. The other girls were jealous of her oval eyes and flawless caramel skin, her length, and her grace, which had been an affront to her plain-Jane bedfellows. The boys were always fighting for her attention, so much so that there was usually trouble. Her childhood and teenage years would be filled with insecurity, fear and disappointment. She had lived a long time without an identity. Then one day a lady named Kiki Shaw, an ex-dancer and one of her many foster parents, had complimented her singing voice. She only mentioned it once but that's all it took. After that day Mia did nothing but sing, initially in the hope that her voice would attract the attention and praise she craved, but when neither were forthcoming she did it for herself. When she was fourteen she stole a guitar. She stalked the shop for a full week before making her move. She knew exactly which one she wanted. It was blue and closest to the door. Usually, there were two young guys behind the counter, but on that day there was only one. He went into the back once in three hours, but when he did she ran inside, grabbed the guitar and then ran as fast as her legs could carry her, holding her newly acquired possession high in the air until her legs shook and she was far away from the scene of the crime.

She taught herself some chords from an old book she picked up secondhand. She wrote her first song at fifteen. She left her last foster home at sixteen. Through a placement she got a job as a waitress and the owner let her live in the room above the diner. When she wasn't working she gigged in every dive that would have her. But as hard as she tried and as much as she wanted it, six years later she was still a waitress and the dive above the diner was still home.

She was twenty-two when a beautiful man had come into her world and changed it utterly. He plucked her from obscurity. He dressed her. He styled her. He even named her. He believed in her and in doing so filled her with courage and hope. He had made her feel special, and for a long time she'd thought that he loved her.

Deep down, Mia had long believed herself to be Sam's creation. In him she had found her missing identity. He'd given her a family and her life, and she knew that behind all his inexplicable fear and before heroin stole him away, he had loved her too. She knew this because once upon a time he had been kinder to her than to any other human being on this earth. She couldn't let him go. She just needed one last shot. One last shot to get him back.

But then there was Caleb. She had lied to him, much like she had lied to Mary. Her therapist was in no way involved in her decision to see Sam. In fact, he would be wholly against the idea, and since Sam had left her she had become increasingly dependent on her bass player. Only the previous week he had declared his love for her in a beach house in Malibu. She had spent the night, having fallen into his willing arms, and this was something she didn't take lightly. She had never wanted Caleb to be her casualty as she was Sam's. And she did care for him. He made her laugh and he was kind, and even though over the years he had the option of sleeping with a different woman every night, he didn't. He would forgo a romp with an enthusiastic groupie in favor of winding down in a little café somewhere with her. Even when she did see him with someone, he would act as though he had been caught out. She smiled at the memory of his sheepish grin. She had spent the previous night in London with him and she had promised she would return the very next day. Their relationship, if you could call it that, was new and she had made it clear she was very much on the rebound. He had told her he knew all this and then he kissed her and told her he would wait forever, which was a sweet if not a realistic proposition.

She knew he was deeply hurt by her insistence on the necessity of a final visit with Sam. She also knew that he would forgive her. He always did.

★ ★ ★

Sam was sitting at the bar and talking to the barman as though they were old friends.

"It's a warm night," Sam acknowledged.

"Warm, 'tis almost hot."

"Well, it's nearly summer," Sam smiled before taking a sip from his pint.

"Summer my arse!" the man said quietly so that Mia had to strain to hear him while lounging in the large door-way and behind a well-placed antique plant pot. "We are being globally warmed as we speak. Sure, if it keeps going as it is, in a few years we'll all just be stains on the street!"

Sam laughed. "Well, I guess you'd know better than I would."

"Oh, I would, Sam. I've been a connoisseur of Kerry weather for nigh on thirty-eight years now." He grinned. "So you're here to see your lady friend?"

Mia's heart missed a beat.

"Yeah."

"Well, I wish you the best of luck."

"Thanks, Henry," Sam said.

It was at this point that an elderly lady, who looked like she could be a cousin of the Queen of England and who smelled of roses, approached Mia's hiding place. "Are you all right, dear?" she asked. "You seem a little lost."

"I'm fine. Thank you."

The old woman had managed to gain the attention of

Sam and his friend the bartender so Mia made her entrance. Sam immediately got off the bar stool. Henry followed with Sam's drink on a tray, his demeanor immediately changing from casual to professional. Once they were seated by the window overlooking the bay, he asked if Mia would like something to drink.

"I'll have a dry martini."

"Certainly, madam," he said with a bow, and then they were alone.

"It's a beautiful place," she said, looking out over the water.

He nodded.

"Are you going to say anything?" Mia said, annoyed by his silence.

"What do you want me to say?" he asked, knowing that he was being rude.

"You hate me that much?"

"I don't hate you. I just don't want to hurt you again."

"Is that what you have planned?" she mumbled.

"Why are you here?" he asked at the moment Henry appeared behind Mia and placed her drink onto the table in front of her. Without saying a word he was gone.

She looked from Sam to her drink and back toward Sam. "I don't know," she answered honestly. "To finally say good-bye, to win you back, I don't know." She sighed.

He took her hand in his and kissed it. "Say good-bye."

She nodded. "The trouble is, I know I can get over losing you as a lover, but I don't think I'll ever recover from losing you as a friend."

"You don't have to," he said, unable to hide his relief.

"You've got my back?" she asked playfully.

"I've got your back," he said with a grin.

Later over dinner on the terrace Mia told Sam about her burgeoning relationship with Caleb.

"He's so good to me."

"Like you were to me."

"God, I hope I don't treat him as bad!" She smiled.

"I'm sure you won't. You deserve the very best, Mia. You just have to believe it."

"I shouldn't be here," she concluded.

"Probably not."

"Still, I'm glad I came."

"Me too," Sam said, and he meant it. "Are you in love with him?"

"Yes, I think I am. And you, are you in love with Mary?"

"Yeah, I think I am."

"She's lucky." Mia smiled.

"No. She's pretty unlucky actually."

"You're well matched then," she laughed.

"We're giving each other space."

"She told me. You know what I think?"

He shook his head.

"Space is for astronauts."

Sam had missed his friend Mia and he was glad to have her back even if it was for just one night. They made their way to the restaurant arm in arm and after dinner, during which Mia actually ate something, they traveled down Memory Lane. She worried that her career would suffer without him. He reminded her that she was the talent and that every good student outgrows their mentor. She had discussed her fears for the album. It was good. She knew it was good but it needed one more song, a signature tune, something she could hang the album on. He agreed to listen to the rough cuts. She had complained that she couldn't stay more than one day for fear that she'd put on weight and yet she was determined to finish her lobster. It was nice. Over coffee he thanked her for saving his life and this time he actually meant it. At the end of their evening he kissed her good-bye. She hugged him and smiled. "Closure," she mumbled before kissing him one last time. He waited while she walked up the staircase and she didn't look back once.

"Bye, Mia."

Chapter Twenty-four

Holding On, Letting Go

Sam left Mia just after eleven. He was tempted to knock on Mary's door, but her lights were off and he knew from Ivan that she had been having sleepless nights. He had also heard what was a greatly exaggerated account of her breakdown in Gemma's beauty shop. He wondered if she was having that terrible nightmare again. He worried for her as he knew how devastating nightmares could be. He had been haunted by them for as long as he could remember—then again his were based on reality.

He fell asleep quickly. He must have been asleep only minutes but the nightmare woke him. He was starting to panic. That terrible panic he had often succumbed to in his past life. The one he thought he'd escaped. That panic that started in the pit of his stomach before leaking into his system and threatening to debilitate him. It was that panic that had first enticed him into messing around with drugs. Sam hadn't started with heroin—he'd tried pretty much everything else first: marijuana, mescaline, magic mushrooms, acid, china white, LSD, ketamine and cocaine, to name a few, but nothing came close to his first introduction to heroin. The others for the most part he could take or leave, but heroin seduced him instantly and was destined to become his mistress. He lost himself in her.

He made tea while trying to control the tremor threatening to consume his hand. He sat at his kitchen table and tried to remember the breathing technique that Phones had taught him. He closed his eyes and attempted to visualize a calm day, but instead he saw a needle slipping into his vein, liquid slipping into his system and himself slipping into heaven. He shook his head vigorously to empty it. *No. No. Think of the sea or a cornfield or a park; think of the sun, the moon or anything but that. Come on, man, you can do it. If only I could stop this damn tremor. Damn it, what's happening?* But he couldn't stop the memories of the Almighty High flooding back. When he was up he was filled with color, his body felt light and his mind free. He didn't need to be touched or loved. He didn't need to talk or listen. He could just be, wrapped up in his own personal heavenly bubble. He could almost feel the warmth. He stood up and walked around the room. *OK, you want to remember heroin, remember all of it. Remember the bad times. Remember the nightmare,* he told himself, just as Danziger had taught him. He closed his eyes and visualized coming down and it wasn't hard to relive the hell which always followed like a blinding light. His aching head, his ears and skin buzzing and his body screaming. He could see himself in a ball, cold and twisted. His only escape was to slip another needle into his vein. He opened his eyes. *I won't go back there. It's all OK. Everything is fine. I'm fine.* It was the first time he'd really thought about using since rehab. *I'm OK. I'll be OK.* He needed to calm down so he took a hot bath. The techniques his shrink had taught him finally kicked in and his panic slowly dissipated.

He was drying his hair when the doorbell rang. It was after 2:00 AM but he thought that maybe it was Mary.

He answered with a relief which was short-lived.

Caleb pushed past him. "You're a real fuckin' asshole, you know that?" He was holding on to a half-full bottle of Jack Daniel's, the remainder of which was on his breath.

"I didn't ask her here," Sam said, closing the door.

"No, of course you didn't. Why would you? You don't give a damn about her!"

Caleb plonked himself on one of Sam's kitchen chairs. Sam took two glasses out of his cupboard and put them on the table. Caleb snorted at his presumption but poured them both a glass anyway.

"You're wrong," Sam said, after taking a sip of bourbon.

"Oh yeah?" Caleb drawled.

"I do care about her. I just don't love her. Not like you." He drained his glass.

Caleb stopped midsip and put his glass down on the table in front of him. He began drumming his fingers. "She told you about us?"

"Yes." Sam poured another round.

"What is your hold over her, man?" Caleb asked with a voice full of defeat.

"She came to say good-bye," said Sam, "and that's what she did." He put his glass down without taking another sip. Instead, he got up and put on the kettle before turning to Caleb. "She was just looking for a clean slate."

"Easy for you to say," Caleb said, swirling the contents of his glass.

"Why?"

"Because I'm just holding on, man." Caleb sighed.

"I know what you mean," Sam said as he poured coffee into a percolator. "So where you staying?"

"Sheen Falls."

"She's staying in The Park."

"I always thought you were an asshole," Caleb admitted before drinking from his glass.

"You were right. I was, maybe I still am. It's a constant battle." He grinned, hiding the reality of his statement. "She said she's in love with you."

"Don't fuck with me." Caleb looked as though he was about to cry.

"I'm not."

Caleb lowered his glass. "I've loved her since the first day I saw her. Do you think I should go to her?"

"Have some coffee first," Sam instructed.

"No thanks. I must go." Caleb stood up. "You got a bathroom?"

Sam waited while Mia's bass player gargled with mouthwash then emerged pumped up.

"Good luck," Sam said.

"Thanks." He walked outside and suddenly realized

he didn't have a clue as to where he was going. The night concierge had driven him to his first destination and now he was abandoned in a small town next to nowhere.

"You couldn't drive me, could you?"

Sam smiled. "Get in the car."

★ ★ ★

Mary's day had been an eventful one. Although the glitterati often visited Kenmare, Mia Johnson was the first of that particular fraternity to have spent time in her very own home. By coincidence that evening she had invited Ivan and Sienna to dinner at her cousin's behest. He had confided in her that his relationship was starting to suffer slightly under the strain of his children's homecoming. Because their mother was at a rather unfortunate crossroads and one she was determined to take her time to traverse, his new girlfriend could only wonder as to whether or not she had inherited another woman's kids. Of course, she hadn't said as much but she had become slightly snappy, if not downright sulky, especially after a long day's work. She was used to having Ivan to herself and family life was way more difficult than *The Brady Bunch* would have suggested. Mary had agreed to distract his new girlfriend with her famous scallop salad but unfortunately she had fed this to the ravenous rock star. Her father came to the rescue, providing her with fresh sole, which she planned to serve with a risotto. It hadn't been the dish requested but it was the best she could do.

Fortunately, Sienna was partial to sole, and it appeared

that she was so grateful to spend a night away from the kids that a two-liter and a park bench would have sufficed. Mary played an old Bonnie Raitt album, one of her favorites and an artist she knew that the hippie in Sienna would like.

"I love Bonnie," Sienna sighed while sipping a glass of red wine.

Ivan sat at the kitchen table drinking a beer and texting the babysitter.

"We've just left them, Ivan," she said with a voice betraying irritation.

"Sorry," he said after pressing Send.

"Can I help?" Sienna asked Mary.

Mary declined—instead, she told her to sit.

Ivan took her hand in his and she smiled at him. "Cheers!" he said, and they clinked glasses.

"So any news from next door?" Ivan asked.

"No."

"Oh, that's right, you're giving each other space." His voice was laced in sarcasm.

"None of your business!" said Mary.

Sienna laughed at Ivan raising his eyes to heaven.

"Well, I've some news on the subject," Sienna said. "An American booked into the hotel late this afternoon. He asked if his girlfriend was staying."

"Who is his girlfriend?" Ivan asked in awe.

"Mia Johnson." She smiled smugly.

"No."

"Yes." She nodded.

"Did she mention a boyfriend to you?" he asked Mary.

"Hardly."

"Well, now the plot thickens," said Ivan.

"I wonder why she didn't stay in the Sheen?" Sienna said, as much to herself as anyone.

During dinner Sienna revealed the strain Ivan's kids were having on her. It occurred by accident. He was talking about the great day by the sea that he, Sam and the kids had spent before mentioning that she should have come along. She explained that it was hard enough sharing space in a large house with them, never mind the confines of a small boat. Bolstered by the presence of his cousin, he drew her on the subject.

"They're not that bad, surely?" he laughed.

"They hate me."

"They do not," he said lightly.

"Justine refuses to look at me when I talk to her. She doesn't respond when I call her. She won't eat what I give her and instead of using my name she refers to me as 'the woman.'" She drained her glass of wine.

Mary was quick to replenish it.

"Justy is only a baby," Ivan said. "She's just getting used to the situation."

"Neither of them are babies and Chris is as bad. He told me to fuck off the other day." Her voice was rising slightly.

Mary poured her some water in a fresh glass. She ignored it.

"And I gave out to him," Ivan said, tired of the conversation.

"Not enough," she replied.

"Well, what should I have done? Beat him?" he asked, getting annoyed.

"Now you're just being ridiculous," she growled.

The meal pretty much started and finished in that vein. Ivan defended his children's behavior and Sienna defended her reaction to a difficult situation. Mary opened a second bottle of red so that she could drink enough to block out the bickering. The argument ended in a stalemate so they sat in silence in front of the first episode of the second season of *Lost*. Mary and Sienna shared a bottle of red wine and Ivan managed to get through a six-pack of beer and, as compelling as the show was, each person was lost in a world of their own.

Ivan and Sienna left just after ten. Mary stood outside and waved them off. Sam's car was outside but she knew he would be in the hotel with Mia. It was only up the road so he probably walked and his house was dark and still. She had drunk too much wine so she sat out on her wall watching the water. It was still so warm. She wondered what he was doing. She wondered if, when Mia had mentioned her need for closure, she had been telling the truth. After all, why should she? Mary was a stranger. She wondered if Sienna had been right and if Mia was seeing someone else and, if so, why had he followed her on a visit to an ex-boyfriend and why was he staying in another hotel? Mostly she wondered why she couldn't stop wondering about Sam Sullivan. *He's not yours, Mary.*

She went to bed early, hoping for a sound sleep, but woke up to the banging on her neighbor's door a little after two. Despite nearly climbing halfway out the window, she didn't manage to see who was at his door so she convinced herself it was Mia. *He's not yours, Mary,* she reminded herself. *It's for the best,* she lied to herself. "Closure," she muttered before turning off the light.

★ ★ ★

Having deposited Caleb at his desired destination, Sam returned to bed once more. The distraction aside, he was worried that he was slipping and that although a hard battle had been won he was about to lose the war. He had come a long way in six months. Here in this beautiful gentle place he was farther away from his New York self than he could have ever imagined. He knew it wasn't just Mary that had encouraged this change. He knew it was the place and its people and mostly he knew it was his own self. For years he had desperately wanted to escape himself. He always knew that eventually the man he used to be had to die. That man did die one night six months and a lifetime ago yet, just below the surface, a dead man's memories remained intact, haunting him as surely as a determined ghost.

Phones had tried to get him to talk about his past during his stay in rehab. He had employed every trick in the book to get his patient to reveal the depths of himself so that they could work through it. But Phones failed in his objective.

★ ★ ★

Phones had certainly learned a lot though. He discovered that Sam was born to be an outsider. It became obvious early on that his patient's love of his grandmother, although not oedipal in nature, was certainly a form of idealization. And Phones's patient notes included his theory that the timing of her death at the cusp of his manhood would ensure her grandson would find it difficult to ever find another woman, including his own mother, who would or could live up to the woman that his grandmother had become in his own mind. A woman that, had she survived, would have revealed herself to be human and flawed instead of the embodiment of a boy's idea of perfection. This theory was validated by Sam's inability to find a lasting and true love but it did not predicate the darkness that lay deep within his psyche. Something had happened and it was something terrible. Phones was sure that he had not suffered parental abuse; he'd not suffered from terrible poverty or, aside from a dead grandmother, loss. He'd never been to war, nor did he seem to have been involved in an incident that would give rise to post-traumatic stress disorder. *What the hell happened to this guy?* Phones had circled his question twice while doodling on page fourteen of his notes but Sam would never tell.

★ ★ ★

Much later that night, when Sam closed his eyes, he dreamed of the woman only a wall away and all the while unknown to her she dreamed of him. Even as he luxuriated in her warm smile, chasing after her beckoning hand in her world full of color and light, she descended into the depths of his darkness to a place where again she saw the strange hooded teenage boy in a bloody ball hidden behind trash cans. Even as he swam beside her in bright blue water, she stood in a black back alleyway watching the stranger vomit until dry with his mind screaming a scream that was feral and terrifying. His horror was drowned out by city noise but she felt his insides burn and his mind, the part that was connected to his soul, shutting down.

Suddenly, the boy was staring at her.

"Save me!" he begged.

Chapter Twenty-five

Sacrificed

Mary was just outside the Kerry border when smoke began to emanate from under the bonnet of her car. Within minutes she was pulled over at the side of the road with a car full of whiskey for the bar and what appeared to be a clapped-out engine. She called AAA and was told the wait would be at least an hour. The guy joked that she should get comfortable, which served to annoy rather than entertain her. She was sitting static in the car over half an hour listening to some radio DJ talk incessantly about something no one in the world could possibly care about. In her mind she willed him to play a song and cursed herself for forgetting her all-important travel CD collection at the onset of her journey.

It was after she'd grown tired of flicking radio stations that she phoned Ivan. He picked up without too much delay.

"You are not going to believe where I am," she said.

"Where?"

"On the side of the road in a clapped-out car waiting for AAA," she said with a sigh.

"You're not going to believe where I am," he countered.

"Where?"

"Kerry airport."

"Norma!" she gasped.

"She's coming home," he said with a great degree of relief.

"Oh, that's fantastic! So where is she staying?"

"With me and the kids," he answered happily.

"Have you lost your mind?" Mary queried.

"Excuse me?" Ivan asked, a little bemused.

"Your relationship with Sienna is on dangerous enough ground already," Mary pointed out.

"But now that Norma's home it will get better."

"Not when she's living in your house, Ivan! God almighty!"

"All right, calm down. I'll work something out," he sniffed.

"You do that," she said before hanging up.

It was just after seven in the evening and as the tow truck appeared to be light years away she ensured her hazard lights were on, locked her doors and settled down for a snooze with a slight smile on her face. *Now that Norma's home things will get better. Is he mental?*

★ ★ ★

Ivan drove out of the airport with his wife in his passenger seat. The kids were buzzing in the backseat. Aside from her arm being wrapped Norma had made a remarkable recovery. She looked fresh and happy, contrary to everything he had expected. She was grateful for the lift.

"Don't be soft—we were hardly going to let you get a taxi," he scoffed.

The kids laughed at the notion.

"The woman's put flowers in the spare room for you," Justy said.

"Her name is Sienna," Ivan said with frustration.

"That's nice of her," Norma said with a polite smile.

"Chris says they look gay," Justy noted.

"Don't say everything's 'gay,' " Ivan said. "Your uncle Barry is gay." He said it as though that was a good reason to avoid the word.

"I know," Chris replied. "That's why I call him Uncle Gay." He grinned at his mother, who turned to laugh at him.

"Sorry," she said to address Ivan's dirty look but it didn't last.

He quickly broke into a grin.

Just like the old days.

★ ★ ★

Penny's dry spell didn't last as long as she'd hoped, and since she'd tipped most of her booze down the drain, she needed to stock up. Luckily, she'd managed to locate a bottle of vodka in an old suitcase, having conducted a large-scale search operation. Once that bottle was empty she was forced to go to the off-license so she fixed her makeup, brushed her hair and straightened herself up before getting into the car that would take her to town. She picked up a basket and as she did so she noticed, at the corner of her eye and through a reflection on the glass window, that one of the two young Murphy girls behind the counter was pointing at her and making a glugging gesture before mimicking a drunken walk. The other Murphy girl was cupping her mouth so that her snigger would not be heard.

Penny dropped the basket and walked out the door.

Stupid little bitches! she thought before vowing that she would not return to that particular shop ever again. Instead, she decided that the only thing to do would be to shop for her booze in Killarney. This was a good twenty miles away from local gossips and, besides, she could do with the drive.

It was while she was driving to Killarney that she started to panic. Her heart rate increased enough so that she could feel it race. She became hot enough to employ air conditioning, which was usually reserved for only the hottest of days. She felt beads of sweat begin at the nape of her neck before rolling down the natural pathway that was her spine. *What the hell am I doing?* she asked herself. *What the hell is wrong with me?* She realized that her hands were shaking on the steering wheel so she pulled over to the side of the road and stopped. She briefly wondered why she had come over the mountain and supposed it was just habit. There was no one else around, just her sitting in her car, the gray rock towering over her and cascading below. She got out, needing to breathe fresh air. She stood by the small railing which separated her from the glasslike lake below.

And it was there on the still mountain that she admitted what she'd long known and hidden in the deepest recess of her own mind. *I am an alcoholic.* Tears swelled in her eyes until fat enough to tumble. Mary's words and the Murphy girl's imitation ran through her mind. *Oh God help me!* She spent just over thirty minutes crying on the mountain before returning to her car. She cleaned her face with an old tissue she'd located in her glove box and reapplied her eyeliner and some lipstick, and then she drove on to Killarney to purchase much-needed alcohol.

After all, alcoholics drank alcohol.

★ ★ ★

Mary didn't make it home until after 10:00 PM. Mr. Monkels was scratching to get in and she opened the back door to reveal her clothesline had been pulled to the ground along with her washing.

"Reaching for the stars or the birds?" she queried Mr. Monkels whose lowered head and disappearing tail were evidence enough to suggest this minidisaster was one of his making. She was picking up her mud-ridden clothing when she heard Sam's door open. She had an armful of clothes when he peered over the wall at her.

"Hey." He smiled. He looked tired.

"Hey," she reciprocated. She looked tired too.

"Have you had enough space?" he asked candidly.

"Are you OK?" she asked, ignoring his jibe, worried by his look and grabbing on to a wayward sock.

"Not really," he admitted.

"Come inside," she offered.

He made his way over the wall.

"You could have used the front door." She smiled.

"This way is quicker."

He followed her inside. She placed the clothes back into the washing machine and offered him a coffee. He didn't have time to answer before the phone rang.

Mary's face changed seconds into the phone call. Sam knew it was something terrible. She hung up and he looked at her.

"What?" he demanded.

"I need your car." She turned and walked to the door, grabbing her handbag and jacket on the way.

"Excuse me?" he said, following her outside.

"It's Penny. She's been in an accident." Her voice was trembling.

"Is she hurt?"

"Yes."

"How bad?"

"I don't know."

"Where is she?"

"The mountain," she replied in the form of a strangled whisper.

He headed into his house to secure his keys.

"I'll drive," he said when he returned.

He sat in the driver's seat and she sat and strapped herself into the passenger side.

"Don't worry, the emergency services will take care of everything," he said while putting her car into gear.

"We *are* the emergency services."

"I don't understand."

"We can't call anyone—she's drunk," she said before biting down on her lip.

He nodded. "Is this wise?"

"I don't know," she admitted, "but she's my friend."

Sam drove onto the mountain while Mary talked to Ivan, who agreed to meet them at the accident site. She hung up and tried Penny's phone but five minutes previously Penny had warned that her phone was running out of juice. Her speech was slurred and Mary wasn't sure if it was merely as a result of alcohol or a head injury. *We need to get there.* Sam could sense Mary's fear. It was hard not to—she was gripping her phone so tightly her knuckles were white.

"Calm down," he soothed.

"Can't," she replied, staring straight ahead. *I hate this fucking mountain.*

"She's fine."

"We don't know that."

"She can talk, that's a good sign," he said, and she nodded.

"She's crying. She says she's bleeding." The thought of her best friend abandoned and hurt made her well up. "She's really scared." She shook her head from side to side. *I should have been there for her. I should have seen this coming.*

"You couldn't have seen this coming," he said, and she looked at him oddly, wondering if she had inadvertently voiced her thought.

"Is this rock bottom?" she asked.

"Only time will tell," he said.

"We really need to get there."

Minutes later they came across Penny's car smashed into the side of the mountain. The front was crumpled against a dying deer impaled on sharp rocks. Blood leaked from his mouth and Penny was lying crumpled beside him. Mary was out of the car as soon as Sam had pressed the brake. It was the first time since her accident that she had actually put foot on the mountain and, across the road, the close proximity to the edge of a steep cliff was not far from her mind. *Breathe.* She made her way toward her friend, who had passed out when attempting to soothe the dying deer. Mary was scared to turn her friend, afraid of spinal injury. She was scared to touch her at all.

"Penny! Penny! Penny, wake up!" *This is insane.* "Christ, we need to get someone here who knows what they're doing!" she cried out while desperately battling encroaching vertigo.

Sam moved forward and placed his hand on Penny's wrist. "She's got a strong pulse," he said before going to the car and pulling out his and Mary's jackets. "We need to cover her." He placed the jackets on her. It was a second or two before she moved.

"Don't move!" Mary insisted.

Penny ignored her and turned to face her friend. "I'm OK," she said, her speech slurred, with blood streaming from a cut on her forehead. The gash was deep and fleshy, making Sam's stomach turn a little. The current of blood masked broken teeth, a split lip and a badly broken nose, but when Penny arched her head to attempt to change her center of gravity, the damage became all too apparent.

"Oh Jesus!" Mary gasped at her friend's pulverized face.

Sam took off his shirt and handed it to Penny, who up until that second hadn't noticed his unobtrusive presence. She took it and buried her face in it, embarrassed by his assistance.

Ivan arrived before Mary could talk her into lifting

her head once more. As he got out of his car the deer was breathing his last, slow and steady, his breath visible in the air.

Penny lifted her hand to his head and patted it gently as his last breath held and his eyes began to freeze.

"I'm so sorry!" she cried, spitting broken teeth. "I'm so, so sorry!"

Ivan took over then. His previous incarnation as a commercial diver had ensured that he had sufficient first-aid skills to confirm that his friend had no spinal injuries. Her face concerned him most, especially the blood loss from both her forehead and nose. He carried her to his car and laid her on the backseat. He wrapped her in Sam and Mary's jackets and rested her head on a Barbie pillow from the boot that Justy had insisted on bringing home, only to forget about it upon arrival. He then took out ice that he had in a cooler he often used when fishing. He wrapped a pack into a towel and handed it to Penny.

"It slows the blood flow and curbs the swelling," he said.

"What about shock?" Mary asked.

"I think she's drunk enough for shock not to be our biggest problem."

He closed the door on Penny, who was mumbling something about killing Bambi. He went back to his car boot and pulled out a jack. He walked over to Penny's car and with one blow smashed the glass on the driver's side.

"What the hell are you doing?" Sam asked Ivan.

"We need to make it look like the car was stolen. That or Penny goes down for drunk driving. Not to mention that the red deer she killed is a protected species."

"Oh," Sam said.

Mary stood mesmerized by the dead deer, horrified by the terrible death he'd endured. Her nose was running. She wiped it with her hand. She felt faint.

"Follow me," Ivan said.

"Where are we going?" Mary asked, wondering what the hell her cousin was doing.

"Cork. Adam's meeting us at the hospital," he said, getting into his car.

Sam and Mary went to Sam's car with Sam helping Mary, who had now succumbed to a combination of vertigo and fright. Ivan took off with Sam following. Their speed increased significantly to keep up. Mary was attempting to control her breathing as Sam sped around the bend that had once nearly claimed her.

"We'll be OK," he said.

"I know."

"I'm a good driver."

"I wouldn't go that far," she replied.

He smiled. Even when battling terror Mary had the ability to make him smile. Once they had made it off the mountain and were driving on the Cork road, Mary exhaled. She spoke on her mobile with Ivan, who assured her that their friend was OK and had at one point actually attempted to sing the chorus of Phil Collins's "Against All Odds."

Mary hung up and Sam asked how Penny was.

"She's singing," she sighed.

"Anything I'd like?"

"Phil Collins."

" 'You Can't Hurry Love'?"

" 'Against All Odds.' "

"Apt," he said, and despite the desperate situation they both couldn't help but grin to themselves.

A few minutes passed in silence.

Mary couldn't help herself. "Did you have a good night with Mia?"

"Yeah"—he nodded—"it was nice."

"Right," she said, a little put out.

"It was just dinner." He grinned. "Actually, her boy-friend had followed her but I'm guessing you heard that."

"It was mentioned."

"He came to see me."

"Really?"

"Oh, you remember."

"What?" she asked innocently.

"You know, when you nearly fell out the window try-ing to get a look?"

"That is the last time I tell Ivan anything."

★ ★ ★

Adam was waiting at the front doors of the emergency room. Ivan and Sam carried Penny between them with Mary following. Adam gasped at her injuries. Penny started to cry the instant she saw him.

He took her in his arms. "It's all right," he said, "ev-erything is going to be all right." Penny didn't seem con-vinced. She pulled away from his embrace and with her hand attempted to shield her injured face. Once inside and after the woman behind the glass took down her details, she was escorted by a nurse behind a curtain so that her injuries could be assessed.

"How much have you had to drink?" she asked.

"I don't know—a lot," Penny admitted.

"What happened to you?"

"I fell."

"Some fall," the woman said, unconvinced.

After testing Penny's responses the nurse determined that she was not critical, and although she had facial lacerations they weren't considered serious enough to merit her skipping the large queue in the waiting area. She returned to her friends and sat down.

"Well?" Adam said.

"I wait," Penny replied.

"But your face is a mess."

"Thanks."

"This is ridiculous," he said, storming over to the reception desk.

Mary, Sam, Ivan and Penny watched Adam animatedly argue a case for his mistress skipping a long queue. The woman behind the glass window was unmoved. He returned disgusted.

"You'd find a better health system in the third world," he complained.

"It's OK," Penny said from her uncomfortable seat.

"I'll get coffee," Mary offered.

"No, go home," Adam said. "I'll stay with Penny. It looks like it's going to be a long wait."

"Can I talk to you over here for a minute?" Mary said to Adam. She stood up and walked over toward the emergency room door and he followed. An old woman in her eighties lying on a trolley was pushed past them by ambulance men. She was complaining that she couldn't leave the dog at home alone; her weary daughter reminded her that the dog had died in 1987.

"I thought your father died in 1987," the old lady said.

"No, mother, he died in 1977," the woman responded.

"Time flies," the old lady said, shaking her head. "Still, I really do need to get home to the dog."

Adam smiled at the weary daughter and gave her a wink. She smiled back. Mary punched him in the arm.

"What are you doing?" she asked.

"What?" he responded in surprise while rubbing his arm. "I just smiled at her—it looked like she could do with some cheering up."

"Yeah, you're a real humanitarian. I'm not talking about that woman, I'm talking about your marriage."

"I'm not leaving Penny here in that state."

"I'm here," she said. "It's late at night and you have a wife to go home to."

"I'm not leaving."

"OK," she said, shrugging her shoulders, "fine, have it your way."

"Mary—"

"Grow up, Adam," she said, walking back to the others.

After that they debated whether or not it was a better idea to stay in Cork or go home. Eventually, after much negotiation, they all felt it would be a better idea to stay put, at least until Penny was actually seen by a doctor. Mary felt bad leaving Penny but there wasn't enough room in the waiting area for the actual patients, never mind the people accompanying them. Penny insisted she was fine and actually happy to be left alone but Adam insisted on staying. Ivan laughed. Mary gave him a dirty look. He grinned and gave her the finger. She couldn't help but smile. For some reason unknown, something about an adult giving another adult the finger never failed to entertain her.

The others left Penny and Adam sitting in chairs in the regional hospital.

"They're right. You shouldn't be here," Penny said.

"I've already been through this with Mary." He got up from his chair. "I'm getting us some coffee."

"You shouldn't be here," Penny repeated, but Adam was already halfway down the hall.

★ ★ ★

Ivan, Mary and Sam sat in a hotel bar. Ivan and Mary debated their next move while Sam sat drinking a ginger ale in silence. Once her injuries were sorted, Ivan suggested, Penny should be moved to a certain drying-out facility in Dublin. It was well respected. He knew a man from the Tim Healy Pass who up until a few years ago was a falling-down-sleeping-in-the-street drunk, and after a spell with the lads in that fine facility in Dublin he returned a pillar of the community and he had since acquired a golfing handicap of four. Mary wondered whether or not Penny would agree to go to such a place, but Ivan wasn't to be swayed.

"Christ, Mare, she's just killed one of God's most majestic creatures and nearly herself—surely to God she can fall no farther," he said before finishing his pint.

Sam hoped that Ivan was right, being painfully aware that sometimes it takes more than a car crash to hit bottom.

After that Ivan headed into his hotel room so that he

could talk to Norma, who was spending her first night in Kenmare home alone and yet happy, watching over her sleeping children. He phoned Sienna and left a message on her voicemail since she was most likely sleeping—either that or she was pissed off he was housing his ex-wife.

Sam and Mary stayed in the late-night bar, neither wishing to be alone.

"When we were kids she was terrified of the dark," Mary said, reminiscing about her friend.

"Oh yeah?" Sam encouraged.

"She was convinced it would swallow her up," she remembered. "She could get in trouble for this," she added after a second or two.

"She'll be fine."

"You don't deserve to have to deal with this. I'm sorry. I should never have asked you to come."

"I want to be here."

"Why?"

"You're here."

"Jesus," she sighed, "someday soon you'll get sense and then we'll both be very disappointed."

"Not a chance."

"Tart!" She laughed and got up. "Good night."

He watched her walk away.

★ ★ ★

Some time after 8:00 AM Penny was finally seen by a doctor. The long wait had sobered her sufficiently so that surgery could be performed to rectify the damage done to her face. Three hours later she lay on cold steel under glaring lights and beside machines buzzing. The anesthesiologist slipped a needle into her arm and in her head Phil Collins sang "Against All Odds" on repeat.

The next time Penny woke her nose had been reset, her lip, cheek and forehead were stitched and she had the mother of all hangovers. Her teeth were sharp in her mouth and as she ran her tongue across them she realized that her four front teeth had been badly damaged. She dreaded looking in the mirror, having felt the bandages on her cheek and forehead. Her nose felt bigger than her entire head. She cried because she remembered Mary and Adam's gasp at her injuries and she guessed that she'd been disfigured. She cried because she had watched a beautiful animal die a slow and terrible death all because of her. She cried because she really had wanted to stop drinking but she couldn't.

★ ★ ★

It was just after nine when Adam made his way to his own front door. He wasn't sure what he would say to his wife. At least the kids were in school. Maybe he would be lucky and she would be out. Maybe she hadn't noticed that he had been out all night. She was often asleep when he returned home from the restaurant and on delivery days he'd be up and out of the house before the alarm bell rang. He was too tired for an argument. He hoped that the separate lives they had been living since his arrival to Cork would work in his favor on this one occasion. Unfortunately for Adam, this was not to be. He entered the house using his key. The second he opened the door he saw suitcases packed at the end of the stairs. Alina was standing on the upstairs landing. She made her way down the stairs to meet him in the hall.

"Are you going somewhere?" he asked.

"No," she said, "you are."

"Alina!"

"I don't want to hear it, Adam."

"Alina—"

"Leave."

"No."

"Leave."

"I can explain."

"I don't care."

"It's not what you think."

"You were out all night, Adam."

"I know but—"

"You were with her," she said.

"Yes, but it's not what you think."

She walked away from him and into the kitchen. He followed her.

"She was in trouble. She needed me," he argued.

Alina fought the urge to shove his head through the glass patio door.

"Our marriage is over," she said calmly.

"Just like that," he said, shocked. He sat and stared at her.

"You've got your wish, Adam. You're free."

"And the kids?" he asked.

"They've settled in Cork. We're happy here. We'll stay and you will go back to Kenmare. You win."

"I never wanted this."

"Yes, Adam, you did."

"Why now?"

"Because I can't stop hating you. I wanted to for the kids' sake but I can't. I look at you and I want to gut you. It's not healthy." A tear rolled down her face. "I really do hate you."

"I'm sorry," he said.

"Go home," she said, "go on, get out."

He just sat there with the weight of his marriage ending sinking in.

"Get out!" Alina roared, angered by his failure to even attempt to pretend to fight for her but he remained seated. Alina ran at him and pushed him off the chair. "Get out of my house!" she roared, pushing him out into the hallway. He didn't fight her. She opened the front door and threw his suitcases into the garden. He followed them and turned to face her.

"When the kids ask why their dad doesn't live here anymore, I'm going to tell them," she said. "There have been enough lies in this house."

The door slammed shut, leaving Adam alone in the garden.

What have I done?

★ ★ ★

Mary, Sam and Ivan were halfway through breakfast when Adam arrived with his suitcases. He dropped them by the table and sat beside Sam, facing Mary and Ivan.

"What's this?" Ivan asked.

"She threw me out."

"About time," Mary mumbled.

"OK, rub it in," he sighed.

"You know, maybe if one of us had said something a little earlier, your marriage wouldn't be in such a bloody mess and Penny wouldn't be an alcoholic."

"Oh great, this is all I need! My wife, now you! Anyone else want to jump into the ring?"

"She's right," Ivan said. "It was always going to be only a matter of time before it all ended in misery."

"Jesus," Adam sighed. He looked at Sam. "Have you anything to say?"

"No, I think your friend's summed the situation up beautifully."

"I've been a selfish arsehole," Adam admitted.

"Yes, you have," Mary agreed.

"I'm sorry," he said, and he began to cry.

Mary escorted Adam to her room so that he could compose himself. While he took a shower in the bathroom she called the hospital to check up on Penny. She was told that she was in surgery and if there were no complications she could be released as soon as the very next day. She ordered Adam some breakfast, which arrived just before he emerged from the bathroom.

"Thanks," he said.

"Are you all right?" she asked kindly. Any trace of animosity had disappeared upon the emergence of his tears.

"I'm fine," he said. "I'll let things settle down and call the kids tomorrow, or do you think tomorrow is too soon?" Adam seemed unsure for the first time in his life.

"I think tomorrow would be fine."

"OK."

Ivan had phoned his friend from the Tim Healy Pass and he had given him a contact name and number for the facility Ivan had talked of the previous night. He made the call and the woman, a nice lady by the name of Lorraine Ryan, explained that they would be happy to admit his friend but only if his friend was a willing patient. He told her he'd phone her back. He met with the others in the hotel lobby an hour later.

"Do you think she'll agree?" he said, worried.

"I'll talk to her," Adam said.

"I think you should all talk to her," Sam said. "She needs to hear it from all of you."

"Sam's right," Mary said. "It should come from all of us."

"OK. So today we go home and tomorrow we come back and talk to her," Ivan said.

"I'll stay here," Adam said. "She'll be awake later."

"Are you going to tell her about Alina?" Mary asked with concern.

"No," he said, "this isn't about me. It's about Penny."

"At last he sees the light." Ivan smiled.

Adam agreed to phone them that night with an update and, all going well, they agreed to meet back at the hotel the next morning. Adam walked them to the door of the hotel. Mary hugged him and told him everything would be all right. *It's a little late for that,* he thought.

★ ★ ★

Officer Sheehan was on Mary's doorstep just in time for afternoon tea. She made a pot and put out some sandwiches. He patted his round figure and mentioned that he shouldn't indulge but of course he did. He was munching his third sandwich before he even brought up the subject of Penny's car. He took out a pen and notepad.

"And you're sure she left it here?" he asked, referring to the brief details she had provided him over the phone.

"I rang her from the road. She said she'd drop it over. Mine is in the garage and she was going to Dublin anyway," she said, lying through her teeth.

"So you never actually saw it?"

"No. It was gone when I got home. I was waiting for the AAA forever."

"And you're sure she left it here?" he pushed.

"I'm sure."

"Did she phone you and tell you that she had left it?"

"No."

"Then if you didn't see it, how do you know she left it?"

Crap, I should have said yes. "My neighbor. He saw it."

"Well, why didn't you say so in the first place?" He smiled as though the word *Women!* was coursing through his mind.

She smiled, allowing him to indulge in his moment of superiority. After that Sam was summoned into Mary's home to answer the charge that he had witnessed Penny's car parked outside.

"What time?" Officer Sheehan asked.

Sam pretended to think for a minute. "Six or seven."

"Mary, you said you rang Penny around six, didn't you?" Officer Sheehan said, referring to his notes.

"It must have been seven then." Sam smiled.

"Right," Sheehan said, scribbling something down. His phone rang and he excused himself to take the call, leaving Mary and Sam alone.

"Do you think he believes us?" Mary asked in a whisper.

Sam shrugged. He didn't want to panic Mary but guilt was written all over her face.

Officer Sheehan returned. "By the way, did I mention that the car has been found? It was reported as being crashed on the mountain."

"No, you didn't. Is it damaged?" Sam said.

"Any casualties?" Mary chimed in innocently.

"A red deer," Officer Sheehan said, "and, yes, the car is a write-off."

"Right," Sam said, shaking his head.

"Well"—Officer Sheehan pocketed his notebook—"it looks like we are all done here."

"OK then," Mary said, smiling.

Officer Sheehan made his way to the front door. "One last thing."

"Yeah?" Mary responded.

"It would appear that Penny didn't make it to Dublin last night," he said in a manner that reminded her of Colombo just before he revealed a poisonous plot.

"No?" she said with her heart racing.

"No, it appears she only made it as far as the regional hospital in Cork."

"Right," Mary said, nodding her head in a manner that suggested that she was aware that the game was up.

"She could have killed someone."

"I know."

"She was drunk?"

Mary nodded to signal that she was.

"I should arrest you for aiding and abetting. Not to mention attempting to take me for a fool."

"I know. Sorry."

"Is she going to get help?"

"Yes."

"You see that she does," he said.

"I will," she said, "thanks."

"Don't thank me, Mary. I don't know what I'm going to do about this yet," he warned.

"OK."

She opened the front door.

"And, Mary?"

"Yes."

"You really are a pathetic liar."

She nodded her head. "I know that too."

He left.

She sat down on the sofa and Sam joined her.

"I'm not sure what happened there," he said. "Did we get away with it or not?"

"Yes and no."

"It's been a hell of a week," he sighed.

Sam was tired. He hadn't slept well in the hotel and he was weary of drama. Mary was tired too. She had deep black circles under her eyes. He made his way to the door.

"Sam!" she called from the sofa.

"Yeah?" he replied.

"Will you come with me tomorrow?"

"I doubt Penny would be happy about that."

"I know what she did to you but she didn't mean it. She's not like that when she's well."

"I'm sure you're right but I don't belong there."

"It's an intervention. Isn't that the correct term?"

"Yeah," he responded.

"Well, who better to intervene than someone who actually knows what they are talking about?"

He was silent for a moment or two. His head hurt. He really needed to sleep.

"I'll do it."

He was gone before she could say thanks.

Chapter Twenty-six

Clean Up, Clean Out

Sam, Mary and Ivan were waiting in Adam's hotel room. Adam opened the door to reveal a bandaged and broken Penny. She surveyed those in front of her and knew that there would be only one reason for this meeting. Feeling weak, she sat on a chair against the wall, facing a jury made up of her peers.

Adam gave her two painkillers and a glass of water.

"D-day," she said, and her friends remained silent. She shook her head and attempted a smile. "OK."

"We're going to get you some help," Adam said, but she chose to ignore him in favor of concentrating on Sam.

"Is this how rehab happened for you, Sam? Oh no, I forgot. You were brought in on a stretcher."

"Penny," Mary growled.

"It's OK," he said to Mary before turning to address Penny. "You're right. I went in on my back and if memory serves I was also strapped down. You want to go in like that, I'm sure it can be arranged."

"Fuck you!" she spat. Her hands had been trembling all morning. She felt sick, aggravated and badly needed a drink.

"Do you know why you don't like me, Penny?" he asked.

"Enlighten me."

"You look at me and you see yourself."

"Bullshit!" she said, touching the bandage on her forehead.

"I'm an addict and you're an addict too." He leaned toward her so that she was forced to look at him. "I know how hard it is. I know the agony of saying no. I know that if you don't you will die." He looked at her broken face and pitied her with every ounce of him.

Tears rolled down her face, which she tried to hide with trembling hands.

"I don't think I can do it," she whispered to him.

"I know you can do it," he said.

"I don't want to be like this anymore."

"You don't have to be."

★ ★ ★

Penny and Adam found themselves on the 10:30 AM train to Dublin. They sat in the dining section, Adam tucking into a full Irish breakfast and Penny playing with the foil wrapping of her painkillers. She had been silent since she had said her good-byes at the hotel. Mary had cried and Penny had felt like an asshole, remembering her stupid document in which she had spurted venom at those very people who were helping her. When her tremor became so severe Adam feared that she might seize, he made the executive decision to allow her a shot of vodka. While she attempted to sip on it Adam called the hospital to ensure he was doing the right thing.

Penny's tremors subsided, thus allaying Adam's immediate concerns.

"What have you told Alina?" she asked.

"I lied," he lied.

"It's still that easy!" she snorted.

"No, it's not easy. It was never easy."

They both looked out the window at the fields and grazing animals, the towns and houses, all passing them at high speed.

"I want another drink," she admitted.

"I know."

"Thanks for being here."

"It was the very least I could do."

★ ★ ★

The taxi pulled up outside the hospital and Penny sat pinned to the backseat, frozen to the spot and looking much like the poor deer she had destroyed.

Adam paid the driver before reaching for her hand. "Time to go," he said.

"I can't."

"You can."

She shook her head, fresh tears spilling. "I don't want to."

"Yes you do."

She nodded. "I'm really scared."

387

"It's OK to be scared."

He helped her out of the car and the taximan drove away. He guided her toward the door. A nurse emerged with a clipboard. She stood at the door waiting. Penny stalled. Adam put his hand around her waist and she snuggled into him. He spun her around and suddenly they were dancing the way they had danced on the night he'd said good-bye. In her head she could hear Sinéad singing about sacrifice. He kissed her cheek and held her close to him and all the while the nurse watched and waited.

"You're always leaving me."

"I never want to."

He wasn't allowed past the front door. The nurse took her new patient by the hand and Penny smiled through tears and waved good-bye to the love of her life, who stood and waited for her to disappear behind white doors.

I'll always love you, Penny Walsh.

★ ★ ★

Mary sat on the sofa alone that night, Mr. Monkels having fallen asleep on the window seat. She was drinking tea listening to Snow Patrol, and for some reason she felt like crying. That boy from her dreams was haunting her more and more. She didn't have to sleep for him to find her anymore. At any given moment he would appear, looking at her with the most terrible expression on his face. She might have seen things before but they were all so vague and about people she knew in the here and now. Her inclinations had never ever manifested as this one had and, besides, what was it telling her? What part of the story was missing? And why suddenly did he, this boy, seem familiar? Who the hell was he? Emotion welled inside her like an untapped oil supply ready to burst through solid rock and she wondered if she was having a breakdown for the tenth time that month. But then of course she would question herself. It had been so long since she had felt anything. When her child died a part of her had stopped like a broken clock, stuck forever in the past, never to move on. She had been Miss Havisham minus the wedding dress and cruel streak. And then suddenly a stranger appeared and something inside her started to tick and she began to wonder.

★ ★ ★

Sam sat in his kitchen sipping on a glass of Jack Daniel's from the bottle that Caleb had left behind. He hadn't slept properly in a week and succumbed to the shakes earlier like he used to when he was without control. He sat in silence. Penny's intervention had hit him harder than he would like to admit. For some reason it projected his mind to another place. A place in the past when he was a scared-shit teenager running with all his might. *Oh God, no!*

And then he was somewhere else in another time, a time when he was older and successful and an addict. He was in a communal bathroom in a bad area, kicking the shit out of another junkie much larger than himself, but he was beating him down with all his strength, both mentally and physically, despite the fact that he was coming down and needed a fix so badly.

The junkie was crying and begging. "Don't, man! I'm sorry. You don't know!"

But Sam did know. He knew he wanted this fucker dead.

"I've paid for it. I've paid for it a hundred times!" the junkie cried out.

"Not enough," Sam said, kicking him so hard in the nuts the guy vomited.

"I'm a dealer. I can sort you out. I can keep you going, man," the junkie cried, and Sam stopped kicking.

Just like that, he stopped kicking.

★ ★ ★

Ivan was sitting on the sofa with his daughter asleep on his lap. Chris was lying on the other chair and they were watching a show about football. Norma was in the kitchen making the kids' favorite biscuit cake. The doorbell rang and Chris got up.

Seconds later Sienna stood in front of Ivan. He stood up, forgetting his daughter's head was resting on his lap.

"Dad!" she cried, rubbing her eyes.

"Sorry, button."

He hugged Sienna, who seemed a little stiff. Later, when the kids were in bed and Norma had made herself scarce, they sat in the kitchen together.

"I haven't heard from you," she said.

"We keep missing one another."

"We never used to."

"It's just been chaotic. I'm trying to find Norma a place with the kids, there's been madness with Penny and it's just—" He stopped.

"Maybe we should cool things for a while," she said.

"I don't want to."

"You've got your family back, Ivan," she said sadly.

"But I want you," he said, welling up, and she rested her head on his chest.

"I know, but I think this is just a case of bad timing. Maybe when things settle down . . ." After a second or two she added, "You're a good father, Ivan. You're a good man."

"I'll work it all out," he promised.

"I know."

"I love you."

"I hope so," she replied.

He walked her to the door and watched her walk away with a sigh.

You can't have it all.

Chapter Twenty-seven

To Know You Is to Love You

The funeral was lovely. Dick Dogs had been one of Kenmare's best loved. His greyhounds had won many a race and those who backed them had profited time and time again. In his early years he had been a fixture in many a local pub. He had always enjoyed a pint but, unlike some, he knew when it was time to go home. He was kind too, always having time for those less fortunate than himself. He never married, which was a pity because most would say he would have made a good husband. Everyone agreed that it was his time though. He was the last of his generation to go. His friends had led the way and he had openly admitted that he was looking forward to seeing them all again. He had died early in the morning just before the sun rose. He hadn't suffered; instead, he merely stopped. He was found by Sheila Dubury, cold but with a smile on his face.

"What were you dreaming, sweet man?" she'd asked,

and if his corpse had had the power of speech he would have told her that, just before he left this world, he had relived a time when he was a young man and he and his best friend, David Baskin, were standing at the back of a dance hall watching the girls line up in their Sunday best and their hair fresh out of curlers.

Dick had winked at Lena, who shook her head and wagged her finger.

David had laughed at his high ambitions. "She'll never be yours," he said.

"But she could be," Dick had responded.

"She's leaving," David whispered.

"And where would she be going?" Dick had queried.

"We're sending her away."

"Away?" Dick repeated.

"My mother's got it in her head that she'll marry Joseph Dunne."

"But what about me?" Dick asked.

"What about you?" David responded. "She wants something else and what Lena wants Lena gets. She doesn't know it yet but she's leaving tomorrow."

"You're killing me," Dick said, and his friend laughed.

"Take your dance. It'll be your last," David said, not knowing how true his words were, because halfway through that dance the old man reliving the memory breathed his last.

The funeral was held two weeks after Norma's homecoming. She had kept a low profile and Dick Dogs's funeral would be her reintroduction into Kenmare society. She didn't feel ready, still unsteady in herself, still bruised and broken, yet she had always been fond of the old man.

She wanted to pay her respects and her ex-husband encouraged her to do so. She was worried as to what kind of reaction she would receive. She was worried about how she would be viewed and yet her fondness for the man who had dedicated his life to caring for four-legged animals ensured her attendance.

The church was packed, which was odd for a man of Dick's age, especially as he had no family of his own. Ivan stood beside Norma, who was pale and a little shook up. The congregation didn't seem to notice her presence. All heads were bowed in remembrance of an old friend.

It was only when the time came for them to shake hands to give a sign of peace and people had gone out of their way to shake her good hand . . . it was only when she saw men and women who had a perfect right to judge her walk toward her smiling with hands outstretched . . . it was only when she heard the words:

"Glad to have you home."

"Everything will work out."

"You don't have to worry anymore."

"God bless you."

It was only when she stood in front of the people who she'd been convinced would hate her that she realized what it meant to be forgiven.

Thank God I'm home.

★ ★ ★

Mary had spotted Sam standing at the back of the church. She had been standing by Ivan and Norma for the duration of the service. Mary had been suffering a particularly bad migraine over the previous five days and Sam had called every day to ensure she was OK, seeing her at her worst and not seeming to care. The injections that Dr. Macken gave her ensured that the week was full of holes but she did remember Sam holding her hand and wiping her brow and whispering to her. If only she could remember what he had said. She'd continued to have the nightmares, always the same, always unfinished. The lack of progression was frustrating but she knew that there was a time and place and that sooner rather than later the curtain would rise.

She noticed that Sam had attempted to leave the church unseen but Sheila Dubury had nabbed him in the churchyard.

Sheila wanted him to know how much Dick had enjoyed his visit, reliving his affection for Sam's grandmother and times gone by, and how he had talked of it often in the past few weeks. She wanted him to know how glad Dick had been that he'd taken the time to say hello and that the old man had thoroughly enjoyed his gift of ice cream. He thanked her but she wasn't finished. She wondered if he was seeing anyone. He told her he wasn't. She giggled girlishly and asked if he wanted to see anyone and, despite her curves, her black hair and her pretty face, he told her that his heart was somewhere else.

"Pity," she murmured.

"Sorry," he apologized.

"Can't win them all," she noted happily. "So tell me, is Ivan still seeing that hotel girl?"

"No."

"Right," she said, winking. "Well, then, watch this space! After all, every dog has his day!" She laughed uproariously, presumably thinking of the old man laid to rest.

He laughed along. She waved and she was gone. He turned to find Mary standing behind him.

"You shouldn't be here," he said.

"I'm going straight home to bed." She still felt weak.

"How's Penny? Any word?"

"She's still hanging in there. But they won't let me talk to her."

"It's not unusual. It'll work out."

"I know I've seen you but I miss you," she said with a smile.

"I miss you too," he said but he looked sad.

"Maybe you could come for your dinner tomorrow?"

"We'll see how you are," he replied.

He seemed distant and she didn't want to push it. "OK," she agreed, and then she, like the woman before her, was gone.

★ ★ ★

Penny was allowed to make one phone call at the end of a very long week. The week had begun with a urine and blood test which revealed that Penny hadn't a moderate dependence; instead, she was a high risk for delirium tremens. She didn't know what the doctor was saying—it was all Greek to her.

"The DTs," he explained before going on to outline what she could be in for over the next three to four days.

He mentioned confusion.

I think I'm already there.

Agitation was also a possibility.

Stop drumming your fingers, Penn.

Disturbances of memory was next.

396

Not necessarily a bad thing.

Hallucinations were another symptom. He ticked his page again.

Just another Saturday night.

Fever was also on the list.

You give me fever.

She smiled and the doctor asked if she was all right before filling her in on the fact that it was possible she might experience high blood pressure and/or seizures.

"My grandmother died of a stroke," she said.

"We'll be keeping a close eye on you," he promised.

The headache started on day two and it was worse than any hangover she'd ever had. The fever kicked in some time in the afternoon. Her heart rate increased and she was nauseous and dizzy.

"You're doing really well," the nurse said.

"Easy for you to say," she said to both the woman's heads.

Day three was tougher again. She lost track of time. Her eyes leaked something that felt like puss and her body shook. The seizure took hold that evening but Penny was so out of it she had to be told about the incident rather than having any memory of it. By day four she was over the worst of it. She still bore the symptoms but they were milder and the IV fluids and tranquilizers were helping. She had been allowed out of her bed on days four, five and six.

Now, one week on, she sat in a hospital corridor dialing a number she hadn't dialed in a long time. She figured she'd have to leave a message and was quite surprised when her mother actually answered.

"Hello," she'd said breezily as though she had expected a call.

"Mom," Penny said, "it's me, Penny."

"Penny," her mother said happily, "it's been an age, darling. How are you?"

"Fine," she lied.

"Good stuff," her mother replied. "Your father was only talking about you last week saying we should all get together soon. There's a law society function in a few weeks. We've got a spare ticket." She laughed. "There's a few tasty treats attending, I don't mind saying!"

"I'm not looking for a man," Penny said.

"Of course not, let them look for you. Right?" Her mother laughed to herself and continued. "How's all in Kenmare? I really am sorry we got rid of the house. Who knew the bloody house prices would soar?"

"Mom," Penny managed.

"Yes, dear?" her mother replied innocently.

"I'm an alcoholic," Penny said for the third time that day.

"Excuse me?" Her normally unflappable mother sounded a little flustered.

"I'm in a hospital in Dublin."

"Good God!"

"Mom?"

"Yes?"

"Do you love me?"

Her mother took a moment before answering. Her training as a solicitor had ensured that she would absorb all the information laid before her before responding.

"Is this our fault?" she asked.

"No. It's mine. I just want to know."

"You should know. Of course I do. You're my child. I may not be Mary Poppins but I love you with everything in me."

"Mom?"

"Yes."

"Can we try to talk more?"

"Absolutely," her mother confirmed, a little shell-shocked.

"Good," Penny said, relieved.

"Do you want us to come to see you?"

"No, but thanks for asking." She smiled to herself.

"I love you. Your father loves you."

"Thanks, Mom," Penny said before putting down the phone and going back to her room.

★ ★ ★

In the short time Norma had been home she had managed to slip back into the center of Ivan's life, ably assisted by her children. Her intention was not to get in the way—on the contrary, she had no inclination to make her ex-husband's life difficult—but her mere presence had already ended his burgeoning relationship with Sienna. Norma had been upset by this news but he had lied and told her it had nothing to do with her homecoming and that the relationship had simply run its course. In truth, deep down he had known that Norma living under his roof and roaming the halls in a nightgown and making breakfast while his new girlfriend was ringing the bell like a kid waiting on a friend to come out and play was never going to work. But he had asked his wife to stay anyway because that was what was best for his kids.

His mother watched Ivan's wife reentwine herself into the fabric of his life and worried for her son. She asked Norma to join her for a coffee in Jam on the pretext of catching up. Norma was no fool and prepared herself for her mother-in-law's interrogation over tea and scones.

"I see you're doing his washing now?" Sheila said, having witnessed Norma separate Ivan's dark from white smalls.

"Well, I might as well, since I'm doing my own and the kids'."

"He'll miss that when you go."

"I'm sure he'll cope." Norma smiled.

"I wish I was as sure as you. He had a nice thing going with Sienna."

"He said it had run its course."

"He lied," his mother said. "Norma?"

"Yes, Sheila."

"He has strong feelings for that girl. He might even love her, but he would still take you back in the morning."

"You are so sure."

"He'll do what he thinks is best for his family. I'm his mother, I know."

"What do you want me to say?" Norma asked, taken aback.

"Say you'll do nothing to hurt him. The first time I'll forgive, the second I won't," Sheila said while smiling at a passerby.

"I won't hurt him," Norma promised.

"Good." She smiled. "I'll hold you to that."

★ ★ ★

Mossy was frying steak and onions when the doorbell rang. Sam stood at the front door, looking nervous and a little shaky.

"You look like a dead man," Mossy said without concern.

The door swung open and Sam followed him inside.

"I'm wondering if you have anything to buy," he said.

Mossy lit a cigarette and resumed cooking. "Be specific."

"Drugs."

"I thought you were clean," Mossy said, turning to view Sam, whose legs were threatening to give way.

Sam sat down on a hard chair with his head in his hands. "I am. I just haven't been sleeping. I need to sleep," he said in a voice threatening to beg.

"I don't sell," Mossy said.

"Please," Sam muttered.

Mossy took his pan off the heat and turned to view his neighbor. He put his hand through his hair, taking time to scratch his head before answering.

"All I've ever done is hash," he said.

"OK," Sam said.

"I don't feel good about this."

"It's just hash. I just want to sleep."

"I'll give you enough for two joints and then you're on your own."

"Thanks."

Mossy cut a small piece from his own stash. He took out some papers and two cigarettes. "I suppose you know how to roll?"

"Yes."

"Right so," Mossy said. He handed Sam the contraband.

"Thank you."

"Don't thank me," Mossy said. "We both know you're fucking yourself up."

Sam nodded and left without another word.

★ ★ ★

Mary lay on the sofa with Mr. Monkels sleeping on her lap. She had drifted to sleep during *That '70s Show* but woke an hour later with panic rising inside. She knew there was something wrong and everything in her told her to go next door. She lifted Mr. Monkels off her legs. He moaned and moved so as to take up the entire sofa. She made her way next door with a sick feeling inside. She knocked on the door but received no answer. She knocked on the window and still nothing. She knew Sam was inside. Every fiber of her being screamed that something was wrong. She went back inside her own home. In her kitchen she pulled a chair toward the patio doors. She opened them and dragged the chair outside. She placed it against the wall and stood on it before levering herself over the wall and into her neighbor's garden. The back door was open. She slipped inside the empty kitchen. She went to the sitting room but he was not there, and up the stairs his bedroom door was open, revealing an empty room. The bathroom door was closed. She attempted to open it but it was locked.

"Sam!" she called out.

"Go away."

"No!" she said, shaking her head unseen.

"Please go away!" he cried out from the bathroom floor, the well-constructed joint lying on the floor in front of him. For so long had he taken drugs in the bathroom, it had become habit. So there he was, not even halfway through his first year clean, and just about to smoke a joint.

"Come out!" she said from behind the door.

"I can't," he said, flicking the lighter.

"Sam, please don't give up!"

"I'm not strong like you."

"I'm not strong like me! Please come out!" She could sense his terror. She could sense that he wanted to tell her something quite desperately. He just didn't know where to start. She sat on the floor, leaning against the bathroom door.

"Just tell me," she said after the longest time.

"I can't," he said as though expecting the question.

"Why?"

"Because you'll hate me." *Like I hate me.*

"I've never told anyone this." She inhaled before exhaling slowly so as to prepare herself.

Sam waited, leaning against the bath.

"I wanted to have an abortion," she said out of nowhere. "That night on the mountain I told Robert I was pregnant and I wanted an abortion. He wanted to keep it. We argued and he died. When I woke up full of baby, I hated it. I wished it would die. Every day in that hospital and through rehab and right up until he was born I wished my son would die." Tears streamed from her eyes. "And then he did die."

Sam was crying.

"Do you hate me?" she asked.

"No. That wasn't your fault."

"Maybe. Maybe not. Sometimes it's hard to tell."

Sam was silent for a minute or maybe two but Mary waited and her patience paid off. "It was the night I overdosed," he said out of nowhere.

She didn't move; instead, she remained perfectly still, afraid the slightest stir would stall the tale.

"There was this dealer, a guy I knew from school. I'd bumped into him a few weeks before. He was a junkie too. He sold to feed his own habit. He was a *loser!*"

She noted that he spit the word *loser*.

"He'd said he'd fix me up if I ever got stuck. My guy had been lying low. I didn't want to use him. I fucking hated him but I was desperate. I went to his place. He lived in some shithole in the Bronx on the third floor. It took a while to make the stairs. I hadn't banged up in a while."

* * *

Sam was talking to Mary from the bathroom floor in a little cottage in Ireland but right then his mind was in a dank apartment block on 233rd Street. He was walking up the stairs, his legs aching. The damn lift was broken, which was typical. He had an abscess on his foot just at the point where he injected. It burst on the second floor. *Fuck!* He got to the third floor and he could smell piss. He felt sick but he knew if he could make it to 56C he'd be OK. He knocked on the door but there was no answer. He was pissed as the asshole had sworn he'd be waiting. He knocked again, harder and with urgency. He would have broken the door down but it turned out that would have

404

been unnecessary. The door swung open. He entered and it was one room. The kitchen merged with the bedroom, which was also the sitting room. The bathroom was a tiny cubicle just off the kitchen. He knew it was the bathroom because there was a distinct smell of shit coming from it. The guy was sitting on the sofa with his back to him. Sam called out from the door. He noticed the paint peeling down the walls and was desperate to get what he needed and leave the rancid-smelling damp hovel. He called out again and yet the guy just sat there. He closed the door behind him and walked toward the guy. He was annoyed, annoyed that this fucker thought it OK to ignore him.

Then suddenly he was facing him. The guy's skin was a translucent blue against lips of deep purple, a needle still stuck in his arm which was bent and ready to receive. The elastic was still tight around his forearm. His eyes were open and he was hunched as though the end had come in a single second, providing little or no time to slouch.

Sam took a chair and sat close so as to absorb every detail as though the dead man was some sort of macabre museum piece.

★ ★ ★

"Oh my God!" Sam heard Mary say.

Outside his door her hand went up to her mouth. He hadn't spared her the graphic details. Why should he? He wanted her to know. She needed to know what a rotten degenerate he really was. She deserved to be given a fair chance to run.

"After that I robbed him of whatever remained of his stash. I closed the door good and tight and left him to rot." *No more than he deserved.*

"Jesus!" he heard her mumble.

"But just as I was leaving I heard something. I could have sworn I heard him take a breath. It was barely audible and there was no movement when I stared back at him—but I was sure I heard something. An hour or two later I was choking on my own vomit in my Manhattan penthouse." He spoke as though the story had ended.

"I don't understand."

"I lived. He died. What's not to understand?"

"Why didn't you call an ambulance?" she asked, and he laughed as though she'd told a joke.

"Why would I?" he asked bitterly.

"But if he was still breathing?"

"Maybe he was, maybe he wasn't," he sighed, and a tear slipped down his face.

"Why didn't you call the police?"

"I was a drug addict in a dealer's apartment."

"Why did you leave him to rot?"

"Because that's what he deserved!" he shouted.

"Why?"

"Because I wanted him dead!" he roared before standing up.

"Why?"

"I despised him." He got up off the floor and walked toward the bathroom door.

"Why?"

He leaned against the door.

"Why?"

He opened the door and she fell back a little before straightening and getting to her feet.

"You know what the worst thing is?" he asked.

"No," she whispered.

"When I left him I had a fucking smile on my face." He walked past her and into his bedroom.

"Why?" she called out with tears threatening. *Tell me!*

He turned to face her.

"You don't understand. I'm so full of hate, Mary, I rattle with it. Fucking Topher!" He mumbled the last words and fell into his bed and lay there listlessly as though entirely spent.

She flushed the joint and pocketed the lighter. She sat on the floor at the end of his bed.

"Go home."

"No," she said, and then she listened to him cry until at last sleep stole him away.

★ ★ ★

Later, alone and in the half-light, she sat in her sitting room with her sleeping dog by her side. She recalled every aspect of his story, culminating in his final mumbling, "Fucking Topher!" She closed her eyes. She no longer needed sleep to see the boys circle the kid in the hood. She heard the words "Look, Topher's excited!" She saw the kid and ringleader leer. She heard him direct the other boys. "Give Topher a go!" She saw the boy-bear called Topher move toward the kid lying on the ground exposed. *Oh, Sam, what did they do to you?*

Chapter Twenty-eight

Down but Not Out

It was six the following evening before Sam saw Mary again. He had spent most of the day in bed with a head-ache that stubbornly refused to go away. In trying to sleep he employed every trick in the book in a sincere effort to achieve some peace, but counting sheep, hot milk, herbal remedies and even a sleeping tablet didn't help. His mind refused to comply, so busy was it pick-ing apart his previous night's revelation. It churned and churned inside his mind, so much so that his brain felt swollen from the weight of it all. A part of him had wanted to finish the tale. A part of him wondered whether or not in confiding in her he would be finally free from what gnawed at his insides. A part of him wanted her to know everything but the rest of him en-sured that the words that raced around his head stopped short of his mouth. He just couldn't do it. He couldn't look at her and say it. And now, worse than all of it, he feared he would not be able to bring himself to face her. *I've lost her. I deserve to lose her. She's better off without me. Oh God, I can't stand it!*

He was in the kitchen taking two painkillers when the doorbell rang. It had been on the latch since Jerry Letter had dropped in a parcel that Sam hadn't bothered to open. Mary didn't wait for him to answer; instead, she took advantage of her neighbor's lackadaisical approach to home security. She walked into the kitchen with her car keys in hand.

"Let's go," she said, turning on her heel.

"What?"

"You heard me. Let's go." She stopped. "I'm waiting."

"I'm not going anywhere. I'm in my sweats, for God's sake!" He looked down at his unsightly navy sweatpants in an attempt to avoid eye contact.

"We're going," she said, giving him a look that meant business.

"I have nothing more to say."

"There is nothing more I want to hear," she replied.

"You make me crazy," he said, following her to the car.

"You were always crazy, I just highlight it."

She smiled at him and he felt like crying. *I've disappointed everyone who has ever cared about me.* They were driving in silence for at least twenty minutes before he asked about their destination.

"You'll see when you get there," she said, and turned up the volume on her CD player so that Marilyn Manson's ode to "The Beautiful People" filled the car. He turned it down and looked at her but she continued to stare straight ahead, ignoring him.

"What is this?" he asked.

"An ending," she replied.

"An ending?"

"Everything has to end. You need peace. I need to give it to you."

"And you think you can?" he snorted.

"I don't know, but there's no harm in trying." She didn't look at him, eyes fixed on the road. "And then we'll say good-bye."

"I never wanted to hurt you."

"I never wanted to be hurt."

"I'm damaged goods," he sighed.

"We're all damaged."

He fell silent. *Not like me.* It was close to eight o'clock when they arrived at the small strand. Mary parked the car on the hill and handed a flask of coffee to Sam. She pointed at a spiral sandy pathway that led to the beach below.

"Follow the path," she said.

"What about you?"

"This isn't about me." She smiled.

He opened the door, but before he could step out onto the cold sand she grabbed his arm. He faced her with a quizzical look that emphasized his confusion.

"It's going to be OK," she said, and then she pulled him in to her and kissed him on the forehead. "Everything's going to be fine," she said, hugging him tightly as a mother would a child, and he desperately wanted to cry. After she held him for an eternal minute and after he nearly lost himself in her warmth, without another word she pointed again to the pathway and sent him on his way.

He followed her direction and although not really sure what he was doing he was glad of the fresh air. He made his way down the pathway with flask in hand. The glistening water captured him. The tide was high and pink under the last of the May evening sun. The beach was nearly empty save for a woman and her dog and a lonely figure sitting close to the lapping tide. He stood for a moment inhaling.

The man turned around and Sam recognized him as Mary's father. He smiled at Sam and beckoned to him. Sam approached and said hello and Jack patted the ground beneath him.

"Sit," he said.

He looked at her dad, who was still patting the ground, and he complied.

"Jack?" Sam queried. *What the hell was going on?*

"In the flesh," Jack replied.

"I'm not really sure what this is," Sam admitted.

"Me either," Jack replied with a sigh, "but Mary has a way of getting people to carry out her will. She's just like her mother that way."

"What is it she wants?"

"She wants me to tell you a story," Jack replied in a tone that was approaching a whisper.

"A story?" Sam asked, perplexed.

"I've only ever shared this story with one human being and that was my daughter, and only because after Ben died I had an inkling she'd try to follow him. I needed her to know that a lifetime of happiness can't be destroyed in one moment, no matter how terrible or what is lost in that moment." He sniffed the sea air and turned to Sam,

411

who seemed a little scared. "Did you bring the coffee?" he asked.

Sam lifted the flask.

"Good." He took the flask and poured a cup for Sam. Then he pulled a plastic mug from his pocket and poured for himself. "She makes great coffee."

Sam drank half the coffee in one go, then balanced his cup on a rock. He looked back toward the hill and in the distance he could barely make out Mary's car. Jack took another slug before beginning his tale.

"It was the summer of 1957 and I had just turned sixteen. My father had a friend with a farm who offered to pay me half nothing to help him clear out an old stable that needed fixing. I'd been working three days before he came near me and I was exhausted from lifting and hauling all sorts. The place was in a terrible state. He brought me a lemonade drink his wife had made. Jesus, I can still taste the sugar—it was thick with it. I sat down to drink it. He sat next to me. The next thing I know his hands were in my hair. I thought maybe there was straw, but then his other hand was in my crotch."

Sam wanted to stand but his legs failed him. He put his hands to his ears. "I can't," he said, but Jack gently removed his hands from his ears.

"I tried to push him away but he was a strong man. It didn't take much to knock me out, just one clatter of his mighty hand and I was a goner. I wasn't gone for long though. Only long enough for him to have my pants off."

Suddenly, Sam was crying, tears streaming down his

face like a child lost in a crowd of strangers. He was shaking the way he did when the anger took over.

"I understand that kind of hate," said Jack. "I know how it can infect your entire being. I know how it can destroy a soul. I know how you feel, son." His head was held low now like that of a solemn priest awaiting confession.

Sam was sobbing and holding his head in his hands. Jack stayed quiet, allowing the man time to weep. He focused on the tide turning and the birds calling to one another until Sam had collected himself enough to speak.

★ ★ ★

Mary sat in the car with tears streaming. She had seen it all. It had all become clear. She saw him rehearsing above an old launderette. She watched him say goodbye to the others and turn on a street marked 7th. She saw him pass those boys. They were calling out. *Loser, hey, loser, where ya going, loser?* He gave them the finger. They started running. He started running with everything he had in him. Again she felt the concrete under his feet and heard the steam emitting from a grate. She could hear the car screeching to a halt and the horn beeping. She could feel the steel bumper against his thigh as he brushed past it at speed. She could hear them coming and the thud of eight feet moving closer and closer. She could feel his chest tighten and breath shorten. They were closer now, the hairs on the back of his neck standing to attention, warning him of the proximate danger. He tried to speed up but his legs weighed heavily. He slowed down only by a fraction but it was enough. Seconds later they had caught up. The kicking and punching started. He was on the ground, his hood pulled tight around his face and his hands attempting to protect himself from their blows. There was the big guy, Topher, the one they called Bear. He was standing there with a bottle in his hand. He was jumping up and down and laughing.

"Topher's excited. Give Topher a go! Go on, Bear, give it to him! Give it to him!"

Sitting in that car once again, she was lost, lost in another time, when a boy was about to be raped. *"Do it! Do it! Do it!"* The words resonated in her head. She closed her eyes but she could still hear Topher release his buckle and unzip while two of the others held the boy down. She heard them tearing at his jeans. She felt one of them unzip him and felt the cold air hit him as though he'd sat on ice.

"Do it! Do it! Do it!" the boys called out.

"Get him on all fours!" their twisted leader called out, but he was barely audible.

She saw them pulling him to his knees. He wanted to call out, but his voice was gone. He wanted to kick and punch and to make them all bleed but he couldn't. He just wanted to run. It felt like he was tearing inside. It felt like he was burning up and every invasion burned deeper and deeper until time meant nothing. The moment froze. Then and quite suddenly he was alone, covered in blood, shit and piss, and still he couldn't scream out loud, so instead the rage simmered until it infected every part of him.

Mary returned to the present, sobbing out loud and wiping the never-ending stream from both her eyes and nose.

"Save me!" the boy had called out to her.

"Even if it means losing you," she said to her empty car before putting it into reverse and driving away.

★ ★ ★

"If I hadn't given them the finger!" Sam groaned.

Jack nodded. "If I hadn't agreed to the lemonade."

"If I ran faster," Sam said.

"If I had grabbed the pitchfork by the stable wall," Jack replied.

"If I was stronger."

"If I was stronger," Jack repeated.

Sam turned to face him and Jack smiled as best he could.

"If *if* was a donkey we'd all have a ride," he said. "Time to let go"—he nodded toward the sea—"time to turn it around."

Sam watched the sea lap away. "Is that possible?" he asked.

"I'm proof of it," Jack said.

"What if I can't?"

"Then you've allowed those bullies on that night to wage a war that would last a lifetime." Jack sighed. "Don't let them win, son."

They sat in silence until the tide was far away and the cold evening air set in. Then they walked together to Jack's car.

"I have to go home," Sam said.

"No more running away," Jack stated.

Sam nodded. "Mary," he sighed.

"Maybe in another time and place," Jack said with a sad smile.

"Maybe." And Sam was crying again.

★ ★ ★

Mary returned home to Mr. Monkels, waiting with a wagging tail. She sat on the floor and hugged him tight for as long as he would allow her. Earlier that day, when she had asked Jessie and Pierre to watch over the bar so that she and her dad could talk, they had sat in Jack's apartment and she had told him what she suspected about Sam's past. He had sat in silence, listening to her reasoning for her belief, and he had agreed to talk to Sam, as difficult as it was for him.

Before she left, he offered a warning.

"If you're right, he might never forgive you knowing," he said.

"I know," she sighed. "Just help him."

"He might never be able to look you in the face again."

"I know."

"No, love, you don't. So many times I wanted to tell your mother but I couldn't."

"He needs help."

"You could lose him."

"He was never mine to keep."

★ ★ ★

Van Morrison was playing in the dayroom. Penny looked up from one of the books that Mary had sent and marked the page. The phone was free and had been for at least half an hour. She couldn't delay making the call any longer so, after helping Eileen from ward 5 locate the remote control, she dialed Adam's number.

"Hello?" he said.

Adam heard a gulp.

"It's me," she said.

"Penny." He sounded relieved to hear her voice.

"Hi."

"Are you OK? I've been worried sick. Why haven't you let me visit you?"

"I needed time."

"Fair enough." He sighed a happy sigh. "I'm just happy to hear from you now."

"Adam," she began, "I know you're back in Kenmare."

"I made Mary promise to say nothing," he said, a little annoyed.

"Don't blame Mary. I asked about you and, well, you know what she's like. She tried to cover but failed miserably." She laughed a little. "How are you getting on in the restaurant and with your dad?"

"We're fit to kill one another," he laughed. "Still, it's not too bad. We just hired a new chef and he's a pain in the arse but excellent."

"Good. I'm sorry about you and Alina."

"You are?"

"Yeah. I am."

"The kids are OK. I get to have them every second weekend. It's hard but they'll adjust, and they definitely don't miss the arguing."

"That's good."

"When are you coming home?" he asked.

417

"That's what I'm calling about."

"You want me to pick you up?"

"No."

"Oh, OK, what can I do?"

"Nothing."

"I don't understand."

Penny remained silent just long enough for Adam to worry.

"You told me once about the first time you ever saw me," she said after a few moments passed.

"You were wearing blue shoes."

"That's right. I was alone and you said you saw me cry."

"And all I wanted to do was save you."

"Yeah," she said, and tears fell once more. "Well, you can."

"How?"

"Let me go."

"I don't understand," he said with panic.

"I've been such a mess and for so long. I need to be a different person. I need to move on."

"Is that your doctor or you talking?"

"It's the right thing to do."

"No. Penny, please."

"I'm so sorry."

She hung up the phone and Eileen from ward 5 was waiting to give her a hug.

"It's hard to let go," she said, and Penny nodded and dried her eyes.

"Come on, let's see if we can find an episode of *CSI*," Penny offered.

"My favorite." Eileen smiled.

"I know."

* * *

Mary made it home a little after eight. Her body ached and exhaustion was threatening to shut her mind down. Mr. Monkels was waiting by the window. She watched him stretch in anticipation of her key turning. He approached, tail wagging. She rubbed his head and together they walked upstairs. She fell onto her bed and he flopped beside her. It was mere minutes before both of them were sleeping soundly.

She didn't awaken until midafternoon the following day. Her eyes opened to the sound of Mr. M licking himself with a gusto he usually reserved for prohibited foodstuffs. She sat up and looked out her small square window, which revealed a hot summer afternoon. The sky resembled a perfect light blue silk and was cloudless. She stood up and walked toward the light. Below, a woman walked past wearing sunglasses and pushing a pram with a small umbrella protecting a little face from the hot sun. Ivan was varnishing the deck of his boat, something he had been promising to do all year. Chris emerged from the water and raised himself up onto the boat and his father playfully pushed him back in, much to Justy's enjoyment. Mary could see Justy throw her head back laughing, comfortably perched on the side with legs swinging. Mossy sat in his front garden smoking a cigarette and cutting his toenails. His old battered radio was dangling by its cord from the window and from it Van Morrison sang to her about the water and the rain.

And before she even noticed the absence of Sam's car, she knew he was gone.

Chapter Twenty-nine

Those Left Behind

It was a warm September evening. Mary drove home, anticipating a walk in the woods with Mr. Monkels. They loved their walks in the woods and she was determined to make the most of the weather and her time, before the weather changed and she left. She'd stop at the plaque that bore her son's name and walk through the trees with her camera in hand.

Since Penny had returned, she had often joined Mary and Mr. M and, while Mr. M investigated the undergrowth, they'd gossip and laugh about all manner of subjects.

It was during one of these walks some weeks earlier that Mary had confided that she had been accepted into a photography course in London.

"You're joking?"

"No."

Penny smiled warmly. "Congratulations, you deserve this."

Mary was grinning from ear to ear.

"When?" Penny asked.

"Next month."

"I can take Mr. Monkels," Penny offered. "I'd love to help."

"Dad's taking him, but thanks."

"Good for you," Penny said, and they stopped to look at the sun dance on the water.

"You'll come and visit?" Mary asked.

"Absolutely." Her friend smiled and hooked Mary's arm. "Any excuse to shop in London."

"You'll be OK?"

"Absolutely." Penny smiled. "It's all changed. It was the same for so long and now it's all changed."

"It's better?"

"It's much better."

But this evening Penny wouldn't be joining them—she was going to her cooking class.

Mary got home a little after six and called out to Mr. Monkels. He didn't come out of the kitchen or down the stairs. He wasn't stretched out on the sofa or by the window. He wasn't in the garden because earlier he had made it very clear that he had no wish to go out despite the warm weather. She made her way upstairs.

"Mr. Monkels!" she called out. "Where are you, boy?"

She found him asleep on her bed but this time he wouldn't wake. She knew instantly that he was gone. She sat beside him and she kissed his furry face and then called the vet.

After he left Mossy helped her carry Mr. M downstairs.

"He wouldn't stay to see you leave, Mare," Mossy said.

"Yeah," she agreed, blowing her nose.

"It's for the best."

"I know," she said with a sob. "I'll really miss him, Mossy."

"Of course you will," Mossy said, patting her back. "Mr. Monkels was a fine dog, loving and faithful and—"

"Mossy."

"Yeah?"

"Shut up."

"Right."

Mossy made tea while Mary sat rubbing Mr. Monkels. Ivan was the first to arrive with Sienna trailing behind. Their separation hadn't lasted long. In fact, they had only managed one week apart when out of the blue Norma had announced she'd found a job and a new place to live. Once Ivan had approved the house as fit for his wife and children, he insisted on paying the rent. Norma and the kids moved out and one long conversation and a romantic trip to Paris later, Sienna moved in.

Despite the late hour, Ivan and Sienna had managed to secure a wreath in the flower shop before it closed. It read: *Mr. Monkels, we love you.* It was in handwriting on a large card as opposed to script on a ribbon, but the thought was so nice it made Mary's nose and eyes run. All the crying and snots was starting to get to Mossy, who took their arrival as an opportune time to make his getaway.

Adam arrived with a couple of shovels and a large box. This too made Mary cry bitterly so Sienna comforted her while Ivan and Adam dug a hole in her back garden. Penny arrived last, having received the text message at the end of her cooking class. She had shared Mary's news with the entire class, who had all donated their lamb and vegetable stews and lemon tarts so that Mary wouldn't have to cook for a week.

"It's just like a real funeral," Sienna said to Ivan, who took a break from digging to get a glass of water.

"It is a real funeral."

"It's a dog," she reminded him.

"It's more than a dog. It's Mr. Monkels," he said with a sad smile.

When the hole was dug and Mary was ready to say good-bye, Ivan placed Mr. M in the box, and with Adam's help they placed that box into the earth.

"Do you want to say anything?" Ivan asked.

"I think the wreath says it all," Mary said, nodding, with a little sob.

The scene was so sad that Penny and Sienna joined her in sobbing, as did Mossy, who was standing on a beer crate and looking over his wall.

In absence of anything else to do or say, the lads covered him over and placed the wreath on top of the fresh earth. *Rest in peace, Mr. M.* Afterward an impromptu party was held. Jack arrived with a crate of booze, closely followed by friends Patty and Con, each bearing boxes of soft drinks and tonic mixers.

Pierre followed with leftovers from the day's trading. When Mary made a face, he chastised her. "This is perfectly good food, Marie. You Irish are so wasteful."

"You're giving out to me at my dog's funeral?" she asked, managing to hide her smile.

"Say you're sorry," Jessie said, giving him a slap as she passed him.

He nodded his defeat. "You are right, Marie, today is not the day, but as the belle Scarlett once said: 'Tomorrow is another day.'"

Jessie laughed. "I could listen to that man all day but it's an awful shame I have to look at him." She winked at Mary and Penny, who was standing behind her.

"There's something weird with those two," Penny said.

"You're right about that," Mary said.

"What?" Penny asked, mouth agape.

Mary said nothing; instead, she just winked.

"They did not?" Penny said with eyes wide open.

Mary said nothing; instead, she just nodded.

"Jesus, you think you know people!"

Penny walked off into the sitting room, where Mossy was playing the only song he knew on guitar and Ivan was heckling.

Mary watched her pass Adam, who was talking to Norma who'd arrived with the kids who were outside placing flowers they'd stolen from a neighbor's garden on Mr. M's new place of rest. The birds above them were quiet.

Adam called to Penny, who turned and came back to join in their conversation.

Their relationship was being redefined and it was hard on them both, but, watching from her kitchen, Mary guessed that they would be all right.

Steven and Barry arrived—without Pluto as a mark of respect. "We didn't want to rub it in, Mare," Steven said. "After all, Pluto is incredibly cute and alive."

Mary smiled at her cousin's boyfriend. "Thanks, Steve, you really know what to say."

Tin arrived in the kitchen looking for a bin. "Mare,

sorry about the dog dying but still and all you're looking great on it!" he said with a wink.

Before long her house was filled with family, friends, neighbors, well-wishers and music.

It was after twelve and the party was still going strong. Mary sat in her garden beside the mound of dirt covering Mr. M. Penny came out to join her.

"Do you want some company?" she asked, handing her a freshly made coffee.

"Only yours." Mary smiled.

"You're being really brave," Penny said, nudging her.

"I know he was a dog and not a person but . . ."

"But every time you said his name it brought back Ben," Penny said.

"Yeah"—Mary nodded—"it did."

"Everything was the same for so long." Penny repeated the words she had said in the woods.

"But it's all changed now," Mary replied.

"And as hard as it is to let go . . ."

"It's for the best," Mary said sadly. Then she said, while watching Tin and Mossy attempt a two-hand reel in her kitchen, "I received a copy of Mia Johnson's third album today."

"Sam?" Penny asked.

"No, Mia." Mary smiled. "She sent a card."

"Such a nice woman, I still feel like such an arsehole," Penny mumbled. "What did she say?"

"She said that Sam was well and she asked how I'd managed to get him into therapy. Apparently, it was something she could never do. She said he was happy and healthy. She said thanks."

"What did happen between you two?" Penny asked.

"Nothing." Mary said with a smile. "Nothing at all."

Penny smiled and nodded. "OK, you don't have to tell me"—she grinned—"tonight." A moment or two passed. "So what's the album like?"

"It's good. I especially like the track that Sam wrote."

"Sam wrote a song for Mia?" Penny repeated with her mouth agape, much like earlier that evening in response to the hint about Jessie and Pierre.

"He wrote the music. Mia wrote the lyrics. She's a very intuitive woman," Mary said, sighing.

"Did she mention me?" Penny asked, laughing, and Mary joined in. The two best friends sat in a back garden in Kerry absorbing those around them enjoy the present while they acknowledged this present would soon be past and their lives would never be the same again.

Epilogue

It was a cold morning in New York City. Sam stood in the center of the room taking a long look at the white walls and white painted wooden floor. He almost expected to see white sheets covering a white bed complete with white blankets. This room was a much bigger room than the one he had emerged from five years previously. Still, it reminded him of Danziger and Phones and the man he used to be, if only for a moment.

Mia pushed him from behind. "Come on or we'll be late."

"I still don't know what we're doing here."

"You are so impatient," she said, looking at the other people milling around. She pointed to a room off the white room which held plants and a table of white and red wine only.

"Do you want a drink before we go in?" she asked.

"No, I want to go home. Don't you have a husband to do this stuff with?"

"He's in the studio."

"Oh yeah, who with?"

"Does it matter?" she asked, pushing toward the door which led to another white room.

"OK, what about you? Shouldn't you be resting?"

"I'm pregnant, not ill," she responded. "Come on!" She took him by the hand. "You'll like it."

Sam stood in the middle of another white room. Black-and-white photos lined the walls. Mia pulled him to take a closer look. They were all gravesides or memorials, each instilled with a certain sadness that seemed familiar. He couldn't explain it; you had to see the photos to be able to understand. He was lost in a photo of a young girl cleaning a broken headstone. She looked East European; she had a scarf on and couldn't have been more than ten. The headstone listed four names and their deaths were all dated for the same day. He wondered who they were and what they were to her. Was it her family or did she even know them? Maybe cleaning headstones was a summer job, but that didn't explain the girl's sadness.

Mia pulled him along. He passed a photo of an empty soccer goal with flowers intertwining the net and an empty bench in memory of a woman called Emily.

"What do you think of this one?" she asked.

"*We love you, Mr. Monkels*'?" he read, looking at a photo of a dog's grave. "There's only one Mr. Monkels."

"Yes, there is, or sadly was—as the photo can testify to, he's no longer with us," Mary said from behind him.

He turned. "I can't believe you're here."

"I was going to phone, but it's been so long."

"I was going to write. I just didn't know what to say."

"You are both as bad as one another." Mia smiled. "It's a good thing I like to read the arts section."

They were staring at each other intently, signaling to Mia it was time to go.

"I'm going home," she said. "My feet are killing me."

Mary and Sam said their good-byes to Mia and then turned to face one another. It had been a long time and yet no time at all.

"I have one photo I think you'll like," Mary said, and he followed where she led.

She stood in front of a picture of a tree. Light streamed down from the sky above and rain seemed to pour down the bark, running into and past the carving.

```
I will go
My ♥ will stay
LB 1920
```

"LB. Lena Baskin. You found it! I can't believe you found it!"

"It took a while"—she smiled—"but I had some time after you left."

"It's a beautiful exhibition," he said, looking around at the photos of ghosts lining the wall.

"Yeah, well, what else would you expect from Mary of the Sorrows?" She grinned.

"I'm guessing you haven't been that for a long time."

She nodded. "You're right."

"Would you like to catch up over dinner?"

"Very much."

"And if you're free maybe afterward we could get married."

She laughed. "Let's just have a shag first and see how it goes."

And in a moment reminiscent of the closing credits of a Hollywood romance or a French drama, Sam and Mary stood in the middle of the white room and it would have been obvious to anyone who cared to look that all they could see was one another. And if given to fantasy one might expect them to live happily ever after.

Up Close and Personal
with the Author

Your first novel, *Pack Up the Moon,* was a bestseller and award nominee in Ireland. How has your life changed since *Pack Up the Moon* was published? Did that success make the writing of *Apart from the Crowd* more or less difficult?

My working life has changed dramatically since *Pack Up the Moon* was first published. In January 2006 I was a claims handler for an American company called Chubb Insurance. I'm not sure that the success of *Pack Up the Moon* made writing *Apart from the Crowd* more difficult, but I was attempting to adhere to a deadline while still working full time at Chubb. Within a year I was fortunate enough to be able to leave and write full time. By the time *Apart from the Crowd* was completed I was mentally exhausted and physically ill, so there was a part of me that could empathize with both Penny and Mary! My home life happily remains the same. My husband and I have been together for fifteen years, married for five, and most days when he's not regurgitating every single word that comes out of the *Scrubs* character Turk's mouth I'd say we're content. His new favorite is "Oh no he didn't." I believe the fact that I haven't maimed him is a true testament to our lasting love.

Tell us about your writing process. When do you write? Where do you write? Do you plan out the novel before you start writing, or does it organically happen?

I have an office upstairs in my home. I sit at a cream, wooden desk with countless coffee rings on it, which refuse to come off no matter what cleaning product I use. I sit on a cream, hardwood chair, which is not as comfortable as I'd like it to be but, aside from the coffee rings, it matches the table. Beside that is a really old, crappy pink office chair, which my dog, Trudy, sits on. My cat, Maggie, stretches on the cream armchair in the corner of the room, and my large foxhound sleeps on the floor by my feet. I always plan a novel. So far, the stories have just come to me, but I spend weeks creating characters in my head. I have to feel like I know them inside and out before I even dream of beginning chapter one. Mostly I'm in my office by 9 a.m., deal with emails until about 10 a.m., and after that I write. Some days I'll work all day, some days I'll work half the day, and some days I'll take off and instead work throughout the night.

Apart from the Crowd is full of pop culture references: Penny sings "Against All Odds" by Phil Collins after her car crash, Sam thinks about Mary while watching an episode from season two of *The West Wing*, Mary falls asleep watching *That 70's Show*. Do you feel that it's important that a novel be relevant to the culture and time in which it's placed? Are all of the mentions inspired by your personal taste?

I think it's really important to place a story in a specific time and place that is recognizable to those who read it. Each country has its own very specific culture, but popular culture transcends that. It may be trite, but I think in a world full of cultural and political division the global popularity of shows like *Desperate Housewives, Grey's Anatomy, The Office,* or *Father Ted* remind us that we are more alike than not. Plus, I believe that our individual cultures are derived from and informed by our ancestors and the past, but popular culture, whether it be American, English, Irish, or Chinese, speaks of who we are now.

The novel takes place in both America and Ireland, and of course has Sam, an American, as one of its main characters. As an Irish citizen, was it difficult for you to write "American"? What kind of research did you do to authenticate your portrayal of Sam?

I think it's a lot easier for an Irish citizen to write about an American rather than vice versa, unless of course that American is living here. America is such a global force in every way but especially in terms of entertainment. I've grown up absorbing the American culture since I was a child. Also, the Irish have a long history of emigrating to America, and so a lot of first- and second-generation Irish Americans visit or return to Ireland and Kenmare, which is the town featured in the book and the town in which I grew up. I'd worked for an American company for ten years, which also helps. But, having said all that, I prefer to think that every character, whether English, Irish, American, or French, has a voice that is specifically their own.

Sam is explicitly characterized as an atheist in the novel, and there is intermittent discussion of Mary's religious belief and of the afterlife. On page 248, Sam asks Mary why she believes; she answers, "Because if I didn't I'd lose my mind." How do you personally define faith? How did you try to define it in the novel?

I think that faith is a combination of belief and hope. I don't believe that it's the preserve of the pious. Some people have faith in science, in themselves and in those around them, some have faith in God or Allah and the afterlife those deities promise. My mom was diagnosed with Multiple Sclerosis in the late seventies and with each year that passed the illness advanced until she died in 1989. She had faith in God so much so that she often traveled to Lourdes looking for a miracle. I too had faith, but in science; I believed that she would be the beneficiary of a cure. Mom died peacefully and in the way she wanted to die, and I know in my heart that in the end she would have believed a good death to be her miracle. I still have faith that some day, and possibly in my lifetime, we will find a cure. Sam may not believe in an afterlife but by the end of the book I like to think that he has rediscovered faith.

Do you have a favorite character in the novel? Is it the same one that you most identify with? Which character was most difficult for you to write? Why?

My favorite character is Ivan because of his big heart. He's a man's man, not exotic or leap-off-the-page interesting but he's steady, strong, and kind, and when I think of him it makes me smile. The character I most identify with is Mary because I was fostered by my aunt and uncle in Kenmare when I was eleven. Some people tended to pity me because mom was in a care home in Dublin and my dad lived in another town with another family, but I had a far better and happier life than a lot of others. Penny was the hardest character to write. There is alcoholism on both sides of my family, and for a while I lived in Dublin with an alcoholic uncle. I was desperate to get Penny right without exploiting or betraying the real-life stories of the people I know and love.

You majored in marketing in college—so let's talk business! Does your knowledge of marketing influence your writing? Do you consider what might make your novel more "marketable" as you write? What made you leave marketing to pursue writing?

I may have majored in marketing but trust me when I say my knowledge of marketing is minimal. I left after one year. In 1990s Ireland there was no such thing as career guidance, so I picked marketing because I thought it would be creative.

I pictured myself writing funny adverts or jingles and I was devastated when I realized that marketing was simply selling! I left it because I hated the course and I've never considered what stories are more marketable when writing a book. If I had I'd probably have written about a wizard gone bad on a killing spree in downtown Los Angeles, which I think proves the point that I really haven't got a clue as to what sells.

Before becoming a novelist, you worked as a stand-up comedian. Which is more emotionally challenging for you—facing a crowd of people and trying to make them laugh, or being unable to see the reactions of your readers?

Writing is far more emotionally challenging. I enjoyed my short-lived stand-up career. It was cool to make people laugh and the social life surrounding it was pretty good, too. But I wasn't at all emotionally invested. My comedy partner used to get so nervous before a show that she'd pace up and down in the tiny bathroom, pale in the face and hands shaking. I never felt that way. After the show she was buzzed and exhilarated, feelings which totally passed me by. I loved writing the sketch and coming up with the punch line. I received my high the second the joke was conceived; after that it was old news and I wanted to move on. When writing the novels I become so invested in these characters and their worlds that I laugh and cry with them, and when the story is over I find it a little hard to say good-bye.

Ireland has a long and rich tradition of novelists and writers. Can you recommend some of your favorite authors and works? Is there a modern novelist (aside from yourself, of course!) who best captures the Ireland you know?

I'm a big fan of Denyse Devlin, who wrote a book called *The Catalpa Tree*. It tells the story of a thirty-three-year-old man who becomes the guardian of his best friend's fourteen-year-old daughter after the friend's sudden death. Not only is it a great story but the characters stayed with me for a long time after I put the book down. Oh, and she does capture contemporary Ireland, England, and France, for that matter, quite beautifully. I'm also a huge fan of Roddy Doyle. He's written *The Van, The Snapper,* and *The Commitments,* which was made into a movie in the early nineties. In 1993, he won the Booker Prize for *Paddy Clarke Ha Ha Ha.* The first time I read *The Snapper* was the first time a book made me laugh out loud. I love Roddy Doyle.

Do you have any new writing projects planned at the moment? What are your next steps?

My third book has just come out in Ireland, so I'm working on promoting that. I'm also working on a two-part Christmas special TV series for TV3 here in Ireland and once that is in production I'll be starting book four. Then once I complete that I'll be taking a few months off to write a film that I've been dying to write for ten years. I also have another TV project slated with the national broadcaster here in Ireland and hopefully if it's picked up I'll be doing six to twelve episodes. After that I'll be writing book five, and once completed I may take a holiday!